VOL. 1:

ZOEY FOOLS AROUND *and* JAKE FINDS OUT

KATHERINE APPLEGATE *and* **MICHAEL GRANT**

PREVIOUSLY PUBLISHED AS THE **MAKING OUT** SERIES

HarperTeen is an imprint of HarperCollins Publishers.

Grateful acknowledgment is made for permission to reprint a quotation from *The Big Sleep* by Raymond Chandler, Vintage Knopf. Copyright © 1939 by Raymond Chandler. Reprinted by permission.

Originally published by HarperPaperbacks as *Boyfriends Girlfriends*

 For information address HarperCollins Children's Books, a division of HarperCollins Publishers, 195 Broadway, New York, NY 10007.
www.epicreads.com

ISBN 978-0-06-234076-4

Typography by Ellice M. Lee
15 16 17 18 19 PC/RRDH 10 9 8 7 6 5 4 3 2 1
❖
First Edition

ZOEY FOOLS AROUND

PART ONE

Zoey Passmore

Here's the question: Love. What is it? Absolute and unshakable? Eternal and undying? Faithful and true?

Oh, really?

Have you ever been to a dance? Ever seen the way a guy will look right over his girlfriend's shoulder while he's slow dancing with her and give some other girl the eye?

Ever kind of thought about your boyfriend's best friend, or even his brother? Don't lie. You know you have.

So what's love? Something that lasts a week or a month and that's all you can expect? Or is it just that some loves have a short shelf life? You know, like yogurt: after a week or two they go bad.

And how do you recognize the other kind of love, the kind that isn't like yogurt? The kind that is more like . . . I don't know, like peanut butter, that lasts forever and always tastes good?

Okay, maybe not peanut butter. But you get the idea.

So, getting back to the point, what's love? I guess no one can ever be totally sure, and after all, I am just seventeen. Cut me some slack; I can't be expected to know everything. I finally understand the War of 1812, and that's hard enough without having to worry about defining love in a hundred words or less.

Still, I have learned some things about love, especially lately. And I know a lot more about it now than I did, say . . .

. . . two years ago.

TWO YEARS AGO

"JAKE. JAKE. JAKE! WOULD YOU . . . *would you stop it? Jake, I'm serious. Look, stop it, get your hands . . . I'm getting pissed off now. I'm serious; stop it right now." Zoey Passmore slapped her boyfriend's hand away, a startlingly loud sound that made several passersby turn and stare in amusement.*

"Jeez," Jake said, looking wounded and rubbing the back of his hand.

"It's my *ice cream. You ate yours and you've already eaten half of mine." She held it up as evidence. "I'm down to the waffle. You pig."*

"The waffle?"

"You know, the waffle cone. What do you call it?"

"The cone," he said, shrugging his big shoulders and staring at her as if she'd said something utterly idiotic.

"What? What are you staring at me for?"

"It's not called the waffle. *It's the cone. Ice cream* cone." *He shook his head. "Man, you think you know somebody."*

"Well, I'm a complex, mysterious woman." She licked a big dollop

of the chocolate ice cream.

"That's so sexy the way you do that," Jake said.

"Oh, shut up." She glanced around self-consciously, wondering if anyone else had heard him. The crowd on the narrow, cobblestoned street was mostly tourists, people in big, bright shorts and golf shirts, old people and couples dragging small children through the souvenir and fudge shops that lined Exchange Street. Still, here and there were familiar faces, some of Chatham Island's three hundred full-time residents.

"Sorry," Jake said without any hint of remorse. "I'm just feeling good today."

Zoey softened, letting a smile form on her lips. It had been two months since Jake had felt good. "What do you want to do today?"

He leered comically, an expression that seemed out of place on his serious face. "Same thing I want to do every day."

Zoey sighed. Yes, Jake was getting back to normal, for better or worse. "Okay, if you want to go watch sports on TV . . ."

"You know what I meant."

"Yes, but I'm ignoring you." She dodged around a stroller and rejoined him, reaching for his hand. "Why are you feeling good today, anyway?"

Instantly his innocent, happy expression changed. His smile grew cold. "Today's the day Lucas goes off to jail."

She felt her own face stiffen. "Are you sure?"

He nodded. "Of course I'm sure. I thought we might get lucky and run into him. I'd enjoy seeing him go. Just like I'll enjoy thinking of him locked up."

Zoey released her grip on his hand. "You shouldn't talk that way," she said softly.

"Why not? He deserves it. He killed my brother."

"I just don't think it's right. What happened to Wade was terrible, but still, what's happening to Lucas isn't something to be happy about."

"Is to me," he said darkly.

A cute ten-year-old girl came running up, a tornado of knobby knees and silken brown hair. "Jake!" she yelled.

"Hi, Holly," Zoey said.

"Jake, Dad said you're supposed to help him take Mr. Geiger's boat out of the water."

"Oh, crap. I forgot." Jake winced and looked at Zoey apologetically. "I told my dad I'd help out down at the marina today."

"Great, so you just eat my ice cream and take off?" Zoey asked.

Jake leaned close and kissed her lightly on the mouth. "I knew you'd understand. Sorry. But come over tonight, okay?"

"I'll check my calender," Zoey called after his retreating back.

She wandered on through the crowd, feeling the sunshine of the brief Maine summer on her shoulders. This strange, tragic summer was finally close to an end.

She walked past all the familiar shops, following the gentle downhill slope toward the dock. There, in the wider spaces, the crowd was less dense. She could see a line in front of her parents' restaurant and hesitated, unsure what to do. If she went anywhere near the place, she'd get drafted into working. Of course, she could use the money. Sophomore year was about to start, and she needed to replace her now dorky freshman clothes.

But it was just too nice a day to bus tables.

She ate some more of her ice cream, biting off chunks of waffle. Yes, waffle, *she thought defiantly.*

The crowd opened up suddenly, and to her surprise she found herself staring at a guy, standing alone, leaning against a pole by the ferry gate. His blond hair tossed and fretted in the breeze. There were people all around, but it seemed as if a force field surrounded him, leaving him utterly separate and apart.

Lucas.

The image leapt at her, a picture of loneliness. He was gazing with sad, despairing eyes at the bright town, seeking to memorize every image, seeking to hold on.

The ferry whistle shrieked and she saw him flinch, a strange and telling action. No islander raised to the sound of that whistle ever reacted. Yet Lucas had flinched as if he'd been stung.

Were his eyes filled with tears? She couldn't be sure from this distance. Was he searching the crowd for a particular face, hoping that someone, anyone, would come to say good-bye?

A false hope. No one on Chatham Island would break the isolation that had been imposed on the boy who'd brought tragedy to the island. His father, hard-faced and grim, stood on the bow of the ferry, waiting to escort his son.

Zoey eased closer, moving in dreamlike slowness. Lucas's gaze at last focused on her, his attempt at a smile crumbling, his attempt to hide his tears failing, too.

"Hi, Lucas," she said, lowering her eyes to the ground.

"Hey, Zoey," he said without expression.

She stood there, an arm's length away, not knowing what else to say. He said nothing, only brushed surreptitiously at his eyes. She stared at the remnants of her ice-cream cone. Then she looked up.

She had never looked into sadder eyes.

She reached out with her free hand and gripped his arm. "Look, take care of yourself, okay?"

Lucas looked as if her kind words might destroy his last reserves of control. He nodded.

Zoey started to turn away, but some unseen force stopped her. She stepped forward, paused, then with infinite gentleness kissed his lips.

He stared at her uncomprehendingly.

She gulped hard, flustered and amazed at what she'd done.

"I . . . I just thought someone should say good-bye."

The ferry whistle shrieked again. The final warning.

"I have to go," he said.

"I know," she answered.

"Thank you," he said.

"Here." She held out the last of her ice-cream cone. "You may not get any ice cream for a while. . . ."

He smiled sadly as he accepted her gift. "I guess not."

"There's not much left," she apologized.

He stared at her long and hard. She felt his eyes move from her long yellow braid, to her bare, tanned arms, to her freckled nose . . . and settle on her eyes.

"That's okay. The waffle's my favorite part," he said before he turned away.

YOUTH DIES IN DRUNK DRIVING ACCIDENT

BY LISA SOO

Special to the Weymouth Times

CHATHAM ISLAND—In many ways it is becoming all too common a story. On the evening of June 27, tragedy touched the lives of three Chatham Island youths, leaving one dead, one injured, and one, apparently, directly responsible.

Wade McRoyan, 18, was killed when the car he was in struck a tree along Coast Road on Chatham Island. A second passenger, Claire Geiger, 15, suffered a mild concussion and a broken wrist, along with contusions and abrasions. Ms. Geiger is the daughter of Burke Geiger, president of Mid-Maine Bank of Weymouth. The third occupant of the car, Lucas Cabral, 16, was uninjured. Police say Cabral was able to pull the injured parties from the car and seek assistance.

Police also say Mr. Cabral has admitted to being the driver of the car. The officer on the scene administered a Breathalyzer test, which showed Cabral to be legally intoxicated. Ms. Geiger was tested at Weymouth hospital, and the deceased was later tested by the medical examiner. Both

Continued on Page A2

Continued from Page A1

were found to have blood alcohol levels well above the legal limit for adults.

This is not the first such accident to occur in the greater Weymouth area, but it has hit especially hard in the small Chatham Island community of 300 permanent residents. There has never been a fatal automobile accident on the island, which has few roads.

Police will bring charges of drunken driving and vehicular manslaughter against Lucas Cabral. Contacted by telephone, Cabral refused comment.

Burke Geiger stated that his daughter is in good condition and is not expected to suffer permanent injury. "She's going to be fine, thank God," he said. "This whole thing is such an utterly senseless tragedy. My heart goes out to the McRoyans, whom I know well. I can only imagine the pain they must be feeling."

As to the accused Lucas Cabral, Geiger would only say, "I hope that young man will learn from this very sad episode."

ONE

"FIVE DAYS. FIVE LOUSY DAYS. Not a month or several months or a year, no, not even a full week. Five days." Nina Geiger drew deeply on her cigarette and exhaled clear, pure Maine sea air. "Five. Tomorrow it will be down to four. The next day—"

"I'm guessing three?" Zoey said.

"Two."

"One."

"Then . . ."

"Blastoff?" Zoey suggested.

"School," Nina said, crumpling the unlit cigarette in her hand and tossing it toward the trash can. She was allergic to smoke, but the cigarette went with a certain image she liked, so she smoked without lighting. The cigarette missed the trash and landed on the chipped gray-painted steel deck of the ferry. The bay breeze blew it in little circles.

"Better get that. Skipper Too will throw you overboard for messing up his boat," Zoey said. Skipper Too, who was really named Tom Clement, was the captain of the *Minnow*, which was actually called the *Island Breeze. Gilligan's Island* reruns were always popular on the island.

Nina looked defiant for a moment, then leaned forward to retrieve the cigarette. She was wearing black fishnet stockings, thigh-highs that were artfully ripped in several places. Over them she wore baggy army shorts. She had on a brown leather jacket that clashed with her black Doc Marten boots.

"So you're looking forward to school?" Zoey asked, deliberately provocative.

"Just like I look forward to my period every month. Like I look forward to going to the dentist to have my molars drilled." Nina pulled a second cigarette from her pack of Lucky Strikes and popped it in the corner of her darkly lipsticked mouth.

Zoey waited. There was bound to be a third example.

"Like I look forward to finding out the milk has gone sour after I've already taken a swallow."

"The three-part comic tautology rule," Zoey said.

"You remember that?"

"Nina's First Rule," Zoey said. "Funny examples work best in threes."

"Going from least funny to most funny," Nina added. She sighed. "At least you're going to be a senior."

"Yeah, you'll just be a lowly junior. Whereas I will have all the glory and power associated with being a senior." She shot her friend a sidelong look.

The breeze freshened, caught the bow spray, and flung it against Zoey in a fine, cold mist. She grimaced and zipped up the front of her red fleece L.L. Bean jacket. She wore khaki shorts, white running shoes, and a white cotton blouse. It was just right for the warm day ashore in Weymouth, but the twenty-five-minute ferry ride to Chatham Island always had the potential to grow cold, even on a bright, late summer day.

She bent over to rummage in her ferry bag, a stretch net affair that no islander would dream of traveling without. It was loaded with college-ruled notebook paper, yellow plastic pencils, soft-grip pens, and a three-ring binder decorated with abstract pink triangular designs. It also held the items that had been on her father's list: a dozen bulbs of garlic, an annoyingly heavy bag of eggplant, and a glass jar of saffron. Finally, concealed beneath everything else, Zoey found the cookies.

"Want one?" she asked.

"What are they?"

"Fig Newtons."

"Fig Newtons suck."

Zoey glared at Nina. "Five more days," she said. "And by the way, junior girls play a lot of basketball."

Nina shivered. "Don't be cruel just because I don't like your taste in cookies."

"Lots of dribbling and running." Zoey opened the cookies and popped one in her mouth. "Basketball separates the dorks from the near-dorks."

"At least I won't be the one showering with Claire," Nina said slyly, reaching into Zoey's bag for a Fig Newton. "She separates the melons from the lemons."

"I don't let your sister bother me anymore," Zoey said. "It's stupid to be annoyed at someone just because they have a perfect body and once compared you to the Great Plains. While doing an oral report in front of the class."

"That was years ago," Nina said. "You're not the Great Plains anymore. Of course, you're not the Rocky Mountains, either."

"Jake thinks I'm perfect," Zoey said. She looked ahead toward Chatham Island, drawing closer now. From this point, she knew it would take exactly six minutes to round the breakwater, slow down into the enclosed harbor, sidle up to the town dock, and tie off the ferry. She'd taken the trip a few million times during her ten years on the island. She also knew that as they rounded the breakwater she'd be able to look up the ridge and see Jake's house. He might even be on the balcony, using his dad's telescope to watch them come in.

"You know, these aren't horrible," Nina said thoughtfully as she chewed on a cookie. "You just have to get past the fact that they're all mushy. I like crisp."

The ferry rounded the concrete breakwater and brought the island's only town into view across the calm, gray water. North Harbor was a cluster of red brick, painted wood, and weathered gray-shingle buildings. Shabby-looking wooden lobster traps piled five deep lined the docks around several high-bowed, rough-looking fishing boats with names like *Santo Cristo* and *Santa Maria*.

The highest point in the town was the needle-sharp church spire. But behind the town, the green and pine-wooded ridge rose higher still, forming a barrier to the growth of North Harbor. A few buildings peered out through the trees on the slope, quaint inns that catered to the warm weather tourists.

"Why exactly do you hate school, anyway?" Zoey asked. "When we were little, you liked it better than I did."

Nina sucked on her unlit cigarette. "I was young and unformed then. That was before I realized that school is specifically designed to crush the spirits of people like me."

"It's designed to crush everyone's spirits, Nina. Don't take it so personally. I told Mrs. Bonnard—you'll have her this year for English—I told her I wanted to write romance novels when I grew up, and she said the people who wrote those kinds of things were literary whores. I had to use a bicycle pump to reinflate my dreams."

Nina smiled. "Better to be a literary whore than a literal whore."

"Oh, that's deep. Tell that to Mrs. Bonnard when you see her. You didn't think the bicycle-pump line was funny?"

"I smiled. What am I supposed to do, laugh till I pee?"

Zoey looked up the east slope of the ridge and made out Jake's cedar-sided house. Sure enough, there was a tiny figure standing on the balcony outside his parents' bedroom, no bigger than a fly from this distance. Zoey fought a sudden impulse to aim a rude gesture in his direction. Which would have been inexcusable, she knew. It was just that sometimes it got on her nerves, thinking how ever present Jake could be in her life.

Most of the time, though, it was nice knowing he was always there for her.

She grimaced, confused by the contradiction. Well, consistency was the hobgoblin of little minds. Someone famous had said that. Someone famous who knew what a hobgoblin was.

She let her gaze travel left. She could barely make out the brass weather vane her father had put on their house. Just a few yards up the slope something caught her eye. A guy, far too distant to recognize, standing on the Cabrals' deck.

She glanced at the dock. No, Mr. Cabral's boat was still out at sea. So who was that on the deck? She felt a shiver skate down her spine. Not Lucas. It couldn't be. Lucas was in jail. Or Youth Authority, or whatever they called it.

The thought touched her with gloom. It had been some time since she'd thought of Lucas Cabral. His was not a name that came up very often. Unconsciously she touched her lips, remembering that single, strange, inexplicable kiss almost two years ago. Then she thrust the memory out of her mind.

She looked back at the Cabral house, but the light had shifted just enough so that the deck was hidden in glare. Well, it was probably nothing, anyway.

Zoey said a casual good-bye to Nina at the dock. Nina's house was at the northern end of town, overlooking the lighthouse.

Zoey turned right and crossed the paved open square that served as a parking and dropoff area for the ferry and McRoyans' Marina. It was mostly empty, dotted here and there with island cars—rusted, pathetic wrecks without license plates. North Harbor was only six or eight blocks long, and all of Chatham Island was no more than three miles long, with roads over less than half of that, so people didn't see much need for expensive luxury cars. Real cars were kept on the mainland in a covered lot for trips to the mall, south to Portland, or even to Boston.

Passmores', her parents' restaurant, was only a few feet away, facing Dock Street. Its tiny, three-table outdoor café had one table occupied. She went down the alley to the back door, pausing to stick the lid onto an overflowing trash bin.

The door was open, and she stepped into the cramped stainless-steel kitchen area. A large aluminum stock pot bubbled on the stove, and the dishwasher roared, sending up clouds of steam.

Her father had his back to the door, his hair tied back in a ponytail. He was chopping parsley in quick, decisive strokes, pausing every now and again to shovel the parsley into a pile and take a swallow from a sweating bottle of beer.

"Hey, Dad," Zoey called out.

Her father half turned to look at her. The front of his white apron was stained green and brown. He wore wooden clogs on his feet and a Grateful Dead T-shirt. The mocking, laughing blue eyes were the model for her own. People who saw them together always pointed it out, though the rest of her, the unruly blond hair, the smile that rose more on one side than the other, even the ears that seemed to stick out just a little, were straight from her mother.

"You get my eggplant?" her father asked.

She held up her ferry bag as evidence and began to empty it on the counter. "These were the smallest they had."

"They'll do. You hungry?"

"No thanks," Zoey said. "I ate some cookies on the boat. Is Mom here yet?"

Her father stopped chopping and wiped off the knives. "Yeah, we're both stuck here tonight. Christopher had something or other to do, so I gave him the night off. Your mom's in front, but I wouldn't go out there unless you want to get roped into stocking the bar. Plus she's pissed at me, so she's in a bad mood."

"Thanks for the warning. What are you guys fighting about?"

"I have no idea. She said something about getting fat, I said no, you're not, aside from your butt maybe, you're the same as you always were, and suddenly she's mad. You're a woman, why don't you explain it?"

Zoey shook her head. "I think I'll stay out of it. I guess I'm going over to Jake's house, if you guys are going to be here."

Her father eyed her pile of school supplies. "So, are you looking forward to starting school again?"

"Kind of," Zoey said. "I mean, I'll be a senior."

"Well, you're lucky. I hated school myself. About the only part I liked was cutting classes to go get stoned with my friends." He winced in embarrassment. "You don't do stuff like that, do you?"

"This isn't the eighties anymore, Dad."

"Nineties. Give me a break. I'm not that old." He gave her a comically menacing look. "I could still send you out to count bottles with your mom."

Zoey went over and gave him a quick peck on his stubbled cheek. He smelled of fresh parsley and beer. "I'm out of here."

She walked along Dock Street, swinging her much lighter ferry bag. To her right was Town Beach, a narrow strand dotted with driftwood and seaweed that the tourists avoided, preferring the broader beaches along the western shore of the island.

It wasn't yet five o'clock, Zoey realized, but the sun was already weakening, sliding down toward the low brown-and-gray skyline of Weymouth and turning it into a flat, dark cutout.

No wonder Nina was feeling that sense of impending doom—the days were already growing shorter. Soon the daily routine would involve freezing, predawn ferry rides to school, huddling below in boots and parkas and earmuffs. And return trips in the afternoon would take place with blazing sunsets at their backs.

The island seemed unnaturally quiet, as it often did after a trip to Weymouth. Weymouth was a busy little city, full of rattling delivery vans and gasping buses, music escaping from shop doors and car windows. North Harbor, by contrast, was a place of long silences, broken occasionally by barking dogs, screeching gulls, and the many soft sounds of the water.

Across the harbor, through the masts of the sailboats in the marina, Zoey saw the ferry pulling away, heading toward the two outer islands, Penobscot and Allworthy.

How many trips had she taken on that ferry? Thousands? Tens of thousands? No, not ten thousand. Not that many. Of course, if she lived out the rest of her life here, then it would pass ten thousand eventually.

Not that that was going to happen. She was going to college in California, either UCLA or USC or UC San Diego. Anything involving the letter *C*. She planned to apply to all three and she'd probably be accepted at all three, if she could get the loans and grants worked out.

UCLA would be perfect. Year-round sun, year-round warmth, everybody in convertibles. Lined winter jeans that made you look ten pounds heavier would be a thing of the past. She'd go to classes all week, go to Disneyland or the beach on the weekends. Get a tan. Get two tans. Meet some guy who looked like Liam Hemsworth, only nicer. Fall totally in love and end up having to write Jake a terribly sad letter telling him it was over.

"My dearest Jake," she said aloud to an audience of gulls perched on the seawall. "My darling Jake. Dearest Jake. Dear Jake. Jake. I would do anything to avoid writing you this letter, because I know it will cause you great pain, and that is the last thing I want. You have always been kind and honorable with me, and I know your fondest hope has been that we would wed. Alas, that is not to be.

"Alas?" Zoey laughed out loud. "Right. Try *sadly*. Sadly. Yes. Sadly, Jake, that is not to be. Who can predict the human heart? Who knew I would meet the youngest member of One Direction while in Hollywood? Who could have foreseen that we would fall deeply, hopelessly in love? Who could have guessed that our wedding would be invaded by photographers from *TMZ*?

"Who knew I would suffer from strange delusions about Hollywood boy toys?" she asked herself. "Who knew I'd end up talking to myself?"

A vehicle rattled down the road, a familiar rust-red pickup truck. It braked beside her and Jake stuck his head out of the window. "Hey, babe. I spotted you on the boat with Ninny."

Zoey crossed over and kissed him quickly on the lips. "Funny, I was just thinking about you."

"I'm always thinking about you. Jump in."

Zoey went around, reached through the passenger side window, and used the interior handle to open the door. The outside handle didn't work. She climbed up onto the high bench seat. Jake kissed her again, longer this time. He had great lips for kissing, Zoey had decided. Not too full, but not thin, either. And whenever he kissed her, even if it was just a peck on the cheek, he always closed his dark gray eyes slowly, as if he were falling into a dream. And, of course, he had a major bod, too, all muscle-y and tan, with tic-tac-toe abs and a hard rear that made watching him at football practice a major spectator sport.

Not that Zoey cared much about such superficial things.

His only possible failing was that he wore his dark brown hair fairly short. She would have liked to be able to run her fingers through it.

"Where are we going?" Zoey asked. "I was heading to your house."

Jake shrugged. "I've been home all day. I'm tired of home. I thought we could drive down island and watch the sunset."

"You mean park and make out?"

He grinned. "If we go to my house, my mom will force you to help her make dinner. She's making that scallop thing and those apple things for dessert."

"If I wanted to cook, I could have stayed and helped my dad," Zoey said. "On the other hand, your mom makes great apple things."

"Your dad's still down at the restaurant?" Jake asked.

Zoey made a face. She hadn't meant to mention that. "Yes. That Christopher guy bailed."

"So you're saying there are no parental units at your house?" Jake asked. "It's all ours?"

"Benjamin's home," Zoey pointed out.

"His room's downstairs," Jake argued.

"He has supernatural hearing," Zoey said.

"Right. Just because he's blind does not mean he has any better hearing than anyone else. He told me so."

"That's just what he wants you to believe."

"So we'll be quiet."

"Jake, is making out all you ever think of?"

"No. I also think about what should come next, after making out."

Zoey sighed. "You need to broaden your horizons."

"You're right," he said testily. "And I'd like to broaden them with you. I mean, Zo, we've been going out for three, almost four years. We'll be seniors this year."

"I suddenly have a great desire to be home, watching TV by myself," Zoey said. She opened the truck door.

"Oh, come on, Zo," Jake complained. "Peace. All right?"

Zoey closed the door again. "Okay. Let's go to my house and watch some tube or something." She shot him a sarcastic look. "I think Dr. Phil's doing 'Guys Who Think of Nothing But Sex.'"

Zoey

My romantic life started when I was just thirteen years old. At the time I had long, knobby legs, no chest at all, and stringy blond hair done in a style so awful I've tried to destroy every last photograph ever taken of me in those days. Oh, sure, a person with a keen eye and unusual perception might have looked at me and thought, *Well, there's potential there somewhere.* But I'm telling you, when I would just stand there in front of the full-length mirror in my bedroom, stand there in all my pink, well-scrubbed glory, the image that always came to my mind was of a stick figure. Stick body. Stick arms. Stick legs. A circle for a head. A circle with bad hair.

Jake was my pal in those days. We'd known each other since I moved to the island with my family back when I was seven. We used to play catch, Jake and me, with my best friend, Nina, looking on disapprovingly. And we'd hike up the ridge. And we'd, all of us, Jake and me and everyone, take the ferry into town and buy ice cream and hang at the mall and just generally waste time.

I thought about boys in those days, sure. But I guess it didn't really occur to me that Jake was a boy. Jake was Jake. So you see, it came as a major surprise to me. We were walking up the trail along the ridge one afternoon, the whole gang. Jake and I were well out in front of the others, so we stopped to wait for them by a stream flowing with melting snow. I bent over to take a drink, and when I straightened back up, he kissed me. Kind of clumsy, kind of hurried, and we both blushed and looked away and were glad when the others caught up.

Jake's been my boyfriend since that day. Everyone says we're great together, the perfect couple, and I guess we are. He's a very nice guy. The kind of guy whose arms, wrapped tight around you, make you feel small and protected.

And I really like his parents.

TWO

"BENJAMIN? ARE YOU HOME?" ZOEY knocked lightly on the door to her brother's room.

"Yeah. Come in."

Zoey opened the door and stepped inside. Her brother was sitting in gloom, his feet propped up on his antique rolltop desk, his fingers tracing the tiny bumps of a Braille book. Zoey reached automatically for the light switch. Benjamin turned to look back over his shoulder, aiming his sunglasses in her direction. He had worked hard to maintain the habit of looking at the person he was speaking to.

"Jake with you?"

"He's in the family room, channel surfing."

Benjamin nodded. "What's up with you?"

"Dad's working the dinner shift tonight," Zoey said.

"Yeah, I know. Nina's coming over later to read for me. She just called." He reached with perfect precision for one of the built-in shelves of his desk and pulled out a book. He held it up backward for her to see.

Zoey sighed. This was one of Benjamin's running jokes. Like the way he'd decorated his room with maps and posters but had turned half of them upside down. He lived for the times when someone new visited the house and he could point to some upside-down poster of kittens playing with yarn and go on proudly about how much he loved that particular Matisse print. It was a test of character, he said. People who got the joke were all right. People who froze up or played along out of pity were hopeless.

Benjamin laughed and turned the book so she could read the cover. *The Plague*, by Albert Camus. "It's on the suggested list for this year."

"Great," Zoey said. "Nina was already depressed on the boat. That should send her over the edge."

"Nina is always depressed," Benjamin said. "It comes from living in the same house with Claire."

Zoey shook her head. "No one's forcing you to go out with Claire."

Benjamin shrugged. "I hear she's great looking. And she has a nice speaking voice."

Zoey turned off the light and went back out into the front entryway, then down the hall to the family room. Jake was sprawled on the shabby brown couch, a throw pillow under his head, watching *Dateline.* When he saw her, he muted the TV. "Hi. How's Benjamin?"

"Nina's coming over in a little while to read to him," Zoey said.

Jake groaned. "Great. Your brother and Ninny. So much for time alone."

"You shouldn't call her that. She's my best friend."

"How about when she calls me *Joke*?"

Zoey sat on the couch. Jake put his head in her lap and she stroked his cheek, looking down at him affectionately. "That's different. You're just my boyfriend."

"I think she started it," Jake said. "Back when I was in, like, fourth grade. She was in third."

"Since fourth grade. You ever think maybe we're all falling into a rut here?" Zoey said.

Jake looked up at her. "Me and Ninny?"

"All of us. You, me, Benjamin, Nina, Aisha. Even Claire. My parents, your parents."

"See? This is the way you get when you've been talking to Nina. That's why I rag on her. She has the power to destroy a romantic mood from clear across town."

"It's not Nina. It's just this feeling of things going on the same way forever and ever."

"You have the end-of-summer blues, that's all." Jake raised

the volume on the TV.

Zoey pushed his head off her lap and stood up. She walked over to the window restlessly and looked out at the backyard. It was already growing dark. She stood watching as the color faded from the daylilies in the failing light.

The backyard ended in scrub brush at the base of the ridge. The ridge rose sharply from that point, broken granite boulders and gnarled, stubby trees brightened in the warm seasons by dustings of wildflowers. A few houses were propped on the slope where Climbing Way began its ascent along the ridge. Lights were flickering on in their windows, and curtains were being drawn.

She looked up toward the Cabral home, just above hers on the ridge, remembering the impression she'd had on the ferry that someone was up there.

A movement in the shadow caught her eye. She stared. A dark figure stood there, leaning against the railing, his face red and shadowed in the slanting rays of the setting sun.

"Oh, my God," Zoey said, pulling back from the window. She felt her heart pounding.

"What?" Jake asked, looking at her upside down from the couch.

"There's someone up at the Cabrals' house." Zoey pressed her hand over her heart. "I think it may be Lucas."

Jake froze for a moment, then with sudden speed and grace he was beside her. He leaned against the window and looked up the hill, his eyes intense. "I can't see him very clearly."

"It's probably just someone visiting them."

The figure on the deck moved, and for a moment he was clearly outlined in profile before turning away and disappearing.

Jake stepped away from the window. His lips were drawn back in a snarl. There was an ugly light in his eyes. "It's him. It's Lucas. He's back."

Claire Geiger paced slowly around the rails of the widow's walk, pausing from time to time to look in one direction or another before resuming her regular pacing.

The night was cool, and where she was, high atop the three-story house, the breeze was stiff, bringing with it the smells of salt and seaweed and, occasionally, the faint but unmistakable scents of the roses and fringed gentians in the garden below.

Down in the front yard she could make out a shadowy shape closing the gate and trotting toward the front door. Her sister, Nina.

As Claire leaned over the railing to call down to her, she heard the front door close. Too late. She stayed there for a moment, leaning out into space, her long black hair falling forward, before pulling back.

The rail was just barely waist high, and she sometimes worried that she might fall off, sliding helplessly down the pitched roof, careening between the dormered windows and landing on the hard ground below. Sometimes she wondered if those sorts of worries were secret hopes.

The lighthouse, a squat whitewashed tower on a granite islet, blinked and swept its beam over the corrugated black water. Warmer lights from the rooms below spilled out into the front yard, casting shadows among the bushes and trees. As she paced left, she saw the blinking light on the end of the breakwater, the harsh blue-white lights at the ferry landing, the pinpoints of light shining from the portholes of the boats in the marina. Beyond that were the brighter lights of Weymouth, projecting rippling beams and reflections on the mirror of water. Streetlights blazed, car headlights winked and disappeared.

Another quarter turn and she was gazing out over the town proper, dozens of lights in curtained windows, a green warning light atop the church steeple, floating, disconnected lights poking through the trees on the ridge.

She wasn't sure if she had always been so fascinated by light. She suspected it had begun when she started going out with Benjamin. Being around a blind person made you think about being blind yourself, and somehow that made every color seem more vivid, every light seem brighter.

Right at her feet, a square of buttery light suddenly appeared. Nina's face stared up at her from Claire's room below.

"You up there?" Nina called out.

"Yes," Claire said.

"You coming down?"

"I wasn't planning on it. Not just yet."

Nina climbed the ladder, but kept her head below the opening. She had a fear of heights, at least of wide-open areas like the widow's walk.

Claire stood looking down at her sister's upturned face, so like her own—the same wide Geiger mouth they'd inherited from their father—and yet unique. Nina's eyes were gray, laughing eyes, one just slightly out of alignment in a way that gave her a look of perpetual skepticism. Claire's own eyes were dark within dark.

"How's the weather out there?"

"Didn't you just come in?" Claire asked. "It's the same weather up here as it is down on the street."

"I know. I was being droll."

Claire nodded. Nina found it hysterical that Claire was interested in weather and planned to be a climatologist someday. "It's getting chilly. Some high cirrus clouds to the south. You want the barometer reading?"

"Cirrus? Are you sure they're *cirrus* clouds?" Nina asked mockingly.

Claire pulled her hands up into the loose sleeves of her baggy sweater and decided to let the remark pass. "So, where have you been?"

"I was supposed to be reading some novel to your boyfriend, Benjamin."

"Don't call him my boyfriend. We just go out sometimes. What do you mean *supposed* to be reading?"

Nina gave her a meaningful look. "Reality suddenly got more interesting than fiction."

Claire inhaled the crisp air deeply. "Are you going to explain, or am I supposed to guess?"

"Think good old days."

Claire sighed.

"Now think bad old days," Nina said.

"Nina, you just keep getting stranger. Or are you just getting more droll?"

"Both. Thanks. That's a cool thing to say." Nina met her gaze for just a second. "Lucas is back."

Claire felt her heart miss several beats. She reached for the nearest railing and gripped it tightly. "Are you sure?"

"Zoey and Jake said it was him, up at his mom and dad's house, hanging around the deck, looking Lucas-like."

"Jake saw him?" Claire asked sharply. "What did he do?"

"Nothing. Yet," Nina said. "But he was definitely wired. It was a very tense scene. Jake took off right after I showed up. Zoey was halfway thinking we should go and warn Lucas. Benjamin talked her out of it, though. He said he didn't think Jake would really do anything."

"Warn Lucas?" Claire bit her lip. "I don't waste a lot of sympathy on Lucas Cabral."

"He used to be your one true love," Nina said provocatively.

"That was a long time ago."

"Two years."

"I didn't think he'd have the nerve to come back to the island," Claire said. She looked toward the south, toward the few wan lights at the base of the ridge. One of those lights must be the Cabral house. One of those lights might be his window. He might be gazing out at this very moment, searching for her with his coolly penetrating gaze. She turned away.

Nina shrugged as well as she could while still gripping the ladder. "Where else is he going to go? I guess he's done his time, as they say. Paid his dues. Made his amends to society."

Claire rubbed her right wrist. A bump on the head and a broken wrist, that's all she'd gotten from Lucas Cabral. The wrist still ached when the weather grew cold and damp.

Wade McRoyan, Jake's brother, had died.

Claire shivered, suddenly penetrated by the cool breeze. Something deep inside her had awakened at the mention of Lucas's name. Anger, an urgent, demanding anger. And fear? No. Why should she be afraid?

"I wonder if he'll be going to school," Nina said.

"I doubt he'll stay on the island for long," Claire replied. "I doubt he'll feel very welcome here."

Claire Geiger

I had just turned fifteen. Sweet fifteen? Maybe. I don't know if I was ever sweet anything. I guess I wouldn't have been in the car if I were all that sweet.

And I was in the car, that much I can be sure of. And I guess I'd been drinking, too, just like Wade and Lucas. Beer that Wade had somehow gotten hold of. We had driven down Coast Road, past the end of the paved part onto the rutted dirt road that winds back into the woods, with trees closing in all around and deer leaping into our headlights to stare.

We were feeling pretty cool. Lucas and I grabbed a couple of the beers and went deeper into the woods, intoxicated as much by each other as by the alcohol. We were massively in love. I'd have done anything for him, and I believe he'd have died for me if I'd asked him.

Wade stayed by the car, kicking back and listening to the stereo. He'd just broken up with a girl from the mainland and was a little bummed.

I guess Lucas and I made out for a while in the woods. I guess we eventually came back and collected Wade and drove back toward town. I say I guess because I don't remember exactly. I've tried, and sometimes in a dream, or in one of those strange moments of clarity that come when you see a certain picture, smell a certain fragrance that triggers memory, I'll . . . but then it's gone.

I do know what happened later. I know they took me to the hospital with a concussion and a broken wrist. I know that Wade died. And I know that my heart broke when Lucas admitted that he had been the one driving.

Jake came to see me in the hospital. His eyes were empty, his voice barely audible. I told him how guilty I felt. He told me, No, Claire. Lucas was driving the car. Lucas had rammed that tree. Lucas had killed his brother. Lucas was guilty.

And what was I? Just another one of his victims.

THREE

THE CURTAINS WERE OPEN AND the light was on in Jake's room. Zoey stepped onto the patio and pressed her face against the sliding glass door, searching the room for him. Not on the Soloflex machine. Not sitting at his computer. Not watching his TV.

She tried the door, but it was locked. He was probably upstairs with his parents. Zoey shrugged philosophically. She didn't really want to walk in on the whole family at this late hour, but she felt she needed to see Jake. It had been several hours since they had seen Lucas from her family room window, time enough for Jake to calm down a little, to mellow, as he sometimes did, from anger to his own brand of silent grief and remorse.

She walked up and around the house, arriving at the front door. She knocked, and in seconds Mrs. McRoyan opened the door and squealed her usual enthusiastic welcome.

"Is Jake home?" Zoey asked. "I didn't see him downstairs."

Mrs. McRoyan made a puzzled face, wrinkling her blue eyes. "Should be. I can't imagine he'd go out this late."

A sudden worry flashed through Zoey's mind. Had Jake gone off looking for trouble with Lucas?

"I know it's late, but do you mind if I go see if he's down there?" Zoey asked.

"What late?" Mrs. McRoyan protested. "I only wish you'd been here earlier. I had out the trusty Betty Crocker cookbook and was working on the apple tarte tatin, only this time I was making my own puff pastry. Would you like a piece?"

"Sounds great—like everything you make, Mrs. McRoyan. But I'm kind of full."

"When are you going to start calling me Daisy?" She ushered Zoey inside.

"Oh, probably not till I'm at least thirty," Zoey said. "I think I'll just run on down—"

"Well, you know the way. But if you have time, stop back up here. No one around here appreciates the labor that goes into puff pastry. Sure, they'll eat it, but my husband and Jake and Holly don't understand."

Zoey trotted down the stairs. The rec room light was off, but the door to Jake's room was open. With a sense of foreboding, Zoey hurried forward.

Just then, the door to Jake's bathroom opened wide. Steam

billowed out. She turned and saw him facing the mirror over the sink, his face covered in shaving cream.

His face was the only thing covered.

He turned and saw her. His eyes opened wide.

"*Oh oh oh*, I . . . I . . ." she replied.

He slammed the door shut.

She dived toward his room. "Sorry!" she yelled.

"I just shaved my right cheek down to the bone!" he complained, his voice muffled by the door.

"I said I was sorry." She chewed on her thumb. "I . . . I didn't see anything."

"What is that, an insult?"

"That's not funny, Jake," she chided. She heard him laughing softly.

"Look, all I have in here is a towel. Bring me some clothes."

"What?" she asked, looking around at the room and not seeing anything that might be clothing.

"In my closet, on the hook. I think there's a pair of sweatpants."

She found them, a gray pair with *Harvard* embroidered down the leg. She tapped on his bathroom door. "Here."

He opened the door a crack. A hand emerged and disappeared with the pants. Seconds later he came out, holding a wad of toilet paper to his right cheek.

"I just wanted to make sure you were all right," Zoey said lamely.

"I'm not a Ken doll, if that's what you wanted to know."

"You know what I meant."

"Sure," he said breezily. "I'm bleeding profusely and I'm embarrassed. On the other hand, I had been feeling kind of sleepy and now I'm wide awake. Jeez, I just saw *Psycho* on TV last night. You know, butcher knives flashing in the shower? It's amazing how high you can jump when you get that shot of adrenaline. Coach should have seen me."

He pulled the tissue away from his face.

"I think you'll live," Zoey said.

"I don't know . . ."

She put her arms around his broad bare shoulders, her hands barely meeting in back. "You want me to kiss it and make it better?"

"Actually, yes."

They ended up on his bed, making out. After a while they ended up lying together, Jake with his back against the wall, Zoey reclining against his chest, enjoying the rise and fall of his breathing, listening to the deep rumble of his laugh as they watched Jimmy Fallon together.

At last, as she felt sleep closing in, Zoey got up, stretched, and headed for the sliding glass door. He followed her, peering out at the night over her shoulder.

"Thanks for coming over," he said.

"I just wanted to, you know, make sure you're okay," she said.

He smiled gently. "I am now, Zo. To tell you the truth, I was pretty keyed up before, but then, you always have been able to make me feel great, just by being around."

She nodded, touched by his emotional admission, so unusual for Jake. "You know what?" she asked. "You do the same for me."

He grinned mischievously. "You could spend the night . . ."

Zoey shook her head tolerantly and sighed. "Good night, Jake."

Zoey woke and lay in bed, listening to the music of her clock radio and warming to the fading tendrils of a dream about Jake. It was eight o'clock, earlier than she had been getting up, but she was trying to get herself back on a school-year schedule. Once school started, she would have to be down at the dock by seven forty.

As she closed her eyes again, a thought was prickling the back of her mind, demanding to be remembered. Oh, yeah. Lucas.

She snapped off the radio and climbed out of bed, twisting

her Boston Bruins T-shirt around so that the logo once again faced the right way. Her room had two windows, one on the side that gave a view of the house next door and, if she craned her neck, a sliver of the Cabrals' deck.

No sign of Lucas. Maybe he wasn't even home. Maybe.

She moved to the second deep, dormered window where she had a built-in desk. She leaned across the cluttered desk and drew aside the curtains. The house was perched at the dead end of Camden Street, giving her a view straight down the entire five-block length of the street.

Gentle morning sunlight lit the brick and wood buildings on the left side of the street, leaving the other side in cool shadow. As usual, there was little traffic, only the occasional bicycle, the infrequent island car rattling to or from the ferry. Two blocks down, where Camden crossed the cobblestones of Exchange Street, the old woman who ran the antique store was sweeping the sidewalk in front of her building.

Zoey drew her gaze away from the window and stared at the sides of the dormer. The walls were plastered with Post-it notes—lists and reminders and appointments on the right, quotations on the left. Her current favorite was a quote from Joseph Joubert:

Imagination is the eye of the soul.

She had no idea who Joseph Joubert was, but she liked the quote just the same.

Below that was another.

A man ^or a woman can stand almost anything except a succession of ordinary days.

Goethe had said that, and it had been bothering her ever since she'd found it in a book and duly written it down on the yellow Post-it note. Maybe that was why she'd been feeling restless. Maybe her life was becoming a succession of ordinary days.

She showered and shaved her legs and put on white shorts and a short-sleeve blue-and-white-striped top. Her mother was downstairs in the kitchen with Benjamin. She was wearing a bathrobe, her faded blond hair tousled, reading the newspaper and sipping coffee. Benjamin was making himself a bowl of cereal, keeping his thumb hooked inside the bowl so he'd know when he'd added enough milk. Her father would already be down at the restaurant, cooking for the fishermen and the early morning ferry crowd.

"Good morning, everyone," Zoey said cheerfully.

Her mother looked up from her paper and smiled wanly.

"Don't be so cheerful; my head can't take it."

"Hung over," Benjamin said, walking with his cereal to the table.

"No, smart guy," their mother said. "I just didn't get much sleep last night." She grinned. "Your father and I were arguing, so naturally we had to make up."

Zoey shook her head and reached for the box of muffins on the counter. "Mom, do you think you could spare us the details? We *are* your kids."

Her mother shrugged. "You do know the facts of life, don't you? I mean, you do know where you and Benjamin came from and all?"

"Yes, of course I know. I just don't need to think about it. You're warping me."

"I don't do all that parental crap, you know that," her mother said, waving her hand dismissively. "You want Donna Reed, go hang out with Daisy McRoyan. She likes to stay home and bake pies while her husband's out banging everything in a skirt."

Zoey glared at her mother. "I don't think you should go around saying things like that. What if Jake was over here and heard you say that about his dad?"

"If Jake doesn't know it, he's the only one," her mother said. She rolled her eyes. "Look, I'm sorry. I take it back. Fred McRoyan's a saint. Everybody on this island's a saint. We're all just one big, happy family." She turned the page of the newspaper.

"I'm going out," Zoey said.

"You going over?" Benjamin asked.

"No, I was just going to head down to the circle, see if anyone's around. See if Nina wants to do anything. You want to come? Or did you want me to pick something up for you on the mainland?"

"Nope. Just wondering," Benjamin said. "Take it easy."

"We could use a few hours of your time down at the restaurant later," her mother said. "Just this afternoon."

"No prob," Zoey said. The restaurant was the whole family's responsibility. Besides, her parents paid her for her work.

"Hey," her mother said suddenly, looking up from her paper. "What's this I hear about the Cabral kid coming back?"

Zoey turned. "We thought we saw him yesterday evening. No one's totally sure, though."

"He was a cute kid," her mother said. "Remember how he'd come down the hill in the morning and bring us those sweet rolls his mom made? Now there's a woman who should open a bakery. Your dad's been after her recipe for years."

"I remember," Zoey said. Lucas would sit at the table and drink coffee with milk before walking with Zoey and Benjamin down to the ferry, where they would meet Nina and Claire and Aisha and Jake. And Wade.

No doubt Lucas would be the subject of conversation on the island for some time.

At least for a while, the succession of days wouldn't be quite so ordinary.

FOUR

CLAIRE KNEW THEY WOULD BE there. They were there many mornings, and today, with word of new developments spreading, no one would miss circling.

The circle was at the center of North Harbor, a cobblestoned hub from which five tiny streets spread out like spokes. On one side, the church seemed to stare across the circle and down Exchange to the ferry landing. Around the circle were little souvenir shops, craft galleries, and candy stores that sold fudge to the tourists. On the exterior wall of the insignificant town hall was a compass rose that showed how far it was from Chatham Island to all sorts of cities and locations around the world—845 miles to Bermuda, 1,325 miles to Sarasota, Florida, 14,678 miles to Tahiti, if you wanted to take the long way around.

In the center of the circle was a grassy lawn dotted with a few trees, a couple of quaint, green-painted benches, and a low granite obelisk with a brass plaque bearing the names of the island's war dead since the Civil War. There were nine names altogether, with spare room for more.

Zoey was standing, and Claire's sister, Nina, lounged on a bench beside Aisha, who was trying to catch her mass of springy black curls with a rubber band. Jake leaned against the monument, his head bowed, his big shoulders hunched forward. The usual crowd. Sometimes Benjamin would be there, too. Lately the black guy, Christopher, had dropped by from time to time, obviously not sure whether he was being invited to join the group or not. Hopefully he understood, having seen Aisha, that he wasn't being given the cold shoulder because of his race. It was just that he'd only been on the island since spring.

To Claire's surprise, the conversation was not about Lucas.

"We're the last of a dying breed," Aisha was saying. "I'm graduating this year, Zoey and Ben are both graduating, Claire's graduating."

"Joke will graduate if he can ever get those multiplication tables down," Nina said.

"Chew me, Ninny," Jake said.

"Next year there's not going to be much of an island group at the school," Aisha continued. "Just Nina and my little brother. It will be a few years before Jake's little sister is old enough."

"Kalif's going to the high school next year?" Zoey asked. "I don't know why, but he never seems that old to me."

"Nina and Kalif, that's it. That will be it for islanders." Aisha nodded in agreement with herself.

"You figure one of us should volunteer to flunk so we can keep up the islander tradition at Weymouth High?" Claire asked.

"Would you mind?" Aisha said with her worldly-wise, impertinent grin. "I'd do it, but my folks would be pissed."

"Benjamin would be glad if you flunked, Zoey," Jake said.

"He would not," Zoey said. "Benjamin's not like that."

"Not consciously, maybe," Jake persisted. "But he's not thrilled to be in the same grade with his sister who's a year younger than he is."

"Benjamin's realistic," Claire said. "He lost almost two years being sick and going through rehab. He's already made up half that time." Jake moved away from the monument, and Claire took his place. He had left the granite just slightly warm with his body heat. Or maybe that was her imagination.

"The only bummer is I'll have to ride the ferry alone," Nina said.

"Kalif will be there," Claire pointed out. "Maybe he likes older—stranger—women."

"Are we doing anything today?" Zoey asked, sounding suddenly frustrated.

Aisha shrugged. "I have to help my mom get the rooms

ready. We're booked for the weekend."

"I thought about taking the boat out, maybe do the barbecue thing up at the pond if anyone's up for it," Jake said. He looked questioningly at Zoey, then shot a glance at Claire.

"Just so I know," Claire said, turning to meet Jake's gaze, "since I got here last and all. Did you already deal with the question of Lucas, or are we going to pretend he doesn't exist?"

Jake's expression turned instantly stony. Zoey looked relieved.

"I don't know what there is to talk about," Jake said, almost daring anyone to say anything else.

Claire rolled her eyes. "This is Chatham Island, not Manhattan Island," she said. "It's not like Lucas is going to be invisible. We're going to be running into him, don't you think?"

Jake kicked at a tuft of grass. "This is such crap," he said. "This shouldn't be happening. I mean, what the hell does he think he's doing, coming back here? What does he think we're going to do? As far as I'm concerned, two lousy years in juvy is nothing."

"They gave him the maximum for a juvenile," Zoey said quietly.

"Only because he already had a record," Jake said. "I don't think the judge gave a damn that my brother—" He lost his voice for a moment, and Claire looked away. "He didn't care that Wade was dead. I mean, if Lucas hadn't had a record, the judge probably would have let him off with a reprimand."

"That's not true," Zoey said, but Claire could see that Jake was beyond listening.

"Vehicular manslaughter," Jake said, sneering at the words. "You get faced and you go tearing down Coast Road in the middle of the night . . . It's not like it's an accident. I mean, it's not like you have to be a genius to figure out that you can't drive stinking drunk without someone getting hurt. His lawyer made it sound like it was all just this unfortunate accident. Son of a bitch should have gone to prison, not juvy. See how big a man he is in prison. See how he likes that."

Jake seemed to run out of steam. He slumped down on the grass, resting his elbows on his knees and holding his head in both hands. Claire had heard it all before. They'd all heard it before.

"We all miss Wade," Aisha said at last, breaking the silence.

Claire nodded. She rubbed her wrist. It had been in a cast for two months. The doctor said her being drunk might have accounted for the mildness of her injuries. Evidently it was better to feel relaxed when you stopped very suddenly. Except that theory hadn't worked for Wade.

Lucas had been unhurt.

"So what do we do?" Zoey asked.

"Well, it's not like we can get revenge," Aisha said firmly. "If that's what you're thinking, Jake, then stop thinking it."

Jake shook his head. "I'm not going to touch him. My dad said we're just going to have to live with it. He says he thinks Mr. Cabral will get rid of Lucas eventually."

"His own dad is going to kick him out?" Nina asked skeptically. "I don't think so."

"Mr. Cabral is a proud guy," Jake said. "You know how these old Portuguese fishermen are. Son or not, Lucas humiliated him. My dad thinks sooner or later the old man will force him out."

"Jeez, that's cold, isn't it?" Nina said.

"Cold is what he deserves," Jake said sharply. "You weren't hurt, all right, Ninny? I was. Wade was my brother. And your sister was hurt, too. Don't tell either of us about what's cold."

"All right, get a grip," Nina said. She made a face but fell silent.

"If Jake's dad is right, then I think we should help Mr. Cabral . . . deal with Lucas," Claire said.

"How is that?" Jake asked.

Claire met his eyes. "I think we should make sure he knows he's not wanted by any of us, either," she said slowly. "Cut him off totally."

"There's something about this that makes me uncomfortable," Aisha said. "I mean, I don't know—"

"Look, no one's forcing you to do anything," Claire said reasonably. "But we've always stuck together."

Nina shook her head. "Maybe we should just go all out," she said. "You know, grab our pitchforks, light some torches, and march on up the hill and drive the monster out like the peasants in a Frankenstein movie."

"Let's save that for later," Claire said. She looked around the group and saw them nodding, one by one—Aisha troubled, Nina mocking, Zoey almost distracted. Jake deadly serious.

Claire took a deep breath and let it out slowly. For the first time since Nina had brought her the news, she felt . . . relief.

Yes, that was the emotion, she realized. Relief. But why?

Aisha Gray was still troubled when she left the group at the circle and headed toward home.

She was halfway down Center before she realized that she was going to be passing right by Lucas's house on the way to her own. Avoiding it would mean going some distance out of her way and making a much steeper climb. She didn't feel like doing that. The walk back home was steep enough.

So what did they all expect her to do if she went walking past the Cabrals' and Lucas happened to be out front? Was she supposed to ignore him, refuse to answer if he said hello?

It was ridiculous. Jake, she could understand. Maybe even

Claire. But why on earth would Zoey go along with this primitive reaction? Just because she was Jake's girlfriend?

The road beneath her feet began to steepen and she leaned into it, stretching her calf muscles, pumping her arms.

There it was, right above the Passmores' house, the little gray shingle cottage with the deck that looked down the hillside. She stole a glance at it. The windows weren't curtained, but the interior was dark. Still, he could be in there, watching her walk past.

She barely remembered Lucas. She'd only come to the island a year before Lucas had left. Mostly she recalled an image of long, unruly blond hair and a face too sweet for the eyes.

She passed the house and kept climbing, feeling a mixture of relief and resentment. This island solidarity crap could get to be too much. On the other hand . . .

Her parents had moved to Chatham Island and bought the inn three years ago, just as she was starting high school. It had been a shaky time for her, moving from Boston to this tiny, lily-white enclave. None of the kids her age had bothered even to say hello, and she'd assumed with sinking heart that it was racism on their part. Maybe to some extent it was.

But when she'd taken the ferry to the mainland that first day, there'd been some subtle change. A couple of the kids at Weymouth High had started in with crude remarks about her race. Zoey had told them to stop, but they had persisted. Which was when Zoey had gone to get Jake and his big brother, Wade. Jake and Wade had made it clear that Aisha was one of them. They didn't even know her name, but what had mattered was that she was an islander.

Of course, it had still taken a year before she'd been really accepted on the island itself. And that's when the accident happened, and Lucas was sent away.

Climbing Way turned and brought Gray House into view. It was a two-story brick structure with an attic ringed with dormered windows. The Gray family, Aisha, Kalif, and their parents, lived in bits and pieces of the huge old mansion. The family room, her parents' bedroom, and the small private kitchen and bathroom were built over what had once, long ago, been stables, a wing of the main house. Aisha's bedroom was downstairs, hidden away. The rest of the downstairs—formal dining room, living room, breakfast room, main kitchen, and foyer—were all stunningly decorated in colonial style, like something straight out of a magazine. Upstairs were the three rooms that were rented out, two smaller rooms and a truly magnificent room called the Governor's Room that had a private bath with a huge whirlpool.

It was a lot like living in a museum.

Someone was sitting on her front porch. It wasn't hard to

figure out who. Aside from her own family, there was only one other African American on Chatham Island. This particular one was holding a handful of wildflowers.

Christopher stood as he caught sight of her. "Hi. I was waiting for you. I figured you were down at the circle with your friends."

Aisha nodded. "Uh-huh."

"Here, these are for you." He held the flowers toward her.

"They are?"

"Sure. I picked them in the yard of my apartment building. The landlady said it was okay as long as I . . ." He stammered to a halt. Then he recovered himself. "As long as I was going to give them to a young lady."

Aisha looked from the flowers to his face and back again. He had shrewd brown eyes and an expression that seemed to go from intense concentration to confusion, as if he were always trying to figure something out.

What was she supposed to do? She didn't even know this guy. Still, how could she refuse?

"My mom will like them in the front foyer. We have guests coming tomorrow, and she likes flowers around."

"But these are for you," Christopher said, looking uncomfortable.

Aisha took them, carefully wrapping her hand around the

stems. "Thanks," she said. Then, not knowing what else to add, she pushed past him and opened the door. She turned back to him with what she hoped was a dismissive, yet polite expression. "Thank you. I'll see you around."

"Um, wait!" Christopher bounded toward her. "Listen, I, uh, I was thinking."

"Yes?"

He made a fist and slapped it against his palm. "I was, uh, wondering if you'd like to go out with me."

"No, I wouldn't," Aisha said.

Christopher's jaw dropped. "You wouldn't?"

"Thanks, but no."

"Do you already have a boyfriend or something?"

Aisha shook her head. "No."

"Then . . . you just think I'm a troll or something?"

"Look, Christopher, I don't think you're a troll. I just don't know you, that's all. We've only spoken once or twice, and then it was just to say hi."

"Well, if you went out with me, you'd get to know me, wouldn't you?"

"If I don't know you and don't know if I'd even like you, why would I want to go out with you?"

Christopher tilted his head and gave her a sidelong look. "Are you a lesbian? Is that it? No offense if it is; that's cool."

"No, that's not it. I date guys. Only guys. I just don't know you. Maybe later, after a while, I'll get to know you."

"Okay, I'm lost here. You tell me. How do I proceed with getting to know you if I can't ask you out?"

"Why are you so sure you want to know me?" Aisha asked.

Christopher shrugged. "Because you're very beautiful."

"Thank you."

"Besides, I mean, you and I are, like, the only people of color on this island."

"Ah ha!" Aisha pointed a triumphant finger at him. "See, I knew that's all it was. You figure since I'm the only young black woman around and you're the only young black man around that we *have* to be together. Like I have no other choice. See, I understand. Everyone on the island is starting to say, Hey, Aisha, are you going out with that Christopher guy yet? *Yet.* Like it has to happen. Well, it doesn't have to happen."

"But, you have to admit—"

Aisha shook her head. "No, I don't have to admit. I'm not just waiting around here for you to come and sweep me off my feet. I go out with white guys as well as black guys, so it's not just like, hey, check out my skin, now you have to go out with me."

Christopher nodded. "You know, I'm starting to see something in what you're saying. I think you're absolutely right. We needed to know each other better, see, because if I had known you better, I'd have known you were a bitch." He reached for the flowers. "I'll take those."

"Take them," Aisha said, relinquishing the bouquet.

Just then Aisha's mother opened the door and stepped outside. "Is there some reason I hear shouting out here?"

"I'm very sorry, ma'am," Christopher said smoothly. "My name is Christopher Shupe. These are for you." He handed the flowers to Aisha's mother.

Her mother took the flowers and smiled. "They're lovely. I like to have flowers in the house when we have guests. Thank you. I keep wanting to grow a garden, but I never seem to have the time. Maybe next spring."

"Actually, ma'am, there are things you should be doing now if you want a garden for next season. You need to be putting in bulbs, you know, for daffodils, tulips—"

"Tulips?" Mrs. Gray said, her eyes lighting up. "I love tulips. But I just don't have the time, and there aren't any landscaping companies that operate on the island."

"There's a guy I know who'd do it on either a per-job basis or by the hour," Christopher said. "Me."

"Mother," Aisha warned.

"Aren't you in school?" her mother asked.

"No, ma'am. I've graduated, and now I'm working to put college money together. I cook nights down at Passmores' and

I do repairs around the building for my landlady, but I have several days available."

"Tulips," Mrs. Gray repeated, her eyes wandering over the yard.

"Next spring, just like clockwork," Christopher promised.

"You have a deal, young man," Mrs. Gray said. She turned to go back inside. "And thanks for these flowers."

Aisha shot Christopher a poisonous look. He grinned back.

"Fate," he said.

"I don't believe in fate," Aisha said, closing the door in his face.

Lucas Cabral

At the Youth Authority we slept in barracks, a dozen bunkbeds to a room, twenty-four guys in all. The guy in the bunk above me had tried to poison his father with Drano. The guy in the next bed over had sold LSD to some eight-year-olds. So, you see, even though by Chatham Island standards I was a bad guy, my fellow cellmates weren't real impressed.

I spent the first year being bitter. At my dad for being such a hard case. At Claire for never once writing or visiting. I figured that was the least she could have done. At life in general. But after a while, if you're any kind of a human being, you get past bitterness.

I started reading a lot. Used to help some of the other guys keep up with the lame attempts the YA made to deal with our educations. I grew up a little.

One day I was looking through the Weymouth Times and happened on a picture. Zoey. Zoey Passmore, it said right under the photo of her smiling nervously and standing down by the ferry, the place where she had been the only one of all my supposed friends to say a kind word.

Not that I'm bitter.

The article with the picture said she was one of three

Weymouth High kids who had been selected to contribute articles to the paper's youth page. I read the two she did when they came out. An interview with the new vice principal and a funny review of the cafeteria's food. Echoes of a place I used to know.

I cut out the picture and pinned it on the wall beside my cot. After a while it grew yellow and frayed, but I kept it. I don't really know why, except that I've learned you have to cling to hope no matter how unreasonable, no matter how or when it appears.

Even if it's just a faded picture of a beautiful girl you barely knew.

FIVE

"HE WAS GROPING YOU," NINA said. She pulled the trigger of her pump water gun and let fly a stream of water that caught Zoey in the neck. Aiming the stream higher, she arced it straight into Zoey's open mouth. "Last time we went to Big Bite, Jake was groping you, and I'm just saying if we go this evening, expect gropage. It's the fresh air or something. It brings out his grope reflex."

Zoey lay back on the webbed chaise lounge, swallowed the water, and held up her hand for Nina to cease firing. She pumped her own green-and-orange plastic water rifle and aimed toward Nina, who lay ten feet away on a matching chair. Zoey squeezed the trigger and nailed her friend's belly button.

"Sorry," Zoey said, raising her aim.

"It's okay, it feels good," Nina said. "It figures. A beautiful, perfectly sunny day like this, and the beaches are crawling with tourists. They could at least wait till tomorrow."

"I seem to remember you whining about the tourists all

being gone. Anyway, soon we'll have the island back to ourselves," Zoey said. She fired, and this time Nina caught the stream in her mouth. "In the meantime, we have my backyard."

Nina adjusted her rainbow sunglasses and the straps of her two-piece bathing suit. "This tan has to last us like nine months."

"Dragonfly!" Zoey yelled.

Both girls trained their water guns on the big insect buzzing by overhead. It flew off up the hill, and Zoey settled back on her chair.

"Jake was definitely groping you," Nina said. "I saw movement under your shirt."

"Okay, so he tried a minor grope."

"He used to be such a nice boy," Nina said regretfully. "Well raised, respectful of his elders, the kind who always says grace before he eats. Now he's become a swine."

"Guys will do that," Zoey said tolerantly. "They're gropers by nature. Just as girls are counter-gropers."

"I wouldn't know, would I?" Nina said. She sighed dramatically. "Maybe this year I should get me one of them. One of them thar' boyfriends."

"Plenty of guys ask you out," Zoey said.

"Nerds. Dweebs. Geckos."

"How about George in tenth grade?"

"He was such a gross kisser. Total tongue, like he was trying to lick my liver."

"Thanks for telling me that," Zoey said. "That is the grossest thing I've ever heard."

"No, it isn't. I've told you plenty of grosser things than that."

"Time to turn," Zoey announced. "One, two, three!"

Both girls spun on their lounge chairs, turning at the same time so that they were face to face.

"Hit me," Nina said, opening her mouth wide.

Zoey pumped, aimed, and fired perfectly.

"Not all guys are George," Zoey said.

"You're right," Nina said snidely. "Some are Jake."

"He's a good kisser," Zoey said thoughtfully. "I mean, I think he is. It's not like I have a lot to compare him to."

"Tad Crowley," Nina said.

"Better than Tad," Zoey said definitely. She had kissed Tad at a party when she was mad at Jake. He was the only other guy she had ever kissed. Unless you counted Lucas, and that . . . well, that had been different. She'd never told Nina about that. "You should go out with Mike Monahan. He likes you."

"He told you he likes me?" Nina asked.

"Not in so many words."

"Uh-huh. Well, in so many words I have to go use your bathroom." Nina got up from the chair. She had a webbing pattern across her stomach.

Zoey put down her head and closed her eyes. Nina wasn't back within the expected two minutes, which meant she was either raiding the refrigerator or she'd found something to do for Benjamin. She was letting Benjamin absolutely use her like a servant lately.

Zoey sensed something change, as if the sun had gone behind a cloud. She rolled onto one side and shielded her eyes, staring up at the sky. She saw the outline of a head, with brilliant rays of sunlight blazing behind it.

"Sorry," a voice called down from above. "Didn't mean to block your sun."

Zoey's breath caught in her chest and she sat up quickly, tilting her head to see the face that went with the voice. She knew who it was.

Lucas was gazing down at her from his deck.

"Lucas?" Zoey said in an overbright voice. "Is that you?"

"I wasn't sure you'd remember," he said.

"Of course I remember," Zoey said, still sounding shrill and phony.

Lucas walked to the end of the deck and climbed over the railing. He dropped to the little path that went below his deck and wound down to Zoey's backyard. In an instant he was standing right in front of her.

He had grown in the two years he'd been away. There was more muscle on him now, though he was still less beefy than Jake. His blond hair was long and kept falling forward into his face.

"Hi," Zoey said.

"Long time, Zoey," he said. He looked her up and down, not coyly but openly. "You look good. I always remembered you as being skinny."

Zoey gulped. Why did her modest pink bikini suddenly feel so incredibly revealing? For some reason she felt a compelling need to straighten her hair. At the same time, a confused feeling of guilt welled up inside her. This was Lucas. She wasn't supposed to be talking to Lucas.

"I heard you were back," Zoey said.

"Oh? Who did you hear that from? Not my parents. They don't officially admit I am back." He smiled wryly. "They don't officially admit I exist."

Zoey could only nod. What was she supposed to say? She glanced nervously toward the house. Nina could come back out at any moment.

"Ahh," he said. "I see. You're supposed to be blowing me off, aren't you? Islander solidarity and all that."

"No, no," Zoey stammered, her cheeks burning.

He laughed. "I remember you being skinny. I don't

remember you being a liar. Don't forget, I was born on Chatham Island. I know how it goes." He tilted his head and looked at her speculatively. "Jake McRoyan think he can get rid of me with a little cold shoulder treatment?" He laughed again, this time bitterly. "Where I've been the last two years, you hope that guys don't want to talk to you. It will take more than Jake, and more than my father, to scare me off."

He turned and began ascending the path again. Halfway up, he turned back. "Tell me, Zoey." His face was softer now, his voice more tentative. "How's Claire?"

Zoey shrugged.

"Does she know I'm back?"

"Yes."

He thought for a moment, then nodded. "I notice she hasn't come by to welcome me home. She's with Jake on this, huh?"

Zoey bristled inwardly. Lucas made it sound like it was some secret pact between Jake and Claire. It was more than that. "I'm with Jake on this, too," Zoey said in a voice that tripped as she spoke.

"Yeah, well, give Claire a message for me next time you see her, will you, Zoey? Tell her not to worry so much. Tell her I keep my promises. You tell her that." He gave Zoey a last long look before he walked away.

SIX

ZOEY SPENT THE AFTERNOON DOWN at the restaurant, helping her parents prepare for the Labor Day weekend crush. She moved beer from the storage room out to the bar coolers, unpacked several heavy boxes of new plates and sent them through the dishwasher, helped her father pull down the greasy vents from the hood over the stove, changed the oil in the deep fryer, and cleaned the entire walk-in freezer.

By the time evening rolled around, she was more than ready for escape.

She changed clothes in the restaurant bathroom and went outside into the fresh, warm air of early evening. She could see that Jake already had his father's big boat warming up. Aisha was on the foredeck with Nina. Claire was standing on the bow looking at something Zoey couldn't make out, with Benjamin just behind her.

Zoey crossed Dock Street and walked out onto the floating pier.

"About time, Zo," Jake called out to her from up on the flying bridge.

"All work and no play, et cetera," Claire said.

"Hey, some of us have to work for a living," Zoey said, climbing aboard the big cabin cruiser. "Not all of us have rich daddies."

Claire smiled. "But your dad is cool, as fathers go."

"Yeah," Nina chimed in, "your dad smokes dope and listens to The Who."

"The who?" Aisha asked, looking blank.

"Big rock band of the sixties," Benjamin said.

"No, he doesn't, not anymore," Zoey said. She could feel a flush creeping up her neck.

"Doesn't what?" Claire asked. "Listen to The Who?"

"He doesn't smoke pot anymore. Can we drop this topic and get going?" She told herself she was irritable because she'd been working all afternoon. But a part of her also felt guilty. She hadn't told Nina about talking to Lucas, and that was unusual. She told Nina everything. Almost everything.

"Zoey," Benjamin said, "you're really not responsible for what Mom and Dad do. You don't have to defend them."

"Are we going for a boat ride or are we picking on Zoey?" Aisha asked, coming to Zoey's defense.

"Can't we do both?" Claire asked.

"Somebody cast off the stern line!" Jake yelled down from the bridge.

"Is that front or back?" Nina asked. "I can never remember."

The boat backed out of the slip and Jake turned it around to face toward open water. They rounded the breakwater, and Zoey waved to some little kids Rollerblading along the concrete expanse.

As soon as they were out of the shelter of the harbor, the water grew choppy, with wavetops blown white by the breeze. Jake held the boat a quarter of a mile offshore. Zoey could see the well-preserved Victorian homes that lined Leeward Drive, most of which had been converted into inns or apartments.

Chatham Island was shaped like a croissant, with a big bite taken out of the middle. The bite was appropriately called Big Bite pond, a shallow, sheltered body that nearly cut the island in half. The north half of the island was inhabited, with North Harbor at the very tip. The part south of Big Bite was a wildlife sanctuary, with dirt roads and a very few scattered, isolated homes.

It took less than ten minutes to travel the distance from the breakwater to the inlet. Jake guided the boat through the narrow inlet, and suddenly they were out of the wind, on water that barely showed a ripple. The pond was only half a mile wide from its northern shore, lined with homes on widely spaced wooded lots, to its wilder, tree-lined southern shore.

Jake anchored the boat within a hundred feet of the south shore and they set about lowering the small dinghy into the water. Nina and Aisha climbed down into the dinghy, and Zoey and Claire passed down the cooler filled with cold soda, the bag of charcoal, and the Tupperware containers of meat and vegetables.

Benjamin joined them in the dinghy, climbing down with a hand from Nina, and the three of them rowed for shore.

"You want to do it the easy way or the hard way?" Claire asked Zoey.

Zoey looked toward shore, mentally calculating the distance. "I'll race you. Loser hunts firewood." She shucked off her shorts and blouse, revealing the pale blue maillot underneath. Claire did the same.

"Hey, Jake!" Zoey called. "Bring our clothes when you come ashore, all right?"

Jake nodded and waved from the bridge. He was waiting to be certain the anchor was holding.

Claire grinned and, without warning, dived like a knife toward the water. Zoey cursed under her breath and dove in after her. The water was cold, but after a day spent in the restaurant kitchen, sweating and covering herself with cleaning solutions, it felt heavenly. She surfaced and saw Claire, already two lengths ahead.

Zoey stretched out her arms and went after her. She was the better swimmer but, as usual, Claire had found a way to get an edge. The distance to shore wouldn't be enough for Zoey to make up for Claire's early start.

Claire stood just as Zoey's feet found the gravel bottom.

"Don't you ever get tired of cheating, Claire?" Zoey asked, squeezing the water from her hair.

"Don't you ever get tired of losing?" Claire replied, grinning.

Aisha rowed the dinghy back out to the boat to retrieve Jake. Claire went back into the water, waist deep, meeting the dinghy just as Jake and Aisha neared shore. She leaned over the side and retrieved her dry clothing. Zoey saw the way Jake's eyes homed in on Claire's cleavage, so ostentatiously displayed in her bright red bathing suit.

If I were the suspicious type, I'd think she did that deliberately, Zoey thought. Jake sent her an innocent smile that proclaimed his guilt. She smiled back with her mouth, letting her eyes tell him that she had indeed noticed.

"Who's coming with me to scrape up firewood?" Zoey asked, looking pleadingly at Nina and Aisha. Both of her friends volunteered half-heartedly. Zoey put dry clothing on over her wet bathing suit and tied her shoes.

"Dry wood this time," Jake said as they tramped into the woods.

"Just tend to your little barbecue, Jake," Aisha said. "I'll be hungry when I get back."

"I don't know if I should leave Jake with Claire, undefended," Zoey grumbled as they shuffled noisily over the carpet of pine needles.

"Which one is undefended?" Nina asked.

"You know, guys are going to look," Aisha said. "They always do, even when they say they don't."

"I don't blame him," Zoey said. "It's Claire, always parading those big buffers of hers around."

"You know Jake's faithful to you," Aisha said, stooping to pick up a fallen tree limb.

"Yeah, he lacks the imagination for anything else," Nina said dryly. "He thinks life comes with a rule book and a set of instructions. He wants to grow up to be exactly like his dad, only with more hair."

Zoey flashed on what her mother had insinuated about Mr. McRoyan at breakfast that morning. She wasn't sure whether she should bring it up or not. Maybe with Nina alone, another time. Somehow telling *two* people seemed like gossip, whereas just telling Nina would be all right. That made two things she was hiding from Nina.

Zoey pointed ahead. "There. Dead tree. We can break off the branches."

"You know what I don't get?" Aisha said. "I don't get Claire and Benjamin."

"No one gets that," Nina said. "Claire's been getting by on her looks since she was twelve. Now she's going out with the one guy who can't be totally sure she isn't a gorgon. Go figure. Not to mention the second part of the equation—what's a nice guy like Benjamin doing with my sister?"

"I don't know about Benjamin being such a nice guy," Aisha said. "No offense, Zoey. I don't mean he's not nice, just that he's . . . he's got an edge to him."

"Of course he does," Nina said before Zoey could answer. "I mean, cut the guy some slack. He's dealing with being blind, which makes you feel weak and vulnerable. So naturally he reacts by keeping his distance from people."

"I think it's all you island people," Aisha said. "You all grew up here together, you're stuck together, so you all get kind of protective of your space."

"We do not," Nina said. "Hey!" she yelled at Aisha. "Don't touch that stick. That's *my* stick. It's much closer to me."

"Very funny," Aisha said with a smile.

"Keep an eye out for ticks," Zoey said.

"Oh, Zoey!" Nina whined. "Did you have to say the word ticks?" She began examining her bare legs.

"Ticks," Zoey repeated.

"Bats," Nina countered.

"Too early for bats," Zoey said confidently.

"It will be dark soon," Nina said. "That's when the bats come out with their leathery wings and their sharp little teeth."

"Well, at least we haven't seen any snakes yet," Zoey said gleefully, enjoying the crestfallen look on Aisha's face.

"Yeah, they're worse than bats and ticks put together," Nina agreed solemnly.

"Don't start with me," Aisha warned.

"Psssss!"

Aisha jumped, looking down at the ground where Nina was pointing. Then she shook her head. "Oh, you're very funny, Nina."

"I think we have enough wood," Zoey said.

"Snakes and ticks and bats, oh my!" Nina said.

"Let's just get our wood and follow the yellow brick road back to the beach," Aisha said to Zoey. "See if we can get your boyfriend off her sister."

"It's a dangerous world," Nina said in a low, trembling voice. "Bats and snakes and ticks . . . and Claire!"

• • •

The bonfire burned noisily, sending up Fourth of July fireworks in showers of sparks, cooling as they fell to earth before they could reach the dark, overhanging trees.

Clouds had moved in, concealing the stars but letting through the bright diffuse glow of the full moon. Away from the circle of the fire the air had grown brisk, but sitting with her back against Jake's chest, his thick, muscular arms wrapped around her, Zoey was warm. Her toes were close to the fire, and from time to time she had to pull them away to cool off.

Claire and Benjamin were on the opposite side of the fire, visible only in flashes between the flames, sometimes kissing, other times just holding hands. It was odd, always had been, for Zoey to see her brother being romantic. Benjamin, of course, could not see her, or even know that she could see him. It was one of the compensating advantages of being blind, she supposed—you could pretend to have a level of privacy, even when there wasn't any.

Nina and Aisha were down by the water, outlined as shadows against the glittering surface of the pond, having a deep philosophical discussion of some sort as they studiously avoided looking at the two couples.

"Nina needs a boyfriend," Zoey said to Jake.

"Nina needs a personality first," Jake said.

"A guy would be very, very lucky to get her."

"Aisha's the one who needs a boyfriend," Jake said. "I can't believe that new guy Christopher hasn't asked her out yet."

"Maybe he isn't attracted to her."

Jake made a dismissive noise. "She's got a nice bod, pretty face."

Zoey twisted around to look at him. "She can read and write, too."

"You know what I meant," Jake said. "The first thing a guy looks at is . . . is looks. Later he gets into whether a girl is smart or has a good sense of humor."

"How much later?"

"Zoey, is it just my imagination, or have you been busting me a lot lately?"

Zoey tilted her head straight back and closed her eyes. Jake kissed her lips and tightened his grip around her, letting his hand slip upward from her waist to just beneath her breasts.

"We've never kissed that way before," Jake observed. "I mean, upside down like that."

"Do I taste like barbecue sauce?"

"We both taste like barbecue sauce," Jake said with a laugh. "Can I have some more?"

"Upside down?"

"Too strange," Jake said. He guided her into turning around. They sat face to face, Zoey's legs over Jake's. She kissed him again, enjoying the feel of his lips on hers.

"That was nice," she said, pausing to breathe.

"Mmmm," Jake agreed.

His eyes reflected the yellow flames, two separate bonfires burning in dark pools. He undid the top button of her blouse and let his fingers slide beneath the fabric.

"Jake, my brother is like ten feet away," Zoey said in a whisper. Worse yet, Nina wasn't far away, and if she saw Jake in action, she'd be bound to start another round of discussion on groping.

"Your brother is always like ten feet away," Jake said. He let his fingers caress the slope of her breast. "It's not as if he can see what we're doing."

Zoey took his hand and moved it away. She kissed him again, but his response was less than enthusiastic. "Claire isn't blind."

"She's not watching us," Jake said. He reached for her again.

Zoey stood up. "I'm going to talk to Nina and Aisha."

Jake stood up and grabbed her arm. "Just tell me one thing, Zoey," he said. "Is this the way it's going to stay? I mean, I'm supposed to stay on first base until we get married?"

Zoey spun around and faced him. The fire no longer reflected in his eyes. They were just shadows within shadows now. "Excuse me? Did I just hear that?"

"I was just asking whether we're ever going to do it, Zo."

"You said *until we get married*, Jake. I don't remember ever even discussing anything like that." Zoey put up her hand, palm outward, to keep him at a distance. "We're not even seniors yet."

Jake shrugged. "I didn't mean anything by it."

"Good."

"You know I love you, Zoey," he said softly.

Zoey held her breath. It was not the first time he had said those words. She had even said them to him, once or twice. Maybe she had even meant them, who could be sure? Maybe Jake meant them, too, in his own way. She let Jake draw her close again.

"Don't you ever think about the future, Zo?" he asked in a low voice. "I mean, you know, after high school and all. You ever think about what it would be like to get married and have kids and a house? Maybe a dog."

"Sometimes," Zoey said, feeling uncomfortable.

"I do," Jake said solemnly. "I know we're young, but I think about having a family of my own. Some kids. Maybe a boy."

"Don't you think we should enjoy being wild, irresponsible teenagers?" Zoey asked, hoping to jog Jake out of his serious mood.

Jake smiled crookedly. "I'm not very good at being a wild

and irresponsible teenager, am I?"

There was something in his tone that was deeply melancholy. He was right, Zoey knew. Jake was seventeen and already acting like he was thirty.

"You're good at being a horny teenager," Zoey said, leaning her forehead against his.

Jake laughed softly, then grew silent again. "You know what today is?"

"Saturday?" Zoey said.

"Yeah, that too." He nodded his head slowly. Then he turned to look over the placid waters toward the far shore, where house lights shone bright amid the trees. "Wade's birthday."

Zoey felt her heart sink. How could she have forgotten? What perfect timing on her part. This day of all days, she'd stood around chatting with Lucas. She hugged Jake from behind. He took her hands in his and sighed heavily.

"Two years," he said. "I figured I'd be over it after two years. He'd be twenty now, did you know that? Probably a sophomore in college."

"Of course you still miss him," Zoey said.

"Yeah," Jake said. "Someday I'm going to have a son and name him Wade."

Zoey looked away. Benjamin was resting his head in Claire's lap now, sunglasses in place, eyes staring sightlessly up at the gray-black blanket of clouds. Claire stroked his hair in a distracted way and watched Zoey.

No, Zoey realized as Claire's eyes were lit by a spurt of flame from a falling log. It was Jake she was watching.

Aisha Gray

I used to live in Boston, which is a great city, although school there was a drag. I was one of the black kids who got bussed into south Boston so that the previously all-white junior high schools there could be integrated. What fun. One day some of the white kids, cheered on by their parents and with the assistance of their older brothers and sisters, decided to turn our bus over. With us still inside.

My folks freaked and decided that was enough of Boston, which was too bad, because really, setting aside that one incident, Boston was a very cool city. Great shopping.

Naturally my parents, being the people they are, managed to come to the conclusion that the perfect place for us was Chatham Island, a place where people aren't even tan, let alone black. They've never been able to explain their logic. Mostly I think my mom just lost it when she saw this inn for sale and started hallucinating about quilts and valences and canopied beds.

At first I thought people here were even worse than in south Boston. They treated me like I was invisible. They treated my parents and my brother the same way. Always polite, but sort of like we weren't entirely real.

I finally got pissed off and yelled at Zoey. I knew her from school by this point. I said, What is the deal here? You seem too nice and normal to be racist. She was shocked. Racist? I don't care that you're black!

Then what's the damn problem? I said. I'm not invisible.

Of course not, she said. You're just from away.

Away. That's Maine-speak for the entire rest of the planet.

Eventually I stopped being from away. Now I'm not so sure I trust people from away. I mean, I'm polite and all, but still, you don't want to pay too much attention to them for the first year or so.

SEVEN

AISHA HAD TO RUN THE last several blocks down from Climbing Way, fighting to keep gravity from drawing her too quickly. She made her way down the even steeper drop that was a shortcut over to Dock Street and bypassed Lucas's house, then shifted gears into an all-out sprint along the waterfront as the ferry blew its piercing final warning whistle. She yelled frantically as they raised the gangway, blowing through the gate as she waved her ferry pass in the air. She leapt over the few feet of water that now separated her from the ferry and landed, thankfully, on the slowly moving boat.

Gasping for breath, she bent forward at the waist, hands on her knees, as the eleven-ten ferry pulled away from the dock. Too close. She'd promised her mom she'd go into town, buy potpourri, of all things, at the mall, and pick up the drapes from the dry cleaner. The drapes went in the inn's most expensive room, and the guest who'd reserved the room was arriving on the four twenty-five—which, incidentally, would be the same ferry Aisha returned on unless she managed to get everything done in less than an hour.

Once she caught her breath, she made her way to the bow, squeezing through the cars that jammed the open deck. The car ferry didn't usually make this run, but this time of year the last of the elderly summer residents—the Living Dead, as Nina called them—were starting to bail out, avoiding the Labor Day tourist crush and heading back to their condos in Florida.

She leaned against the railing and looked idly down at the water below, split into two plumes of white by the knife edge of the hull.

"Hi," a voice said behind her.

She turned. Christopher. "Oh, hi," she said coolly.

"Nice run," he said.

"Excuse me," she said, and walked away, squeezing back through the cars toward the stern. She leaned against the rail, watching the wake.

"Hi," he said again.

Aisha sighed. She turned to face him squarely, folding her arms over her chest. "Where are you from?"

He looked surprised. "I was born in Baltimore."

"I see. So you're basically a southerner. That would explain it. See, here in Maine, people have a different attitude toward things than people do in Baltimore. Here, the idea is you leave people alone, they leave you alone, everyone gets left alone." She returned her gaze to the ferry's wake.

"I doubt that you were born here," Christopher said, laughing. "There's no such thing as a black person born in Maine."

"I'm from Boston originally," Aisha said. "But I have embraced the Maine way of life."

"Do you say *ayuh*?"

"Look, no one says ayuh except very old fishermen. And when they do say it, they don't say it like that."

"Do you say *wicked* when you mean something's good?" he asked.

Aisha drummed her fingers on the metal rail. "Sometimes. But that's not what being a Mainer is about. Let me explain again. Whereas someone from Baltimore would go up to a stranger and say hi, a Mainer wouldn't go up to a stranger. Understand, stranger?"

"Ayuh. And it's a wicked good way to be," Christopher said. "Only I'm not a stranger. I'm Christopher Shupe. You're Aisha Gray, a lovely name, by the way."

"I'm also a bitch, or don't you remember that?"

"How could I forget? You're still a bitch."

Aisha narrowed her eyes and glared at him. "Then I would think you'd want to stay away from me."

"Can't. Tomorrow I'm starting in on your mom's garden.

That's where I'm headed right now, to the greenhouse for bulbs and fertilizer. Besides, we live on the same small island. Anyway, I kind of like the bitch act. On you it works."

Aisha decided to treat him to silence. Sooner or later he would get tired of annoying her and get the message.

"Your mom seemed nice," he said. "So unlike you. And, no offense, but I think she's got the edge on you in looks, too."

"Excuse me?" Aisha said, breaking her three-second-old vow of silence.

"Maybe it was just that her hair was nicely done, her makeup was very professional, and she has a certain style in the way she dresses." He grinned at her. "But I like you just the way you are—scruffy and bitchy."

"Does this kind of sweet talk work with a lot of girls?"

"I tried to give you flowers."

"I didn't ask you to bring me any damned flowers," Aisha snapped.

"I know. It was sweet of me, don't you think?"

"Sweet," Aisha said poisonously. "Yes, that's just the word I would apply to you."

"Aisha. It means *life*."

She looked at him in surprise.

"I looked it up. You know what Christopher means?"

Aisha coolly looked away.

"You know what Christopher means?" he repeated.

"I don't care what it means."

"It means *boyfriend*."

"No, it does not."

"It will eventually," he said smugly.

"I don't think so."

For once he was quiet, staring off toward the skyline of Weymouth. She began to wonder if she had finally managed to discourage him.

"I have to tell you something," he said.

So much for discouraging him.

"Just look at me, listen to me for one minute. Less, even, if I talk fast, and then I'll leave you alone for the rest of the trip."

Aisha sighed dramatically, and lazily, reluctantly, met his eyes. They were flecked here and there with gold highlights amid the deep brown.

"The day will come, Aisha *Life* Gray, when you and I will stand here on this very boat, wrapped in each other's arms, our lips joined, our eyes closed to everything else around us. Not because you're the only black chick on the island, not because everyone expects us to get together, but because when I first saw you walking down Exchange Street, I froze, I stopped moving, stopped breathing, stopped thinking. In that instant I knew that you were the reason I was on the island, in Maine, on planet Earth."

He moved closer, and Aisha realized she herself was no longer breathing. He raised his fingers to her cheek as if to draw her close. She felt her eyelids grow heavy, her knees grow weak.

Then he stepped back. "No, I'm not going to kiss you now."

Her eyes flew open, suddenly alarmed.

"But soon," Christopher said. He turned his back to her and started to walk away. Then he hesitated. "And when I do kiss you, you'll stay kissed."

Zoey paused outside Benjamin's room. From inside, she could hear Nina reading, her voice barely muffled by the door.

"I sat down on the edge of a deep, soft chair and looked at Mrs. Regan. She was worth a stare. She was trouble. She was stretched out on a modernistic chaise longue with her slippers off, so I stared at her legs in the sheerest silk stockings. They seemed to be arranged to stare at."

Zoey knocked.

"Yeah," Benjamin's voice called out.

Zoey opened the door. Nina was seated in the rocking chair, eyeing her a little impatiently. Benjamin was lying on the floor, his head on a pillow, legs propped up on the edge of his bed.

"I have the feeling that is not *The Plague* you're reading," Zoey said.

Nina held up a pastel paperback. "*The Big Sleep.* Raymond Chandler. Much cooler than Camus."

"And that's on the suggested reading list for this year?" Zoey asked skeptically.

"No, but it ought to be," Benjamin said. "I was reading it in Braille, but this is easier."

"I volunteered," Nina said, looking a little embarrassed. But then, maybe the color in her face was the result of their sunbathing yesterday.

Zoey decided against bringing up the point that her parents paid Nina to read schoolbooks, not mystery novels. It wasn't exactly her business, and the last thing Benjamin would put up with was his little sister acting like she was his mother.

"Sounds good," Zoey said. "Look, Nina, I'm heading down to the restaurant. They asked me to wait tables for the dinner shift."

"That's okay," Nina said. "I'll stay a little while."

"No," Benjamin said dismissively. "I've been hogging your time enough, Nina, go ahead. I'm being a jerk making you sit here and read to me all afternoon."

"No, you're not," Nina said quickly.

Benjamin yawned. "Truth is, I think maybe I'll catch some Z's. I'm going over to your house later anyway, to see Claire."

Nina closed the book with an audible snap. "Okay, whatever." She smiled frostily at Zoey. "I guess I will walk down with you."

They walked down Camden toward Exchange, threading their way through the crowds of sunburned tourists in their Chatham Island T-shirts and Bermuda shorts. Soon, Zoey knew, these narrow streets, these brick sidewalks, would be empty. You could sled down Camden in the winter when the snow fell.

"I spoke to Lucas," Zoey blurted suddenly.

Nina stopped dead in her tracks and grabbed Zoey's arm, stopping her, too. "You spoke to Lucas?"

"Yesterday," Zoey said, looking away. "When we were out in the yard and you went in to use the bathroom. He came down and said hi."

"He came down and said hi?" Nina repeated.

"Actually, he guessed we were all trying to blow him off. He said it wouldn't work."

Nina fumbled nervously in her purse and produced a cigarette. She popped it in her mouth.

"That is a really strange habit, by the way," Zoey said, starting down the street again.

"Sorry," Nina said. "I started as a goof; now I can't quit. Come on, Zoey, spill."

Zoey took a breath. "He asked if Claire knew he was back, and he said to tell her not to worry so much. Something about keeping his word."

"Hmm." Nina sucked on the unlit cigarette. "How come you didn't tell me earlier?"

"I was . . . embarrassed," Zoey admitted. "I mean, we're supposed to be doing the big ostracism thing, and right away I blow it."

"What were you supposed to do?" Nina asked. "Turn your back on him?" She grabbed Zoey's arm again. "So. How does he look? Still gorgeous? Or is he all tattooed and mean-looking from being in prison?"

"It wasn't a prison, it was a youth authority. Reform school." Zoey called to mind the image of Lucas, first a silhouette against the sun, then a slightly sullen, somewhat gorgeous guy, standing with arms crossed in her own yard. "Sure he's cute," Zoey admitted. "Not my type, of course."

"No, I wouldn't think so," Nina agreed, giggling as if at some private joke.

"Well, it's not that funny."

"Yeah, it kind of is, Zo. I mean, Lucas is the classic bad boy. Even before he got in trouble over the accident, there had been other stuff. The only thing you ever got in trouble over was that time in seventh grade when Ms. McQueen caught you cheating."

"I was *not* cheating," Zoey said hotly.

"See, that's my point. While you were *not* cheating, Lucas Cabral was probably shoplifting."

They reached Exchange and Zoey glanced at her watch. She had already, strictly speaking, walked a block out of her way. "I better get on down to work. You could come and hang out if you want."

"I know I have no life, Zoey, but even I can think of better things to do than sit around and watch you work. Besides, now I have to go tell Claire what Lucas said."

"No!" Zoey said. "She'll know I talked to him."

"Relax. I'll tell her *I* talked to him. I'm not afraid of my sister."

"It's not Claire; I don't want Jake finding out. He'll think I'm a traitor or something. You know how he felt about Wade. He idolized him."

"Yeah," Nina answered thoughtfully. "You know, Benjamin said something about that. We were talking about Lucas being back. Benjamin says Jake is overdoing it. He said something . . . It sounded really cool the way he said it. It was something like *the best part of Wade's life was the end of it.* Only it sounded cooler than that."

"*Nothing in his life became him like the leaving it,*" Zoey said. "Shakespeare. I've seen it in my quote books. Kind of a rotten thing for Benjamin to say."

Nina shrugged. "Maybe your big brother knows something you don't."

Zoey

I started working on this idea for a romance novel soon after I first kissed Jake. I guess I figured it would sort of be about Jake and me. I know, it's a dopey idea. What's really embarrassing, though, is that I'm still kind of working on it and I'm almost a senior. Every month or so I'll get this great idea and I'll start writing away at top speed, filling page after page of the big journal I bought just for this purpose.

So far I've written chapter one about twenty times. There is no chapter two.

Sometimes it's a historical romance and I'm the usual lusty yet virginal heroine, a plucky maiden who is captured in a raid on my small village by the hero, who is a lusty, fiery, yet strangely sensitive knight or Viking or prince about to reclaim his throne. The one thing you can be sure of is that he's lusty, fiery, and yet strangely sensitive.

I know it's corny, but that's the way these things are written. I didn't make up the formula. Besides, I do think Jake would look pretty good in armor.

Other times I go with a more contemporary story. Say, one about a lusty yet virginal heroine who, let's say, lives on a small island off the coast of Maine. This requires less research.

Unfortunately, I have a basic problem with this scenario. You see, one so seldom encounters a lusty, fiery, yet strangely sensitive knight, Viking, or prince along the coast of Maine.

EIGHT

ZOEY DIDN'T GET AWAY FROM the restaurant till after ten o'clock, her apron stuffed with forty-two dollars in quarters, singles, and the occasional five-dollar bill. Her feet hurt from running and her back from hoisting heavy trays.

The night air was like a slap of cold water on her face. Getting away from the smell of food and beer and people's cigarettes to breathe the fresh, salt air revived her. The thought of heading straight home to sit in her room or watch TV downstairs with Benjamin held no great attraction. Neither did the idea of going over to Nina and Claire's house. The last thing she wanted was to face a cross-examination by Claire.

Instead she stayed on Dock Street as it curved along Town Beach, enjoying an unusually clear sky filled with stars. It was the sort of sky you saw in winter, when the sky got so clear and cold that it seemed like nothing lay between earth and empty space.

She reached the end of Dock, where it merged into Leeward.

She'd expected to head over to Jake's house, just a hundred feet away, a blaze of lights amid the pines. Instead she turned right, following the dark road that led to the breakwater.

There was a sign at the head of the sandy patch that connected the road to the breakwater, stating that no one was to be there after dark. The town had put up the sign after some tourist kids had been swept away by high surf and badly battered before they could be rescued. Naturally, no resident of the island paid the slightest attention. Unlike tourists, residents knew better than to parade around the breakwater when a freak summer storm was sending fifteen-foot waves crashing over it.

To the right, the bay was placid within the shelter of the breakwater. To the left, the sea kept up its relentless attack, churning and surging. Every so often it sent explosions of spray up into the air, carrying on the breeze as a salty dew that condensed on Zoey's warm skin.

It was one of Zoey's favorite places, a walk that never failed to affect her, at once deeply calming and exciting. The slowly flashing green light at the breakwater's tip glowed like a firefly. Across the harbor, she could see light spilling from the restaurant she had just left. Up on the ridge she could pick out the lights from Aisha's inn. And across the four miles of water, Weymouth.

But for Zoey, the better view was always the view north,

straight out into a profound darkness unaffected by man-made lights, indifferent even to the stars and the moon.

She neared the end of the breakwater before she saw him sitting on the wall, his legs hanging over the side, seemingly oblivious to the crash of waves at his feet. A fountain of spray erupted, drenching him in a salt shower. He tilted back his head and smoothed his hand over his hair.

Zoey stepped back, hoping to walk away before he noticed her.

"Too late, Zoey," Lucas said. "I've watched you all the way from your folks' restaurant."

"I was just heading over to Jake's house," Zoey said, pointing, as if that would help convince him.

Lucas brought up his legs and stood, shaking his head to throw off a new dousing of water. "I saw you hesitate down at the crossroad. You like it out here? I do. It's one of the places I kept thinking about while I was away. I kept thinking of a night just like this, and the smell of the sea."

Zoey nodded. "It is nice out here."

"You have no idea," he said softly. "You've never had it taken away from you."

"I guess you're right." She paused, gazed back over her shoulder at the lights of Jake's house. "Well, I have to go."

He fixed her with his gaze, curious, confused. Then he

smiled a faint half-smile. "Oh. You're scared of me, aren't you?"

"No, I'm not. I mean, you and I used to be friends. You know, neighbors, anyway."

"I used to bring my mom's sweet rolls down and hang out with you and Ben and your mom for breakfast. Your dad would already be down at the restaurant. You'd be telling your mom about school, or what Nina said, or getting upset over the hole in the ozone or whatever." Lucas looked at her and smiled. A real smile this time. "And your mom would be nodding and muttering *uh-huh,* having no idea what you were saying because she hadn't had her first cup of coffee yet. Ben would be sitting there, pretending to read the newspaper upside down." Lucas laughed at the memory. "Does he still pull stuff like that?"

Zoey smiled despite herself. "He's added a few tricks. He walked into a classroom with a substitute teacher last year and acted like he thought he was in the boys' bathroom. He pretended to believe the teacher's desk was a urinal. The sub totally lost it."

"Did he . . . ?"

"No. He's not crude, just strange."

"I always did like Ben. I always liked your whole family. You seemed so nice and normal to me."

"Normal? I don't know about normal. Personally, when I want normal, I go over to—" She fell silent and looked away.

"You can say Jake's name," Lucas said. "That feud is all one-way. I have nothing against Jake McRoyan, except that he hates my guts."

Zoey glanced over her shoulder again, her heart fluttering. For the second time in two days, she found herself talking to her boyfriend's greatest enemy.

"Did you tell Claire what I said?" Lucas asked.

Zoey shook her head. "Not exactly. I told Nina, though." She looked down at his feet. "What did you mean about Claire didn't have to worry, and you kept your promises?"

"Nothing," Lucas said. "Old news, old history. We were kind of close before the accident, Claire and I."

"I know. She's going out with Benjamin now."

"Poor Ben," Lucas said.

"He doesn't think so, I guess. They've been going out for a year almost."

"And you're still with good old Jake, huh?"

"Yes, still." It was so odd, Zoey realized. Here she was, talking to Lucas as if he were a stranger. Except he was a stranger who knew all the people she knew, knew much of her life, her history. Sometimes when he spoke it was like the old times, an easy, familiar feel, as if he were still the same guy who dropped by for breakfast. Then, suddenly, she would remember what he had done, and why he had been away.

And why Jake, the guy who loved her, and whom she loved in return, so hated him.

"You're looking confused," Lucas said, reading her thoughts. "You don't know how to treat me, do you? Am I the enemy? Or am I still a friend?"

"I guess I don't know," Zoey confessed.

"I know how I feel about it," Lucas said. He turned to look off toward the town. Lights were being extinguished as North Harbor began to go to sleep. "When you're locked up, you spend a lot of time with your memories. At first you tend to focus on all the bad stuff, like how it was you came to be locked up. But you can't spend almost two years reliving the bad times. Eventually you start to remember all the good times. All the places you enjoyed. This place, for example. And all the people you cared for." He looked at her again, his smoldering dark eyes wide and glittering with reflected moonlight. "I remembered Claire, yes. And Nina and Ben and Aisha. I remembered Wade, too. I even remembered all the times I was out with my dad, working, hauling up the lobster pots, him cursing at me in Portuguese. Even though they weren't all happy memories, they were a million miles away from my cellmates and our cinder-block walls." A dark shadow crossed his face, like clouds momentarily blotting out the moon. Then he looked up at her again, his expression peaceful.

"I also thought about you, Zoey. Strange, because I don't think I'd ever paid much attention to you when we saw each other every day. I don't know that I'd ever really seen you until that day when you . . . when you gave me that ice-cream cone. Still, I found my thoughts returning to you. I think in some way you came to represent everything that I had lost."

Zoey's throat had gone dry. She swallowed hard. A jet of spray shot up, landing as noisy rain in the space between them.

"Now you're really worried, aren't you?" Lucas said.

Zoey shook her head, not trusting her voice.

"It's okay, I understand," Lucas said. "Don't take me too seriously. I've just been around guys who don't talk much except in four-letter words and threats. And then there's my folks. My dad hasn't spoken a word to me. He's forbidden my mother to speak, too, although once when he wasn't around, she . . ." He stopped as his voice broke. He took several deep breaths. "Sorry. They say it takes a while to readjust to normal life. You'd better get going. This island is so small, somebody's likely to see you."

He was giving her the opportunity to leave. And that's exactly what she should do, Zoey knew. This was Lucas. Lucas Cabral, the person responsible for Wade's death.

More important, Jake, Claire—everyone—was determined to make Lucas a pariah. It was a matter of islander solidarity. And if they knew she was giving any sort of support to Lucas, she herself might be the next one cut out of the group.

"Go on, don't feel bad about it," Lucas said. "I know how it is."

Zoey nodded and turned away. She took a half-dozen steps before she turned back. "Lucas!" she yelled.

"Yeah?"

"Why don't you stop by for breakfast sometime?"

"Why don't you stop by for breakfast?" Zoey muttered into the darkness of her room. Was she nuts? Was she coming unglued? Was she absolutely begging for trouble? She tossed in the bed, flipping from her left side to her right side, scrunching the pillow up under her head.

Not enough that she had talked to him, no, not nearly enough. Jake might have forgiven that. After all, he knew she was no good at being mean to people. But no, she'd had to go that one step further. She'd had to make the leap from *dumb, but we can overlook it* to *what on earth were you thinking?*

Still, Lucas had seemed so sad. Sad and alone and . . . well, face it, kind of gorgeous, if you liked guys with smoldering, melancholy eyes. What was she supposed to do? Add to his sadness? Stomp on his sort of sexy vulnerability? What if he'd gone out to the breakwater thinking about suicide? What if it was like the guy in that movie, *It's a Wonderful Life*, that Christmas movie where the guy was getting ready to kill himself and the angel came along to rescue him at the last minute? What if the angel had said *Screw you, pal, no one wants you around*?

It would have been a very different movie.

And it really had nothing to do with the fact that Lucas had great dark eyes.

Nothing.

She was just being nice.

See, Jake had great eyes, too. And Jake didn't end up going to reform school.

Whereas Lucas probably hadn't even seen a girl for two years.

She threw back her covers and twisted her Boston Bruins shirt she was wearing back around. She went to the cramped desk in the dormer window and looked for a while down the street, dark under an overcast sky.

She snapped on the little brass light mounted on the wall and sat down, pulling out her journal. She found the paper clip that marked the end of her last version of the romance novel and checked the draft number. Picking up her pen, she wrote:

Chapter One–Draft #23

She'd been wrong all along, she realized. It shouldn't be a story about the lusty yet virginal maiden who is carried off by the lusty, fiery, yet strangely sensitive knight, Viking, or prince. It should be a story about the same knight, only he was lying wounded, nearly dead after a terrible battle. He'd been wandering lost, perhaps not even knowing who he truly was anymore. Wandering lost, bloody, thirsty, hungry, and alone.

He would wander into the maiden's village, where she lived with her ancient, gnarled uncle after her entire family had been killed by marauding barbarians.

The very barbarians who had wounded the knight. That way there would be a connection between the two.

The maiden would take him into her humble, historically accurate yet clean house and lay him tenderly on her straw mattress. She would remove his armor, piece by piece, and hide it in the woods, so if the barbarians came looking for the knight they wouldn't know it was him.

What would he have on under the armor?

A leather jerkin. Whatever that was. But that would have to be removed, too. And the wound would have to be cleaned and bandaged. And the rest of him would have to be cleaned as well. After all, dried blood and so on.

Then she'd spoon-feed him some soup. He'd thank her and ask her name, which would be . . . Meghan. Or Raven. Or Chastity.

Chastity for now, anyway. Later, when the knight recovered . . .

Zoey put down her pen and sat back in her chair. She had covered three and a half pages with her looping, disorganized handwriting, but now a wave of sudden sleepiness reminded her that it was, after all, the middle of the night.

She snapped off her light and went back to her bed.

She was letting her imagination run away with her, something it often did. All that had happened was she'd spent a few minutes talking to Lucas on the breakwater. It didn't mean anything. Besides, he'd said he remembered her as skinny.

He'd also said she represented everything he'd lost. What did he mean by that?

And why did she care?

Zoey fell asleep with that question running slower and slower around in her mind. And the memory of Lucas's eyes.

NINE

"IF YOU HAVE A TOUCH-TONE phone, please press one now."

Aisha pushed the one.

"Hi, this is Christopher. If you'd like the accounting department, please press two. If you'd like the lingerie department, press three. If you'd like to be connected to the space shuttle, press four."

Aisha pressed four.

"Hi, this is Christopher. If you'd like to join a suicidal cult, press pound and five. If you'd like to speak to one of our sales representatives, press star-nine."

Aisha pressed seven, two, and four.

"Hi, this is Christopher. If you'd like to order pizza, press ninety-nine. If you'd like to eat fish, press *E: none of the above*."

Aisha wrapped the cord around her finger and yanked it from the wall.

"Hi, this is Christopher. If you'd like to know what *Zeitgeist* means, press the *Zeitgeist* button. If you can spell *waba waba waba*

waba, please press *press*."

Aisha threw the phone at the door.

The door opened. Christopher stood there, grinning his cocky grin. "Hi, this is Christopher," he said.

Aisha woke up in a cold sweat, eyes wide, breathing heavy, and heart pounding. Sunlight blazed around the edges of her curtains. Outside she could hear a familiar *peet-weet, peet-weet* from the sandpiper who had been coming by in the mornings before heading down to the water.

Aisha liked birds. Although she would be relieved when this particular sandpiper decided it was time to head south for the winter. He'd been waking her up lately.

At least he'd put an end to that dream. That *nightmare.*

She put her feet down on the braided rug and rubbed her eyes. The clock said six ten. Thanks to her sandpiper friend, she was already back on a school-year schedule.

Aisha got up, put on her blue terry-cloth robe, and forced a comb through her hair. Because her room was downstairs, just off the common area used by guests at the inn, it was important for her to look somewhat civilized when she came out of her room in the morning. She had to walk through the foyer to reach the little downstairs powder room, where she quickly splashed cold water on her face, taking care to wipe the sink down afterward with paper towels. Everything the guests saw had to be perfect at all times.

The shower in the family bathroom was upstairs in the semidetached wing that included her parents' bedroom, the family room, the small family kitchen, and her mother's office. Her brother Kalif's room was just around the corner in the main house, right beside one of the guest rooms—which meant he was doomed to have a stereo- and TV-free room, lest he annoy a guest.

Aisha could hear her mother in the formal downstairs kitchen, preparing coffee and the usual amazing spread of fresh-baked muffins, poached eggs, bacon, and fresh-squeezed orange juice for the guests, at least one of whom already seemed to be waiting in the breakfast room at the rear of the house.

"Aisha," her mother called out from the kitchen in her cheery, fake, for-the-guests voice, "would you be a dear and get the paper for Mr. and Ms. O'Shay?"

Aisha rolled her eyes. Days like this she really wondered about the whole idea of running an inn. Sure, her father's job as a librarian in Weymouth wouldn't let them live like millionaires, but at least wherever they lived it would be all theirs.

Fortunately, winter wasn't far away, and then it would be many weeks between guests. They would slowly take back the huge house, and she'd be able to do wild and crazy things like step out of her room without having her hair combed and a cheerful smile plastered on her face.

Tough, looking quaint and cheerful when you'd just woken up from a nightmare.

Aisha opened the heavy front door and walked out onto the steps. The papers were halfway across the lawn, and she grimaced in annoyance. She was bending over to pick up the *Portland Press Herald* and the *Weymouth Times* when she heard him. The voice straight out of her dreams.

"Hi," Christopher said.

Aisha spun around like a cat, feeling the little hairs on the back of her neck stand up.

"Sorry, I didn't mean to scare you," he said. He was wearing overalls with no shirt on underneath. There was a dirty trowel in his hand.

"What the hell are you doing here at six in the morning?" Aisha demanded, pressing her hand over her beating heart.

"I'm starting on the garden," he said.

"The sun is barely up," Aisha said, outraged.

He shrugged. "I have to start early. Mr. Passmore wants me to come in and cook the lunch shift today. Besides," he said with his all-too-familiar grin, "I've been up a long time. They bring the newspapers over on the water taxi at one a.m. the night before and drop them at the dock. I have to pick them up and have them bundled and ready to go before five so the fishermen can have theirs to take out with them for the day."

"Wait a minute, you also deliver the papers? Since when?"

"I just started two weeks ago."

"Exactly how many jobs do you have?"

"Just what I told you: I cook part time at Passmores', I deliver the morning papers, I do a little work around my apartment building, and now I'm starting to do yard work. Also, sometimes I do shopping on the mainland for some of the older folks."

"Are you involved in working with telephones at all?" Aisha asked sourly.

"No. Why?"

Aisha waved off his question. "Never mind. Are you going to school?"

"That's what I'm working for," Christopher said. "I'm accepted for U Mass next year. I have some scholarship money, but I need to save some up, too."

Aisha nodded and started to walk back to the house. On the steps she looked back over her shoulder. "Business major, right?"

"How'd you guess?"

Zoey woke up late and hungry. The day before she had worked straight through what should have been dinnertime. After that she'd had the chance encounter with Lucas at the breakwater and since then, she hadn't really thought about food at all.

She trudged toward the shower, scratching her head and trying to pry open her left eye. She brushed her teeth and started running the water in the shower. It always took a good minute for the hot water to come.

This time, however, it didn't come at all.

"Oh, man," she groaned through a foam of Crest. The hot-water heater must have gone out again, a regular occurrence. Either that, or Benjamin had taken one of his half-hour showers.

She rinsed and stomped barefoot down the stairs, feeling grumpy and sleepy and a little dopey. "Four more and I'd have the seven dwarfs," she muttered.

"The damned hot water is out again!" she yelled as she reached the kitchen.

"I'm sorry to hear that," a voice said calmly.

Zoey jumped, and spun around. She clapped her hand over her heart.

It was Lucas.

Her brother was nowhere to be seen. Neither was her mother. Only Lucas, who was sitting in the breakfast nook and sipping a cup of coffee. A plate of sweet rolls was on the table, two left.

"Your mom invited me to wait for you," Lucas said. "She had to go to the restaurant, then catch the eleven-ten ferry. Ben went with her. Something about school clothes."

"Oh, Lord," Zoey muttered under her breath. She reached for her tangled mess of hair and tried to shove and pat it into something human-looking. But then she realized that with her hands over her head, her Bruins T-shirt rode perilously up toward her cotton panties. She slapped her arms down to her sides and tugged the shirt hem downward, which had the effect of drawing the fabric taut over her breasts. She released the hem and started on her hair again, then crossed her arms over her chest and tried her best to look nonchalant.

"You did invite me for breakfast," Lucas pointed out.

Zoey nodded. "Yes. Yes, of course, because I hoped you'd bring some of those delicious sweet rolls and I see you did so I guess I was right in inviting you . . . not that that was the only reason, I mean it's not like you're the baker or something I mean I . . . we, I mean my mom and Benjamin . . . I also, you know . . . you know, we're like friends and all from before."

Nicely expressed, Zoey, she thought.

Lucas smiled his serious smile. "I guess I kind of surprised you."

"Why? Do I look terrible?" She cringed and took another stab at untangling the bird's nest on her head.

"No, you look wonderful."

"I don't think so," Zoey said, laughing wryly. "I mean, usually I try to wear something more than a T-shirt."

"Trust me, you look wonderful."

"Not that I'm wearing *just* a T-shirt," Zoey added quickly. "I mean, I'm wearing underwear." Instantly she felt the blush rising in her cheeks. She gulped and looked down at the table.

"Me too," Lucas said, grinning at her discomfort.

Zoey sighed. "I'm not exactly awake. When I'm awake, I babble a little less. I still babble, but less."

"Want some coffee? There's still some in the pot your mom made."

"Normally, no, but since the hot water's out and I'm making a fool of myself, maybe I could use a cup. Or six."

Lucas got up, went to the kitchen counter, and poured. She sat down at the table and reached for a sweet roll. With the first few sips of coffee, her confidence began to return. So she'd babbled, big deal. After all, it wasn't like Lucas had a lot of other alternative conversational partners on the island.

This thought brought guilt with it. Her stomach churned. A mental picture of Jake formed in the air just over Lucas's head.

"Your mom can still cook," Zoey said.

"Yeah," Lucas agreed affectionately.

"Is she . . . are you two talking?"

Lucas shrugged. "My mom is trying to play it safe. She wants to make peace, but if she defies my father outright, well . . . You know my father. He's very 'old country.' He thinks he's the absolute ruler of the house, period, just like he is on the boat."

"Still, he's letting you live there," Zoey remarked, taking a bite of the roll.

"It's all a part of the same thing," Lucas said. "He's Portuguese, *Acoreano.* He's an islander going back in his family to long before Chatham Island had even been discovered by whites. Family is very important, and you have to take care of family no matter what, so no, he won't just kick me out. Not until he can figure out something to do with me, anyway." He rolled his eyes. "Like I said. Very old world."

"But isn't your mom from the Azores, too?"

"No. She emigrated from the Netherlands. The Dutch are a bit looser, I guess." He used his fingers to rake a strand of hair that had fallen over his eye. "That's where I got my blond hair," he said. "Just think Little Dutch Boy."

Zoey patted her own hair with her free hand. "Just think sparrow's nest."

Lucas was about to say something else, but he bit his lip and fell silent. The silence stretched awkwardly for a moment.

"Are you going to be going to school?" Zoey asked.

"Yeah. I still need a year, what with the Youth Authority

being so much better at locking people up than it is at education. So, yeah, I'll be going to Weymouth High. I know everyone on the island will be thrilled to find that out."

Zoey nodded glumly and chewed the last bite of her roll thoughtfully. "I guess it will be kind of rough for you."

"And for anyone who befriends me," Lucas said, his voice dropping. "Which is why I want to say something. You've been very sweet, Zoey, but I don't expect you to talk to me in public. I understand how it is. I promise it won't hurt my feelings if you blow me off."

Zoey hesitated. What was she going to do about this? It seemed awfully hypocritical to talk to Lucas here, even to enjoy talking to him, and then pretend that she couldn't stand him later.

Lucas grinned crookedly. It was meant to look tough and indifferent, but the corner of his mouth collapsed a little. "I'm a big boy," he said. "I can handle it."

"No one can handle it," Zoey said. "You can't live life totally cut off."

Suddenly she stopped. She had reached for him without thinking. Her hand, dripping with sugar glaze from the roll, was covering his. Slowly, Lucas's fingers entwined around hers. Neither of them was breathing. Zoey's heart was beating so loudly she was sure he could hear it.

"I . . . I got you all sticky," Zoey said, her voice a squeaky gasp.

Lucas raised their locked hands to his lips. He brought her sugary index finger to his mouth. His eyes were nearly closed, his every movement in slow motion.

The doorbell rang. Zoey snatched her hand away. He withdrew his as well.

"The door," Zoey said breathlessly. "Probably Nina."

"I'll leave through the back," Lucas said.

"You don't have to—"

"Yes," he said regretfully, "I do." He turned away as the doorbell rang a second time. At the back door he paused, looking down at the knob. "Thanks," he said. And then he was gone.

TEN

THE FRONT DOORBELL RANG A third time before Zoey reached it. She hoped Lucas was smart enough not to let Nina see him as he climbed back up the hill. "I'm coming, Nina," she muttered. "Jeez, hang on a minute."

She paused for a moment, closed her eyes, and tried to catch her breath. Nina knew her too well. She might easily notice the furious blush on her neck.

Zoey opened the door. Her breath caught in her chest. Claire stood there, looking grim. A few steps behind her, looking uncomfortable, was Jake.

"Claire?" Zoey asked. And then, in a more suspicious tone, "Jake?"

"Morning, Zoey," Claire said coolly. "Do you mind if we come in?"

We? As in Claire-and-Jake *we*? Zoey held open the door. Claire glided past. Jake came up and leaned forward to plant a light kiss on her cheek. She sent him a questioning look, but he just shrugged and made a point of pressing on, like he was in a hurry to get past her.

Claire led the way to the family room, as if she were in her own home escorting guests. She seemed to be barely suppressing some urgent need, but intent on acting in control. She sat on an easy chair, legs crossed like a man, arms wide. A forced smile on her lips was betrayed by a cold, dangerous light in her eyes.

Jake flopped on the couch, alternately scowling and averting his eyes. He shifted every few seconds, uncomfortable with himself, yet clearly sullen and angry as well.

Zoey stood with her arms crossed, looking from one to the other. There was no point in pretending that this little visit was normal.

"What's up?" Zoey demanded.

Claire affected a casual shrug. "We just wanted to talk to you."

Again with the *we*.

"You. And Jake. At nine forty-five in the morning."

Claire made a show of noticing Zoey's nightshirt. "I hope we didn't wake you up."

"No, I was up," Zoey said.

"Won't you sit down?" Claire asked, motioning toward the couch.

Jake patted the cushion beside him.

"Excuse me, both of you, but this is *my* house," Zoey said. "I'll decide whether I want to sit down or not. Now, I haven't had a shower yet, and I'm not up for a long discussion about the weather, so why don't you two tell me what's on your minds?"

Claire met her gaze and held it, her black-on-black eyes boring into Zoey's. Zoey looked away, then looked back.

"I think you know what this is about," Claire said. "My little sister isn't a very good liar, you know. She said *she* spoke to Lucas, but Nina is weak on making up convincing details."

Zoey tried not to flinch or show any guilty reaction, but the result was that she just stood there in the middle of the room, staring stonily.

"Look, Zo," Jake said, "it's no big deal if, you know, he kind of took you by surprise and you talked to him for a couple of seconds or whatever. I mean, like I told Claire, you're a nice person. Your natural instinct is to be nice."

"How nice of you to defend me to Claire," Zoey said sarcastically. "When did this little discussion take place?"

Jake wrinkled his brow and looked upset, but Claire stepped in smoothly. "I called him last night. Also, we discussed it on the way over here."

"On the way over? You live on the point, Claire, and Jake is down island from here."

"I asked him to pick me up in his truck," Claire said blandly.

"This is amazing," Zoey said. "What is this, the Spanish Inquisition?"

"We're just asking, Zo, did you talk to Lucas?" Jake smiled placatingly. "That's all. Simple question."

"What if I don't want to answer your simple question?" Zoey said, trying to buy time. What could she say? They were just asking about her very brief conversation with Lucas in the backyard. They didn't even know about the breakwater, or that he'd been there just minutes before, raising her fingers to his lips—

"You're no better at lying than Nina is," Claire said contemptuously.

"Are you calling me a liar?" Zoey asked, loading her voice with outrage.

"I'm saying you talked to Lucas Cabral," Claire said, unintimidated. "It's a yes or no answer."

Zoey glanced desperately toward Jake, but his gaze had hardened, drawing on Claire's determination.

"I spoke to him."

"Damn it!" Jake exploded. He shot to his feet and began pacing angrily back and forth.

Claire nodded. "So. What did he have to say?"

"Who cares what that creep had to say?" Jake stormed. "I thought you understood, Zoey. I mean, what were you thinking of? Did you at least tell him to hump off?"

"He caught me by surprise," Zoey protested weakly. "I was out back sunbathing and suddenly he's talking to me. I didn't know what to do." She flopped her arms at her side.

"Tell him the truth," Claire suggested. "I'm sure he won't be surprised. Just tell him we don't talk to people who do the kinds of things he did."

"I don't think he did it on purpose," Zoey said. Instantly she realized she'd made a mistake.

Jake whirled on her, his face contorted in rage. "On purpose? Who the hell cares if it was on purpose? He was drunk and he got behind the wheel of a car. Maybe he didn't say, 'I'm going to ram this car into a tree and kill Wade McRoyan,' but he knew he was drunk and he knew he was driving, end of damn story. If I go running around town shooting off a gun, maybe I don't *plan* to kill anyone, but if I do, I can't just shrug my shoulders and say, 'Hey, sorry, pal, I didn't plan to kill you.' It doesn't matter. You're just as dead."

Zoey recoiled, startled by Jake's rage. But at the same time his words hit home. He was right, wasn't he? Lucas might seem like a perfectly nice person, even a sad, lonely person in need of a friend, but did that change what he had done?

Wade was dead. That was reality. The guilty thrill she'd felt when Lucas told her she looked wonderful, the disturbing warmth that had flowed through her when he kissed her hand . . . that was illusion. Reality was Wade. And Claire, not her closest friend, perhaps, but not an enemy, either. And Jake, his fury now softening into a look of confused betrayal.

The line had been drawn very clearly. On one side: Jake. And Claire, and to a lesser extent Nina and Aisha. On the other side Lucas. Just Lucas.

Zoey drew in a deep, shaky breath. "I . . . I'm sorry. I guess . . . I mean, it never affected me directly. I didn't really know Wade that well, him being older and all."

"You know me well," Jake said softly. "I know you didn't mean any harm, Zo. But this is important to me. See, I want that bastard out of my life, and I want it to work out peacefully, no trouble for anyone. And that only works if we all stick together on this."

"I understand," Zoey said numbly.

"If you love me . . ." He smiled crookedly. "If you just even care about me, you'll stay away from Lucas Cabral."

Zoey nodded mutely and bit her lip.

Claire smiled brightly, as if everything were perfect again. She slapped the arms of her chair and rose to her feet. "Well. That's over, at least."

"You want me to drive you back?" Jake asked.

"Not necessary," Claire said magnanimously. "It's nice out."

"You want to do anything today?" Jake asked Zoey, striving for an air of normalcy.

"I still haven't had a shower or breakfast yet," Zoey said, adopting his tone. "How about if I come over to your house later?"

"Sounds good," Jake said gratefully. He kissed her on the lips, a hurried, uncertain kiss.

Claire was at the door to the breakfast nook, looking thoughtfully at the table. In a flash, Zoey realized one of Mrs. Cabral's famous sweet rolls was still on the table.

Claire went on toward the door, Jake following behind. "I realize this is tougher for you, in a way, than for the rest of us," Claire said, eyeing Zoey thoughtfully. "After all, Lucas is your next-door neighbor."

Jake opened the front door and walked out into the morning sun, looking as if he were glad to be escaping some prison. Claire waited till he was halfway across the lawn, then she favored Zoey with her cool smile. "Plus, Lucas always was cute. Those soulful eyes. That slightly lost look of his. Hard for any girl to resist."

She let the faintest sneer form and then disappear, swallowed up in a brightly artificial smile.

She knows, Zoey realized. *Not everything, not the details, but she knows he was here this morning.*

"He had a message for you," Zoey blurted.

The way Claire's mouth opened in surprise and her face seemed to pale was very rewarding.

"Oh. Did he?"

"He said you shouldn't worry so much. He said he keeps his promises."

Claire's brow furrowed. For a moment her eyes were genuinely troubled, far, far away as if she were listening to some faint, distant music. Then, with an impatient shake of her head, she put her mask of indifference back in place. "How cryptic."

"What does it mean?" Zoey asked.

"I have no idea," Claire said.

Zoey ended up taking a cold shower, which did very little to improve her mood. To make things worse, she forgot to rinse the shampoo out of her hair, which meant she had to get back under the cold spray after she'd already started drying off.

It had been a completely unsettling morning.

She dressed and spent a few minutes looking through her quote books for some insights. The only things that stood out made her feel worse, not better. Good old Confucius saying, *To know what is right and not to do it is the worst cowardice.*

It sounded good, but of course her problem was that she didn't know what was right. She was perfectly balanced between two opposite points of view:

1. Lucas had paid the price for what he'd done and had a right to be forgiven.
2. No, he didn't.

And there were complications making either point of view hard to completely accept.

Complication #1:

Her boyfriend and one of her friends would completely turn against her if she didn't go their way, and others would follow them.

Complication #2:

Whenever she remembered Lucas kissing her fingers, her knees buckled, her throat seized, her eyes closed, and her head tended to loll back and forth as if there weren't any muscles in her neck.

Complication #3:

Complication #1 made her seethe. Jake actually *conspiring* with Claire.

Complication #4:

Complication #2 made her feel like a treacherous, disloyal, lowlife tramp.

Her eye settled on a well-known saying from Thoreau: *If a man does not keep pace with his companions, perhaps it is because he hears a different drummer. Let him step to the music which he hears, however measured or far away.*

Easy for Thoreau to say. He wasn't trapped on a tiny island with people who knew everything you did within twenty-four hours of the time you did it.

Still, she wrote down the quote and stuck it on the wall beside her window. Then, after a moment's hesitation, she added the Confucius quote, too.

Okay, so maybe she was a coward. Or maybe she was just confused.

She had to get out of here, that much was certain. Any minute now Nina would come by and she'd have to go into the whole thing blow by blow, word by word. And if she told Nina about the breakwater, or worse yet, what had happened that morning with Lucas (knees buckling, throat choked, eyes very heavy, head sinking toward her right shoulder) . . . well, she'd inevitably spill it to Claire, who would undoubtedly have to talk it over with Jake.

Zoey pressed her lips into an angry line. The nerve of those two, coming over and trying to discipline her like she was a naughty child.

Definitely had to get out of the house. She glanced at the clock on her dresser. No, off the island! She could just make the eleven ten if she didn't blow-dry her hair.

She had completely forgotten what Lucas had said about her mom and Benjamin taking the eleven ten until she saw them up by the front rail of the *Titanic.* Benjamin was leaning over the rail, his hands clasped. Her mom was sitting in the passenger seat of a van, chatting with the driver, who happened to be the woman who ran the island grocery store. Her mother noticed her and waved a casual hello.

"Hi, Benjamin," Zoey said as she came up beside him.

"Hey, Zoey."

The whistle blew shrilly and the ferry began backing away from the pier.

"You decide to come shopping with us?" Benjamin asked.

"Actually, I didn't know you'd be here," Zoey said.

Benjamin turned to show her a dubious grin. "Lucas didn't tell you?"

"Maybe he did, but I forgot," Zoey said, feeling a little annoyed. She'd escaped a cross-examination by Nina, only to run into one from Benjamin.

"So, you *did* talk to him this morning."

"Kind of."

The ferry began to pull clear of the dock and headed across

the harbor, blasting its horn at a careless sailboat that was getting too close.

Benjamin removed his shades and rubbed his eyes with his free hand. "Damn pollen is thick today. It doesn't seem fair if your eyes aren't going to work that they should itch."

He turned toward her, his dark eyes blank, their focus aimed just slightly to the left of her. Then he pulled a tiny bottle of Visine from the pocket of his jeans, tilted back his head, and settled two drops in each eye.

Zoey felt relieved when he replaced his shades.

"A little eerie?" he suggested.

"What?"

"My eyes. They look weird, don't they? I mean, I can imagine. Like the lights are on but no one's home inside?"

"Benjamin—" Zoey stopped herself from saying something kind. Benjamin was always laying out these little traps, looking for some sign of pity that he would pounce on unmercifully. "Actually, you just looked like you were very interested in my left ear."

"Roger." He gave a little salute. "Adjust three points to starboard. Nice day, huh? Partly cloudy?"

"Yeah. Although the sun is getting lower on the horizon every day."

"It will do that. So, aren't you worried Jake will have a hissy fit if he finds out you're talking to Lucas? You're crazy if you think he won't hear about it."

"He already has. He and Claire came over this morning. Nina told Claire—you remember her, your girlfriend?—Well, Nina told her I spoke to Lucas the other day. We exchanged about a dozen words at the time, so naturally it called for a major inquisition." She related the events of that morning to her brother, leaving out all mention of certain things Lucas had said and done.

"Claire, huh?" He nodded thoughtfully.

"Don't worry," Zoey said. "I don't think it's like she's interested in Jake or anything. I think it's just that they both are all hot about this whole Lucas thing."

"If Claire decides it's to her advantage, she'll find a way to get interested in Jake real fast," Benjamin said. "You know how she is. Or maybe you don't."

"You make it sound like she's the one behind all this," Zoey said impatiently. "It was Jake's brother who died. He's the one who's most involved. He's the one I'm worried about hurting."

"Then why is Claire getting in the middle of it all?"

"She was hurt in the accident. I guess she figures she could have been killed, too."

"But she wasn't."

"No."

"So why the big push from Claire?"

She looked at him quizzically. He must have felt her gaze because he smiled at her. "Are you trying to tell me something?" she asked.

He pursed his lips. "I can't tell you anything, little sister. Only . . . you remember that first time we went whale watching? Maybe not, you were pretty young. But it's one of those memories I hold on to from when I could see." He made a wry face. "Like I remember your face, except you'll always look about ten years old. Anyway, I remember the way you could watch the surface of the water, the way it would seem to bulge, almost imperceptibly, and you'd know the whale was right there, just below the surface. You couldn't see him yet, but you knew he was coming up."

"I do remember that. Like a bubble."

He nodded. "That's what we have here. Something big, just below the surface. You can hear it in Claire's voice since Lucas came back. You can feel its outlines in strange things like the two of them coming to see you this morning. And then there are all the little things that don't quite fit in."

Zoey looked at him sharply. "What little things?"

"I'll give you one." He held up his index finger. "The car they were all in that night was an old VW bug, right? Two seats in front and no way a third person fits in."

"Okay."

"So one person's in the backseat. Wade. Lucas. Claire."

"Either Claire or Wade," Zoey said, but the little hairs on the back of her neck were standing up.

"Yep. Only . . . only you'd figure the two in the front would be the two who were most badly injured in a head-on crash into a tree." He shrugged. "Wouldn't you figure that?"

"Have you ever mentioned that to Claire?" Zoey asked.

He shook his head. Then he grinned. "But you'll mention it to Nina, which is almost as good."

"So . . . So what are you saying?"

Benjamin made a "who knows?" face. "You know me," he said, waving his hand dismissively, "always picking at details."

Claire

My mother died when I was thirteen. She had breast cancer.

Naturally, I was overwhelmed. I couldn't eat, couldn't sleep without having horribly sad dreams. My dad was great, doing his best to take care of me, sending me to counseling, even asking if I wanted to start going to church.

We'd always been close, my dad and I. Just like Nina had always been closer to my mom. Everyone said they were so alike, not just in looks but in personality. Nina went away to stay with our aunt and uncle for a couple of months, so I didn't see much of her during this time. And when she came back, she seemed so changed. Maybe I was, too.

I know that from then on, things were different between Nina and me. Maybe she resented being sent to stay with my aunt, but I know my dad did what he thought was right. He said that as close as Nina was to my mother, she needed a change of scene.

After the crash that killed Wade McRoyan, my father never left my hospital room, even though the doctors told him it really wasn't a big deal, just some minor injuries. He asked me who was driving, and that's when I realized I didn't remember anymore, which was kind of frightening.

He said he'd get to the bottom of it. I shouldn't worry. One way or the other he would protect me. He believed in me. He trusted me. He knew I was going to be just fine, because he would never again let anyone or anything hurt me.

It was what I needed to hear right then, with my mind a scrambled mess of half-memories and confusion. At a time like that, you need to hear that it's all going to be okay. You know?

And it was. I healed right up. Lucas confessed. Over time my confusion diminished. Life went on.

ELEVEN

"IT'S FINE BY ME," NINA said. "I hate to be responsible for their deaths, anyway. Screaming as they hit the boiling water, crying out to their lobster gods for mercy."

Claire laughed. From time to time, amid the general weirdness, Nina could actually be funny. "Lobster gods?"

"Oh, absolutely," Nina said solemnly. "Lobsters are quite devout. I've never seen a lobster covet or bear false witness."

"What's the holdup?"

They turned and looked at their father. Burke Geiger came up to the seafood counter, pushing a grocery cart that held a bottle of white wine and a loaf of French bread.

"No lobsters," Claire said.

"No lobsters?" her father echoed disbelievingly.

"We're too late," Nina said. "Labor Day's a big day for lobsters, I guess."

"We have to have lobsters," Mr. Geiger said flatly.

"They have no lobsters," both girls said at once.

Mr. Geiger made a face, wrinkling the tan brow that contrasted so sharply with his prematurely white hair. "Let's walk down to the dock and see Roy Cabral."

"If he had any lobsters, he's probably sold them," Nina said, sounding hopeful.

"He'll take care of us," Mr. Geiger said easily, abandoning the basket and leading them toward the door. "Hell, I own half his boat."

Claire hurried to keep up with him. Her father habitually walked as if he were late for a meeting with the president, even when, like now, he was not at work. "Since when do you own part of Mr. Cabral's boat?" Claire asked. She always tried to show an interest in her father's business. He had no one else to talk to.

"And which part?" Nina mumbled, bringing up the rear.

Mr. Geiger shrugged. "You remember a couple of years back, the price of lobster was way down—"

"Sure," Nina said ironically. "You know how I keep up with seafood prices."

Mr. Geiger ignored her. "He was hurting for cash, so I helped out a little. No big deal."

They reached the dock and veered across to the spot where Mr. Cabral's boat was tied up. He was on the boat, hosing down his deck, wearing high rubber boots over dirty overalls. His face had little in common with his son's, Claire reflected, at least as she remembered Lucas's face. Maybe the mouth was the same, but the rest was as hard as chiseled stone, weathered a deep chestnut color.

"Hi, Roy," her father called out.

"Mr. Geiger," Mr. Cabral said, nodding. He turned off the hose and wiped his hands on a rag.

"Roy, I'm in a bind. No lobsters, and my housekeeper is set on cooking up some lobster tonight."

Mr. Cabral nodded again, as if this were indeed a terrible tragedy. "I have lobster. Not all sold yet. Only maybe not so big." He shrugged.

"I'll take whatever size you have, Roy, and thanks."

Mr. Cabral walked back to the hold and began banding and boxing lobsters.

"Smaller are better, anyway," Mr. Geiger said to Claire. "People think you need a lobster the size of a Volkswagen, but the smaller ones are so much more tender."

"Volkswagen," Nina echoed, looking puzzled.

"Yes?" Claire said, batting her eyes condescendingly at her sister.

Nina shrugged. "Nothing. Zoey was talking about Volkswagens today. Wasn't that the car—you know, the big crash, wasn't that a Volkswagen?"

"I don't know one car from the next," Claire said dismissively. "It was small. Are Volkswagens small?"

Nina shrugged again.

"What was she asking about the car for?" Mr. Geiger said, sounding casual and keeping his gaze fixed on Mr. Cabral.

"I don't know," Nina said. "I was trying to get her to loan me this pair of shorts she just bought. She said she and Ben were talking about it on the ferry this morning. Volkswagens and whether they were small. Ben said he thought it was strange that everyone didn't get crushed."

"That's a little morbid," Claire said disapprovingly.

"He's *your* boyfriend," Nina said. "If you don't like him, maybe you should—"

"Here you have," Mr. Cabral said, lifting a box of sluggishly moving lobsters onto the pier.

"How many?" Mr. Geiger asked.

"Six, half-dozen," Mr. Cabral said. "Two each because so small."

"Could you add a couple more?" Mr. Geiger asked. He turned to Claire. "I thought maybe we'd invite Benjamin over tonight. It's been a while since we've had him to dinner."

Claire leaned against the railing of the widow's walk and watched him approach. He had his cane out, swinging it back and forth in a short arc that was more a formality than a necessity. It wasn't the cane that told him precisely when to stop, stretch out his left hand and place it within three inches of the latch to her gate.

There was always something a little amazing in the way Benjamin managed to find his way through the narrow streets of North Harbor, going the length of Camden, crossing four other streets, taking the right turn on Lighthouse, crossing yet another street, finding her gate among the others on the block, finding the door and the knocker, and ending up there under the porch light, looking as if it were nothing.

He had explained it to her before: seventy-one steps from his house to the first street, and eleven steps to the other curb. Then a hundred eight steps, and ninety-seven steps more. And with all the counting went the sounds: the barking Labrador retriever, the beeping of the video machine just inside the grocery store, the way the sounds of the dock echoed up the cobblestones of Exchange, the lapping surf when you reached Lighthouse.

It was one of the things that made her like him, the way he paid such close attention to all that went on around him. When she spoke to him, he heard her every nuance, focused his full attention on her. Most guys sent every third glance in the direction of her chest and heard only half of what she said.

It also made her uncomfortable at times, the way he always seemed to be paying unnatural attention to details no one else even noticed.

"Hi," she said, panting a little from the hurried descent from her room.

"Yes, I'd like some fudge, please? With walnuts."

"Come on in," Claire said.

"You mean this isn't Mrs. Laskin's sweet shop?"

Claire slipped her hand around the back of his neck, drew him toward her, and kissed him on the lips.

"Why, Mrs. Laskin. I didn't know you cared." He folded the collapsible cane and set it on the small table at the base of the stairs.

Claire's father came out of his study and clapped a hand on Benjamin's shoulder. "Ben, good to see you."

"Evening, Mr. Geiger. How's business? Foreclosed on any widows or orphans lately?"

Mr. Geiger managed a pained but tolerant smile. "Mid-Maine Bank never forecloses on widows or orphans, Ben, you know that. We don't give them loans in the first place."

Benjamin laughed, which delighted Claire's father. Mr. Geiger had made it clear he was somewhat uncertain of Benjamin's prospects, but at the same time he clearly liked him, which was an improvement over Claire's previous boyfriends.

In fact, he'd seemed almost eager that Benjamin come for dinner tonight.

"I think Janelle has dinner just about ready, so we can go on into the dining room," Mr. Geiger announced. "Nina!" he shouted up the stairs.

"I'm here, I'm here," Nina said, appearing at the top of the stairs and trotting down them loudly.

"You might try wearing something decent when we're having someone over for dinner," Mr. Geiger said disapprovingly. Nina was wearing bib overalls under an unbuttoned red plaid flannel shirt.

"Really, Nina," Benjamin chided. "Where's your sense of style?"

Dinner was served in the formal dining room, patterned china and lead crystal glittering brightly beneath a brass chandelier. Janelle, the live-in housekeeper Claire's father had hired soon after the death of Mrs. Geiger, served in courses of a cold scallop appetizer, a salad, then the lobsters for everyone except Nina, who had decided in the end that she couldn't cause any more lobster suffering. She had broiled cod instead.

"So, are you looking forward to school starting tomorrow?" Mr. Geiger asked as Janelle poured coffee.

Benjamin shrugged. "It will be my senior year. I guess I'm looking forward to getting it over with."

"And then?"

"You mean after I graduate?"

"It's not a million years in the future, is it?" Mr. Geiger asked.

"He's sizing you up as a marriage prospect," Nina said darkly, stirring sugar into a cup of coffee.

"Me?" Benjamin asked in astonishment. "Marry your father? Well, naturally I'm flattered, but—"

Claire reached across the table and put her hand on Benjamin's. "Don't pay any attention to my annoying sister."

"He never has," Nina muttered.

"I was just curious," Mr. Geiger said. "You're obviously too bright to miss out on college. But at the same time I know your folks have to send both you and Zoey at the same time. Quite an expense."

"Daddy," Claire chided. Her father had a tendency to be rather blunt where money was concerned.

"Oh, Benjamin's a big boy. He knows I hold the loans on Passmores' Restaurant. There's nothing sinister in it. I'm the president of the bank; I'm supposed to know how much money everyone has." He made a deprecating face. "Ben's dad knows what everyone likes to eat, his mom knows how much of what poison everyone on the island drinks, and I know how much money people have."

"Like a dentist knows how many teeth everyone has," Benjamin said. "Or a proctologist knows how big—"

Claire squeezed his hand sharply.

"Thank you, Ben," Mr. Geiger said, shooting Claire a look that was half-amused, half-annoyed. Claire kept her expression innocent. "What I was getting around to was reassuring you that if you need a little boost with the old college funding, I'm sure we at the bank can work something out."

Claire felt the sudden tension in Benjamin's hand. Or perhaps he was just responding to her own surprised reaction. Her father was volunteering to help pay Benjamin's way through college? What was this all about? She stared closely at her father's face, but he was blandly spooning up the ice cream Janelle had put in front of him.

"That's very nice of you," Benjamin said guardedly.

"See?" Mr. Geiger said. "It's not all foreclosing on widows and orphans. Sometimes being a banker you get to help someone out."

Benjamin smiled. Her father smiled. Even Nina smiled, in a sort of perplexed way.

Claire pushed away her dessert. No, this was not what it seemed. Not that her father was incapable of being generous; he was. But Claire knew him too well. They were two of a kind in many ways. Her father had some motive for this sudden display of openhandedness.

As usual, Benjamin went with unerring accuracy right to the point. "So, if I end up taking out a loan, Mr. Geiger, what do I have to sign over to Mid-Maine Bank? This isn't one of those deals where I have to sell my soul, is it?"

"Dad doesn't believe in souls," Nina said.

"Of course I do," Mr. Geiger said. "I'm not just a materialist—I believe in patriotism, honor, right and wrong." He paused to take a sip of his coffee. "And of course, loyalty. Loyalty is especially important to me."

HOPES . . .

Zoey

My hopes for this school year? Well, I'm hoping to get good grades, of course. And I'm also hoping I get a locker combination that's easy to remember. I'm hoping no one talks me into running for student government again because last year when I came in fourth behind Carla Bose, Jed Froman, and Captain America, it was totally humiliating. Although I beat Thor by two votes.

Claire

Hopes? Hmm. I'd like teachers who understand that homework is an infringement on my private life. I'd like to learn that George Noble had a sex-change operation over the summer so he'd stop asking me out. I'd like people to quit coming up to me and asking what's the deal with my weird little sister, is she nuts or what? That would be nice. Oh, and

I'd love to catch the weasel who wrote my phone number in the boys' bathroom and hurt him badly.

Aisha

Desks with some padding. That's it. And lighter books. I mean, what's the matter with paperbacks? Is there some rule that schoolbooks have to weigh fifty pounds? Also, I hope the lunchroom will figure out that vegetables are not actually supposed to be gray and so overcooked, you can suck them up through a straw. I'm serious. I could show you green beans that would make you cry.

Nina

Hope? Absolutely! I'm brimming with hope. I'm blowing chunks of hope. I hope everyone will like me, and I'll like them, and all my wonderful teachers will fill my head with useful yet interesting information, and all our teams will be in first place and then, yes, I'll be voted queen of the junior prom! Hooray! Failing that, I'm hoping school isn't the usual dark, mind-numbing, spirit-destroying hell it was last year.

TWELVE

"**'CAUSE I KNEW YOU WERE** *trouble when you walked i-i-i-n . . .*"

"Oh, shut up, Taylor." Zoey slapped the music alarm and threw back her covers. She stood up, feeling pins and needles in the soles of her feet as they hit the floor. She twisted her Boston Bruins shirt around and groaned.

The light coming in through the dormered window was watery and gray. A light that signaled it was too early in the day for people to be up and walking around and scratching themselves. She glanced at the clock. Six twenty-one.

Then she remembered. School.

The day before, Labor Day, had passed in a whirl of work. One of the waitresses at the restaurant had quit, and another had fallen off a bike and bruised her hip. Zoey had been stuck working a double shift, which left hardly any time to think about the fact that in the morning . . . *this* morning . . . she'd be going to school.

At six twenty-one in the morning.

It seemed like a million years since she had gotten up this early to go to school. She had to make the seven-forty ferry. Get to Weymouth at five after eight. Make it up to the school by eight thirty. Catch the four o'clock coming home, arriving four twenty-five.

The times of her life. The rigid schedule of her days. Freedom a thing of the past. Sleep also a thing of the past. Homework.

Still, she realized with a slow, building excitement, she was a senior.

How did a senior dress? Should she do her hair differently? Would she no longer get zits now that she was a senior? Would her hair be easier to manage? Would she acquire great wisdom?

She felt a little clenching in her throat. It would be the same old school, yes, but *she* would be different.

And that could change everything.

"Can we go back, this is the moment . . ."

"No, no, please say it isn't so," Nina groaned, pulling her pillow over her head and reaching for the button to silence Macklemore. "How can summer be over?" she demanded of her pillow. "How?"

She peeked from under the pillow at her clock. "Six twenty-five? Why? Why can't they start school at noon? No, after noon. Then we wouldn't have to eat the food."

She sat up and stared across the room. "Notebooks," she cried, glaring hatefully at the pile of school supplies. "Number-two pencils! Oh, and three-ring binders! It's not right, it's not fair, why me, O Lord, why?"

She kicked at her tangled covers, and continued to kick after they had all fallen off the bed. Then she swung her feet onto the floor and fumbled in her bedside table for her pack of cigarettes. She popped one in her mouth and sucked on it.

School. School. The horror. The loathing. The bad food.

The crush of bodies in the halls between classes. Bells going off. Lockers that jammed. Other girls who all had great hair. Teachers who droned on and on and on till your head started nodding and your eyes grew heavy, heavy, and . . .

Nina snapped herself awake. She had drifted back onto her pillow. No, missing the ferry would not be a smart way to start eleventh grade.

Eleventh grade. A junior. Big deal.

Of course, now with school starting up again, she'd have to spend even more time reading to Benjamin. And maybe Claire would find some new guy. And Lucas was back.

No. No point in trying to work up any enthusiasm. It might be occasionally amusing, but it was still school.

• • •

Beethoven's Seventh Symphony, the melancholy, majestic second movement, woke Benjamin from his sleep. He had set up his iPhone with this wake-up music, chosen from his eclectic collection of songs.

He let it play on as he rose from his bed. Right from the front corner of his bed, one, two, three to his bathroom door. The music played in there, too, pumped through two waterproof speakers.

He turned on the shower, waiting till it reached the right temperature, and climbed in. He dropped the soap and had to feel around the bottom of the shower stall for several seconds before he located it, sweeping his hands methodically over the tiles.

He toweled off in front of the sink, facing the mirror that he knew would be steamed and opaque. He wondered, not for the first time, what it would show. Here he was, first day of school, new people to meet, new teachers to deal with, and he had no idea what he looked like.

People told him he was very good-looking, but then, people tended to be kind. Besides, even if he were, what *kind* of good-looking? Good-looking effeminate? Good-looking rugged? Good-looking cute?

"I could be a simp. I could be a toad," he said philosophically. Beethoven swelled toward a stately crescendo, and Benjamin grinned at the darkness where his reflection would be. "Still, at least if I am, I'm a senior toad."

Claire woke through gauzy layers of dream, surfacing, breathing deeply as if she'd been submerged. The alarm was buzzing, and she silenced it and listened for the sounds of the house. The radio on Nina's alarm was playing rock and roll, a faint but unmistakable sound. Her father's shower was running. Outside, a light breeze turned the twin brick chimneys into flutes, playing a tuneless melody.

She slid out of her satin sheets and wrapped her nude body in a brocaded silk robe. Then she climbed up the ladder to the widow's walk as she did every morning, throwing back the hatch to emerge in low, bright sunlight.

The sky was almost clear except for some low cumulus building to the north, but with the breeze out of the southwest, the sky would soon be perfectly clear, a rare phenomenon for this part of Maine.

First day of school. Her first encounter with Lucas, no doubt. The first chance to observe how Zoey and the others would react. Had she and Jake succeeded in isolating Lucas?

"Is that really so important?" she asked herself. A fragment of dream nagged at her consciousness, but when she tried to recall it, it slipped away.

"Why is it so important?"

She tried to remember Lucas, the way she had known him. She tried to imagine the ways he might have changed in two years' time. And how she would feel when she saw him.

Was that it? Was it that she was afraid she might still care for him? Was that the reason she felt so compelled to push him away?

Maybe. Yes, maybe that was part of it.

And what was the rest of it? Claire asked herself. That was the question. In the meantime, she would follow her instincts.

And eventually things would work out the way she wanted. They almost always did.

"What, what?" Aisha woke up startled, eyes wide.

Her little brother, Kalif, was smirking down at her. "Mom said to wake you up."

"So you scream *the house is on fire*?"

"I tried whispering *wake up*, but it didn't work," Kalif said, heading out the door.

Aisha looked at the clock. The alarm must not be working. No, she'd forgotten to set it. But good old Mom had remembered. Thanks a lot, good old Mom.

She stumbled to her closet, found her robe, and put it on over the new bottle-green pajamas she'd worn to bed.

"Shower first or eat first?" she asked herself, pausing in the foyer. From the kitchen came the smell of coffee and her mother's fresh-baked muffins.

Well, if she ran late, would she rather show up at school hungry or dirty?

The first day of school was always such a fashion show, everyone trying to establish themselves. No one would know if she was starving. Everyone would notice if her hair was sticking out on one side of her head.

She sighed. Shower it was; food could wait.

"Can we go back, this is the moment . . ."

"Good start to the day." Jake's covers were already off, lying in a twisted pile by the foot of the bed, as usual.

He did a sit-up, stretching down to touch his toes, then rolled out of bed. He stretched, right arm arcing up over his head to a count of forty, then did the other arm. Then, bending at the waist, pulled his forehead against his left knee, counted to twenty-five, and the same on the right side.

He did twenty-five push-ups, fifty stomach crunches, and several more stretches.

Then he stood up and took a look at himself in the full-length mirror on his closet door. He flexed a bicep, looking at the result critically. Then he slapped his ridged, flat stomach, satisfied with the muscle tone.

Yes, he'd have no trouble making the football team again this year. He hadn't let himself go over the summer, like a lot of guys.

He glanced at the clock. The stretches and exercises had taken nearly ten minutes. It was six thirty-four. No time for a run this morning. He'd have to work on getting up half an hour earlier.

Lucas had been up since six. Six A.M. had been wake-up at the youth authority. Five minutes to get your act together, grab your soap and towel before they marched you down to the showers, where you confronted the unappetizing sight of several dozen naked guys. And if that didn't ruin your appetite, the food, usually runny scrambled eggs and fatty ham, would.

He leaned against the railing of his deck, a cup of delicious coffee in his hand, steam curling up, the aroma intoxicating. The air was fresh scrubbed, salty and clear, just some low clouds to the north, nowhere near obscuring the sun as it rose from behind the ridge.

The town below was all sharp morning shadows and gold-drenched brick and clapboard. The sun turned the church spire into a brilliant gold needle. Through the trees and building clutter he could just see a slice of the harbor, his father's trawler chugging around the point, heading for the patch of water where he set his lobster traps.

Closer at hand, he could see Mrs. Passmore at the sink in her kitchen, dumping the seeds from a cantaloupe. He longed to see Zoey wander in wearing that nightshirt of hers. It would be nice to go down for another breakfast with her, but school started today. She'd have enough on her mind.

He certainly had enough on his.

"You know, Nina, you're not going to be able to do that in class," Zoey said, indicating the unlit cigarette in Nina's mouth.

"Why not? It's only against the rules to *smoke* cigarettes."

"That's like saying it's only against the rules if you *shoot* heroin, Ninny," Jake said.

"Or *fire* a gun," Zoey added.

"Or *spend* money after you steal it," Aisha offered.

Nina shook her head glumly. "Here it is. Officially our first pointless discussion on the way to school of the season."

They gathered on the right side of the ferry, back toward the stern where they had always gathered last school year, and the year before that. It was the place. From there they could watch all the other passengers on the upper deck, stay out of the line of sight of Skipper Too and the bridge, and get the best view of Weymouth as they came in, right down to the flagpole in front of their school at the end of Mainsail Street.

Mr. Gray, Aisha's father, and Mr. Geiger, Claire and Nina's father, were down below, where, by custom, they stayed out of the way of their kids, reading their papers and drinking coffee from steel thermos bottles.

Claire leaned against the stern rail, gazing off toward the bank of clouds to the north. Zoey knew she'd long had a fixation of sorts for weather phenomena. Not that Claire ever really spoke of it. She just spent a lot of her time gazing at clouds, referring to them not just as clouds but as *cirrus* or *cumulonimbus.* Nina said she often sat up on her widow's walk in the middle of storms. It was a strange fascination, but then, Claire was a strange girl. She was a friend, Zoey supposed, and yet there was always something a little withdrawn, a little preoccupied about Claire. Especially lately.

"Damn. There he is," Jake said, gritting his teeth.

Zoey didn't have to ask whom he was talking about. Lucas had come up the stairs to the upper deck. He looked in the direction of the group, turned away, and sat down toward the front, out of earshot but impossible not to see.

Had his gaze focused on her? Zoey wondered. Certainly not so anyone would notice.

Jake put his arm around her shoulders, drawing her to him. "I wasn't sure he'd have the nerve," he said.

"He has to go to school," Nina said. "How else is he going to get there?"

"He can swim," Jake said.

"Aren't you going to rush right up and beat the hell out of him?" Benjamin asked from the bench behind them.

Jake scowled. "I get into a fight and I could screw up my eligibility for the team."

Benjamin laughed. "Isn't that the reason the Swiss are always giving for staying out of wars? They don't want to screw up their chances of making the team."

"Come on, babe," Jake said, standing up and pulling Zoey to her feet.

"Where?"

"I want to stretch my legs," Jake said.

Zoey glanced nervously in Lucas's direction, but his back was turned to them. Reluctantly she fell in beside Jake as he walked slowly down the aisle toward the front of the boat.

"Jake, don't start anything. You know Benjamin was just trying to goad you."

"I'm not starting anything," Jake said. "I'm just taking a little walk around the deck."

Jake kept his arm around her shoulders and she could feel the tension in his muscles. Unfortunately, they were already so near Lucas that he would be sure to overhear if she argued with Jake anymore.

Nevertheless, she whispered through her teeth, "Jake, this is stupid."

"What? What are you talking about?" Jake said in a bad parody of innocence.

He turned and crossed in front of Lucas, Zoey still almost a prisoner in his strong grasp. Lucas's long legs were stretched out in front of him, and he slouched into the collar of his jacket, staring fixedly down toward the bow of the boat as it sliced through the water.

"You want to move your feet?" Jake said, his voice deadened.

Lucas slowly pulled his legs back, never looking up at Jake.

"Thanks, killer," Jake said. He turned his back on Lucas and leaned against the railing. Then he bent low and, to Zoey's amazement, kissed her on the lips. She pulled back in surprise.

Jake's eyes flared angrily, but she could tell he didn't want to say anything in front of Lucas.

"Let's go sit down, Jake," Zoey said tersely.

"No, I like it up here," he said, waving his arm expansively. "Up here I can look out and see the water. Sitting back there I found my view was obstructed by a piece of garbage. I hate looking at garbage, don't you, Zoey?"

Zoey shot a glance at Lucas, who was still sitting, staring calmly at nothing. Was Jake trying to pick a fight or just showing off?

Jake leaned his back to the railing, releasing Zoey. He stared straight down at Lucas. "I don't think Zoey likes garbage, either. I don't think anyone on the island likes garbage. You hear me, killer?"

Lucas took a deep breath and let it out slowly. "If you have a problem with me, Jake, don't drag Zoey into the middle of it."

"In the middle?" Jake demanded. "No, she's not in the middle. No one's in the middle. See, there's all of us on one side, and then there's you on the other, killer."

With a look of resignation, Lucas got to his feet. "Go ahead, Jake. Get it out of your system. You want to take a shot at me? Fine. Here's your chance."

Before Zoey could open her mouth, Jake's fist flew through the air, catching Lucas in the stomach and doubling him over. A second blow caught the side of his face and knocked him down onto the steel deck.

"Cut that out!" Skipper Too's angry voice blasted from the P.A. system.

Jake danced back on his toes, fists ready, daring Lucas to get up.

And somehow, before she knew what she was doing, Zoey

was on her knees, wrapping protective arms around Lucas's hunched back.

"Get away from him!" Jake roared. "He had it coming."

"Don't do this, Zoey," Lucas whispered, gasping for air.

Aisha and Nina rushed forward to grab Jake's arms and pull him back.

Zoey dug in her ferry bag for her little packet of Kleenex, pulled them all out, and pressed the wad against the flow of blood from Lucas's nose.

Skipper Too appeared, shoving Jake back and shouting, "I'll ban you from this boat, Jake, damned if I won't, if you don't get back there and sit down."

"That son of a bitch killed my brother!" Jake yelled hotly.

"I said sit down! By God, I'm the captain on this tub and you'll do what I tell you."

Jake backed away several feet. "Come on, Zoey. Leave that creep to bleed."

"Oh, shut up, Jake. Shut up!" Zoey cried.

"Go," Lucas said, trying to push her away. "Don't be stupid. I'm fine. I've taken worse."

"Zoey, damn it!" Jake yelled.

Zoey helped Lucas back to a sitting position, dabbing at him with her Kleenex in a vain attempt to keep the blood from staining his shirt. She could see Jake storming back to the others, shooting bitter looks of betrayal at her. Aisha and Nina seemed stunned, uncertain what to do as they stood halfway between Jake and Zoey.

As Zoey watched, Claire reached out and let her fingers settle on Jake's arm. Then her hand curled around his arm. It could have been a gesture of support, or comfort, or . . .

It all happened so quickly. No time to think. And now she knelt at Lucas's side, feeling very, very far away from the only friends she had.

THIRTEEN

"ALL RIGHT, LINE UP, GIRLS," Coach Anders said, giving a blast on her whistle that made Aisha wince. "Line up here on the sidelines. That's right. No, a *line*, not a gaggle."

Aisha jostled Zoey, who was on her left. "No gaggling," Aisha said under her breath, trying to get Zoey to laugh. Zoey could only manage a wan smile. Not that Aisha expected more, after the terrible scene on the morning ferry.

Aisha had handled that badly, she felt. She should have gone to Zoey, shown her some support. Zoey had looked so stricken and abandoned. And it wasn't like Aisha was on Jake's side.

Of course she wasn't on Lucas's either.

Why were there suddenly sides, anyway? Zoey was going to have to patch this up with Jake and quit feeling sorry for Lucas or it was going to put Aisha in a difficult spot.

"We are going to get right into it this year," Coach Anders announced, taking wide, swaggering steps along the line of girls in their gym shorts and Weymouth High T-shirts. "This," she held up a white-and-black ball, "is a soccer ball."

The class groaned in unison. Across the soccer field, a class of guys was running, one after another, toward a high jump, and, one after another, knocking the crossbar down.

"I know, you think because you're seniors you shouldn't even have to take gym class. Or else you think maybe it should just be aerobics or some such thing. Wrong." She stopped, dropped the ball to the grass, and put her foot on it. "Now, the school board did not approve my proposal to get you girls into weight training, but this will be just as tough."

"Oh, good," Aisha said under her breath. "It's important to be sweaty and bruised by the end of third period."

"Did you have something to add, Ms. Gray?" Coach Anders demanded.

"No, ma'am."

"Fundamentals!" Coach Anders shouted. "It's a game of fun-da-men-tals. And we are going to work on those fundamentals again and again until every woman here can thread this little ball through a field of opponents, get within scoring distance, and nail that goal."

A collective sigh of depression went through the group.

"Now, where are my balls?" Coach Anders demanded, looking down the field toward the gym.

Aisha snorted. Several girls giggled. Even Zoey cracked a smile.

Their coach's eyes flashed angrily, but she showed no sign that she understood what was funny. "There we go," she said, nodding in satisfaction. "Come on. Let's get moving!"

"Sorry, Coach, but one of them had a leak and I had to put on a patch."

Why was that voice familiar? Aisha wondered. She turned to look, but her view was blocked by Claire and several of the other girls.

"Women," Coach Anders announced, "meet our new equipment manager."

He ran up, wearing black shorts and a rugby shirt, carrying a large sack of balls slung over his shoulder.

"His name is Christopher Shupe. He'll be taking care of the balls, bats, nets, and so on. Mr. Forbes, who you may remember from last year, has moved to Florida."

"Hi," Christopher said, waving his hand to everyone and grinning directly at Aisha.

"It's a nightmare," Aisha muttered wonderingly. "Everywhere I go, there he is."

"Christopher was also on his high school varsity soccer team," Coach Anders went on, "so he's going to help us out with a few pointers."

Of course, Aisha thought darkly.

"Chris, why don't you pick out a volunteer, and we'll demonstrate some of the fun-da-men-tals."

Gee, I can't even begin to guess who he's going to choose, Aisha thought sarcastically. After all, the entire world, including her own mother and her gym teacher, was conspiring to get them together.

Christopher sent her a dazzling grin, then walked up, pointed his finger, and said, "All right, I sort of know Zoey, here. Maybe she'll give me a hand."

Zoey?

"Um, I'm really not . . . you know, very sporty," Zoey said lamely. "Wouldn't you like to get Aisha?"

Christopher shook his head. "No. No insult intended, but Aisha has somewhat large feet. I'm worried she might trip over herself."

Aisha felt her jaw drop open. She snapped it shut. *Somewhat large feet?*

"I'd never noticed before," Coach Anders said, looking down thoughtfully at Aisha's feet.

"I wear size nine," Aisha cried in protest. "That is not large!" Well, maybe nine and a half, but still . . .

"Nothing to be ashamed of," Coach Anders said heartily.

"I don't have big feet," Aisha repeated. "This is amazing.

The first day of school and I'm being insulted. I can play soccer as well as anyone here."

"Are you interested in playing soccer?" Christopher asked. "Because desire goes a long way, as I'm sure Coach Anders will agree."

"Desire is half the battle. The other half is fun-da-men-tals."

"I have the desire not to have people think I can't play soccer," Aisha said hotly.

"Great. We were thinking of putting together some intramural teams," Christopher continued. "You sound so enthusiastic, Aisha. Meet me after school—we'll get together and see if we can get this thing started."

"Excellent," Coach Anders said, nodding vigorously. "I know you two will get the ball rolling, so to speak. Ha, ha."

Christopher just smiled.

"I'm so glad we're back in school," Nina said, wrinkling her nose at the food on her tray. "I don't get nearly enough tamale pie in my life."

Zoey looked at her own tray. "Oh. Right."

"You need to snap out of it, Zo," Nina chided, leading them toward a table. "You're walking around in a trance."

"Sorry," Zoey said. "I guess I'm distracted."

Nina shrugged. "Guys fight all the time. If they were left on their own, that's all they'd do. Don't take it so seriously."

They found an empty table, round with four orange plastic chairs. "It's not the fight, Nina. It's the fact that Jake thinks I betrayed him."

"I'm not eating this," Nina said. "These people need to make some kind of arrangement for those of us who don't eat dead cow. Jake will get over it."

"You really think so?"

"Well, not if you keep being nice to Lucas. But if what you want is to keep things together with Jake, you have to make a choice."

"Jake picked that fight," Zoey said.

Nina picked at the fruit cocktail on her tray. "Isn't it supposed to be *my boyfriend, right or wrong*?"

Aisha dropped into one of the vacant chairs. "Did you see what happened in gym class?" she demanded of Zoey. "That jerk played me like a fiddle."

"Like a fiddle?" Nina echoed, shaking her head disapprovingly.

"Okay, like whatever. He totally manipulated the situation. Zoey will tell you."

"Zoey, what's Aisha talking about?" Nina asked.

"Christopher," Aisha answered angrily. "How many jobs

does he have, anyway? Now Toni LaMara is calling me *Big Foot.* That's the kind of thing you don't want getting started. I told her I'd spread the rumor she slept with George Amos."

"Toni slept with George Amos?" Nina asked.

"No, of course not. Eew," Aisha said. "Don't gross me out. But she won't be calling me Big Foot again anytime soon."

"I guess this is some of that ultrasophisticated, worldly-wise stuff you seniors understand," Nina said.

Aisha hooked a thumb at Zoey. "She still depressed?"

"I'm not depressed," Zoey said. "Not exactly. I'm just trying to figure out what to do."

Aisha shrugged. "You have to pick a side and stay there. Which one do you want, Jake or Lucas?"

"It's not that easy," Zoey said.

"*Joke* has more muscles," Nina said. "Especially between his ears."

"But Lucas is kind of sexy," Aisha reflected.

"He's done time, Eesh. He's a guy who's had a mug shot, and probably had a number stenciled on his clothes. He probably has a tattoo that says *Born to Raise Hell* on his chest," Nina said. "No, he's more Claire's type."

"He's not good enough for your best friend, but he'd be just fine for your sister?" Aisha said, laughing.

"They used to be tight, don't forget. Besides, it would be

so much fun if Claire brought Lucas home to meet our dad. He loves Benjamin. He wants to pay Benjamin's way through college. He'd chew porcelain if he thought Lucas was going out with his precious Claire."

"Hmm. Then Benjamin would be free, I could ask him out, and that would so blow Christopher away," Aisha said.

"You and Benjamin? No way. Incompatible," Nina said dismissively. "Totally wrong."

"I can't believe I took Lucas's side against Jake," Zoey said, shaking her head.

"Your nurturing instinct just took over. Apologize to Jake, blow off Lucas, get on with your life," Nina said.

"Tell Jake you can't stand the sight of blood, so you just lost it when he punched Lucas," Aisha advised. "He'll believe that. Besides, you two have to work it out; you're one of the Solid Couples."

"Really," Nina agreed. "You and Jake are pillars of Weymouth High society. People count on you. You're the very stable, slightly boring couple that other couples look to and say, Gee, why can't we have the kind of dull, predictable relationship Jake and Zoey have?"

Zoey smiled, in spite of the fact that she knew Nina was deliberately trying to goad her. "You're such a keen observer of other people's relationships, Nina. I guess it helps not to have one of your own to distract you."

Nina clapped a hand to her chest. "Ooh, straight through the heart."

"I'm not going to blow my relationship with Jake," Zoey said, trying to sound firm and decisive.

"I *am* going to blow my relationship with Christopher," Aisha said. "Whatever it takes. He cannot just barge his way into my life."

"I'm going to become a lonely, shriveled-up old lady," Nina said.

"Don't look," Aisha said urgently, leaning forward over the table. "It's Lucas."

"Is he coming this way?" Zoey asked, forcing herself to keep her gaze rigidly locked on Aisha.

"Yes. No. Wait a minute," Aisha said, throwing repeated glances across the crowded lunchroom.

"I'll call him over," Nina said.

"Nina!" Zoey cried.

"Kidding. Jeez, don't wet yourself."

"He's sitting down," Aisha said, leaning back with a sigh.

"I haven't seen Jake anywhere since homeroom," Zoey said.

"You'll see him on the ferry after school," Nina pointed out. "Just have a talk with him. He'll have his testosterone under control by then."

"He may not talk to me," Zoey said glumly.

"Then go to lip lock," Nina said.

Aisha nodded sagely. "Lip lock. That will do the trick."

"Slippery lippery."

"Mouth to mouth."

"Tongue twistage."

"Molar mining."

Zoey sighed. "I'm so glad I'm a senior now. Our conversations are so much more intelligent than they were last year."

FOURTEEN

TO ZOEY'S SURPRISE, NEITHER JAKE nor Lucas was on the four-o'clock ferry home. In fact, only Nina and Benjamin rode the ferry with her. Aisha had been roped into seeing Christopher about soccer. Claire, Zoey figured, could be waiting to take the water taxi home with her father. After all, they could afford it. Jake had probably decided to catch the later ferry, or arranged for his dad to pick him up in their boat.

As for Lucas, who knew? Zoey was not going to concern herself any further with Lucas Cabral. Jake was her boyfriend, and she owed him some loyalty and support. Obviously, this whole thing with Lucas had been difficult for him. She should have seen that and tried to help.

The trip home went peacefully, twenty-five minutes of gossip about the first day of school, teachers, classmates, and in Nina's case, a lengthy diatribe on the soul-crushing nature of school.

Zoey said good-bye to Nina and walked the rest of the way

home with Benjamin.

"Nina said something about Mr. Geiger wanting to pay your way through college," Zoey said. "Or was she just exaggerating?"

Benjamin shrugged. "He did say that. I think he's hoping I'll marry Claire someday. He figures I'll be easier to control than some other potential sons-in-law."

"Doesn't that kind of piss you off?"

Benjamin smirked. "You think I'd really be easy to control?"

Zoey chuckled. "Not hardly."

"I don't take it seriously," Benjamin said.

When they reached the house, Zoey said a quick hello to her father, leaving him to cross-examine Benjamin about school, and went up to her room.

She sat down at her desk in the dormered window and closed her eyes. What a day. Not bad enough that it had been the first day of school, no, it had to start with a fight between her boyfriend and . . . some guy she barely knew.

Lucas. Why had she sided with Lucas? The obvious answer was because he wasn't the one who had started the fight, and he *was* the one who got hurt. That was the obvious answer. But was it the whole truth?

What *did* she feel for Lucas? And what did she feel for Jake?

She pulled out a yellow pad and wrote *JAKE* at the top on the left side, *LUCAS* on the right. Then she drew a line down the middle of the page, creating two columns.

She thought for a moment, then, under the name *JAKE,* she wrote *Known him for years.* Since she was just a kid. He was the first guy ever to kiss her. He'd taught her to water ski. He had believed her when she'd denied the rumor going around that she was seeing Tad Crowley. (She'd only kissed Tad once at a party, that was it.)

Under *LUCAS* she wrote *Barely know him.* Strictly speaking, she'd known him since she was little, too. But he'd been away for two years. Things changed a lot in two years.

And then, not to be crude, but if you put the two of them side by side wearing little Speedos like those bodybuilders on ESPN, it would be no contest. And why shouldn't she think that way? Guys did.

Under *JAKE* she put *Great body.*

Not that Lucas had a bad body. Not at all. He was tall and lanky. He had long legs and broad shoulders. Seeing him in a Speedo wouldn't make her want to run screaming from the room or anything.

Under *LUCAS* she wrote *Okay body.*

So far, Jake was out in front. She went on, line after line, noting that Jake was a great kisser, while Lucas was an unknown in this category. You could hardly count that one little kiss two years earlier. He hadn't even moved his lips.

The further she went, the more obvious it was that Jake was totally superior in every category to Lucas.

After filling half the page, she wrote *Jake makes me feel . . .* She hesitated. What did Jake make her feel? She imagined the many, many times they had lain together, out on the beach by a blazing campfire, or just on the couch in the family room. She could feel his big arms wrapped around her, holding her close.

. . . safe. That's what Jake made her feel. Like nothing could ever harm her when she was in his arms.

And Lucas? *Makes me feel . . .* she wrote.

She remembered him on the breakwater, waves crashing around him. And she remembered the queasy, unsettled, disturbed feeling after he had lifted her hand to his lips.

She quickly crossed out the line. She added the fact that Jake clearly had a very excellent chest, all smooth, tan muscles, while Lucas probably had a tattoo there.

Then she looked down the list. It certainly was one sided. A person looking over this list would reach only one conclusion. Obviously, Jake was the right choice.

Still, maybe she had been slightly unfair to Lucas. He did have better hair than Jake, in her opinion. Even so, it was no contest.

"Of course it isn't," she said aloud. "Jake is your boyfriend. Jake loves you. Jake does not have a tattoo."

She hid the pad in her drawer and stood up. She would go to Jake, apologize, make some good excuses, and then, as Nina and Aisha had suggested, go to lip lock.

And life would be back to normal.

Her eye settled on the Post-it note bearing the quote.

A man ^or a woman^ can stand almost anything except a succession of ordinary days.

She took it down and crumpled it, letting it drop in the wastebasket. What did Goethe know about life on Chatham Island?

The List

JAKE	LUCAS
-Known him for years	-Barely know him
-Great body	-Okay body
-Like his mom	-His dad is a little intense
-Very good kisser	-?
-Never got anyone killed	-Probably got someone killed
-Everyone likes him but Nina	-No one likes him
-Thinks he's going to marry me	-Says he thought of me a lot
-Getting kind of gropey	-Hasn't seen a girl in 2 years
-Friend as well as boyfriend	-Neither
-Makes me feel safe	-~~Makes me feel~~
-Excellent chest	-Possible tattoo?
-Don't like his hair	-Nice hair

• • •

"Yes, I did have an interesting dream," Claire admitted. She leaned back against the cool leather, enjoying the crackling sound it made. Dr. Kendall raised her eyebrow expectantly. Dr. Kendall loved dreams, Claire had discovered. Unfortunately, most weeks Claire had no dreams to tell her psychiatrist, at least none that she could remember.

"As usual, I don't remember it perfectly."

"Do the best you can."

Claire smiled coyly. "I'm afraid there's no kinky sex or anything in it."

Dr. Kendall just nodded. Claire knew this was because Dr. Kendall believed *everything* was something psychological. If Claire sat up straight, that meant something. If she slouched, that meant something, too. If she yawned, it couldn't just be that she was tired; no, it had to be something of a deep-seated psychological nature.

She'd been seeing the shrink since her mother had died. About the time of the accident her father suggested she might want to drop the sessions, but by that point Claire had gotten used to it. It was a familiar ritual, comforting, sort of like some people said church was.

"Well," Claire began. "It was in the car again."

"*The* car?"

"Uh-huh. Only it was a lobster. You know, a four-wheeled lobster with a stick shift."

"Go on."

"Lucas was there. And Wade. And we were skidding around but laughing just the same. All three of us."

"Yes." Dr. Kendall nodded wisely.

"That's about it. Except that we started to crash, and Lucas was trying to grab the wheel out of my hand."

"Lucas was—"

"I mean, I was trying to grab the wheel away from him, only my hands were slippery."

"I see. And then?"

"Then we crashed. And I woke up." Suddenly an image flashed in Claire's mind. A sharp, clear picture. She shook her head angrily.

"Is there something else?"

"Nothing. Just that I suddenly had this weird flash of Benjamin, standing by the side of the road after we had crashed."

"Benjamin? This is your male friend, right? The unsighted one?"

"The blind guy, yeah. He was staring at us, very solemn, and it was his actual eyes, not his sunglasses. I mean, it's like in my dream he could see or something."

Dr. Kendall nodded.

"So?" Claire asked, dismissing the lingering effects of the dream image. "So what's it all mean?"

"It could mean any number of things," Dr. Kendall said.

Claire rolled her eyes. Well, there you had it: the perfect shrink answer. "Come on, I have the kind of weird dream that my sister Nina has every night—and sometimes during the day—and it doesn't even mean anything?"

Dr. Kendall smiled her noncommittal smile. "Dream interpretation can be tricky. Perhaps you simply ate a lobster and remembered it in your dream."

"Actually, I did."

"There you go."

"Well, I'm disappointed. You ask me for dreams and I finally bring you one loaded up with twisted imagery, drivable lobsters the size of Volkswagens, blind guys who can see . . . I don't really think I can get much crazier than that."

"We don't use the word crazy, Claire. And in any event you are an extremely sane person. For your age, one might even say you're abnormally sane. Apart from the fact that you don't remember certain events surrounding the accident, you appear to be quite well adjusted. In fact, you show great self-awareness and excellent coping skills."

"Are you telling me I shouldn't keep coming?"

Dr. Kendall looked at her thoughtfully. "Claire, you may never remember. It may simply be physical, and not in any way psychological. You did suffer a concussion in the accident."

"Oh, I see."

"Certainly you can keep coming here, if you feel you need someone to talk to, if you're lonely."

"I'm not lonely," Claire said quickly, dismissively.

"No?"

"No. Of course not. I'm just ... solitary. A loner."

"There's nothing wrong with being solitary," Dr. Kendall said with a reassuring smile. "Still, if you'd like to schedule another session for next week—"

Claire felt an unfamiliar pang of confusion and doubt. "Maybe I . . . maybe I should." Claire shrugged. "You know, sort of taper off slowly."

"We could make your next visit in *two* weeks."

"Okay." Claire stood up. "Well, I have to catch the ferry." She reached the door, then hesitated. "You know, though, if I come every two weeks, I'm bound to forget whether I'm supposed to come or not, so maybe we should just keep doing it every week. You know, just because it's easier."

Zoey walked from her house down to Dock Street where it ran along Town Beach, feeling nervous and a little annoyed for some indefinable reason. Yes, yes, she knew she had to go and work things out with Jake, but still, it was annoying. It wasn't like she'd committed some big crime.

From the point where Dock merged into Leeward Drive she could look up and see Jake's house, brightly lit so that even in the black of a moonless night, you could see the red of the cedar.

She walked on, the agitated waters of the bay on her right, a breeze rustling the pines on her left. High, thin clouds like gray lace scudded overhead. The skyline of Weymouth glittered brightly, the office buildings no doubt full of hardworking types catching up after the three-day weekend.

She climbed the twisting, steep driveway to Jake's house and cut along the well-known path around the side and down to the flagstone patio.

She peeked tentatively around the corner. After that last visit she didn't want any more sudden revelations. Through the sliding glass door she could see Jake, wearing only a pair of shorts, leaning back on his bed, watching TV and throwing a football up into the air while he tried to catch it with his left hand.

Standing there in the dark, she knew she was invisible.

"See?" Zoey reminded herself. "Great body."

She stepped forward into the pool of light and tapped on

the glass. He looked at her, seemed to hesitate for a moment, and then, with a show of reluctance, got up and opened the door.

"Hi, Jake."

"Hi, Zoey," he said in a voice several degrees colder than hers.

"I thought we should talk."

"Do we have something to talk about?"

"I think we do," she said. She slid past him into the room. He closed the door behind her but remained standing, still holding his football, while she sat on the edge of his bed.

"Let me just get this out right away," Zoey said. She took a deep breath. "I'm sorry if what happened this morning made it seem like I was choosing sides against you."

"That's what it was," he said.

"No, it wasn't, Jake. I . . . I just can't stand violence. My first reaction was to help Lucas because he was hurt. I don't think that makes me a bad person," she added plaintively.

"He wasn't hurt," Jake growled. "If I'd really wanted to hurt him . . . well, I could have if I'd wanted to."

"His nose was bleeding," Zoey said.

"He had it coming."

Zoey suppressed an urge to point out that it was Jake who had picked the fight. That wouldn't help. "I'm sorry," she said.

"I thought you were—" To Zoey's amazement, Jake's voice actually broke. "I thought you were, like, being interested in him. You know?"

"You mean as in *romantic* interest?" Zoey said, loading her voice with disbelieving surprise. "Lucas?"

Jake made a wry, embarrassed grin. "Maybe I was just imagining things."

"You were jealous?" Zoey said a little shrilly.

Jake shrugged. "I was kind of upset at the time."

Zoey got up from the bed and crossed the room. He waited for her to come, offering no overt encouragement. She put her hand on his arm.

"Jake, you and I have been together forever. We're a couple. Today at lunch Nina said we're the couple everyone looks up to."

"Ninny said that?" he asked skeptically.

"Well, something like that," Zoey admitted, grinning.

Jake smiled back. "I can just imagine what she really said." Then his face grew somber again. "It's just, look, I love you. You know that."

"Yes, I do," Zoey said softly.

"I have to be sure you're on my side."

Zoey nodded. "Of course I am. Just don't go around getting into fights. You'll get in trouble."

"Okay. Deal. No more fights."

He slipped his arm around her waist and pulled her to him. She responded, entwining herself around him, opening her mouth to accept his kiss.

It felt wonderful. It felt as if the world that had been torn was now neatly sewed up. Life was back to normal, things once again as they ought to be.

Draft #24

. . . and with a roar, the white knight swung his gleaming broadsword, shattering the shield in Sir Luke's hand and knocking him to the ground.

"I yield!" Sir Luke cried, holding up his arm as if to ward off the final blow.

"Yield?" the white knight roared. "You are no gentleman, whatever your title. You have no honor, and thus I give you no mercy." He raised the broadsword high over his head. "For all the suffering you have inflicted on the peasants, and for your base treason, I send you straight to hell!"

"No!" Raven cried, gathering her skirts and rushing to the fallen Sir Luke. She spread her arms, shielding the villain, though she well knew the terrible suffering he had inflicted on the people.

"What?" the white knight cried. "You would protect this knave?"

"Nay," Raven cried just as fiercely, "it is you I protect. The king has ordered that this foul creature, though his sins are ~~manifest~~ ~~manifold~~ many, should be taken alive."

"Out of my way, woman. My vengeance will not be delayed."

"Stay your hand, my lord," Raven said. "If you strike, you will make yourself as base as this evildoer. You must obey the king!"

"I care not for reason!" The white knight raised his sword higher still. "Stand aside, Raven, and let him meet the devil, his master!"

Raven threw her arms tightly around the cringing shoulders of Sir Luke. "If you strike him, you will destroy me as well."

The white knight's eyes blazed. But Raven knew his love was even greater than his rage. Slowly he lowered the sword till its point was in the dust. Then, with a quick, decisive thrust, the white knight sheathed his sword. "I thank you, fair maiden, for you have kept me from committing a grave error in my righteous rage."

Sir Luke breathed a sigh of relief. "You saved my life," he told Raven.

"Nay," she said, "for your judgment still awaits at the hand of the king."

~~"Nevertheless," Sir Luke said. He raised her hand to his lips. Raven felt~~

FIFTEEN

"SEVERAL ANNOUNCEMENTS THIS MORNING," CAME the gravelly voice of the principal, Mr. Hardcastle. "Several announcements, if I may have everyone's attention, please."

Zoey caught Aisha's attention and rolled her eyes at the P.A. Homeroom lasted fifteen minutes and came just before the first lunch. By this point in the day, everyone was hungry, and no one wanted to hear Mr. Hardcastle go on about rules, regulations, meetings, events, rallies, and the other stuff he went on and on and on about every day.

To make matters worse, the day before, Ms. Lambert, their homeroom teacher, had demonstrated the annoying habit of taking all the announcements seriously and actually asking them questions afterward to see if they had paid attention. Ms. Lambert was new, of course, this being her very first class. Sooner or later she'd learn to chill a little.

". . . a matter has come up that requires some clarification,"

Mr. Hardcastle said. "It is against school policy to allow students to smoke cigarettes on campus. This policy applies whether or not the student actually *lights* the cigarette."

Zoey and Aisha exchanged a look and laughed. Zoey scribbled a quick note on her pad, tore off the slip of paper, and when she was sure Ms. Lambert was looking away, started it on its way from hand to hand toward Aisha. The note said,

Nina will be thrilled. She'll think she's a celebrity.

". . . although as far as we know, an *unlit* cigarette does not pose a health hazard, we feel it is important to be consistent in enforcing . . ."

Aisha received the note, read it, and scribbled one back. It changed hands three times before reaching Zoey:

Nina will be thrilled. She'll think she's a celebrity.

You know how Nina loves to provoke. Speaking of which, I was too busy doing homework on the ferry this a.m.; what happened with you and Jake? Kiss and make up?

". . . turning to student government, and the fact that so far we have no nominations—no *serious* nominations—for any of the offices . . ."

Zoey glanced at Jake, in the back of the room, looking like he might fall asleep and let his head crash onto the desk at any moment.

Slippery lippery, as you and Nina put it so maturely. All better now. How about you and soccer practice?

". . . include student council president, student council vice president, head of the school spirit committee, which is responsible for . . ."

Aisha grimaced as she read the last part of Zoey's note. She scribbled a long note and sent it back.

". . . and that concludes the morning announcements. Have a nice day."

The sound of a chair scraping the floor startled Zoey, coming in the sudden silence. "Well, *I* have an announcement to make," Ms. Lambert said, getting up from her desk and walking deliberately down the center aisle of the classroom. She stopped beside Bella Waterton and held out her hand. "I wish to announce that note passing is a no-no. A rather juvenile no-no for a class of seniors. Give it up, Ms. Waterton."

Bella shrugged apologetically at Aisha and handed the folded note to the teacher.

Ms. Lambert unfolded the note and read it over. She carried it back to her desk.

She wouldn't read it out loud, would she? Zoey wondered, aghast at the possibilities.

"My policy will be to read aloud any note I intercept in this class," Ms. Lambert said. "Homeroom is not just a time for you to play around." She held the note out at arm's length. *"Christopher is such a jerk to trap me into that. I'm going to kill him. I blew him off, even though it will probably piss Coach off. Although I will—"* Ms. Lambert blushed a little, suddenly appearing uncomfortable. But she took a breath and went on. *". . . although I will say he has a cute little butt, running around in those shorts."*

Aisha was sinking slowly under her seat as the room erupted in hoots and catcalls. Anyway, Zoey figured, Ms. Lambert had gotten a lesson in why it was a bad idea to read notes aloud.

"Zoey, wait up," Lucas said as the class poured out of last period and into the boisterous hallways.

Zoey pretended not to hear and kept walking, making a beeline for her locker. Then she felt a hand on her arm. She turned around, fixing an indignant look on her face.

"Look," Lucas said, "I know you're trying to avoid me and

that's fine. I understand. I just stopped you to say that we don't have to pay any attention to what Mr. Bushnell said back there."

"I wasn't planning to," Zoey said. Mr. Bushnell taught French, and Lucas and she had the same class. The teacher had suggested that all the students form partnerships, with someone they saw regularly with whom they could converse in French. He'd suggested, for example, that since Zoey and Lucas were both island kids, they could speak to each other in French on the ferry rides to and from school.

This suggestion had caused Zoey to turn white. The idea that she would be gaily chattering away in *French* with Lucas while Jake sat a few feet away was a little hard to picture.

"Cool," Lucas said. He released her arm and seemed to sink back within himself.

"It's not—" Zoey began. *No, shut up, Zoey,* she chided herself. So he looked like the loneliest human being on earth. That was not her problem. She had no interest in him.

After all, she had made a list.

"It's not that I'm trying to be a jerk," Zoey said lamely.

"I know," Lucas said.

"If it were up to me, sure, I'd be glad to . . . to talk French with you."

He grinned. *"C'est la vie."*

Zoey smiled back, glancing nervously down the hall for any

sign of Jake. But of course he would be out on the field, getting in some practice for the football tryouts.

"Oui, c'est la vie, mais c'est . . . um, *c'est une bêtise, tout le même."* She made a face. "Did I say that right?"

"That's life, but it's dumb, just the same," he translated. "I'm not sure. It sounded right to me. But then, it's been two years since my last French class."

Zoey nodded. The reminder that he had been "away" for the last two years made her tense up. She really had to cut this off. Maybe she could go out to the field and watch Jake run. "I guess there's not a lot of French spoken at . . . at that place."

"It's not all that common, no," Lucas said.

An awkward silence descended. *I need to get out of here,* Zoey reminded herself. *Maybe Jake's not around, but Claire might be, or even Nina or Aisha.*

"Was it really bad?" Zoey blurted. "The reform school?"

"YA. Youth Authority. Although we called it a few different things." He shrugged and looked away. "It wasn't Devil's Island or anything. The food was pretty bad."

Zoey smiled. "So, then, I guess cafeteria food must seem pretty okay?"

"Nothing could make the cafeteria food seem good," he said. "Still, you end up missing a lot of stuff while you're in there. Like pizza. Like McDonald's. The funny thing is, I was never all that crazy about McDonald's, but when you can't have a Big Mac and fries, they start to seem like the most important thing on earth. You lie in your rack at night thinking, Man, I'd give anything for a Big Mac and fries."

"So did you run out first thing to Mickey D's?"

"Haven't been yet," Lucas admitted. "I've been on the island until yesterday. And yesterday after school I had to go see my caseworker. You know, have her tell me to stay off drugs and so on."

The hallway was emptying fast as kids piled out the doors, and the two of them, standing there talking, were becoming ever more conspicuous. All it would take would be Jake coming in for a drink of water or something and there would be a major blowup. Even if it seemed rude, she had to get away.

"Well, I'll see you in class," Lucas said, turning away.

"Wait!" Zoey said. "Um, my parents' real car is in the lot down the street, and I have the keys, and we could maybe run out to the McDonald's by the mall and still get back in time for the ferry." Her face was flushed, her head was spinning, and her mouth was saying things she didn't want it to say.

"Zoey, you don't have to—"

"I'm hungry, that's all," Zoey said.

"I doubt anyone from school would be out there," Lucas reasoned. "I guess if they were, they'd be *in* the mall. But there is one other problem. I don't have any money."

"My treat." What was she thinking?

It took five minutes to arrive by back roads at the parking garage, and ten minutes to reach the restaurant. Lucas and Zoey decided by unspoken mutual agreement to eat in the car. As soon as they'd paid for a Big Mac, large fries, and a milk shake they drove out past the airport and away from town. There was still the chance that someone from school might show up in the restaurant itself. And the sight of Zoey Passmore sharing a milk shake with Lucas Cabral would instantly become *the* gossip the next day at school.

They listened to the radio and Lucas wolfed down the burger. He remarked from time to time on the sights—a new shopping center that hadn't been there the last time he'd driven this way, a new car model he had seen only on TV.

They joined the coast road, heading north through tall pines and flashes of rocky shoreline. Zoey found it strangely liberating. Off the island, away from school, she felt a delicious sensation of freedom. Sometimes it was a relief to be where nobody knew you, where your every action wouldn't become common knowledge within minutes.

"Pull in there." Lucas pointed with a french fry down a small, single-lane road.

Zoey turned so sharply that it threw Lucas against her. He apologized, and they both laughed nervously as he retrieved several spilled fries from her lap.

"Where are we going?" Zoey asked. The narrow road forced her to slow down. Then, quite suddenly, it reached its end, a gravel patch beyond which was nothing but wide sky and the ocean.

"Come on," he said, opening the door. "You'll like this."

She followed him across the gravel to the edge of the bluff. A hundred feet below them, the churning sea worked its slow, endless destruction on the rocks, relentlessly grinding them into sand. Sea gulls flew by at eye level, soaring on the wind that rose from the cliff. Across the water was Chatham Island, a dark mass dotted here and there with barely visible points of color and light.

"I can't believe I've never been down this road," Zoey said. "What a great view. The old island looks downright romantic from here."

"My father has his lobster pots ranged just out there." Lucas pointed down the coast. "The red markers with green stripes."

Zoey could see the familiar wooden floats that marked the locations of lobster traps. Lobstermen carved out territories, sometimes handed down through a dozen generations. Mr. Cabral had acquired this area from a cousin of his, an old

Portuguese fisherman who had died twenty years earlier.

"Are you going to take over from your dad when he retires?" Zoey asked.

Lucas shook his head. "I think once he wanted me to, but I'd have to say it's pretty unlikely now. By mutual agreement."

"It's hard work," Zoey said.

"Yep."

They fell into silence. Zoey listened to the sounds of the gulls, the crash of water, the grinding of rocks, the far-off whistle of the ferry. Later she'd have to come up with some story for why she'd missed the four o'clock. Later. Right now she was far from prying eyes and hours away from excuses.

"Sorry," Lucas said. "Now I guess we're stuck till the six thirty."

"I don't mind," Zoey said. She smiled at him. "You have special sauce on your mouth."

He reached to wipe it off but missed. Zoey reached up and wiped his face.

"Thanks," he said softly.

"Uh-huh." She found she was staring at his lips. She found she was remembering the list she'd made, and the way she'd had to put a question mark under his name on the subject of kissing.

She found that they were standing closer, without either of them having moved.

And she found her heart thudding, so loud it was drowning out the cries of the gulls, and the crash of the water, and the grinding of the rocks.

His hand on her arm. Hers on his shoulder. Her eyes closing. His arm around her waist. Her breasts crushed against his chest. The feel of sinewy muscles in his back. His thigh and hers.

His lips on hers, soft, gentle, terrible urgency restrained. Her lips on his, trembling, surprised, uncertain.

Her mouth opening. And his.

Her fingers now entangled in his hair, unable to stop, just making things worse.

And sudden desire for more, knowing he wanted her, the unsettling realization that she wanted him as well.

Then withdrawal, both exerting control, both smiling sheepishly, and kissing again, more tentatively.

Well, Zoey thought, at least she could fill in the blank spot on her list.

SIXTEEN

FROM THE FRONT OF THE ferry Benjamin heard the sound of the heavy rope being cast off, slipping up the piling, and falling on the wooden slats of the dock. He had heard the feet of the crewman, running to the stern to cast off that line. He waited for the shriek of the whistle.

It sounded.

So. No Zoey. She would have come over to say hello.

Beside him he felt Claire's arm strain as she turned to scan the deck. What did she see? Not Zoey. Lucas? No, not Lucas, either, because whatever she was looking at had caused her to relax.

So, no Zoey and no Lucas. Interesting.

And Jake? Yes, Jake, that's who she was looking at, he was almost sure. She wouldn't spend this long focusing on Aisha. That left Jake, and now she was tilting her head slightly, a movement that translated as her shoulder pulling away.

"What's the weather like?" Benjamin asked.

"Oh, it's nice, a little overcast."

Yes, she was staring at Jake, and thinking about him. Claire never gave an answer about weather as simple as *a little overcast*.

The ferry was pulling away now, backing into a turn to head toward the bay. He could feel the heat of the afternoon sun, slowly moving from his face, to the side of his face, to the back of his neck, until the ferry was pointed out to sea.

"I have to run down to the girls' room," Claire said.

A lie. "It's called a *head* on a boat," Benjamin said.

So, she was going to talk to Jake. And she didn't want him to know. How interesting. Of course Claire would have noticed that neither Zoey nor Lucas was on the ferry. And if Jake hadn't noticed, or if he hadn't become suspicious on his own, Claire was going to plant the seed.

He strained to hear their conversation. They were far away, and the boat throbbed and vibrated, obliterating much sound. Still, he could hear snatches. It wasn't that blind people's hearing was any more acute, as he'd explained to Claire, it was just that without the distraction of sight they could concentrate much more intensely on hearing.

It wasn't Claire he could hear, though. Her voice was soft. Jake, fortunately, had a voice that carried well.

". . . last night, I mean . . . fine now, we talked . . . way . . .

maybe she . . . shopping with Nina. Oh. I didn't see Ninny over . . ."

Oh, so Nina was on the ferry, Benjamin noted. And yet she hadn't come over to say hello, to him or to her sister. Well, Nina could be moody at times.

". . . Lucas? How would I know? . . . yeah . . . back in jail . . . I'm just not the suspicious . . . uh-huh . . . not worried . . . okay . . . sure . . . about Benjamin? . . . I guess, sure . . ."

Benjamin kept his face blank. He heard Claire approaching, the familiar sound of her walk, the smell of her perfume, her shampoo.

"Sorry. There was a line." Claire lied smoothly.

"Women's bathrooms are always that way," Benjamin said. *Just what game are you playing, Claire*? he asked silently. *What game? And do you even know you're playing it?*

"Is Nina around?" Benjamin asked.

"Yes. You want me to call her over?"

"No. I just wanted to set something up for some homework reading. Where is she?"

"Um, last bench, over on the other side."

"Thanks. I'll be right back," Benjamin said. He stood, turned a sharp left, checking with his left hand for the end of the bench. He counted the steps, reached for and found the railing, then followed it right.

"Nina?" he said when he knew he was close.

"Hi, Benjamin," she said. Her voice sounded just slightly sulky.

He sat beside her. "Is Jake nearby?" he asked in a low voice.

"No," she said, dropping to a conspiratorial whisper. "He's up at the front. Why?"

"Just wondering. It's nice to know who's listening when you talk to someone."

"I guess so."

"Look, Nina, you and I are friends, right?" Benjamin said.

"Um, sure." Her voice was a little strained.

"You know I hate to ask anyone anything. I mean, unless it's something I just can't do myself."

"Sure."

"Well, this is something kind of embarrassing, so if you don't want to answer, don't. It's just that I can only do so much without being able to see. I have a question, like I said, an embarrassing question."

"I'll do my best," Nina said doubtfully.

"Just now Claire was talking to Jake, wasn't she?"

"Uh-huh." A guarded answer, like she was hiding something.

"She's with him right now, again, isn't she?"

"Kind of."

"Well, maybe that answers my question," Benjamin said, muttering darkly.

"What question?"

He sighed. Even with eyes, it was hard to see into a person's heart. "Look, is Claire . . . is she, you know, interested in Jake?"

Nina was silent. He could feel her staring across the deck.

"She's never said anything," Nina said evenly.

"Okay, okay," Benjamin said, letting his frustration show, "but right now, as you look at them, as you *see* them talking, as you see them making eye contact or not, touching or not touching, sitting close or keeping their distance: Is she interested in him?"

"Jeez, Benjamin," Nina said.

He waved his hand, annoyed at his display of frustration. "Never mind. Forget it, Nina. I was just—"

"Yes," Nina said, blurting the word out. "She is."

He sat back down. "Damn."

"I mean, that's how it looks to me, anyway, not that I would know."

"Damn," he repeated softly. "Why?"

"I have no idea. I never really saw why Zoey liked him, either. Claire's always said he's good-looking, but I never thought she was interested, you know?" Nina said, sounding as if she were thinking out loud. "But then, who knows? I mean, I guess sometimes a girl suddenly looks at someone she's known a long time and all of a sudden, well, he seems different to her. Or maybe she's the one who changed. Maybe the guy . . . maybe he doesn't even realize she's interested or anything."

"Yeah," he said flatly. "She'll make sure he knows."

"Maybe she's shy," Nina said very softly.

"What? Claire, shy?" Benjamin said derisively. No, she wasn't shy. Not really. Not when she wanted something or someone. And now, suddenly, it seemed she wanted Jake. Why? Because she suspected Zoey might be releasing him? Or was it just that she was tired of being with a guy who couldn't even tell her she was beautiful?

Well, fine. He didn't care. He'd known it would end eventually.

"Thanks, Nina," he said. "I guess."

"Yeah, right," she said, sounding angry. Probably Nina didn't appreciate being used as a spy, although she should have a little concern for him. It was his feelings that were being trampled, not hers. He was the one left looking like a fool.

"Troll. Maggot. Tweedledum *and* Tweedledumber." Nina raged around her room, kicking aside piles of clothing on the floor, throwing her arms wide, then clapping them on her hips. "Blind? Blind isn't half of it. If he could see, he'd still be blind.

He's sputum. He's a bad odor. He's a stain!"

What did it take, anyway? She'd been pretty obvious. It wasn't like Benjamin was incapable of grasping subtleties, the jerk. He could figure out someone's entire life history after hearing them say three words. But oh, when it came to her, well, *then* he was utterly impervious. Blank. Blank squared. Duh to the tenth power.

"It's not like I'm asking all that much," she said to a poster of Ed Sheeran. "I'm not talking ravishment here. I'm not saying, Hey, let's move immediately to a Condition of Maximum Erogenization. It's just that he's like the first guy in my whole life I ever thought, Yes, yes, I could steam some glass with this guy. The stinking scab."

Okay, so he was going out with her sister. Sure. But she didn't love him and he didn't love her.

Did he?

How could he? How could he love Claire, the ice queen, a girl who could make Lindsay Lohan take a step back and say, *Whoa, that girl's a real bitch.*

After all, it wasn't as if Benjamin could be transfixed by her beauty. He was the one guy around who couldn't be, which should mean that he could concentrate on inner beauty, soul, heart, conscience, sensitivity. And what with Claire having *E: none of the above*, it should be an open-and-shut case.

No way he could really be in love with her. Especially now, with her licking her lips for Jake.

"And what's that all about?" she asked Ed suspiciously. Just Claire's usual need to be drooled over by every male over the age of nine?

There was a knock at her bedroom door. "Nina? Are you talking to someone in there?" Claire called through the door.

"I'm having a psychotic break and talking to the voices in my head!" Nina yelled.

"Oh. Just the usual. Zoey's on the phone."

Nina stomped to the door and threw it open.

"I'll hang up downstairs as soon as you pick this phone up," Claire said, trotting down the stairs.

Nina snatched up the phone in the hallway. "Zo?"

"It's me. Is Claire around?"

"I thought you wanted to talk to me," Nina said a little crossly.

"I do, and I don't want her listening in."

"Claire!" Nina yelled down the stairs. "I got it. You can hang up the phone now." In the receiver she heard the scuffling clatter of the other extension being hung up. "Okay, spill. What's the secret?"

"I'm still in Weymouth. I just wanted to know if Jake took the four o'clock with you guys."

"You just need to know that, huh?"

"Yes. Was he on the ferry or not?"

"You're going to have to do better than that, Zoey." Nina glanced left and right down the hallway. "Come on, come on. This has something to do with . . . with *L*, doesn't it?"

Zoey's end of the line was silent.

"*He* wasn't on the four o'clock," Nina said. "You and *L*, neither of you was on the four o'clock."

"Damn."

"You think I wouldn't notice a little coincidence like that?" Nina said.

"How about Jake?"

"I'll tell if you tell."

"You first."

"He *was* there, so if what you want to know is whether it will be safe for you and *L* to take the next one home without being seen, the answer is yes," Nina said quickly. "However—"

"However?"

"However," Nina continued, "I think I can guarantee that your absence was not unnoticed by certain people, initials *J* and *C*."

A heavy sigh.

"So. Now it's your turn," Nina said. "What have you been doing?"

"(mumble) went for a drive."

"Excuse me? Who went for a drive?"

"Just felt like going for a drive," Zoey said.

"Who. Not why, who?"

Another sigh. "Swear to me on a stack of Bibles."

"You and Luc—you and *L*?"

"He wanted a Big Mac."

"Right. He wanted a Big Mac," Nina sneered.

"Really. That's what he wanted."

"Yeah? And what did he *get*?"

"Don't be crude."

"Oh, my God, did he try to kiss you?" Nina's mind went into overdrive. Zoey and Lucas? *Oh, my God.* That would mean sooner or later Jake would find out. Then, what would keep him from going to Claire? And then, Benjamin would be free! Unless Claire lost interest in Jake as soon as he was truly available. Claire was capable of that.

Suddenly she realized Zoey hadn't answered. "Zoey?"

"Yes."

"You kissed him, didn't you?"

"Kind of."

"You slut. Do you realize what this will mean? What about Jake? What about the fact that Lucas is a jailbird?" *What about Benjamin?* she added silently. "The entire structure of our lives is going to crumble now because you wanted to fool around with Lucas."

"The entire structure of our lives?" Zoey repeated incredulously.

"Not to be unkind here, Zo, but look at what Lucas did to the entire structure of Wade's life."

"Nina, stop it!" Zoey ordered. "Maybe it's not as simple as that. Maybe Benjamin really is on to something."

"What? Zoey, *what* are you talking about?" Nina asked crossly.

"About the accident. About how the car was a little Volkswagen and there were only two seats in front. You remember," Zoey went on in a rush.

"I remember," Nina said. "Well, you know something? Benjamin isn't exactly Sherlock Holmes sometimes. As my dad pointed out, Lucas pleaded guilty, so there wasn't much point in asking questions about who was in what seat. We all know who was driving and what happened."

"You told your dad?"

Nina stiffened a little, feeling defensive. It wasn't very often she had anything to say that would interest her father in the slightest. And this had. "It just came up, all right? I didn't think it was a big secret or anything."

"Well, *this* is a big secret, just so you know."

"I'll wait for you at the dock. I will require details, full, complete details."

"Just keep your mouth shut, all right?"

"Locked. Sealed. Crazy glued," Nina vowed.

Zoey hung up the phone. Nina settled the receiver back in its cradle, but just as she pulled it away from her ear, she heard a second soft but unmistakable click.

SEVENTEEN

CLAIRE BACKED AWAY FROM THE phone, staring at it as if it were a snake ready to strike. Already she could hear Nina coming down the steps.

"Claire! You weasel, were you listening in?"

Claire backed through the living room into the dining room just as Nina reached the bottom of the stairs and burst into the living room.

"I guess not," she heard Nina say.

Claire ducked quickly out the sliding glass doors that led from the dining room onto the patio.

It was a lot to digest all at once. Too much. Zoey falling for Lucas, that was bad.

Not that Claire could deny Lucas's attraction. Yes, she remembered that about him, the way he could make your insides melt with a look or a touch. And now he had broken the solid wall of resistance. Now it would be infinitely harder to get rid of him.

And then there was Benjamin's little theory. What was that all about? Some question about who was driving the car? What did Benjamin suspect, that *Wade* had been driving? Could that be? Was Lucas truly innocent?

No. Lucas wasn't the martyr type. He would never have confessed. Why would he? To protect Wade's reputation? Hardly. Jake might have turned Wade into some larger-than-life hero in his mind, but Claire knew better. Wade McRoyan was a selfish, even cruel person, well on his way to becoming a serious drunk.

"I have to think," Claire said aloud, squeezing her head with both hands.

She followed the path around the side of the house, through the rosebushes and flowery shrubs in the front yard. She glanced at her watch. Six twenty-five. Zoey would be on the six-thirty ferry, arriving at ten till seven. She needed to see Benjamin before that. Find out just what was going on in his head.

And then, Jake.

She walked quickly through the center of town, just five minutes to Benjamin's house. She rapped at his window, letting him know she was there. Mr. Passmore often took a nap in the early evening.

She waited by the front door until Benjamin came and let her in. She followed him to his room. Here in his own home he moved with all the ease and assurance of a sighted person.

She gave him a little kiss, just brushing his lips.

"I didn't expect you," Benjamin said, sitting down on his bed.

"I didn't know I had to make an appointment," Claire said, trying to sound pleasant and unhurried. Inside she was boiling with impatience. It was strange. She wasn't an impatient person.

"Of course you don't," Benjamin said. "Why don't you come here and give me a real kiss?"

She felt anger flare. He was so smug, so sure he was smarter than everyone else around him, with his so clever upside-down posters, his eerie impersonation of a sighted person, his terrible concentration on everything and everyone around him. What a relief it was to be with someone like Jake. Jake was so easy to be with, so straightforward.

"You know, Benjamin," Claire began, hearing the false notes in her own voice, "lately, with Lucas coming back and all, I've been thinking a lot about what happened. The accident, I mean."

There it was: the hint of a smug grin, quickly repressed but not quickly enough.

"Uh-huh," he said, drawing out the last syllable to ironic extreme.

"You know I've never been able to remember that whole thing."

He waited for her, silent. She fidgeted, sticking her fingers into the pot of aromatic herbs hanging in front of his window, and looking down the street, half-expecting to see Zoey come walking up. "I mean, Lucas pleaded guilty, didn't he?" She yanked her hands back to her sides. Amazing. She was trembling. Her voice was shaky. He couldn't help but hear it.

"Yes, he did," Benjamin agreed.

"So he must have been driving, right?" Claire demanded.

Now Benjamin let his slow, infuriating grin spread across his face. "Ah. So. It's always interesting to watch how long it takes for information to travel across this island. But I was sure you'd already heard about my speculations."

"I haven't heard anything," Claire snapped, not really expecting him to believe her. "What bull are you spreading around? That's all I want to know."

"You're ready to climb a wall," he said wonderingly. "I don't think I've ever seen you like this before."

"I don't like lies and rumors, that's all," Claire said. "If Lucas confessed, why are you going around trying to get everyone to believe Wade was driving that car? Why are you trying to help Lucas?"

To her amazement, Benjamin actually laughed. "I'll be damned, Claire. You really *don't* remember, do you?" He shook his head. In a low, kind voice he said, "Poor Claire. I was too cynical; I'm sorry. I assumed from the way you were acting, the frantic way you were attacking Lucas, that weird offer from your dad . . . But you actually don't remember."

"What the hell are you talking about, Benjamin? Why don't you just wipe that smug look off your face and spit it out?"

Benjamin stood up and crossed to her. He fumbled for and found her, holding her by the shoulders, his face now sincerely sad. "I'll always stand by you, Claire. I want you to know that. Whatever you decide. Not because your dad tried to bribe me."

Claire pushed him away violently. He fell back onto his bed. "You're scaring me!" she shouted.

You're scaring me!

She felt as if a bolt of electricity had shot up her spine. She reached for the wall, pressing her palm against it, trying to regain her balance in a spinning room.

Stop it. Pull over. You're scaring me.

"It's coming back, isn't it?" Benjamin asked softly.

"No!" Claire cried.

"It wasn't Lucas driving," Benjamin said, the words tumbling out at top speed. "He was the only one who was uninjured. He was in the backseat, wasn't he?"

"I have to get out of here," Claire said. "I—I have to . . . I—" She reeled toward the door.

"Claire, wait!" Benjamin cried.

Claire ran.

BENJAMIN PASSMORE

I had wondered from the start, from the first few moments after the initial shock of the news had worn off.

Maybe it's because I can't see. Sight is very convincing. When you see something, you don't doubt that it's true. You see something, ~~instnalty~~ instantly you know what it is, and you know it to be real, absolutely, with utter confidence. It doesn't take a lot of interpretation. You don't spend much time guessing.

Hearing, smell, ~~tuoch~~ touch are all so much less certain. And when you have to rely on those uncertain senses, when you have to rely on senses that you are trained to believe are unreliable, you find certainty very much harder to achieve.

I won't say being blind has made me suspicious; that would be the wrong word. But where sighted people are in the habit of simply accepting what seems obvious, I'm in the habit of guessing, reasoning, imagining.

So when all my sighted friends learned that Wade McRoyan had ~~sied~~ died in a car with Lucas and Claire, and when they had *seen* the body, and *seen* Claire's injuries, and *seen* the car crumpled around that tree trunk, those sights became all-important.

Whereas I could only imagine. I had to imagine a car. And imagine three people sitting in it. You see, I had to place them there in my imagination, and at that point the question arose: Who was in the backseat?

One dead. One injured. One uninjured.

Wade. Claire. Lucas.

I couldn't be sure at that point who *was* driving the car, but I was pretty certain who was not.

And then, Lucas confessed. And Claire couldn't remember.

I figured I was wrong. I didn't guess the full truth until Lucas came back and I saw how Claire reacted.

I don't know how much she ~~rememmbared~~ remembered over time, or half-remembered, or suspected. She's a person who will act on intuition, and I guess that's what she did. I like to think if she had known the truth two years ago, she'd have told it. Claire is a decent person underneath all her compulsive manipulation. If she'd remembered the truth back then, she never would have let Lucas pay the price he did.

I have to ~~beleive~~ believe that. It's the only way I can keep on loving her.

EIGHTEEN

"LOOK, THE IMPORTANT THING IS you have to act like you just happened to be passing by," Nina said for the dozenth time.

Aisha rolled her eyes. Like Nina was the person to be giving lectures on how to be discreet. Nina, who had spilled the news about Zoey and Lucas to her within fifteen minutes of having heard it.

Now they were standing around the dock, practicing so they'd look casual when the ferry came in with Zoey and Lucas aboard. Aisha was supposed to pretend she had just been passing by and *Oh, there's Nina, I'll go over and say hi, and oh, there's Zoey on the ferry. What a major coincidence!*

"I'll be totally cool, all right? I mean, I'm not personally quite as worked up over this as you are."

"Zoey and Lucas?" Nina said incredulously. "You think that's no big deal?"

"Well, it's big, I mean as far as gossip and so on, but I don't think it will be a life-altering experience for me." She looked at her watch, then glanced out toward the setting sun. "There's the *Minnow.*"

"Okay, now run away."

"Away where?"

"I don't know. Jeez, Aisha, do I have to think of everything?"

"This is your particular insanity, Nina," Aisha said.

"Run over to Passmores'. If she sees you there, you'll just say you went in for a Coke."

"Should we synchronize our watches?" Aisha asked. "That's what they do in the spy movies."

"Would you rather I just hadn't told you?" Nina asked.

Aisha considered that question as she trotted across the parking area to Passmores'. There were two tables filled in the outdoor seating area, and the sound of more diners inside.

Aisha lurked by the alleyway, self-consciously keeping her head down as the ferry chugged across the harbor.

So, Zoey was fooling around with Lucas. It was juicy, no question about it. Stupid, too, probably. But then, Zoey did have this suppressed crazy streak deep down inside that you didn't really notice till you'd known her awhile. Plus, she was hopelessly, pathetically romantic, which was the kind of character trait that got people into trouble. Much better to be rational.

It was one thing to look at a guy and think, Hey, not bad.

But that didn't mean you acted on it. Otherwise, you'd constantly be getting led around one way or another, a prisoner of whatever chance happened to bring a good-looking guy your way.

The ferry whistle split the calm night. None of the diners at the cafe flinched or jumped, which showed that they were locals. Aisha looked at them more closely. Pastor what-was-his-name and his wife. And the two gay guys who had the house on Pond Road.

Zoey and Lucas. Definitely running counter to peer pressure on that one. Not that peer pressure should be your guide. If it were, well, she'd be going out with Christopher, wouldn't she?

She flashed on an image of him, tight, very tight shorts, running down the field, keeping the ball just ahead of him, his cute little . . . But then, that was exactly the point. Zoey was the kind of person who'd let that get to her. Aisha was not. She could separate out the fact that he was good-looking and not be influenced in the slightest. And she could ignore everyone's expectations.

Aisha nodded, feeling content.

Besides, Nina didn't have a boyfriend, either. Lots of girls didn't have boyfriends.

"Order up." She heard the familiar voice close at hand, but muffled. She jumped around and stared down the alley. "Come on, pick up, it's getting cold."

Of course. Christopher cooked at Passmores'. It was one of his seemingly endless profusion of jobs. The kitchen door was just down the alleyway.

Aisha glanced anxiously toward the ferry. It was nosing into the dock, but it would take four more minutes before they tied it off and lowered the gangplank.

She sidled down the alley, stepping carefully so as not to make a noise. Hot, moist, aromatic air blasted from the doorway, along with the crash of aluminum pots and the roar of a dishwasher.

"You need drawn butter with that," Christopher said.

Aisha flattened herself against the brick wall and peered around the corner. The kitchen was blazingly bright, fluorescence gleaming off stainless steel. Christopher was only a few feet away, his back to her as he placed a green garnish on a plate of fish.

He was wearing a white apron over cutoff shorts and a blue T-shirt. On his head he had a baseball cap turned backward.

He moved from the range to the broiler, shaking a frying pan here, lifting a plate there, sailing a steak through the air to land on the grill. It was almost graceful. Almost like a dance of some sort, and he did it well.

He bent over at the waist, reaching into a low refrigerator, and pulled out a cake, sliced it, spooned strawberries over it, and, with a flourish, sprayed a mound of whipped cream on top.

"Here," he said, turning very suddenly to face her.

Aisha leapt back, but it was too late. He leaned out of the door and handed the strawberry shortcake to her, producing a clean spoon from the pocket of his apron.

"I . . . I . . ." she said.

"You are hungry, aren't you?" he asked smugly. "I mean, that is why you came sneaking down the alleyway, right? You wanted something to eat? Surely it wasn't to see little old me."

"I just happened to be here."

"I see. On your way to—" He made a point of turning his head slowly. "On your way to the brick wall at the end of the alley."

"I'm waiting for someone," Aisha said furiously.

"Uh-huh. I know you are, but I'm working right now, Aisha." He grabbed her hand and thrust the dish into it. "Try this, it may satisfy at least some of your craving." He winked outrageously and disappeared back into his kitchen.

Aisha threw the dish hard against the bricks. "Why can't I get rid of you?"

He leaned back through the doorway, looking serious and a little angry. "If you really want to be rid of me, you can," he said. "I'll never speak to you again, never look at you, put you out of my mind permanently. If that's what you really, truly want. You have three seconds to say *Get out of my life.*"

"I, uh, I—" she stammered.

"One."

"Look—"

"Two."

"Christopher!"

"Three." He nodded cockily. "Didn't think so."

The creep, Aisha thought grumpily.

Claire walked for several hours, through the narrow, familiar streets of North Harbor, along the breakwater, in the sand on Town Beach. She sat on a bench in the circle for a while, till the bells from the steeple rang eight and roused her from her thoughts.

She knew she should go home, but she knew she couldn't. Not yet.

Inevitably her feet found Coast Road, and she turned south. It was a mile, more, till the houses, some bright, some shuttered and empty, thinned out, leaving her with only the crashing surf for company. The last of the widely spaced streetlights fell behind, and now only the milky light of a startlingly bright moon showed her the way. It was another half-mile to the intersection with Pond Road, down which she saw more homes, more light, but she plunged on into lonely darkness.

In two years she had not returned to the spot, and she wondered if she would know it when she got there.

But then a chill breeze raised goose bumps on her arms and shoulders. Her steps faltered on the sand-blown blacktop.

Yes. This was the place. The moon's diffuse glow seemed to cast a spotlight on the vast white scar, the tree trunk naked, its bark ripped away long ago.

She stood there, staring, not really thinking, just letting her mind go blank. And then, after a while, she realized she was crying.

"Zoey, how *could* you?"

They sat in the middle of the circle, Zoey lying back on the grass, Aisha with legs and arms crossed sitting on the bench, Nina pacing back and forth, chewing her unlit Lucky Strike. The sun had set, plunging North Harbor into darkness softened by a dusky moon overhead.

Zoey had met the two of them at the dock, instantly realizing that despite their lame attempt to make it look like a coincidence, Nina had, of course, told Aisha everything.

When he'd seen them, Lucas had squeezed her hand and prudently disappeared into the disembarking crowd.

"You don't understand," Zoey said, trying to calm her

heart, trying to keep her head from spinning. "It's like—it's like you're happy with regular old store ice cream until you discover Ben and Jerry's."

Aisha rolled her eyes toward Nina. "Look," she said, leaning forward, "I think you're kind of missing the point a little, Zoey. I mean, sure, right now all you see is the good stuff with Lucas—"

"—whatever that might be," Nina interjected.

"But you can't ruin your life just because some guy gives you a case of heaving bosom."

"I know," Zoey said dreamily.

"Do you realize what this will do to everyone?" Aisha asked. "We've always gotten along all right, the six of us. You, me, Nina, Claire . . . most of the time, Benjamin, Jake. We're a group, we're buds."

"We're all stuck with each other, trapped together like rats in a cage," Nina said. "Every morning we're on the ferry together, every evening the same thing. In between we go to the same school and live so close together that you could just about throw a baseball from your house to anyone else's house."

"I know," Zoey said, more seriously this time. She sat up and wrapped her arms around her knees. She took a deep breath and closed her eyes. "I know this will really hurt Jake."

"It's not just that," Nina said. "I don't care if Jake gets hurt.

It's that, I mean, we won't be a group anymore."

"You hate being part of a group, Nina," Zoey pointed out. "You're the raging nonconformist here."

"I know, but still, I need a group to rebel against."

"It will be like civil war around here," Aisha said glumly. "You and Lucas on one side, Jake and Claire on the other. We won't be together anymore. Don't try to fool yourself, Zoey. This isn't just like you're seeing another guy; it's like you've decided to go steady with Satan or something and you're trying to convince yourself that everyone will accept him eventually."

"Really, Zo," Nina said.

"So what am I supposed to do?" Zoey shouted in sudden exasperation. "You want me just to give Lucas up because it will keep the group together?"

"Sounds kind of unromantic when you put it that way," Nina said.

"Look, romance is not the only thing in the world," Aisha said. "People do stupid things for love. How about the Trojan War? Paris and Helen go at it and Agamemnon ends up being chopped up by his wife while he's taking a bath."

"Excuse me?" Nina said. "Could we stick to reality here?"

"I can't stop feeling something because it's inconvenient," Zoey said.

"Of course you can. I do it all the time," Aisha argued.

"You're right, though," Zoey went on, talking almost to herself. "Things won't be the same, will they? It's like we've all been going along in this pleasant little dream and I'm going to screw it up."

"Forget about us," Nina said, suddenly serious. "What about you, Zo? You won't be part of Zoey and Jake anymore. You won't be the couple everyone looks up to. Barbie and Ken. You'll be part of Zoey and Lucas.

"It's your decision, Zo," Nina went on. She looked at her friend, for once without a hint of irony in her eyes. "Only it's maybe bigger than you think."

Claire found her father in his study, a dark-paneled room lined with expensively bound books and lit from green-shaded lamps. He was in a deep leather wing chair, smoking a cigar, sipping a glass of scotch, and reading through a sheaf of official-looking papers with a detached look.

"Daddy," she said.

"Oh, hi there, honey. Where've you been?"

Claire came into the room and sank into a chair opposite him. She tried to meet his eyes, but looked down at the carpet instead. It took a while to put the words together. "How did you get Lucas to do it?"

"What?" His voice was confused. He pulled the cigar from

his mouth and set the glass on a table. "What was that?"

"How did you get Lucas to confess that he was driving the car?"

"Me?" Her father made an effort at a smile.

"Daddy, I remember," Claire said in a choked voice. "It wasn't Lucas."

"I don't know . . . what are you—"

"Lucas wasn't driving the car," Claire said flatly. "He was in the backseat. He was complaining, he was saying we were all too damned drunk to be driving and we should walk back into town. He was making a joke out of it. *Stop it. Pull over. You're scaring me.* He was joking, but he was serious."

Her father's confused look vanished. "I think you're just imagining things, honey. I know how much you've wanted to remember—"

"Have I?" Claire snapped. "How hard have I tried?"

"It's not your fault. You had a concussion, for God's sake."

"He wasn't hurt, Lucas wasn't hurt; Benjamin's right. Because he was in the backseat. He was in the back yelling that we should pull over and not try to drive."

"Look, memory's a tricky thing—"

"But he confessed. Why? To protect Wade? Why? He didn't care about Wade. No. He cared about me, though. He was in love with me."

"Love," her father snorted.

"Tell me the truth, Daddy," Claire begged. "It wasn't Lucas driving."

"Wade, then," her father said. "Maybe you're right. Maybe it was Wade."

Claire laughed bitterly. "It was me. It was me!" Her voice broke and she buried her face in her hands. "I was driving the car. Me."

For a long while, neither of them spoke. Then her father, in a dull monotone, said, "There was no conclusive evidence."

"Until now. Now I remember."

And not before? Or had the truth always been there, just below the surface of her dreams? Why else had she been so frightened when Lucas reappeared? Why else had it been so important to get rid of him? Had she sensed somehow that his coming would prod her guilty memory?

Fear. That's what she had felt, learning he was back. Unreasoning fear. She'd done her best to shut him out. And in her fear she'd turned away from Benjamin, probing, suspicious Benjamin, and felt herself drawn to Jake. Jake would be her ally against the common foe. Safe, dependable Jake.

"Old Officer Talbot, hell, you know they send the old cops over here to take it easy till retirement," her father said, gazing at her with unfocused eyes. "He'd been at a desk since the eighties, hadn't investigated anything for years. But he was bound and determined, it was a crime, dammit, someone had to pay."

"It should have been me," Claire whispered.

"Everyone knew the Cabral kid had been in trouble before. What was it to him? He'd have ended up in jail sooner or later."

"Oh, God."

"At first it was Lucas's own idea, do what he must have figured was the manly thing: protect his girlfriend by taking the rap for her. For you." Her father nodded. "It was probably the only really gutsy thing he'd ever done. But I was worried sooner or later someone would think about it: Why was he the only one not hurt? The driver's side of that car was crushed like a beer can. Only someone small could have been behind that wheel and survived. The McRoyan kid was six three. Lucas Cabral was smaller, but he'd at least have been badly hurt, not untouched." For the first time he met her gaze. "No. I couldn't be sure it was you driving, sweetheart, but it was most likely, and if I could figure it out, so could someone else."

"I remember now," Claire said in a faraway voice. "The door was popped open by the impact and Lucas had to get my seat to recline before he could get me out. I could barely breathe from the wheel pressing against me."

"I told Lucas I thought he was taking it like a man, confessing to what he'd done." Her father hung his head. "I told him

I hoped he would have the guts to stick to his story. We never really admitted out loud that he was innocent. He never claimed he was, and I really didn't want to know for sure that he was." He closed his eyes and sighed profoundly. "Still, we reached an agreement. His father's business had been slipping for a while, lots of problems with the boat, prices for lobster were at rock bottom. Cabral was a razor's edge away from losing his boat altogether. I told Lucas I'd be able to help with that."

"Oh, God, Daddy," Claire whispered.

"I didn't think he'd go to jail," her father said sadly. "Everyone figured he'd just get a slap on the wrist, being a juvenile and all. You have to believe that. I didn't think . . . And it was easy to see how shaken up he was when the judge handed down the sentence. But he took that, too, and just as they were leading him out of the courtroom he said to me, 'Don't worry, Mr. Geiger. I keep my promises.'"

"All this time," Claire whispered. "He thinks I knew. He thinks I've let this happen to him, that I just abandoned him. It's sickening. I feel like throwing up."

Her father's gaze was steely. "I do whatever I have to to protect you. Whatever. Even perjury."

"Perjury?" she asked, uncomprehending.

"That's what they'd call it, I imagine: subornation of perjury. If you ever told anyone what we've just discussed, I might even wind up in jail myself."

"He went to jail to protect me, and to save his father," Claire whispered.

Her father smiled bitterly. "People do all sorts of things to protect the ones they love."

Claire felt the weight of his words settle on her. Yes, people did all sorts of things to protect the ones they loved.

And now, it would be her turn.

"You know I love you, honey," her father said.

"I love you, too, Daddy."

The List

JAKE	LUCAS
–Known him for years	–Feel like I ~~Barely~~ know him well
–Great body	–Okay body
–Like his mom	–His dad is a little intense
–Very good kisser	–~~?~~ Excellent kisser
–Never got anyone killed	–Maybe ~~Probably~~ got someone killed He paid for it, though
–Everyone likes him but Nina	–No one likes him—but me
–Thinks he's going to marry me	–Says he thought of me a lot
–Getting kind of gropey	–Hasn't seen a girl in 2 years
–Friend as well as boyfriend	–Neither ?????
–Makes me feel safe	–~~Makes me feel~~ Makes me feel amazing
–Excellent chest	–Possible tattoo?
–Don't like his hair	–Nice hair

Zoey stared thoughtfully at the list. Things had definitely improved for Lucas, she realized. Definite, major improvement. But when she'd made the first list, she hadn't really known Lucas, not like she did now.

She snapped off the little lamp over her desk and gazed out the window. The moon was so bright, it must be full. The cobblestones were painted silver; the shadows were soft and benign.

She craned her neck out of the small window to try to get a glimpse of the Cabrals' deck. Too bad her window didn't face the other way. Then maybe she could look up at him, and he'd be able to see her down below if he stepped out onto his balcony.

Maybe he was already asleep, possibly even dreaming of her. Was he a guy who would dream? Probably. He was thoughtful and intelligent and romantic, even though he tried to hide it under typical male toughness.

Yes, he certainly dreamed. And if he did dream, why not of her? She was certain she would dream of him. Oh, definitely; in fact, it was the best reason ever for going to sleep early.

At least in their dreams they wouldn't have to worry about how Jake would react—no guilt, no feeling that you were betraying someone you thought you loved.

And in their dreams there would be no Claire, no Nina

shaking her head like she had, saying, Jeez, Zoey, do you really want to do this? No Aisha making snide remarks about how naive you were. No group to be split for the first time ever into angry camps.

She pushed her chair back impatiently and began pacing the room. It was the island. It was too small, too intimate. Anywhere would be better. In a big city who would even notice whom she went out with?

Was he still awake? Probably; it was early still. Too early for dreams, but still, he might be thinking of her, right now, this very minute, only a few dozen feet away.

She lay back on her bed. Was he lying on his bed?

She closed her eyes and pictured him, the look in his eyes when they had separated after that first earth-shattering kiss. Was he remembering that same moment, right now, lying on his bed?

She jumped up, impatient, agitated, sleep an absolute impossibility. She would never fall asleep, not this night. Not the way she felt, her mind racing, her insides jittery, her limbs rattling with too much energy.

Had she felt like this with Jake? *Honestly,* she scolded herself, *did you ever feel this way with Jake*?

No. Yes, sort of, in a way. But not this way, not this precise way.

Was she falling in love with Lucas?

What a ridiculous thing to think. They'd only spent one afternoon together. And that time on the breakwater. And when he had met her at the breakfast table.

Was that enough?

She opened the door to her room stealthily and crept to the guest room. It was at the back of the house, with windows that looked up toward his.

Kneeling and looking up, she could just see the Cabral house. The lights were off. Of course, those were the lights in his parents' room, not his.

Suddenly a delicious thrill went through her. She was going to go and see. She had to know if he was awake or asleep.

She tiptoed back to her room and quickly put on her sneakers. With the Boston Bruins nightshirt, a slightly unfashionable outfit.

Walking at a snail's pace, she descended the stairs, reaching far to skip the one that squeaked. Then it was out the front door into the night.

The cool night air surprised her, blowing through and under her shirt. She felt wonderfully dangerous, creeping around her house, finding the narrow path through the bushes.

She climbed carefully, fell and scuffed her bare knees on the dirt, and almost dissolved in nervous giggles. This was basically a pretty dorky thing to be doing at nearly midnight. Mr. Cabral would probably wake up and think she was a burglar.

She reached the top, panting a little from exertion and excitement, and made her silent way around to the front of his house. There was a single window on the second floor, dormered like hers. The light was off.

So, he was in his bed. Asleep and dreaming, or awake, unable to sleep for thinking of her.

Or neither, some dark, unromantic comer of her mind suggested.

"Zoey?"

"Ahhhh!"

"Shh," Lucas said, clapping his hand over her mouth. When she was quiet he removed his hand, and smothered her giggles with his lips. She melted into his arms, letting her hands travel down his back and making the shocking discovery that he wore no shirt.

He pulled away, then kissed her again, a kiss that lasted so long she was sure the moon would have set and the sun come up by the time they drew apart again.

His eyes glittered darkly, so near she might fall into them and never find her way out again.

"I . . . I just wanted to see if your light was on," Zoey admitted. Would he think she was an idiot, prowling around in the dark on such a ridiculous mission?

He nodded. "I couldn't sleep either. I was thinking of you."

"Me too. I mean, of you."

He held her close, but now Zoey sensed a heaviness, a sadness in him that made him cling all the harder.

"What's wrong?" she asked, craning back to look into his downturned face.

He sighed. "I, uh, I had a fight with my father," he said.

"Was it bad?"

He nodded and pulled away, withdrawing his touch. "He wants me gone," Lucas said in a flat, monotone voice. "He's arranged with my grandfather for me to go there, until I can graduate."

Zoey felt her heart stop. "Your grandfather?"

"Yeah. My grandfather who lives in Texas." He clenched his fists and turned away.

Zoey flew to him, wrapping her arms around him, pressing her cheek against his back. "You have to talk to him, make him change his mind!"

"My father's never changed his mind about anything," Lucas said bitterly. "A few weeks from now—"

"No, Lucas, no," Zoey said desperately. "We'll figure something out; you can't . . . I can't . . ."

"Just kiss me again, Zoey," he said. "When you kiss me, nothing bad can happen."

They kissed in the moonlight, desperate with longing, afraid, their tears mingling, and slowly, slowly, the rest of the world faded away, leaving them perfectly alone together.

JAKE FINDS OUT

PART TWO

Zoey Passmore

Who is my boyfriend? Ha. Good question.

Truth is, I've sort of been torn between these two guys: Jake, my long-time boyfriend—a great guy, a nice guy, the right guy (according to all my friends)—and Lucas.

Lucas (according to all my friends) is the wrong guy. Very wrong.

See, a couple years ago, Jake's brother, Wade, was killed in this car crash, and Lucas was driving the car. Lucas spent two years in jail for it. Then he got out, moved back here to Chatham Island, and, well, to make a long story short, I fell for him big time. Not <u>that</u> big time, just, you know, kisses that stopped the moon in the sky and made my knees rattle.

I haven't told Jake yet. Maybe he won't care.

No, that's stupid. Of course he'll care. He loves me, he hates Lucas. The thought of me with Lucas will . . . I guess I don't know what it will do, except that it's bound to start trouble in our group. Living on a small island like this, it's very difficult to ignore how other people feel. And to show you just how popular Lucas Cabral is around here, his own father is planning to send him away. Mr. Cabral's very old-fashioned. He says Lucas brings shame on his family.

My friend Aisha thinks I'm being an idiot and that bad things will come from my being with Lucas. But I can't really believe that my loving Lucas could ever result in anything bad. I mean, it's love, right? And love conquers all. At least, I think it's love. Does probable love conquer all?

Probably.

Aisha Gray

Boyfriend? Don't start with me on the subject of boyfriends. There's this guy named Christopher who thinks he's my boyfriend. He thinks we're destined to become boyfriend and girlfriend because we're like the only two black kids on Chatham Island, if you don't count my little brother.

But I don't go for destiny. I don't go for fate. I am a rational person who is not going to be swayed just because some guy thinks he's hot, and everyone else I know thinks he's right for me. Zoey's the romantic in our group, which is why her life is a mess. I don't turn my life around just because some guy with a cute butt comes along.

Did I say that? What I meant was, I don't turn my life around just because some guy with a big mouth comes along. That's what I meant to say.

Anyway, if I wanted a boyfriend, there's a whole big world of opportunity: black, white, brown, yellow, red. I'm open-minded. And I make my own decisions. I'm my own woman.

So the answer is no, I don't have a boyfriend.

And if I did, it wouldn't be Christopher.

Nina Geiger

Don't have a boyfriend, never really wanted one. To me a guy is about as necessary as a training bra is to a python; as necessary as an inflamed appendix; as necessary as an electric blanket in hell.

See, that's my three-part comic tautology rule: If you're doing funny examples, do them in threes. Yes, tautology. Look it up. Use it in your next English class and watch you teacher fall over in a dead faint.

Of course, there is this one guy—Zoey's brother, Benjamin.

Yes, he is my sister Claire's boyfriend, but that's a mere technicality. He doesn't really love her. I mean, how could he? We're talking Claire, whose soul is an automatic icemaker. I'm sure that if Benjamin ever thought about it and realized how much I like him, he'd immediately see that we're right for each other.

If he ever even noticed that I'm alive. If he ever bothered for one second to realize that I am not just his buddy, that I am a young woman, and, by the way, not a complete gorgon or anything. If he ever MANAGED to pay the SLIGHTEST bit of attention to the fact that he's the ONLY guy I've ever been interested in in my LIFE, the arrogant, self-centered TOAD . . .

Well, then I think we'd be just right for each other.

Claire Geiger

I suppose Benjamin is my boyfriend. Either that or he hates me, I'm not sure. And I'm not sure how I feel about him anymore, either. A lot of things are up in the air since I remembered.

See, I honestly didn't remember; that is the truth. You have to understand that. For the longest time I tried to remember; at least I believe I tried. I would never have let Lucas go to jail for me. I would never have kept silent for those two years if I'd remembered.

But now I do remember. I was driving the car when Jake's brother, Wade, was killed. Me, not Lucas.

Benjamin suspects the truth. No one knows for sure except

me and Lucas and, unfortunately, my father. But Benjamin suspects.

My dad was just trying to protect me. He guessed the truth right from the start, but he made a deal with Lucas and Lucas stuck to it. Why? I don't know. Lucas used to be in love with me, that's one reason. Plus my dad said he'd help Lucas's father out with his business.

And now, if I tell the truth, I don't know what would happen to my father. And if I tell the truth, Jake is sure to turn against me, and I was just starting to realize how much I like him.

But if I don't tell the truth . . . then what kind of person am I?

Who's my boyfriend? Who's the guy I love? Benjamin? Jake? Is there even some lingering feeling between me and Lucas? Like I said, I don't know anymore.

ONE

"SO, THIS IS YOUR ROOM," Lucas said, letting his dark eyes roam over Zoey's unmade bed, taking in the bookshelves, the journal on her nightstand, the half-open dresser drawer that spilled out white cotton panties and bras.

"This is it." Zoey Passmore waved her arms awkwardly to encompass the room, then let them flop at her sides. Why had she invited him up here? And especially, why had she invited him without bothering to clean up? "Pretty exciting, huh?"

Lucas smiled as Zoey sidled over to close the dresser drawer. "It's been two years since I've been in a girl's room," he said. "It's nice. It smells nice in here."

"It's that subtle interplay between baby powder and dirty laundry," Zoey said.

Lucas leaned into the deep, dormered window. Zoey's father had built a small desk in there where she could do her homework and look down Camden Street, enjoying a view of the slow, gentle life of North Harbor, Chatham Island's only town. On the right wall of the dormer she tacked notes and lists and reminders about appointments. On the left she put quotations on yellow Post-it notes.

"'Imagination is the eye of the soul,'" Lucas quoted, reading her favorite. "Who is Joseph Joubert?"

Zoey shrugged. "He's the guy who said 'Imagination is the eye of the soul.' That's all I know. I guess maybe someday I should find out."

"I like the quote," Lucas said. He tilted his head sideways. His long, unruly blond hair hung down. "'If there is anything better than to be loved, it is loving,'" he read.

Zoey gulped and felt a blush rising in her cheeks. She ran a hand through her own unruly blond hair. "Yeah, I just, you know . . . kind of liked the way it sounded."

"Anonymous, huh?" He grinned. "Anonymous said a lot of very interesting things."

Zoey laughed. "Yes, he or she has always been one of my favorites."

Lucas stood back, nodding as he looked at her little alcove. "This is how I'll picture you from now on," he said. "Whenever I'm in my room at night, thinking of you, I'll imagine you sitting at this desk, watching the sun setting over the town, the way it is now, and searching for wisdom in quote books." He looked at her with his usual startling, unsettling directness.

"Better than picturing my messy bed, I guess."

Lucas smiled an impish half smile. "Oh, I'll probably think of you there, too," he admitted. "But I'll try to keep those thoughts under control."

"Good," she said.

He reached out for her and she took his hand, just holding the tips of his fingers with hers. For a while that might have been seconds or hours, they just looked at each other. Then Zoey felt his grip tighten on her hand. Lucas drew her to him.

Or perhaps she drew him to her. It was always hard to tell.

His lips met hers, a tender, gentle collision that grew in intensity, escalating so suddenly and explosively that when at last they drew apart, Zoey's lips felt bruised. Her hands shook. Her heart pounded wildly. She could not trust her voice to speak.

The effect Lucas had on her was startling, like nothing she had known before. It was as if she were driving along at ten miles an hour on a quiet street one minute and then, a split second after their lips met, she was doing warp factor nine and blowing past Jupiter. The mental image made her smile.

"It's amazing," Lucas said, grinning a little foolishly and shaking his head in disbelief.

"You mean—?"

"Kissing you," he said. "It's just . . . " He shook his head again, at a loss for words.

"You too?" Zoey asked shyly. "I thought maybe it was just me."

"Oh, yeah. Like someone shoved a thousand-volt wire up my—" He stopped himself and made a wry face.

"That's a really romantic image," Zoey said, laughing.

"Well, I'm quite a poet," he said self-mockingly.

"Maybe we'd better do it again," she suggested.

"I think we'd better," he agreed.

His lips had just brushed hers when there was a knock at her door.

They flew apart, both looking flustered and guilty.

"Your dad?" Lucas asked in a hoarse whisper.

"He's down at the restaurant," Zoey said. "So's my mom."

The knock came again. "It's just me," a voice said.

Zoey sighed in relief. Benjamin, her older brother. She opened the door. Benjamin slipped inside and closed the door behind him.

"I hope I'm not interrupting anything," he said, turning his dark sunglasses roughly toward the spot where Zoey and Lucas were standing.

"We were . . . uh, going over some homework," Zoey said lamely.

"Of course you were," Benjamin said smoothly. "But in case you weren't just going over your homework, I thought I'd come up and warn you that Jake is downstairs in the family room."

"Jake?" Zoey cried.

"Yeah, you remember," Benjamin said, "your boyfriend? Big guy, muscles, dark hair? He was going to just come on up, but I convinced him you were waxing your legs and you'd be annoyed if he barged in and saw you like that."

"I don't wax my legs," Zoey said.

"It's all I could think of, all right?" Benjamin said. "It was either that or tell him you were up here playing tongue hockey with his worst enemy."

Lucas frowned. "Maybe we should just get this out in the open."

"No!" Zoey said. "I mean, I want to prepare him for it."

"You'll never be able to prepare him for it," Lucas said reasonably.

"He's right," Benjamin said, nodding agreement. "But there might be a gentler way of doing it." Suddenly he froze, cocking his head to listen. "Damn. He's coming."

A second later Zoey heard Jake's quick, heavy tread on the stairs. "Oh, no." She looked pleadingly at Lucas. "Would you mind hiding? Quick?"

Lucas hesitated, as if he might argue, then shook his head in disgust and dropped to the floor, bending over to look under her bed. "What's all this junk under here?"

Jake's tread was closer now, turning the corner at the top of the stairs. "Zo? Are you decent in there?"

"I can't fit under here," Lucas whispered.

"In the closet," Benjamin hissed.

Lucas jumped up, dashed for the closet, slipped inside, and wormed his way back through dresses and jackets and blouses.

Jake knocked on the door. Then, without waiting, he opened it. Zoey's clothes were still rustling and swaying, and far toward the back of the closet, she could still clearly make out a pair of battered leather boots that were definitely not hers.

"Hi, babe," Jake said. He crossed the room to take Zoey in his muscular arms.

"Jake," Zoey said with phony brightness. "Benjamin told me you were here."

"He told me you were waxing your legs," Jake said, giving Benjamin a dubious look.

"I'm all done," Zoey said.

Jake grinned slyly. He hugged her to him and let his hand slip down her side. "Can I feel?" he asked wickedly.

Zoey was sure she saw the boots in her closet begin to move. "No, Jake," she said sharply.

"No, Jake," Benjamin echoed helpfully. "You really shouldn't flirt with my sister while I'm in the room."

And Lucas is in the closet, Zoey added silently.

Jake released her, and Zoey almost sighed in relief. "Are you going to be ready anytime soon?" Jake asked, looking at her skeptically.

"Ready?"

"Yeah, you know. We're all going over to The Tavern for dinner. You, me, my folks."

"That's tonight?" Zoey said, sounding shrill. "But I—I don't have anything to wear to The Tavern." Instantly she saw Benjamin wince and shake his head imperceptibly. Her eyes flew toward the closet.

Jake gave a long-suffering look and marched to the closet.

Oh, no.

"You always say you don't have anything to wear, Zo. How about that blue dress? You know, the one that's got the slit up the side?"

Zoey gulped. She felt frozen in place. Jake was riffling through her clothes now. In a matter of seconds his hand would encounter a warm body amid the silk and cotton.

"Where is that thing?" Jake demanded.

"I . . . I don't think I . . ." Zoey stammered.

"I'm sure it's in here," Jake said. "You know the one I'm talking about." He gathered a bunch of clothes and shifted them to the right.

"Let me!" Zoey yelled, leaping forward.

Jake turned to look over his shoulder.

The dress, the blue dress, suddenly appeared, thrust forward from the back of her closet.

Zoey stretched, shoved past Jake, snatched the dress, and spun to block Jake's view. "Here it is," she said breathlessly.

Jake stared hard.

Zoey felt her smile crumbling.

"Amazing," Jake said. "A girl can just reach right in and find something. I probably could have looked for hours." He clapped Benjamin on the shoulder and laughed. "That's the way it always is. It's the same with a girl's purse."

"Yeah, women," Benjamin said, smiling blandly. "Well, as much fun as it might be to stay, I have to head on over to the Geigers'. Nina's reading for me."

"An evening with *Ninny*," Jake said, making a face. "I thought you could do better than that."

Benjamin shrugged and turned around, walking in his precise way to the head of the stairs. "You shouldn't be jealous just because Nina can read, Jake."

Jake laughed good-naturedly and slipped his arm around Zoey's waist. "Hmm. I believe your brother may just have insulted me, Zoey." He drew her close and bent down to kiss her, just as he had so many, many times before.

Zoey reached with her free hand and pushed the closet door.

Her lips opened to Jake.

The door closed on Lucas.

Lucas waited until he heard Jake leave, then stepped out of the closet. Zoey was standing there, holding the blue dress, looking confused and guilty.

Lucas forced a smile. There was no point in making things worse for her.

"I'm so sorry," Zoey whispered.

"You did what you had to," he said flatly.

"I need to tell him," Zoey said, worrying the fabric of the dress in her hands.

Lucas shrugged. "Either that or I'll have to get used to hanging out in closets." He looked at her sideways, told himself not to ask the question that was burning around his brain, then ignored his own good advice. "You kissed him, didn't you?"

Zoey flushed and looked down at the floor.

"Thought so," he said.

"Look, I . . . It was the quickest way to get rid of him," Zoey said.

"And now you're going to spend the night with him and his parents."

"It's something I agreed to a long time ago," Zoey explained.

She looked thoroughly miserable, and Lucas told himself to relent. But he couldn't let go of the image of her standing right here, not three feet from him, kissing another guy while Lucas could still taste her lips.

"It's a little hard to take," he said grimly.

"I just need some time, Lucas," Zoey said. She touched his arm. He didn't respond. "You're really mad, aren't you?" she said.

"No," he lied, shaking his head as if it would clear out the disturbing images. Then a more alarming thought occurred to him. "You're not sleeping with him, are you?"

Zoey drew back, arching her eyebrows angrily. "No, Lucas, I'm not. And if I were, which I'm definitely not, do you think I would now? Now that you and I are—"

"Are what?" Lucas said. "That's the question, isn't it? Are we . . . *we*?"

"We're *we*," Zoey said softly.

Lucas tried not to let himself feel too pleased, since he was enjoying feeling resentful, but a wry smile escaped. "You and me?"

"Yes, you and me," Zoey said, smiling shyly.

"No one else?" Lucas demanded.

"I'll tell Jake tonight," Zoey promised. "If, you know, if there's a time when I can do it."

Lucas grimaced at the dress. "That looks kind of low-cut."

Zoey rolled her eyes. "With me, how low-cut could it be? I'm not exactly Adriana Lima."

"Too low-cut for Jake," Lucas said grumpily.

"I have to change," Zoey said. "And Jake is still downstairs waiting."

"Sure, go ahead."

"Lucas."

He smiled sheepishly. "I guess you want me to get back in the closet."

"Just turn your head and promise not to peek."

"Okay." He turned away.

"Nice try, Lucas. Turn the other way, *not* toward the mirror."

He laughed. "Mirror? I didn't even notice there was a mirror there." Behind his back he heard the sound of clothing dropping to the floor, of dresser drawers opening and closing, and the sound of silk against skin.

"Ta-daa," Zoey said.

He turned, prepared to make some leering remark, but somehow the sight of her, perfect, so perfect, choked off the words.

"You don't like it?" Zoey asked, looking crestfallen.

"No, it's just . . ." He had to stop and swallow down the lump in his throat. "It's just that you are too beautiful. I can't believe you're real, and that you're mine." As he spoke the words he felt their truth. She *was* too beautiful. Too smart and funny and decent. For him.

Anyone could see that she belonged with Jake, not with him. How could he ever live up to her? What chance was there that this could last? His father was trying to convince his grandfather to take him in, and any day he could be told to go. Was it right to ask Zoey to give up Jake for a guy whose future was an open question?

Zoey laughed self-deprecatingly. She held out her arms and looked down at herself skeptically. "You know, you have been living with just guys for the last two years. It obviously doesn't take much to impress you." She gave a twirl, then stopped and looked at him doubtfully. "What's the matter? You look grim."

"Nothing," he said. "I just wanted to say, you know, you can take a while to tell Jake. I'll understand."

"I want to do it as soon as I can," Zoey said. "I want it to be out in the open." She reached for his hand again, and this time he grasped her fingers. "I'll be thinking of you all night."

"Yeah, right," he said, drawing her close.

"Well, just in case, you'd better give me something to remember," she said softly.

He kissed her, feeling waves of desire and pleasure. Waves that almost washed away the lingering realization that these same lips, only moments before, had been on Jake's.

TWO

CLAIRE GEIGER WAS WALKING DOWN Center Street carrying a plastic sack of groceries when she saw Benjamin ahead of her, outlined against a darkening sky as he crossed the street and aimed for her house.

She slowed her pace, hanging back so as not to overtake him. He was using his cane, swinging it from side to side, but only in the most casual manner. North Harbor was such a small town that he had counted out every street and knew exactly how many steps there were from corner to corner.

On this familiar turf Benjamin could move with the easy confidence of a sighted person, lithe and almost graceful. His dark Ray Bans, an integral part of his handsome, serious face, gave him a mysterious, strangely alert look.

Claire held her breath, hoping he didn't know she was here watching him, wondering whether she was ready to talk to him. They hadn't seen each other since he'd told her he knew the truth. That he *thought* he knew the truth.

She made a decision and quickened her pace, breaking into a run to catch him before he reached her gate. "Hey, Benjamin."

Benjamin stopped and turned, his shades aiming just slightly to the left of her. "I was wondering if you were trying to avoid me," he said.

"Avoid you?" She touched his cheek, directing his mouth, and kissed him lightly on the lips.

"Yes. You know, when you stopped by the kite shop." He smiled his knowing half smile. "You have a distinctive walk, Claire. And you're wearing thongs. You can't sneak around when you're wearing thongs."

Claire laughed as nonchalantly as she could. "You know, most girls would think the cool thing about having a boyfriend who's blind would be that he couldn't keep track of them. But, of course, they'd be wrong about that."

"Actually, I think what most girls would like about a blind boyfriend is that he would never know if they were beautiful or not." He reached toward her, letting his hand drift slowly at the right height, till his fingers touched her face. "Although I hear that's not something you'd ever have to worry about, Claire." He looked at her wistfully. "Eyes as dark as your hair, Zoey tells me. But then, I still remember that from when we were little."

"Were you heading over to my house to see me?" Claire asked, sidestepping his compliment. People had told her all her life she was beautiful. Her relationship with Benjamin had been one of the few she'd had where her looks played no great role.

"Yes."

"Just dropping by?" she asked, trying to make the question sound innocent.

"Nina's going to read to me," he said. "And I wanted to talk to you."

An island car went by, rattling along the cobblestones, its punctured muffler roaring.

"Let's go down to the rocks for a minute," Claire suggested. "Nina will wait."

"All right," Benjamin said.

They walked the few yards to the end of the street and crossed Lighthouse Road. Claire kicked off her thongs and climbed out onto one of the many tumbled boulders that lined the shore at the northern tip of the island. Benjamin could only follow slowly. He used his cane to outline the nearest boulder, carefully defining the angle of its surfaces. Then he stuck out his left foot, felt the hard surface with the toe of his sneaker, and hopped onto it.

He stayed on a flat rock while Claire set down her bag of groceries and climbed a little farther out. The sea was calm, just a low swell running past the point, crashing and receding in quick, hushed strokes. The tidal pools formed by the crevices of the rocks rose and fell, but only gently.

Definitely a front coming in, Claire noticed, with her usual keen attention to the sky. A line of red-and-gold-trimmed clouds off to the southwest was advancing, as if fleeing the dying sun. There might be rain, she realized, possibly even a small storm. A storm would be nice.

"I haven't seen you all weekend," Benjamin said.

Claire was startled to hear his voice so close by. He had managed to work his way out to her and now stood confidently on a slanted slab of granite. One pants leg was wet from a mis-step along the way.

"I didn't realize I was obligated to see you every day," Claire said.

"You're not. It's just that the last time I saw you . . . well, you were reeling around the room and acting like the world was coming to an end."

"Oh, that," Claire said dismissively. "I was just woozy. I had a lousy night's sleep the night before, and I'd swiped a beer from the refrigerator before coming over."

"So that's all it was," Benjamin said, sounding neither skeptical nor convinced. "I thought maybe your reaction had something to do with my little theory."

"Theory?" Claire said, trying to keep from sounding brit-tle. Benjamin had a deadly accurate ability to read tone of voice.

"Yeah. My theory that you were the one driving the car when Wade McRoyan was killed. That theory. Slipped your mind, huh?"

"No, it didn't slip my mind. And really, the truth is, Benjamin, it shook me up for a while. As you know, I've never remembered what happened that night, so I began to wonder if maybe you were right. I had to ask myself if it was possible." She watched his reaction closely. The subtle superior smile faded. His jaw tightened. Claire grinned triumphantly. *Yes, I thought that might be the way to handle you, Benjamin.*

"You're saying you still don't remember?"

"No, I don't," Claire said. "Which doesn't necessarily mean you're wrong, Benjamin. You may even be right. Maybe it was me driving drunk that night. For that matter, maybe it was Wade himself." *There, let it go,* Claire told herself sternly. *Don't try to push it. Don't overdo it.*

It was always a chess match with Benjamin. She had to be on guard all the time, particularly when she wanted to deceive him. He was not a guy who could be misled by an innocent look or a pretty smile.

She had turned him aside for now, but she could tell Benjamin was far from convinced. In the end, if she was going to keep her secret, she would have to get him out of her life.

Benjamin started to say something, then stopped. His brow

furrowed in concentration. Claire could see herself reflected in his black sunglasses. At last his brow cleared. "Claire, if you did remember . . ."

"Yes?"

"If you did remember, and what you remembered was that it was you, and not Lucas, who was driving the car, would you tell?"

Claire stared straight into the distorted reflection of her own face. "Yes, Benjamin. Of course I would. What kind of person do you think I am?"

A ghost of a smile formed on his lips. "I don't know, Claire. Do you?"

Nina looked from her window and saw Benjamin and her sister, side by side, coming across the road from the water. They were holding hands. Claire was carrying a bag of groceries. Benjamin was carrying her thongs.

Nina glanced at the clock beside her bed. He was fifteen minutes late.

Fifteen minutes. Well, fine, if he wanted to run around with Claire and waste fifteen minutes. She still got paid by the hour to read homework to him, and she was going to charge the Passmores for the fifteen minutes. After all, she could have used the time doing something else. She was a busy girl. It wasn't like she was just waiting around for Benjamin to show up so she could read to him.

Wasn't like that at all. She had a life.

And if he spent the next ten minutes downstairs making out with Claire, fine, she'd charge his parents for that time, too. Ten dollars an hour. Ten minutes of making out, that would cost them . . . ten minutes was one sixth of an hour, into five . . . it would cost him about a dollar sixty-six. Maybe she would just point that out to him.

She grabbed the bottle of *Miss Dior* she'd bought at Porteous and sprayed a little on her wrists. She smelled it, shrugged, and checked herself in the mirror. She looked okay, in a great shirt she'd picked up at the Goodwill thrift shop in Weymouth, under a loose-fitting army shirt and shorts. She shoved her dark hair into approximately the right location. Pointless, really, since for all Benjamin knew she could be wearing a clown suit and a Bozo wig. But maybe the perfume would get his attention. After all, he could still smell.

He knocked at her door.

"Come in," she said loudly.

He opened the door and stood there. "Is it safe for me to come in? I mean, have you strewn your floor with clothes like last time?"

"No, the floor is clear," she said sharply, bending down

quickly to snatch a single boot and a bag of Doritos out of his path. "You're late, you know."

"Sorry."

"I do have a life, you realize."

Benjamin tilted his head at her quizzically. "Are you in a bad mood? We could make this another time."

"No," Nina said quickly. "No. Let's do it now. Sorry I snapped."

Benjamin made his way to her bed and sat down on the edge, then pushed off his sneakers and lifted his feet, making himself comfortable. He handed her a book. "It's poetry. Sorry about that."

Nina rolled her eyes to the ceiling and shook her fist at an invisible fate. She hated reading poetry. She could never get the rhythm right. And Benjamin would correct her. *No, it's supposed to be accented on the third syllable.* It was so much harder than just regular reading. She hated it. "No problem," she said.

"Thanks," Benjamin said. "We're supposed to read Shelley."

Nina made a face and silently mimicked, *We're supposed to read Shelley.* We were supposed to read Shelley fifteen minutes ago, but you were too busy playing slippery lippery with the ice princess.

"Percy Bysshe Shelley."

Percy Bysshe Shelley, Nina mimicked. *Why don't you get Claire to read Percy Bysshe Shelley to you?* She turned to the table of contents, found the right section, and dragged her chair over by the bed.

Benjamin frowned. "Is that . . . is that perfume?"

Finally. He noticed. "Um, I guess so. I mean, someone gave me some, and, you know, I may have spilled it or something."

"Hmm," he said.

Hmm? Hmm? That was it? Seventy dollars on her dad's charge account for *Hmm?*

"Does it bother you?" she asked.

"Naw. It smells a little like melons, doesn't it? I think the poem is called Indian something."

Nina gritted her teeth and considered giving Benjamin the finger, but that seemed mean. It wasn't nice to take advantage of the fact that he couldn't see. Then she did it anyway, because it made her feel good. Then she did it with both hands because that made her feel even better.

She began to read.

I arise from dreams of thee
In the first sleep of night—
The winds are breathing low
And the stars are burning bright.

It was a love poem, Nina realized. She looked sharply at Benjamin. A love poem? Was this really on the senior curriculum, or could it be possible that he was trying to tell her something?

I arise from dreams of thee—
And a spirit in my feet
Has borne me—Who knows how?
To thy chamber window, sweet!—

Wait a minute. Here he was, in her chamber. Okay, probably just a coincidence, but still, the first thing he'd asked her to read was a love poem.

The wandering airs they faint
On the dark silent stream—
The champak odours fail . . .

"Champak?" Benjamin asked.

"That's what it says," Nina said. "Champak."

"Would you mind looking it up?"

Nina got up and rummaged on her bookshelf for the dictionary. "Champak. It's some kind of tree that has fragrant flowers."

"Oh," Benjamin said. "Maybe that's where your perfume came from."

Nina smiled. That was better than *Hmm*. He was relating the poem to her. She hurried through the rest of the second verse, which had somehow dragged a dead nightingale into the story. But the third verse was better.

O lift me from the grass!
I die, I faint, I fail!
Let thy love in kisses rain
On my lips and eyelids pale.

Okay, this was definitely a love poem. And was it just her imagination, or was Benjamin listening to her more attentively than usual? Especially around the kisses raining on my lips part.

My cheek is cold and white, alas!
My heart beats loud and fast.

Nina gulped. Actually, her heart was beating fast. She shifted in her seat. It had to be deliberate. Benjamin was amazingly subtle, for a guy. He had to have known that having her read a poem like this, full of kisses and champak odors, while he lay back on her very bed . . .

O press it close to thine own again
Where it will break at last.

Benjamin nodded thoughtfully. "You're getting better at reading poetry. You got some real feeling into that."

Nina swallowed hard. "Well, it was more about something I . . . you know, I mean, it was more about . . ." She was sinking into her seat, her voice growing lower as she sank.

You're mumbling, Nina! she chided herself. *Why are you mumbling? You never mumble with anyone else. Stop mumbling and spit it out.*

"You mean it's something you identify with more," Benjamin said helpfully.

"I guess so," Nina mumbled.

"It's a love poem," Benjamin said.

"Yeah, I kind of thought so, too," Nina managed to say.

Benjamin smiled. "I never thought of you as a romantic type, Nina. Is it anyone in particular, or is that none of my business?"

Anyone in particular? Had he already guessed? Was he just waiting, hoping that she would tell him how she truly felt about him?

It was the perfect opening, the perfect opportunity. He'd asked her to read a love poem, then he'd asked her if it meant anything special to her. Plus, he loved her perfume. Or at least he had noticed it.

All she had to do now was open her mouth and say, Benjamin, I am totally in love with you. All she had to do was open her mouth and say—

"Benjamin?"

"Yes?"

"I . . . I . . . was just wondering what you'd like me to read next."

Claire paused at the door to Nina's room. She could hear her sister's voice droning on and Benjamin's occasional interruptions. Good. They would be busy for the next hour at least, then probably Benjamin would stay for dinner.

She mounted the stairs to the next level, her room, perched alone atop the house. There was a small metal box on her desk, a miniature weather station that gave temperature and wind and barometer readings. She noted the information with satisfaction.

Then she climbed the ladder that ran up one wall, pushed open the trapdoor, and climbed out onto the widow's walk. It was her favorite place in the world, quiet, inviolate, with a view of the town, the island, the water, and the overarching sky. It was the reason she loved this house. The reason she would have a hard time leaving it to go away to college.

The sun was dying over Weymouth, turning the tall buildings there into black rectangles of shadow, turning the water red.

She walked to the west end of the widow's walk to the tall brick chimney that rose beside it and quickly found the right brick. It came out easily. Claire reached inside the hole and pulled out a small leather book.

Claire glanced down at the yard, though she knew it was empty and that no one could have seen her behind the chimney anyway. She sat down on the roof, leaned back against the railing, pulled a pen from the pocket of her jeans, and opened the book to the next empty page.

She put the date and the time at the top of the page. Then the temperature and the wind's speed and direction.

Diary:

There appears to be a front moving in from the west-southwest. But the barometer is only dropping slowly, so we're porbably not in for a storm.

On the personal front

She sighed and looked down at the challenging blank page. This was a momentous entry, probably an ending to a long chapter in her life.

I had a talk with Benjamin just a few minutes ago. I think I've thrown him off for now. I told him I still didn't remember anything. I don't know if he believed me or not. He is pretty good at hiding his true feelings. I've never even really known how he feels about me.

Something we have in common, maybe, an ability to keep our private lives private.

Maybe that's why I've been thinking more about Jake lately. Maybe because he wouldn't be constantly trying to dig below the surface like Benjamin. My relationship with Benjamin can be exhausting at times.

"But that's not the real problem," Claire said aloud. "It's not just about whether I end it with Benjamin or not." As sad as that thought made her, it was only part of the problem.

But that's not the real problem. The real problem is, what do I do now that I remember what happened that night? Do I tell the truth, or do I keep up the lie?

If I keep lying, it hurts Lucas. And I guess it hurts Zoey, too, because I'm pretty sure she's falling for Lucas. She thinks she's keeping it secret, and I guess she is from Jake, but Jake's just a guy and not the most perceptive guy on earth, either.

If I tell the truth, I hurt myself. People would be convinced I'd been lying all along. They'd be sure I deliberately let Lucas go to jail to protect me.

And there's Dad. He says what he did, offering Lucas's father help with his business, would look like a bribe, or perjury or whatever.

So I can either hurt Lucas and Zoey, or I can hurt my dad and me.

I want to do what's right.

She closed the book. "What's right," she sneered. She knew perfectly well what was right. The right thing was to tell the truth. But was it the smart thing to do? After all, Lucas had already suffered, and there wasn't anything she could do about that. How would it help for her to suffer as well, and maybe drag her father into it too? In his business, reputation was important.

She opened the book.

But what is right? Is Zoey's little flirtation with Lucas really more important than my own father? Besides, Lucas came out of it okay. Maybe he's got some problems with his family—who doesn't? And it's not like Lucas was ever a plaster saint.

If I keep quiet, everyone survives okay. The only real trouble comes if I open my big month.

She closed the book and stood up. It wasn't a pleasant decision, but it was the smart decision, she told herself. She hid the diary again, replacing the brick.

Which left only the question of Benjamin.

Benjamin would have to go. He was too hard to deceive, too dangerous to have around. The realization gave her a sharp stab of pain. Benjamin had been part of her life for a long time. He was so much like her in many ways: private, aloof, independent, difficult, challenging.

Relentless when he wanted something. And he wanted the truth.

When she thought of Jake, the whole picture changed. Being with him would be so easy. And she had always been attracted to him. It wasn't like this was a sudden decision, not really. She'd thought of him often. Sooner or later Zoey would drop Jake. And then Claire could pick him up.

Her lies would go on unchallenged and everyone would be happy. Except, of course, for Benjamin.

Nina

Okay, picture me in fifth grade. Braces, hair from hell, clothes from the Miss Young Dork collection, zero buffers, permanent nose zit. Such a dweeb even I didn't want to hang out with me.

Still, there was this guy named Sketch. Really, I wouldn't make that up; his mom was an artist. He had a brother named Canvas. Anyway, I was in major love with Sketch, who was in sixth grade but was held back in my math class. I drew little hearts on my notebook with "Sketch and Nina" inside. I held imaginary conversations wherein I would try out lines like, "Meet my boyfriend, Sketch," or "Allow me to introduce my husband, Sketch."

Often I would become distracted and start coming up with sentences like, "This is Sketch, he's a bit of a lech, but he's fetched a job as a sketch artist in Saskatchewan."

But to get back to the point, which is my pathetic love life. Sketch seemed somewhat unaware of my love for him. In fact, he seemed somewhat unaware that I was alive. So I decided to come up with a foolproof plan to make him love me. It had five steps:

1. Try to sit next to him at lunch.
2. Let him copy off my math tests.

3. Always smile at him but don't show braces.

4. Try to run into him at the mall.

5. Get Claire to find out if he likes me.

I didn't have much success with steps one through four. But five worked beautifully. Claire agreed to find out if he liked me.

He didn't.

He did, however, like Claire, who was his same age and had no braces, no zits, perfect hair, and the Grand Tetons.

All of which taught me one very important thing. I should have come straight out with it and told Sketch how I felt.

It probably wouldn't have worked any better, but at least he wouldn't have ended up going out with my sister.

THREE

"WAIT A MINUTE," AISHA GRAY said. "You had Lucas in the closet."

"Yes."

"And Jake in your room," Nina said, giving Aisha a sly look. She shook her head and took a drag on the never-lit cigarette stuck in the corner of her mouth. "And here Aisha and I don't have even *one* boyfriend between us."

"It wasn't a moment to be proud of," Zoey said darkly.

They were standing together at the stern railing of the *Minnow*, the ferry that ran from the islands, Chatham, Allworthy, and Penobscot, to the mainland city of Weymouth, where all the island kids of high school age attended school. It was a gray, overcast, chilly morning, too chilly for the second week of September, but then, Maine could grow cold without warning.

Zoey looked over her shoulder at the rest of their friends. Claire sat reading her history book, her long, glossy black hair lifting in the breeze. Benjamin sat beside her, tilting his head to better hear the cries of the gulls floating along in the air beside the ferry. He smiled as a wisp of Claire's hair floated across his face.

To their right, up in the front corner of the open deck, sat Jake, staring stonily ahead, arms spread across the bench back, feet propped on the railing.

Lucas was in the far-left corner reading a book, occasionally combing his hair back with his fingers.

Zoey shook her head and sighed.

"Yeah, things have changed," Nina said, as though Zoey had spoken aloud. "Used to be we all sat together, more or less."

"The good old days of last week," Aisha said.

Zoey bit her lip. Aisha did not approve of her decision to be with Lucas. She thought Zoey should be able to control her romantic impulses. Aisha was taller and thinner than either Zoey or Nina, with an explosion of long, springy hair pulled back from her skeptical, high-cheekboned face. She used her extra inch of height to look down, arms crossed over her chest, shaking her head at Zoey's folly.

"And you haven't even told Jake yet," Aisha added in a low whisper. "You need to tell him, Zoey. It's only fair. You should have told him already."

"I'm going to go sit down," Nina said.

"No," Zoey said, grabbing her friend's arm. "You guys have to stay here with me. If we sit down, I'll have to either sit with

Jake, which will hurt Lucas's feelings, or else sit with Lucas."

"Which will start World War III," Nina said.

"If we just stand here and look like we're talking about girl stuff, neither of them will care."

"Girl stuff?" Nina turned the phrase over. "Girl stuff? You mean like we should be discussing our favorite brand of tampon or something?"

"Or we could all just huddle together and giggle," Aisha suggested acerbically.

Zoey rolled her eyes. "Look, we can talk about peace in the Middle East if you want, just so long as neither guy thinks I'm avoiding him."

"See, this is what I said would happen when you started fooling around, Zoey," Aisha said. "Now Nina and I are dragged into it and everyone is lying to everyone else."

"You don't have to lie," Zoey said, stung by Aisha's words.

"You're lying to Jake, Nina and I are lying to Jake and Claire, Benjamin knows, so he's obviously lying to Claire, too. Lucas is lying by pretending he doesn't care about you. I mean, jeez, Zoey. A week ago we were all close friends who more or less told each other the truth."

"More or less," Nina added.

"Look, I'll tell Jake soon," Zoey said. "I promise."

"Like that will fix everything right up," Aisha muttered.

"You're going to dump a guy you've been going with forever so you can be with a guy who, according to you, is about to get shipped out of town by his own father. People get led around by their hormones, and this is what happens."

"So," Nina said brightly, "let's talk about tampons."

"Aisha, just because you have no romance in your soul doesn't mean that those of us who do are idiots," Zoey said defensively. Too much of what Aisha was saying was hitting home.

"But you have *two* romances in your soul at the same time," Nina pointed out.

Zoey hung her head. They were right. She was putting her friends in an awkward position. She was forcing them to choose between her, on the one hand, and Jake and Claire on the other. And worse than that, she was basically making a fool out of Jake behind his back. Plus forcing Lucas to deny his own feelings.

She raised her head. "Please, you guys, I know this is bogus, but I need your help. Just until I tell Jake, which I promise will be soon."

"Look," Nina said, nudging Aisha. "She's got a tear in her eye. Right there in the corner."

"That is so manipulative," Aisha said, shaking her head. "I'll bet she can't squeeze it out."

"I wish I could do that," Nina said. "The ability to generate tears is very useful."

"Yeah, it works even on me," Aisha admitted. "All right, Zoey, cut it out. I'm not mad at you, I'm just saying you should focus more on controlling your emotions."

Zoey smiled and wiped away the tear. "You know something, Eesh? You talk tough, but someday you're going to fall so hard over some guy it's going to be pathetic to watch."

"Not me," Aisha said confidently.

"It's Jake," Nina hissed. "He's coming over, and Lucas is watching him."

Zoey kept her gaze focused away. She made quick eye contact with Nina and Aisha. Aisha nodded imperceptibly.

"No, no, I really prefer the plastic applicator," Aisha said.

"But they're not biodegradable," Zoey argued loudly.

"Hey," Nina nearly shouted. "What's the matter with good, old-fashioned Kotex? I'm talking maxi-pads, big, thick, like walking around with a mattress down your panties."

From the corner of her eye Zoey saw Jake freeze. His lip curled; he made a disgusted face and veered away.

"Gets 'em every time," Zoey said. "Now, getting back to peace in the Middle East . . ."

Jake stopped at midcourt, dribbling the basketball and looking over the defenders. Well, well, he was in luck. Lucas was right between him and the basket.

"Move the ball, McRoyan!" Coach Zane yelled from the sidelines. This was just regular gym class, but Coach Zane also coached the varsity basketball team, and he had been trying for some time to get Jake to abandon football in favor of basketball.

Jake saw one of his teammates running a pattern that would set him up perfectly for a pass, but Jake didn't want to pass. He wanted to take the ball to the net himself. And he wanted to take it right through Lucas Cabral.

He made his move, plowing forward, big, unstoppable, aiming straight for Lucas. Jake dropped his shoulder, football style, and hit Lucas squarely in the chest. Lucas was knocked back, falling spread-eagle toward the hardwood floor.

But as Lucas fell, his foot lashed out. Probably just an accident, Jake realized; still, it landed with deadly accuracy. Jake took two more steps before the pain hit him. He let the ball roll free and doubled over, clutching at himself.

"Foul!" Coach Zane yelled. "Come on, McRoyan, this ain't football. You can't just hit a man." He came running over and looked down at Jake, now on his knees. "You all right? Serves you right, taking a cheap shot. Okay, that's the period, hit the showers," he said as Jake got to his feet.

The thirty guys in the class all ran for the showers, stripping off sweaty shirts and shorts the minute they were inside.

"You gonna live, Jake?" Lars Ehrlich asked, grinning as he twirled the combination to his gym locker.

Jake gave him a sour look. "I wish I knew whether that was deliberate," Jake said, glaring across the room at Lucas, who had slipped under the shower head and was lathering a bar of soap.

Jake removed the rest of his gym clothes, stuffed them loosely in the bottom of his locker, and headed for the shower himself. Lucas moved away as he approached.

Jake snorted. Probably afraid Jake was going to start something. But no, he'd promised Zoey he wouldn't go after Lucas, no matter how sick it made him to have to be in the same room with the guy.

"Don't worry, killer," Jake said. "I'm not going to hurt you."

Everyone in the shower room instantly shut up and all eyes turned toward Lucas. Lucas stuck his head under the spray and said nothing.

"Looks to me like he's ignoring you," Lars said.

Jake watched Lucas closely. It was possible that kick had been deliberate, which meant Lucas could be fast and accurate, even while falling. Still, Jake had thirty or forty pounds on him.

"He's afraid if he tries to say anything, he'll burst out crying," Jake said dismissively.

Lucas squeezed the water out of his hair and met Jake's eye. He seemed to be debating with himself, then shrugged and shook his head. He walked out of the shower, picked up his towel, and slung it over his shoulder.

After he'd dressed he came back toward Jake and planted himself squarely, feet wide apart, in front of Jake's locker.

Jake finished buttoning his shirt and faced him, hands loose at his sides.

"I've really been hoping we wouldn't have to go through this, Jake," Lucas said in a low voice. "But you're the kind of guy who just won't let things go."

"Things? You mean like I should just get over the fact that you killed my brother?"

"I'll say this once. There were three of us in that car, and all three of us were drunk. I pleaded guilty and I've done my time, and it's over."

Jake felt anger boiling up inside him. "I promised someone I wouldn't beat the crap out of you," he said through gritted teeth.

"Don't let that stop you," Lucas said.

Jake clenched his fist, but then, with an effort, he relaxed. He smiled coldly. "You're not worth it. You're gone, anyway. Your own father is kicking you out."

"Zoey told you that?" Lucas demanded sharply.

It took several seconds for the implication of Lucas's question to sink in. *Zoey told you that*? Zoey?

"Your father let my dad know he was shipping you off," Jake explained in a halting, disconnected voice. His brow was deeply furrowed, but his eyes unfocused. "What was that about Zoey?"

"Nothing," Lucas said, but his eyes betrayed the truth.

"You've been talking to Zoey?"

"Who I talk to is none of your business."

"You son of a bitch."

"She's not your property, Jake."

Jake swung fast, but wild. Lucas caught his fist against his right arm, then drove his own fist into Jake's neck. Jake gasped for air, choking, and a second blow caught him in the stomach, doubling him over. He sank to his knees on the tile. Lucas stood over him, a cold look in his eyes. Jake reached to grab him, but Lucas backed away, out of range.

"I gave you one free shot last week on the ferry," Lucas said. "Don't try me again, Jake. I've spent the last two years with a very unfriendly crowd, learning how to take care of myself. Don't push me too far." He turned and walked out the door.

Jake got up, feeling humiliated and furious.

"He sucker-punched you," Brian McNeil said.

"You'll get him next time," Lars said sympathetically.

Jake nodded and leaned his head against his locker. His stomach hurt, but he would survive that. Worse by far was the growing realization of what was happening. Zoey wasn't just *talking* to Lucas.

She's not your property, Jake, Lucas had said.

Impossible. Could Zoey actually be interested in Lucas? Was she actually seeing Lucas behind his back? His worst enemy? No, that was impossible. Not Zoey. She wouldn't do that to him. He was imagining things.

With numb, unfeeling hands he closed his locker. The room was emptying as guys went off to their next classes.

Zoey and Lucas? He had to know. Even the faint suspicion was too much to bear. He had to know.

FOUR

"OH, BROWN GOO ON WHITE bread, my favorite," Nina said, looking down at her lunch tray.

"I think it's turkey," Zoey said doubtfully. "You can tell by the peas. Turkey always comes with peas. If it was Salisbury steak, there would be gray beans."

"Where is Salisbury, anyway, and why do they force their steaks on the rest of the world?" Aisha demanded.

"Salisbury's not far from Turkey," Nina said. "And you two are supposed to be seniors. Pay attention during geography, and you'd know that Turkey is separated from Salisbury by Greece."

"Greece," Zoey groaned. "That's bad."

"Yes, and Frankfurt and Hamburg aren't in Germany, either," Nina said, grinning mischievously. "Nope. They're in Ireland."

"Ireland? I don't get it," Zoey said.

"Actually, in County *Mayo,* Ireland. Mayo. Get it?"

"Now I get it," Zoey said darkly. "I wish I hadn't."

"She gets it, she just doesn't relish it," Aisha added.

"Please stop," Zoey said politely. "I'm armed with red Jell-O. Don't make me use it."

They paid for their lunches and headed toward a vacant table. Zoey noticed Claire coming out of the other lunch line. "Hey, Claire," Zoey said quickly before Nina could poke her in the ribs, "would you like to join us in our sumptuous feast?"

"Sure," Claire said unenthusiastically. It was an unwritten rule between Nina and Claire that they spent as little time near each other as possible while they were at school. But Zoey had felt there was some undefined tension between herself and Claire. It had been evident on the ferry ride that morning. And Aisha's warning about the group becoming divided had hit home with Zoey. The island kids had always hung together.

She caught sight of Lucas, sitting several tables away at a discreet distance. He looked even more solemn and withdrawn than usual.

"Are you going to eat that?" Claire asked Nina as they sat down. "I thought you weren't eating anything that involved animal flesh."

Nina shrugged. "I'm starting with cows and pigs. I'll work my way down to chickens and turkeys."

"How about fish?" Aisha asked.

"That's stage three," Nina said.

"Stage four is you starve to death," Claire said. "You know, this vegetarian thing is—"

"Uh-oh," Aisha murmured.

Zoey felt a hard tap on her shoulder and turned around in annoyance. Jake stood over her, looking huge, his face distorted by cold anger.

"Hi, Jake," Zoey said.

"I need to talk to you," Jake said in a low, dangerous voice.

"Um, okay, pull up a chair," Zoey said.

"Alone. Now."

"Jake, I'm eating—" She gestured vaguely toward her tray.

"I don't give a damn about your food," Jake snapped. "I want to know what's going on, Zoey."

Zoey felt the hush that was falling over the lunchroom, a ripple of whispers and strained attention. Nina and Aisha's eyes were aimed down at the table. Claire watched with calm detachment, her dark-in-dark eyes curious and alert.

"What are you talking about?" Zoey asked, buying precious time.

"You and Lucas," Jake said. "I'm talking about you and Lucas. You and that dirtbag."

Zoey felt her throat clenching up. Everyone was staring at her. She glanced toward Lucas and met his eye. He was grim, waiting for her to answer.

She hung her head and answered in a whisper. "Jake, I was going to tell you—"

Jake interrupted with a string of expletives, slamming his fist onto the table. He started to walk away but instantly turned back. Zoey flinched. Lucas started to rise from his seat.

"Why?" Jake demanded. His eyes were wide, but no longer with rage. Now they pleaded, and Zoey felt like she'd been stabbed in the heart. "Why would you do this to me?"

"Jake—" she began desperately.

"I love you, Zo. We've been together since . . . forever, it seems like. I thought you loved me, too."

"I . . . I do. I mean, I did." The final word came out in a barely audible whisper. "I didn't mean to hurt you."

"Didn't mean—" He smiled a desolate, desperate smile, and to Zoey's horror she saw that there were tears in his eyes. He tried to speak, but the words wouldn't come out. He stood there, his big body seeming strangely shrunken and sagging.

"Jake," Zoey said. But there was nothing else for her to say.

He looked at her hopefully, as if she might still change her mind and tell him it was all just a terrible joke. At last he turned away.

A thundering silence followed him as he strode from the room. Then a nervous laugh from somewhere in the crowd. And whispers that rapidly grew in volume.

Lucas sat with his head in his hands, looking nearly as unhappy as Jake. Even Nina looked at Zoey with accusing eyes.

"I didn't think . . ." Zoey began helplessly. "I never wanted to hurt him. I loved him. I still do, it's just . . ." Zoey bit her knuckles. Nothing like this had ever happened to her. People were staring at her, no doubt thinking she was the bitch of all time. Then another thought occurred to her. "How did he find out? Did one of you tell him?"

Aisha gave her a dirty look. "Don't take it out on us, Zoey. As of right now, the three of us are the only friends you've got."

Claire stood up slowly, lifting her tray. "Make that two."

Dear Jake:

I'm writing you this letter because the truth is, I'm afraid to try to talk to you. Not that I'm saying I'm afraid of you, because of course I'm not.

Dear Jake:

I know this probably seems strange, me writing you this letter. I'm going to ask Nina or Aisha to bring it to you because I want you to get it right away. I just want to try to explain, and I know that if I went over and saw you right now that we'd end up arguing. I don't blame you for hating me.

Dear Jake:

Look, I'm sorry about the way things worked out, but I can't help how I feel, any more than you can help how you feel. Which I guess is pretty mad right now. I didn't deliberately try to humiliate you.

Dear Jake:

First of all, I am so sorry. So very sorry. Lucas explained to me what happened.

Dear Jake:

First of all, I'm sorry about how things turned out. I was a thoughtless jerk not to let you know in some kinder way. I am ashamed of myself and I probably feel as bad about this as you do. Honestly, I don't think I've ever felt so down and depressed.

You and I were together a long, long time, Jake, and I hope you know I'll always love you.

Dear Jake:

First of all, I'm sorry about how things turned out. I was a thoughtless jerk not to let you know in some kinder way. I am ashamed of myself and I probably feel as bad about this as you do. Honestly, I don't think I've ever felt so down and depressed.

You and I were together a long, long time, Jake, and I hope you know I'll always care for you as a close friend. You and I have done so much together and been so much to each other. I also hope that someday you will forgive me for hurting you.

If I could have somehow stopped feeling for Lucas the way I

Dear Jake:

I've tried to write this letter about ten times and it keeps coming out wrong. I keep trying to find some way to ask you to forgive me. But I guess that's really just selfish of me. You're mad at me and I deserve it. I should have been more up-front. I know it still would have hurt you, but the way I handled it makes me feel like scum. Sorry.

You know me well enough after all the time we've spent together that you can probably guess I'm crying as I write this. I hate hurting people, especially a person I will always, always care about.

Maybe I'm just losing my mind. I know I didn't plan for any of this to happen. Now that it has happened, I can't stand thinking of the pain I've caused you. It's tearing me up inside.

I don't want you to hate me, and I also don't want you to hate Lucas. I want somehow for everything to be all right and back to normal, with all of us being friends, friends like we were a long, long time ago, before everything happened.

I'm writing this because I know if I call you on the phone, I'll just end up blubbering. And I'm asking Nina or Aisha to take it over to you right away so that at least you'll know I'm thinking about you, and caring about you and wishing there were some way for me to make the pain go away.

I guess that's all I have to say, Jake. Except that I really did love you all those times I said I did. And I really am sorry that I changed.

Your friend,

Zoey

Zoey grabbed a tissue from the box of Puffs on her desk and pressed it against her streaming eyes. Nina leaned over her shoulder and read the letter silently.

"I feel like crap," Zoey said through the tissue.

"It's a good letter," Nina said thoughtfully. Zoey felt the pressure of Nina's hand on her shoulder. Then Nina picked up the letter and handed it to Aisha, who was sitting on Zoey's bed.

Aisha read it over and handed it back to Nina. "It's nice, Zoey. It's about all you can do, except for dumping Lucas real fast and going back to Jake."

"I can't do that," Zoey said, wiping her eyes dry with a

second tissue. "I think I'm really in love with Lucas."

Aisha seemed to be biting her tongue.

"I know what you're going to say, Eesh," Zoey said, breathing deep to clear away the sobs. "I thought I was in love with Jake, too."

"Well, you have to admit, you are a little unreliable on this," Aisha said. "What is different about the way you feel with Lucas? I mean, is it just exactly like Jake, only ten percent more or something?"

Zoey shrugged. "I don't know. I always really liked Jake. I always thought he was really good looking and sexy."

Nina shivered and made a face. "Don't mention the words sexy and Jake in the same sentence."

"I think he's sexy," Aisha said. "I'd go along with that. Maybe a good solid eight on a scale of ten."

"It's not that I suddenly didn't like Jake anymore," Zoey said. "It's just that all of a sudden there was Lucas. And it was like . . . " She searched her mind for a comparison. "It was like, you know, how at night the moon can seem amazingly bright, but then you get days when the moon is still up in the sky, but the sun is up, too? And then the moon looks pale and the sun looks so incredibly bright?"

"So Jake is the moon and Lucas is the sun," Nina said dryly. "Zoey, have you been working on your romance novel again?"

"Which one of us is supposed to deliver this letter to Jake?" Aisha asked unenthusiastically.

"I don't want to do it," Nina said.

"You think *I* do?" Aisha asked.

"I'll flip you for it," Nina said, pulling a quarter from her pocket.

"I hope you know what you're doing, Zoey," Aisha said.

"I do," Zoey said, trying to sound confident. "I've learned my lesson. I want to get it all out in the open. That's the only way things will ever get better."

"I meant that I hope you know what you're doing, choosing Lucas over Jake," Aisha said.

"I know what I feel in my heart," Zoey said softly, but with conviction.

"Call it," Nina said, tossing the coin in the air.

Claire

Here's something that Zoey never found out. I had already kissed Jake, long before the two of them broke up.

It was just last year, Christmas vacation. Zoey and Benjamin had gone off with their parents to stay with their grandparents for a week. While they were gone, we got about a foot of new snow. I happened to run into Jake, who was roaring around the beach on a snowmobile his dad had just bought. Being Jake, he didn't offer me a ride because, after all, what would Zoey think if she found out?

So I asked him, and he couldn't really refuse. We raced on down along the beach, half a mile or more, kicking up a big plume of snow while the surf crashed just beside us, me holding on to him from behind.

He stopped after a while and said something about how cold it was. He said his lips were frozen stiff. So I said I'd have to do something about that.

The kiss lasted maybe one second. No big deal to me, just a whim, but you would have thought Jake had been caught selling crack to five-year-olds inside a church. He made me swear ten times I wouldn't ever tell Zoey. It could never happen again, he was faithful, he was in love with Zoey, blah, blah, blah.

I was a little insulted, to be honest. But since then I've noticed that he can't always keep his eyes off me. When I'm in a bathing suit or tight shorts or something, he'll always look, and then get all guilty and turn red and immediately start paying complete attention to Zoey.

It's kind of fun to watch. One harmless little kiss, but for him it's this big moral dilemma. That's Jake. The kind of guy who thinks he's committed a felony just because he likes to look at a pretty girl.

Faithful, honest, straight-arrow Jake. You can read him like a book, and you always know just where he stands.

Kind of naive, even a little ridiculous. But then again, after a Lucas and a Benjamin, there are times when you want a Jake.

FIVE

AS ZOEY WAS SIGNING THE letter, Claire was riding her bike the eight blocks from her house to Jake's. She stuck to the shore along the rocks, going past the dock and along the beach before turning into the steep driveway. It was too steep to ride her bike without getting hot and sweaty, so she leaned it against the McRoyans' mailbox and walked the rest of the way to the house.

She knocked at the front door and stood there on the porch, swatting away the flies that buzzed around the porch light. There was no answer, and when Claire looked, she noticed that there were no lights on inside.

She walked around the house, following the path past the garbage cans to the lower level where Jake's basement room opened onto the patio. Light spilled from his room.

"Claire?"

Nina's voice. She had come from the other direction, appearing through the bushes.

"What are you doing here?" Claire asked.

Nina grabbed her and pulled her away, out of the pool of light from Jake's room. "What am *I* doing here? What are *you* doing here?"

"I'm stopping by to see Jake," Claire said calmly.

"You're stopping by to see Jake," Nina echoed incredulously. "Since when do you stop by to see Jake?"

"Since he asked for my history notes."

"Puh-leeze."

"You know, I don't have to check with you before I stop off and see a friend," Claire said icily. "But since you've poked your nose into *my* business, how about if you tell me why you're here?"

"Just passing by," Nina said.

But Claire noticed a white envelope stuck in the waistband of her sister's shorts. "What's that?"

"Nothing," Nina said instantly.

Claire laughed. Nina never had learned the knack of lying very well. "Okay, you don't have to tell me. But I'll bet it's something from Zoey."

Nina's eyes flared in unwilling acknowledgment.

"What, some mushy letter? Is she apologizing for making him look pathetic in front of the whole student body?"

"Does Benjamin know you're *visiting* Jake in his bedroom at night?" Nina asked sharply.

"I don't think so," Claire said.

"I bet he would be a little suspicious if he did," Nina said.

Claire made a wry smile. "Benjamin is always suspicious of one thing or another." She started to walk away, but Nina held her back.

"Claire, this is pretty sleazy, don't you think? Even for you. I mean, I don't even know if Zoey and Jake have officially broken up yet. And I know you haven't officially broken up with Benjamin."

"I'm just stopping by to give Jake my history notes," Claire said flatly. "Besides, Nina, I know how happy you'd be if I did break up with Benjamin, so don't try throwing that in my face."

"What are you talking about?" Nina demanded, a little too shrilly.

"Give me a break. Benjamin's the one who's blind, I'm not. I know you're all hot for him." She walked away, relieved that Nina said nothing further to stop her.

Well, that had been a piece of unfortunate luck. Nina was sure to tell Zoey, and she might even work up the nerve to tell Benjamin.

On the other hand, so what? These were minor secrets, in the grand scheme of things. As long as she could keep the real secret from all of them, everything would be all right.

Jake sat on his bed, staring at a dusty cardboard box, and took a long swallow from the beer. It was lukewarm, from one of the cases his dad kept in a corner of the unfinished rec room for times when he had a bunch of people over for a barbecue.

Two empties lay crumpled in his trash basket. A third empty lay on its side on the floor.

He took the lid from the cardboard box and sneezed at the dust that rose from it. The box was marked JAKE'S JUNK in black Magic Marker. He turned it over, spilling the contents onto his comforter. A Red Sox pennant, from the time Wade and he drove all the way down to Boston to watch a game, just the two of them. Come to think of it, that had been the first time he'd ever had a whole beer. Wade had used his fake ID to buy them some. By the end of the game, it was Jake who'd had to drive all the way home, even though he was just fifteen and didn't have so much as a learner's permit.

Great day. The only time he'd gone to a ball game with Wade. Great day.

He drank some more of his beer, ignoring the sour taste, and opened a scrapbook. Newspaper clippings of Wade when he was the star full-back on the Weymouth High football team. A photo of the whole team together, Wade right at the front, looking cocky, as always. A ticket from Wade's junior prom. He was dead before his senior prom.

And the newspaper article about the accident, a sort of dividing line in the scrapbook. Before that article, most of the stuff was Wade's. After, it turned to pictures of Jake himself, standing with the whole team and looking cocky.

A ticket from his own junior prom. He had taken Zoey, of course.

He finished the fourth beer and fumbled on the floor for the next one, cracked it open, and grimaced as he swallowed.

Zoey, of course.

He didn't dance very well, couldn't seem to keep track of the rhythm, and anyway he looked like a big trained bear wearing a suit or tuxedo, but Zoey had never minded.

Well, maybe she had. Maybe that was it. Maybe she was tired of dancing with a big trained bear who couldn't keep the beat. Maybe that was it. Maybe.

There was the picture of them together in front of a snowman they'd made in the circle. They were both wrapped in parkas and hats and laughing out clouds of steam.

And there they were on Town Beach, the ferry in the background. He was lifting her up, holding her in his arms, and she was smiling and laughing. Of course, Ninny had taken the picture, so most of his head had been cut off.

He closed the book and rocked forward, not caring that tears were rolling down his cheeks. He couldn't look at any more pictures. He wasn't drunk enough yet to think about her. He might never be drunk enough.

It took several seconds for him to realize that someone was tapping at his sliding glass door.

Zoey. Only Zoey came this way, straight to the sliding glass door.

He got up and forced himself to walk slowly to the door. If she thought she could just come and apologize and right away he'd take her back . . . well, she should think again. He wasn't going to let her off the hook that easily.

He wiped his face and slid open the door, forming a cold, forbidding expression on his face.

"Hi, Jake."

He stared, wondering if the beer was distorting his vision. "Claire?" he said at last.

"Yes," she said. "I'm sorry I'm not Zoey."

"I'm not," he said.

"Can I come in? I knocked upstairs at the front door, but—"

"My folks and my sister are over in Weymouth at some movie."

Claire glanced at the pile of mementos on his bed. "I don't want to interrupt you if you're busy," she said.

"Just junk," Jake said. He swept it back into the box and dropped the box onto the floor. He looked around uncertainly. The only chair he had was over by his desk. But Claire solved the problem by sitting at the end of his bed. He sat at the head, crossing his legs.

"I just mostly stopped by to tell you how sorry I am about you and Zoey," Claire said.

Jake nodded. It was safer than trying to speak on the subject of Zoey. He found the last beer of the six-pack and held it out for her.

"No, thanks. I haven't been interested much in drinking since . . . you know, since the accident."

"Well, I never drink and drive," Jake said. "I'm not Lucas." The name made him crumple the can in his hand. Some of the beer spurted out of the top and he drank it before it could stain the bed.

"No, you're definitely not Lucas," Claire said.

He looked at her sharply.

Claire smiled. "I mean, you know how I feel about Lucas. I can't understand why his father hasn't gotten rid of him yet." She leaned closer and put her hand on his. "Are you okay?"

He took a deep breath and let it out slowly, trying to still the quaver in his voice. "Yeah, I'm fine. It was just kind of a surprise, was all."

He fell silent, slipping back down into darkness, memories of Zoey, always laughing or smiling. That's how he thought of her. Always smiling, always so small in his arms.

"It's tough," Claire said, interrupting his thoughts.

"I'm sorry, what?"

"I said, it's tough. Losing a girlfriend. Or a boyfriend," she added with a wry smile. "I mean, I've lost a few of those over the years. Remember that guy Rick I used to go out with in eighth grade?"

"Yeah. Whatever happened to old Rick? What happens to old boyfriends when their girlfriends dump them?"

"He started going out with Courtney Howard. They've been together ever since."

Jake smiled ruefully. "So what you're telling me is don't worry, there are other girls?"

"I thought I was being more subtle than that," Claire said.

Jake smiled, but the smile couldn't last. His face fell, and Claire's eyes grew sad and sympathetic. She moved closer, sitting beside him, and put her arm around his shoulders.

"It's okay if you want to be sad, Jake," she said softly. "I won't like you any less if you cry. And I would never tell anyone. I'm good at keeping secrets."

Jake let her pull his head against her shoulder, and his tears did run down onto the white cotton of her blouse.

For a long time they lay that way, silent. Jake felt waves of bitterness, waves of anger, followed in turn by terrible sadness, loneliness.

Except that in his loneliness he felt Claire's warmth beside him. Felt her arm around him. Even, to his embarrassment, felt the soft swell of her breasts.

Soon the tears dried up. *That's enough*, he told himself. *Enough tears for Zoey.* Right now Zoey was probably in Lucas's arms, kissing that creep. And he doubted very much that she was even sparing a moment's thought for him.

Strange what you learned about people. He would never have guessed that Zoey could be so cold-blooded.

And he would never have guessed that Claire could be so sympathetic.

"Thanks for coming over," he said, looking up into her dark eyes. The first words spoken in a long time.

"Anytime, Jake," she whispered.

Her mouth was so close to his that he could feel the words. So sweet to hear his name from her lips. So nice to be this close, to know that he wasn't really all alone.

Her lips were different from Zoey's. Fuller, softer, yet more forceful. It was she who kissed him, she who parted his lips with hers.

They had kissed once before, a long time ago, it seemed. Back then, he had been overwhelmed by feelings of guilt. Now it was as if all the life that had drained out of him came rushing back. And guilt wasn't even a memory.

SIX

AISHA HAD LEFT ZOEY'S HOUSE soon after Nina had gone to deliver the letter. She had fully intended to walk on up the hill and go home. But Zoey had put her in a bad mood. It was hard to be exposed at close range to all that weeping and sadness and regret without having it affect you at least a little. Frankly, Aisha resented it just a bit. Emotional people were always like that, always dumping their problems on you.

And it wasn't like anyone with half a brain couldn't see it coming. She'd told Zoey that getting involved with Lucas would lead to trouble. Why Zoey would decide to trade a nice guy like Jake for Lucas was totally beyond her. Lucas had been in one kind of trouble or another even before he decided to drive drunk, plow a car into a tree, and kill one of his few friends.

As she walked down from Zoey's toward the beach, Aisha passed Jake's house. Nina was probably still there, delivering Zoey's letter and waiting for Jake's reply. She considered waiting to see if Nina came out, but decided against it. It would just mean more of the same. More *then he said, then I said.*

The night was cool but not cold, with wispy clouds concealing, then revealing stars, one moment hiding the moon and plunging the road into darkness, the next moment letting the moon shine bright and turn the road silver. The surf to her right broke on the beach with comforting regularity, a crash followed by the rattle of small stones being sucked into the undertow, a lull, then a new crash.

Across the water Weymouth was going to sleep. Most of the office buildings were dark, except for a few scattered lights where cleaning crews were at work.

To her left, many of the buildings she passed were dark. The tourist season was officially over now that Labor Day was past, and the big Victorian bed-and-breakfasts were mostly empty. Aisha herself lived with her parents and brother in an inn up on the ridge, and they had only a few reservations for the next month or so, and none past October.

Only one car had passed as Aisha walked along, rattling and belching as most island cars did. The roads were never exactly busy, even in July. It was expensive to bring cars over on the ferry, and there wasn't really anywhere to go that couldn't be easily reached on foot. And with a crime rate that was in essence zero, the island was infinitely safer than Boston, her childhood home.

She heard the whir of the bicycle just seconds before it blew past.

The rider applied his brakes and stopped twenty yards down the road and waited, straddling the bike and leaning on the handlebars.

"Christopher, tell me that isn't you," Aisha said wearily.

"I don't know, Aisha, I hate to start lying this early in our relationship."

"What do you do, follow me? I mean, every time I turn around . . ." She came up even with him and kept walking. "And don't tell me it's fate."

He rode slowly, keeping pace beside her. He was tall, just around six feet, and muscular in a wiry way. Walking or riding he always gave the impression that he was leaning forward, as if he were being propelled, or as if there were something he had to see first, before anyone else could pass him.

"I think it's just that we're on a small island together," Christopher said. "We're bound to run into each other. It's the law of probabilities." He caught her eye and smiled. "I would never say it's fate. I know how you feel about fate. You don't like anything you don't control."

Aisha started to object, but when she thought it over, she had to admit Christopher was right. "It's not so much that I want to control everything, it's just that I don't want to be controlled.

Not by fate, not by some guy, not by school or parents or hormones or emotions. I make my own decisions." She nodded in satisfaction. That had sounded just right.

"Wow," Christopher said. "Sometimes your smugness absolutely amazes me. Takes my breath away. No one is that much in control. It doesn't work that way."

"It doesn't work any other way," Aisha said. "I just spent the evening with a certain friend who shall remain nameless, who doesn't even *try* to control herself. And she's been weeping and wailing since lunchtime today and will probably be weeping and wailing by lunch tomorrow. Plus, thanks to her, certain other people, who shall also remain nameless, are completely humiliated and depressed. Why? Because she believes in true romance, in true emotion, and she doesn't stop and ask herself, *Hmm, let's think this over and see where it's all likely to lead*. Even though certain of her friends, namely me, told her so all along."

Christopher laughed. "So the whole evening you've been sitting there with Zoey—who shall remain nameless—and having to resist the urge to jump around yelling *I told you so, I told you so*." His broad smile was just visible in the moon's glow. "That must have been very, very hard for you."

"It was hell," Aisha admitted, laughing good-naturedly.

Christopher stopped. "I live right there." He nodded toward

a sprawling Victorian with a tall turret on one end topped by a cone roof that gave it the air of a medieval castle.

"I've noticed the place before," Aisha said. "Cool turret."

"I have the top room in it," Christopher said. "It's small, but the landlady rents it to me cheap since I help out as the handyman."

"One of your ninety-four jobs."

"Just five jobs at the moment. I still cook at Zoey's folks' restaurant, but I'm getting fewer hours now that the season's over. The newspaper-delivery thing I still have, plus equipment manager and part-time soccer coach at your school, and the landscaping business. Still, if you add it all up, I'm only working about fifty hours a week. I'd like to do more, but jobs are scarce."

"Of course they're scarce," Aisha said. "You have them all."

"A man's got to eat and pay his rent. Not to mention saving for college. You want to come upstairs and see my palatial apartment?"

Aisha made a point of looking at her watch.

"Five minutes," Christopher said.

He parked his bike and led her inside a somewhat shabby foyer and up a set of stairs that creaked with every step. "My landlady usually rents out five different rooms," Christopher said as they climbed, "but right now there are only two other people staying here aside from her, so there's no one else on my floor."

They reached the top of the stairs and Christopher showed the way to his door, opening it onto an octagonal room with tall paned windows on three sides and a smaller window that opened onto the pitched roof. A single bed, neatly made, stuck out from one wall, and a desk was positioned by a window, giving him an excellent view of the beach and the waves during the day. Now it revealed a postcard-perfect view of Weymouth by night.

On one wall he had nailed up a dry marker board, where his work schedule was laid out on a red, blue, and green grid.

Instead of a closet, an iron pipe was suspended from the ceiling. On it hung white coats for cooking, overalls for landscaping, and shorts and rugby shirts for his work at the school. The room showed very little in the way of personal touches—no posters, no pictures, no mementos.

"It's very neat," Aisha said.

"It's a place to sleep," Christopher said.

"No pictures of your family or anything?" Aisha asked.

Christopher's face grew somber. "I like it uncluttered," he said flatly. Then he softened a little. "I don't get along all that well with my family."

"Who does?" Aisha joked.

"No, I mean we don't really communicate anymore. I

haven't seen them or spoken to them since I graduated four months ago and came up here."

Aisha realized she was on touchy ground. This was the first time she'd ever seen Christopher seem uncomfortable or unsure of himself. "I guess you'd like me to drop it, huh?"

Christopher shrugged. "It's no big deal. We're just the typical screwed-up inner-city family. No father. My mom's on welfare. She was on crack for a year, but she got off that and now she just drinks. My older sister's living with a creep who takes all her money." He made a derisive noise. "Not much like your family, Aisha."

Aisha was stunned. It seemed impossible that this arrogant, confident, often annoying guy should come from a background like that.

She had always been comfortably middle class. Not that her parents didn't sometimes have money problems. In fact, they acted like they'd go broke if Aisha bought one too many outfits or failed to finish the food on her plate.

"How did you end up here in Maine, on Chatham Island?" Aisha asked, looking at him with renewed curiosity.

"Baltimore's very hot in the summer," Christopher said wryly. "I decided if I was getting out of Baltimore, I was going to head north and at least stay cool."

"Wait till you check out February. You may change your

mind. Kids here compete to come up with new descriptions for the cold. Last year's most popular entry was *icicle enema.* And it's not an exaggeration." She tilted her head and stared at him thoughtfully.

"What?"

"I just didn't picture you coming out of the projects."

"Coming *out.* Staying out. Never going back," he said with quiet conviction. "I learned two things growing up there. One, life isn't fair. Some people are born with everything, others are born with nothing and it just gets worse—bad neighborhoods, bad schools, bad teachers, bad parents or no parents at all. Guns and drugs and violence all around. It's like some huge conspiracy to keep you from staying alive, let alone making anything of yourself. Most people fail. Most people don't have a chance."

Aisha looked at him thoughtfully. "And the second thing you learned?" she asked softly.

"I learned that I'm not *most people,*" he said, focusing an intense gaze on her. "I don't care how impossible it is to succeed. I like it that way. Impossible doesn't bother me. It's going to take more than that."

"I did sort of notice that you are persistent," Aisha said dryly.

"I make a point of getting what I want," he said, stepping closer.

"But there are *some* things even you can't get."

Christopher broke into a grin. "You could just give in now and save us both a lot of trouble."

"Oh, no, I don't think so, Christopher," Aisha said. "Besides, you just said you like it hard. And I have to get home." She turned and headed for the door.

"You do know we're going to keep running into each other," Christopher said.

"It can't be totally avoided," Aisha said.

"Tomorrow night is bargain night at the movies," Christopher said casually. "Two-dollar tickets. Do you ever go?"

"Occasionally," Aisha admitted.

"Then we might accidentally run into each other there, too."

Aisha hesitated, her hand on the doorknob. It wasn't like a commitment. It wasn't like he was asking her out on a date. Not really. He was just pointing out the obvious. It was a small island and a small world and people sometimes ran into each other. "Like I said, it can't be totally avoided."

"Hello, Passmore residence."

"Hi, it's me."

"Nina? What are you doing calling? Where are you? I thought you were coming straight back here after you gave Jake my letter."

"Well, it is kind of late."

"So what did he say?"

"Um, nothing."

"What do you mean, nothing?"

"I mean, I didn't give him the letter."

"Nina! You said you'd do it."

"I tried, only . . ."

"He wasn't there?"

"Um . . . I'm not sure if he was there."

"Look, Nina, just tell me whatever it is you're trying so hard not to tell me."

"I can't, Zoey. It will be like tattling or something. I mean, you're my best friend and all, but jeez, I can't be spying for you."

"Spying on who?"

"Anyone. It's not really up to me to tell you certain things. It's up to certain people to tell you certain things. I only called because I had to tell you that I couldn't deliver the letter. Otherwise I wouldn't have called at all."

"Nina. Just tell me why you didn't give Jake the letter."

"Zoey—"

"You said you don't know if he was home or not, which means whatever your reason is, it couldn't be because he wasn't home. Right?"

"Zoey—"

"Was someone else there? Is that it?"

"I have to go now."

"Who was it? It wasn't Benjamin; he's here. Obviously it wasn't me or you or Aisha because she left after you did. Are you telling me Claire was there?"

"I haven't said anything, I want the record to be clear on that. I never said—"

"There is no record, Nina. Claire was with him. Claire was over at Jake's house at night. That's it, isn't it? Well, it didn't take her long, did it?"

"She was probably just bringing him some homework or something."

"Right. Homework. That bitch, if she's going behind my brother's back, I'll kill her. That would really tear Benjamin apart, and the least she could do is break up with him first."

"You mean like you told Jake before you started letting Lucas stick his tongue down your throat?"

"Oh."

"Sorry, that was rotten. I shouldn't have said that, but I feel bad I told you about Jake and Claire. I don't handle guilt well. I lash out."

"No, I deserved it, Nina. It's true."

"Yeah, but best friends aren't supposed to tell you the truth about yourself."

"Do you think it was . . . I mean, do you think Jake and Claire . . ."

"I didn't stay and watch, Zoey. But she's still not home."

"Oh. Oh, God. I guess I'm getting a taste of my own medicine. It seems strange to think of Jake with some other girl. Jake with Claire. I guess it's not really any of my business, is it?"

"Are you going to tell Benjamin?"

"I don't think so. I mean, I don't want to look like I'm spying around."

"You mean like me."

"Sorry, Nina. I seem to be turning into a major hypocrite."

"Well, don't hang yourself, Zoey. You had to fall off your pedestal of perfection sooner or later. It's kind of reassuring, actually, seeing you screwing up your life for once."

"Thanks."

"I didn't think you were capable of causing this much trouble all by yourself."

"Thanks."

"I mean, it's like you're a one-woman disaster, with ripples of hostility and jealousy and distrust—"

"Okay, Nina, enough."

"—engulfing Jake and Benjamin and Claire and even me and Eesh."

"I'm so glad you called, Nina."

"Just remember, I never told you anything."

"I'll remember. At least now I'm not feeling so much pity for Jake."

"Funny, I'm feeling more. Poor *Jake*, being comforted by Claire."

"I wonder if he kissed her?"

"I doubt it, Zoey. Besides, you don't care, right?"

"Right."

"Okay, see you tomorrow."

"Bye, Nina."

Claire

12:42 a.m. Fifty-seven degrees. Wind at eight knots, gusting to twelve, out of the southwest. Barometer stable. The front that came through yesterday just dropped a little light rain and moved on. Tonight we have wispy clouds and a warm evening.

I went over to Jake's house tonight to see if he was okay. He was pretty depressed over Zoey, naturally. But by the time I left, I think he was feeling better.

We made out for a while. He's very different from Benjamin. Like he's not quite as in control and cool as Benjamin always is. It's funny, because Benjamin's only a year older than Jake, but in some ways he seems so much older. I don't think Benjamin would ever have let himself cry in front of me, or seem so out front about the way he feels. Benjamin's always a mystery, which is exactly what he says about me. Jake is different.

I really didn't expect to make out with Jake, not that I wasn't interested. But it happened so naturally. He was so sad over Zoey and also, I think, from remembering Wade.

I guess I'm partly responsible for what happened to Wade. I don't think I'm completely responsible because all three of us, Lucas and Wade and I, were drunk. Any one of us could have been driving.

Still, I guess I am at least partly responsible. So I think I did the right thing taking Jake's mind off at least some of his trouble.

I'll have to tell Benjamin soon. I don't want to do to him what Zoey did to Jake. I owe him a straightforward explanation.

Besides, Nina is incapable of keeping a secret, so it's bound to come out before long.

I've decided. I'll tell Benjamin it's over. Tomorrow, on the ferry, before he can find out some other way.

The one thing I can be sure of it that he won't be as devastated as Jake was.

It was strange with Jake. I was strange with Jake. I felt different. Like at that moment he was really glad I was there. Like he needed me. That's exactly what it was, I felt like Jake needed me.

Benjamin never needs anyone but Benjamin.

SEVEN

CLAIRE HELD HER BOOKS CLOSE to her chest like a shield and climbed the ramp onto the morning ferry. Lucas, Zoey, and Nina were already up on the top deck, standing at the back of the boat. Zoey looked down, refusing to meet Claire's eyes.

Turning, Claire could just see Jake trotting across the parking lot, followed closely by Aisha. Benjamin was seated toward the bow, alone.

Now would be the time, Claire told herself. Now, before Jake got on board.

She walked purposefully up to Benjamin, feeling at once determined and nervous. The nervousness bothered her. She had blown off guys before. Never quite this way, and never someone she'd been with as long as she'd been with Benjamin. But still, that was no reason for feeling almost sick.

She sat down on the bench beside Benjamin. "Hi, Benjamin," she said.

"Claire," he said in his neutral voice.

She sat there for a moment, trying to remember all the things she had memorized to say. Something about how people could change, and that was good, not bad. Something about how it wasn't like Benjamin would have a hard time finding another girl to go out with. And something else about how neither of them had ever said this was forever.

"Shouldn't you be sitting with Jake?" Benjamin asked.

Claire's mouth dropped open. "What . . . what do you mean?"

He laughed scornfully. "Come on, Claire, you can do better than that stuttering act. I've known for a long time that you were setting your sights on Jake."

"Nina told you?"

"No. Nina told Zoey, and Zoey's my sister. She loves me." He said the last words with a tinge of bitterness.

"Look, Benjamin," Claire said, flustered, "no one ever said it was going to last forever between us."

"That's what you practiced up to say?" Benjamin demanded, sending her a wry, deprecating look. "What else? We'll always be good friends? Come on, Claire. I'm disappointed in you. I expected some style."

"Sorry I didn't write better material. Maybe if I'd opened with a few jokes—"

"Jake will be an interesting change for you, Claire. You've

always needed to find a guy you could feel superior to." He smiled sadly. "That's what you thought you were getting with me."

"That's not true," Claire said.

"Sure it is. You're an isolated, lonely, superior person, Claire. You sit up there on your widow's walk and watch the clouds overhead and the little people down below. And they have to be below you, that's the important thing, because you can't tolerate an equal for long."

Claire realized her hands had formed fists. He was hurting her deliberately. He knew none of what he said was true, he was just saying it to get back at her for leaving him. "I think you're talking about yourself, Benjamin. You're the one who is isolated and . . . what was it? Lonely? Superior?"

Benjamin nodded. "Yeah, that's it. And it's why, sooner or later, you'll get bored with Jake and come back to me. Because we are so much alike, Claire, you and me."

Claire gathered her books and stood up. "You know, I was feeling bad about breaking up with you, but now I feel better. I'm glad I'm breaking up with you. You're a jerk, Benjamin. You are arrogant beyond belief."

Benjamin nodded. "Enjoy life with Jake, for as long as it lasts."

"It will last as long as I want it to," Claire snapped. "Just like our relationship."

"Or until Jake learns the truth."

Claire froze. "What are you talking about now?" she asked, loading her voice with weary disinterest.

"It's a small island, Claire. Too small for big secrets to be hidden for long."

"You think anyone will believe you if you go around saying I—" She glanced around and dropped her voice to a whisper. "You think you can go around telling people I'm responsible for the accident? No one's going to believe you. They'll just think you're trying to hurt me for dumping you."

"I would never tell," Benjamin said sincerely.

"There's nothing *to* tell," Claire snapped.

"Of course there is, Claire. You really think you can lie to me? I know you've remembered. Just a week ago the only people who knew the truth for sure were Lucas, and, I believe, your father."

Claire gasped involuntarily.

"In one week we've gone from two people knowing to four. Your father won't tell, and neither will I, because as strange as it feels to admit this, Claire, I really do love you. But what about Lucas? How long will he keep your secret?"

Claire glanced sharply at Lucas, standing at the far end of the boat, laughing at something Nina had said, his hand casually intertwined with Zoey's.

"You want my prediction?" Benjamin asked in a soft voice. "I think in the end you'll be the one to tell the truth."

"Me?" Claire asked incredulously. "If what you're saying *were* true, why would I do that?"

Benjamin shrugged and smiled his wry half smile. "Because in the end, as self-serving and ruthless as you are, Claire, when the line is drawn between right and wrong, I think you'll do the right thing."

"You okay?" Zoey asked her brother, sitting down beside him.

"Yeah," Benjamin said. His head was bowed forward. "It was okay. At least I deprived her of the pleasure of dumping me. Thanks to you."

"I don't think even Claire would have gotten much pleasure out of that," Zoey said. "I'm just starting to realize how painful it can be."

Claire and Jake had gone below to the lower deck, out of sight, but not out of Zoey's imagination. It bothered her, thinking of them together, thinking that Jake was probably comparing her to Claire. Claire was beautiful in a dark, sultry way that lots of guys seemed to like. She had great, long silky black hair and a disgustingly perfect body. Probably by now Jake was glad that Zoey was out of his life.

"Anyway, it's over," Benjamin said. "For now at least."

"You don't think it will last between Claire and Jake?" Zoey asked.

Benjamin grinned. "Two weeks." He stuck out his hand.

Zoey shook his hand. "I say six weeks, for ten bucks."

"Make it five bucks," Benjamin said. "I already bet a guy at school five bucks that you and Lucas wouldn't last three months."

Zoey punched her brother in the arm.

"Oh, fine, beat up on the poor, helpless blind guy," Benjamin said.

"Helpless, right," Zoey said. "Look, you want to go to a movie tonight? We could pick something with a good sound track."

"A movie on a Tuesday?"

Zoey sighed. "It's a long story. Aisha wants to go because she kind of told Christopher she would, only, if she shows up alone, it will look like she's going on a date with him. If there's a bunch of us, Aisha can act like it was just a coincidence. So Lucas and I are going, too."

"I won't even try to make sense out of that. But I don't think I should go. I'd be the fifth wheel, no date."

"Nina's coming, too," Zoey said.

"Nina's not exactly a date," Benjamin said. "But sure, why not?"

"See, that's perfect, because then you and Nina won't really be on a date so Aisha can say that she and Christopher weren't really on a date, they were just like you and Nina."

"Well, as long as it all makes sense to you."

"I've decided that where romance is concerned, nothing ever makes sense," Zoey said a little wistfully.

EIGHT

1. The major Axis powers in World War II were

   a. Germany, Japan, and France

   b. Japan, Russia, and England

   c. Germany, Japan, and Italy

   d. All of the above

Nina chewed her number-two pencil and looked up at the ceiling. All of the above? Possibly. But all six of them couldn't be *major* Axis powers, that seemed obvious. So, it wasn't *d*. That left three possibilities.

Benjamin would know. He'd know right off the top of his head. Of course, he was a senior, and she was only a junior. Maybe that was the problem. Maybe he just didn't want to date a junior. So she'd have to try to be extra sophisticated tonight at the movie. No dumb jokes, just the occasional witty observation. Fortunately, with Benjamin you didn't have to worry how you were dressed because there'd be no time to get back to the island and change.

But you did have to worry how you smelled. Extra-long shower in gym.

Axis was the bad guys, so it couldn't be England, right? Weren't they the good guys usually? Except during the Revolution. And the War of 1812.

Wait a minute. Germany was definitely involved, so that eliminated *b*, anyway. So, it was down to *a* and c. Either France or Italy was the third bad guy. France or Italy.

Would they be able to sit together? Zoey was sure to sit next to Lucas, but maybe Aisha wouldn't want to actually sit next to Christopher. Aisha might sit on one end, then Zoey and Lucas, then . . . either Christopher or Benjamin. If Nina got between the two of them, she was okay. But what if Christopher was on the far end and she ended up the last person, with Benjamin too far away?

France or Italy. Mussolini! Yes, Mussolini! It was all coming back now. Mussolini was one of the bad guys, and that was definitely an Italian name.

She filled the little circle beside *c*.

Zoey, Fourth Period

"In the second book in the series the author creates a

hurricane that we first see as a distant threat, far offshore from our mythical small beach town. At first we don't think it will be important, but because the author keeps coming back to it, reminding us that it is out there waiting, she . . . she does what? Um, Zoey?"

"Excuse me?"

"What do we call this technique?" the teacher asked. "Daydreaming again, Ms. Passmore? We call this foreshadowing. The author is foreshadowing."

Foreshadowing.

Zoey wrote in her notebook. Of course.

Foreshadowing. Like when you let the reader know that something is probably going to happen later in the book and that way the reader is anticipating it.

Like when one of your friends tells you you'd better be honest and let your old boyfriend know that you're breaking up. That would be foreshadowing. Or when you've noticed some girl who is always making eyes at your old boyfriend and when you do finally break up she rushes in to grab him without even waiting a day. That whole thing had been foreshadowed, but

Zoey was still surprised. Right now Jake and Claire were whispering to each other. They had changed seats so they could sit side by side. What did that foreshadow?

"It was foreshadowing by use of a metaphor. Claire? Metaphor, if you can stop whispering long enough to answer?"

"Metaphor is when you use one thing to describe another. Like, um, like the fog was a blanket, or the clouds marched with military precision."

She's just showing off for Jake.

Suddenly Claire cares about English.

Zoey wrote in her notebook.

"And what is the metaphor in this book, and what does it foreshadow?"

Great, Zoey thought, *I know the answer to that question, but no, the teacher has to jump me when I'm thinking about something else.*

Claire thought for a moment. "Well, I think the hurricane is a metaphor for the heroine's own passion. It's a metaphor for sexual desire. At first it was just out there, harmless, but as it came inexorably closer it became more powerful, more overwhelming, more dangerous, until the heroine was caught up and swept away by it."

Zoey rolled her eyes. Half the guys in the room were now

sitting there with their tongues hanging out. Including Jake. And it wasn't even the right answer. The metaphor in the book had nothing to do with sex.

"Absolutely correct," the teacher said.

AISHA, FIFTH PERIOD

"The square root of two *x* plus *zy* over *p* prime?" Aisha said.

"Correct, except that you have to remember your parentheses," the teacher said.

Aisha winced, then shook her head good-naturedly. "Of course. I meant to say that."

"It is important to be precise."

Aisha nodded in complete agreement. It was absolutely important to be precise. Leave out a variable or misplace a parentheses and the whole meaning of the equation would change.

"Has anyone solved this yet for *x*?" the teacher asked.

Aisha had, but she didn't want to be a show-off. When she saw that Louis Goldman was getting ready to raise his hand, though, hers shot up quickly. No one was a bigger show-off than Louis, and she couldn't let him sit there and gloat. Not after she'd forgotten her parentheses.

She should never have worn this top. It was cut too low. Not slutty low, just low enough that Christopher would probably think she'd worn it for him.

"Aisha?"

"*X* equals negative three."

The teacher winked. "I see you remembered the parentheses when you solved the equation. Correct. *X* equals negative three."

Of course it did, Aisha thought. All around her kids wrinkled their foreheads and went back to their notebooks. Obviously a lot of them had come up with the wrong answer, which was hard to understand. How could you look at a simple equation and not understand it? It was so logical.

If everything in the world were so logical, life would be . . . well, it would be logical. One plus one equals two. It never equals three. That was how everything should be.

Christopher was bound to think it was a date. Which meant he would probably try to put his arm around her. What should she do? She didn't want to make a big scene, but by the same token she didn't want anyone to misunderstand.

"Now, let's talk about parabolas," the teacher said.

Parabolas, good. She'd read ahead into this section, and it was really interesting stuff. In fact, she'd much rather be spending her evening understanding parabolas than going to a movie with Christopher.

No, not *with* Christopher. *Near* Christopher. Maybe not

even so near. They didn't even have to sit together. She could sit between Zoey and Nina. Or she could sit between Benjamin and Zoey, if Benjamin sat by his sister. Or . . .

Wait a minute. This could be an equation. Zoey would be *z,* Nina *n*, Benjamin *b* . . . It was a lot of variables, but with a little work she could have a strategy for every possible arrangement of points—or people—along a straight line, which was to say, a row of seats.

Nina, Sixth Period

Okay, Lucas goes down the aisle first, then Zoey. That leaves me, Benjamin, Aisha, and Christopher. So I say something funny like, Hey, all you couples should be together and leave us single people to ourselves. Of course, then Aisha gives me a death look, but she's trapped, right? She has to go, either her first or Christopher first, which means either way Benjamin and I end up sitting together.

What if it's Aisha first? Then naturally Christopher would go next, followed, hopefully, by Lucas and Zoey. Unless Benjamin jumps in there and ends up between Christopher and either Lucas or Zoey.

"—I'm sorry, would you repeat the question?" Nina snapped back just before the teacher came down the aisle, prepared to pull her famous rap-on-the-head wake-up.

"The question, which you would have heard the first time if you had been paying attention, Nina Geiger, was 'What do you call a verbal construction that involves a repetition of examples all making the same point?' And since I very much doubt that you know the—"

"That would be a tautology," Nina said.

The teacher's mouth hung open, and thirty heads turned to stare at Nina.

Nina grinned back. *Ha. Thought you had me there, didn't you?*

"Do you think you could offer an example?" the teacher asked poisonously.

"Yes, ma'am. Um, okay, like a funny example would be if I say that I love this class like a hungry baby loves his mother's nipple, like a . . . like a drunk loves a toilet with plenty of room to kneel, like a hooker loves a sailor on leave . . . Wait, one more—like a teenage guy loves his hand."

When the laughter died down, the teacher asked Nina if she knew the way to the principal's office. She did, and went off down the hall shaking her head.

Never should have gone for that fourth one, she chided herself. *I've always said three was the right number. When I tell this story to Benjamin tonight, I'll leave one out. After all, I'm going for sophisticated.*

• • •

"I'm not going to see a slasher movie," Zoey said firmly. "I don't see how people can find it entertaining to watch women being murdered. Sorry."

They stood in a little gaggle outside the multiplex at the Weymouth Mall. Night was falling as cars with their lights on cruised through the parking lot, trying for parking places near the entrance. The crowd outside was sparse. Tuesday was not a big movie night, at least not now that school was back in session.

"It isn't really a slasher movie, and besides, lots of people get killed, not *just* girls," Lucas countered without much conviction. "It's an action movie. It's what's-his-name, Dwayne, um, Statham or whatever. The karate guy."

"I don't like violent movies," Zoey said. Maybe it wasn't a major moral stand, Zoey thought, but she had decided after the last violent movie she'd seen, and the subsequent case of willies, that she was going to avoid similar stuff in the future.

"Me neither," Aisha agreed.

"Okay, there's seven other movies," Christopher pointed out.

"Six," Benjamin said. "Because I'm not sitting through another movie about animated characters who save the rain forest or whatever. Shrill, shrieking voices bitching about the environment and every now and then breaking into a bad, bad song. It makes my skin crawl."

"I agree with Benjamin," Nina said. "Crawling skin should be avoided."

"How about *My Sister's Boyfriend?"* Zoey suggested. "It's supposed to be hilarious."

"I heard it sucked," Nina said quickly. "I mean, who cares? A movie about some girl going out with her sister's boyfriend? I mean, so what, right?"

"Three down, five to go," Aisha noted, looking uncomfortable standing beside Christopher.

"The lawyer movie?" Benjamin suggested.

"I'll bet it won't be as good as the one with Tom Cruise," Aisha said.

"You know, he's really short," Lucas said. "About five one."

"And I heard he never takes a shower," Benjamin suggested.

"You guys are so pathetic," Zoey said, giving Lucas a playful shove.

"How about the Christian Bale movie?" Aisha said. "I like Christian Bale."

"I like him, too," Zoey agreed.

"I like him, but not when he was Batman," Lucas offered.

"I like Batman, but not when he was Christian Bale," Nina said. Then she seemed to glance nervously at Benjamin and smiled only when he laughed. What was with Nina tonight? Zoey wondered. She seemed jumpy or something.

They bought tickets and munchies and paraded into the theater, arguing about the relative merits of Milk Duds versus Raisinettes. When they came to an aisle toward the middle of the mostly empty theater, Lucas led the way with Zoey. They went down six seats and sat. Then Zoey realized no one was following.

"You guys don't like these seats?" Zoey asked.

"They're fine. After you, Aisha," Nina said.

"Well, are you coming next?" Aisha asked.

"What do you care?" Nina asked suspiciously.

"I don't, I was just wondering. Because I'll go sit down, but, you know, uh, who would go next?"

Zoey exchanged a mystified look with Lucas. "Excuse me, but is this really that great a challenge?" she asked Nina and Aisha.

"Well, how about if I go sit down next?" Christopher said.

"Fine," Aisha said. "Then you can go, Nina."

"What, and you'll sit on the aisle?" Nina asked Aisha.

"Excuse me, but *I* have to sit on the aisle," Benjamin said. "I have a hard time navigating over people's feet."

"Let's see," Zoey said, "Benjamin's on the aisle, Christopher's next to me; by my count that leaves two seats and, oh, surprise! Two of you. Or should I try to find my calculator?"

"After you, Eesh," Nina said, standing back.

"No, really, go ahead," Aisha said, stepping still farther back.

"Have those two finally lost their minds?" Zoey asked.

"Nah," Christopher said, contentedly munching his popcorn. "It's just Aisha doesn't want to sit next to me because then this would be a date."

"Oh," Zoey said. Of course. "Well, then, what's the matter with Nina?"

Christopher laughed. "I thought Nina was always like this."

"You have a point there," Zoey said

"The movie is starting," Lucas said.

"Aisha," Christopher said, raising his voice a little. "It's not a date, all right? You have amnesty. I will not count this as a date. I won't even try to put my arm around you."

Aisha's eyes blazed, but she stomped down the aisle, plopping next to Christopher. "That wasn't the problem. The problem was Nina wouldn't make up her mind."

Nina promptly took the next seat and Benjamin fumbled for and found the aisle seat.

"I have an idea," Lucas said brightly. "Let's all change seats again."

Lucas

This movie chews. Jeez, I thought it was supposed to be a comedy. My hand is numb. I've been holding Zoey's hand for forty minutes and now I can't feel my fingers. Plus, my hand is sweaty. I'd like to kiss her, but her brother is just a few seats away. I know he can't see, but still. Not to mention her friends. It would be like having an audience going, oh, that was a good one, or worse yet, ooh, bad lip noise. We give a thumbs-down, way down, for that kiss.

Zoey

It's so romantic, the way he's just happy to hold hands and doesn't have to try to feel me up like Jake always did. He's probably nervous with everyone here. Besides, the movie is so good, who wants to spend the whole time making out? Especially with Aisha sitting there, probably thinking what a backstabbing bitch I am making out with Lucas while Jake is probably home alone. Maybe I am a backstabbing bitch. Am I?

Christopher

Her thigh is touching mine. She must be aware of it. I mean, it's like all I'm aware of right now. Skin to skin. Thank God I wore shorts. Thank God she wore that top. Thank God the air conditioning in here is so cold. Afterward, if we go get something to eat, I have to remember to sit across from her. She's so beautiful. I'd sell my right arm to have her. As long as it could be removed painlessly. Although that might screw up working. Can't cook with one arm.

Aisha

If I pull my leg away, he'll think, Aha! I got to her. She got too excited, so she had to pull away. If I just leave it there, though, he might think I like it and I don't. I'll bet he can't believe I'm not paying more attention to him. Mr. Ego. He probably figured I'd be sitting here by now playing kissing face. Although he hasn't tried anything yet. And the movie is half over. Is it the Red Hots? Did they give me bad breath?

Nina

Maybe I could just kill myself. Maybe I could just wedge my head in the seat and suffocate. He leans over, we're in the dark, his lips actually almost brush my ear, I can feel his warm breath on my neck, and what do I do? I inhale a piece of popcorn. Very nice, very romantic. As he leans close I suck popcorn and say HKKKTH HHGHAGH. He's probably getting ready to say, I've just realized, Nina, how much I like being with you; you're so funny and yet sexy, so sophisticated and yet playful, unlike your sister, ice woman. And as he's getting ready to whisper this in my ear, I say HKKKTH HHGHAGH, a sound that will make him associate the name Nina with the word mucus for the rest of his life.

Benjamin

Wow, I wonder if this movie's any better if you can see? Probably not. I miss Claire. When I went to a movie with Claire, I didn't have to worry if the movie was any good. It makes me sick how much I miss her. It makes me sick thinking of her with Jake. Not that I blame Jake. Everyone says she's beautiful, and after getting dumped by my sister, Jake probably feels like going out with Claire erases his humiliation. Plus she's probably kissing him the way she used to kiss me. Maybe I should learn from Jake. Maybe I should find some girl to date, at least until Claire and Jake break up. But who? There's really only one girl I know who . . . But I guess she's going out with Christopher. Damn, I miss Claire. I wonder what she's doing right now?

NINE

CLAIRE SAT BESIDE JAKE ON the bench seat of his beat-up old pickup truck. A song was playing over the speakers as they drove at no more than five miles an hour, making their progress along the shoreline last. There was no traffic on the road, no one in a hurry, and even with the music playing Claire could hear the surf pounding, the crunch of loose sand and rocks under the truck's tires.

"What's this music?" Claire asked.

"Lyle Lovett. It's one of my dad's favorites, but I kind of like it."

Claire nodded. The songs struck her as melancholy, but then, maybe Jake was in a melancholy mood. They came to an intersection. The road going left led along the north shore of Big Bite Pond, the inlet that nearly cut Chatham Island in half, like a huge bite taken out of the middle of a croissant. Ahead, the road led out onto the Lip, a peninsula that was a favorite make-out location.

Jake hesitated.

"Let's drive out onto the Lip," Claire said. "I like it out there. It's so isolated."

They drove the few hundred yards of gravel road and stopped at the dead end. On the left was the placid, glass-smooth pond; just to their right, the more agitated water of the sea itself. Across the inlet was the Lower Lip, home to a colony of puffins, part of the nature preserve. The spit of land they were standing on was so narrow that thirty steps would take them from pond to sea.

Claire climbed out of the truck and looked across at the puffins, who were hopping around the rocks, purring and croaking and from time to time yelling out what sounded like *Hey, Al!* The tide was going out, sucking water through the inlet, and in the sky towering thunderheads floated over Weymouth, sending occasional jagged bolts of lightning down to the city. Directly overhead, the sky was still clear, with darkness falling fast and stars winking into sight, saying brief hellos before the storm clouds could advance and hide them.

"Hi, remember me?"

Claire saw Jake standing a few feet away, hands in his pockets. She must have been lost in thought for longer than she realized.

"Sorry, I guess I was spacing."

Jake looked out at the storm. "You think that's coming this way?"

Claire nodded. "It will be here in about twenty minutes, I would guess. But it's an isolated storm cell, and the wind is veering west, so it may just miss us."

Jake smiled. "Everyone thinks it's strange the way you're so interested in the weather."

"Weather is great," Claire said. "It's what keeps one day from being just like the next. And it's a system of incredible complexity, all sorts of forces interacting so that warm water five thousand miles away in the Pacific and a strong breeze in Africa all have an effect on what happens here." She fell silent, watching the storm. "On the other hand, maybe I am just strange."

"Is that what you're going to do in college? Study weather?"

"Meteorology, climatology, hydrography. Yes. And then later, while I'm working on my doctorate, I'm going to try to get an assignment in Antarctica. Antarctica is the home office of strange, unknown weather patterns."

"Cold, isn't it?" Jake asked lightly.

"That's what I hear," Claire said. "Ninety below zero in some places during the winter. Plus hurricane-force winds."

"Sounds nice," Jake said dryly. "But I guess it must be good to have something you want to do and really care about."

"Don't you?" Claire asked, turning now to face him.

"I like football, and I'll probably make the team in college, but you can't exactly count on making the NFL. It would be great, but you have to have some backup. You know, a *real* job."

"So what are you going to major in?"

He scrunched up his shoulders and made a face. "I have no idea. I thought about criminal justice. You know, become a cop."

She tilted her head and looked at him critically. "I could see you in the uniform."

"I can see you with ten layers of long johns and a fur hood and those big plastic boots, too," he said. "But I like you better this way."

Claire felt a wave of cooler air, a breeze pushed before the onrushing storm. "You just like me because you needed some-one after Zoey hurt you."

Instantly she regretted her words. Jake's eyes showed a wounded look, like she'd slapped him. She would have to try and be a little gentler. Jake wasn't like Benjamin, who seemed to be encased in unscratchable armor. She had gotten into the habit of being blunt and provocative with Benjamin. It was hard to remember just how vulnerable this big, powerful-looking guy could be.

"Maybe that's partly true," Jake said softly. "I mean, I was pretty torn up . . . but that's not why I like you, not really."

Claire took his right hand in both of hers. "I didn't mean that quite the way it sounded."

"I always liked you, as a friend, at least," Jake said. "And I always thought you were sexy." He gave her a deliberately comic leer.

Claire searched her memory for the words Benjamin had snapped at her. "Then you don't think I'm isolated, lonely, and superior?"

"I don't know if you're lonely," Jake said. "Are you?"

"Not when I'm with you," Claire answered.

"Then you'll have to be with me as much as possible," Jake said.

Claire raised his hand to her lips and kissed the hard, rough fingers. She looked at his face as his lowered eyes looked down at her. *Is this real?* Claire asked herself. *Is what I feel for him right this minute real? How could it be, when it all happened so quickly?*

Had she secretly cared for him for months and years? She couldn't remember feeling that way.

Or was this just two people brought together by coincidence, both of them needing someone at the same moment?

Zoey had torn Jake's heart out. Benjamin had forced her to remember a truth she did not want to face. Were they just two drowning, desperate people clinging to whoever came along?

She felt his lips on hers. It was pleasurable, certainly.

Different from Benjamin, different from her memories of Lucas. Certainly there was something wonderful in feeling Jake's powerful arms around her, pressing her to his hard chest, and his shoulders, hunched forward, completed the sense that he was engulfing her, surrounding her with protection.

Jake was hot where Benjamin was cool; straightforward where Benjamin was subtle; bigger, stronger, yet touchingly vulnerable, where Benjamin so often seemed at once frail in his blindness and yet somehow invulnerable.

There could not be a greater difference between the two of them. And she realized that she herself felt different here, with Jake, than she did with Benjamin. As if she were literally a different person with Jake.

A nicer person.

She broke away, feeling slightly annoyed for no reason. She glanced toward the mainland and saw that the storm was advancing fast across the channel, whipping up the water, turning the choppy waves white.

"Here it comes," she said.

"We'd better get back in the truck," he said.

She was about to say that she wanted to go home now. That she wanted to put on her poncho and sit up on her widow's walk alone where she could revel in the storm at close quarters. But she stopped herself. Jake wouldn't understand. He would think she was tired of him, bored, or somehow unhappy with his kisses.

It would hurt his feelings. And she couldn't do that to him.

They all took the nine-o'clock ferry, the *Titanic*, back from the mainland after the movie. It was the last homeward-bound ferry of the night, and missing it would mean being stranded on the mainland or having to pay the exorbitant cost for the water taxi. The *Titanic* was the ferry that carried cars and had a smaller covered space than the *Minnow*, but the rain drove them all inside, watching lightning strikes through steamed windows.

The rain had cleared away by the time they reached the island, leaving behind glistening cobblestones and a fresh, electric smell in the air.

They split up at the ferry landing, Nina heading north, Christopher heading south along Leeward Drive, leaving Aisha looking slightly annoyed. Lucas and Benjamin, Aisha and Zoey walked in a group as far as Camden before Aisha went on ahead, making the tiring climb up the winding road to her parents' inn on the ridge.

Benjamin, always diplomatic, went alone into the house, leaving Lucas with Zoey in her front yard, the first privacy they'd had that evening.

"Well, that was an interesting night out," Lucas said, putting his arms around her. "What's the deal with Aisha and Christopher? Do they hate each other or like each other?"

"I think Eesh really does like him, but she can't admit it to herself yet. She's like a train, you know? She's on track, going a certain direction, and you can't try to distract her."

"I'm glad you're not that way," Lucas said, drawing Zoey close.

"Me too," Zoey said.

They kissed for a while, standing under a dripping tree, perfectly private on the quiet, dead-end street.

"I'd better get inside," Zoey said at last. "Parents."

"Yeah, I understand. Not that my parents give a damn if I come home late. They'd probably rather I didn't come home at all." He spoke lightly, trying to keep the bitterness out of his voice.

"I'm sure your dad will lighten up," Zoey said tentatively.

"At least he hasn't said anything in the last few days about shipping me off."

"See? Maybe he's already calming down."

"Probably," Lucas said, smiling to make the lie more believable. His father never forgot anything, and he had never changed his mind that Lucas could remember. But there was always the chance that Lucas's grandfather in Texas would refuse to take him in. His grandfather and his father were family, but not exactly friends.

"I'll think about you all night," Zoey said, gazing at him with her huge, liquid blue eyes.

"And I'll think about you," he said.

"Maybe we could meet in our dreams," she said, half-seriously, half self-mocking.

He smiled. His dreams about Zoey often took on an explicitness that would have shocked her. He wanted her badly, constantly. But there was no way he was going to risk the one decent relationship in his life by asking for something she didn't want to give. Even though each time she kissed him with her impossibly soft lips, her body pressed to his, he thought he might explode.

"Good night," she said, turning to go down the sidewalk to her front door.

He watched her go, savoring the sight of her, storing up memories of her every movement. "See you tomorrow."

He went around the back of her house and found the dark dirt path that led from her backyard up the steep embankment, under his deck, and around to his front door. He went out onto the deck and looked down, just in time to see in the bright incandescent rectangle of her kitchen window as she walked in, executed a little twirl, and hugged her arms to her.

Her father came in, wearing his bathrobe. He looked at the

ceiling and shook his head, obviously teasing her, but she just pranced over, planted a kiss on his cheek, and left the room. Her father stood at the sink, setting up a coffee machine for the morning, a wistful, reminiscing smile on his face.

Lucas turned away. His own house was dark, as it had been for hours. His father was a lobsterman and got up each day before the sun, piloting his boat along the sheer mainland shore, winching up lobster pots, throwing back the undersized lobsters, replacing the bait, and lowering the pots again.

Lucas crept into his house, carefully climbing the stairs as silently as a burglar. It was a small house, just two bedrooms upstairs, a living room and the kitchen downstairs. But he had the use of his own bathroom, and his own private room where he could open and shut the door whenever he chose. It wasn't much, certainly not a third the size of Jake's house or Claire's. Even compared to Zoey's modest house, it was modest. But it beat a dormitory cell at the Youth Authority.

He waited until he had closed the door of his room behind him to turn on the light. A single bed, a white-painted dresser, a scratched wood desk with a rickety chair. The only personal touches were left over from two years ago.

It was a simple, uncluttered room, so the sheet of paper lying on his desk looked almost ostentatious. He stood over it, reading.

YOU ARE ON THE 11:00 FLIGHT
TO HOUSTON. SATURDAY.

He stared at the words, forcing his mind to accept what was there in front of him. Saturday. Flight. Houston.

You are on.

He sat on his bed, holding the paper in his hands.

It had happened. His father was actually kicking him out of the house, just as he'd said he would.

Lucas had hoped his mother might find a way of changing his father's mind, but now he knew he'd been deceiving himself. It was his father who was the absolute ruler in this house, just as he was the absolute master of his boat.

Lucas inhaled. It felt like he had forgotten to breathe these last few minutes. Saturday. Three more days, and on the fourth . . .

No more Chatham Island. No more Maine. No more Zoey.

He would almost be glad, he realized, if it weren't for Zoey. His grandfather was unlike his father. He had gone down a different path. He was a tough old guy, but decent. Not the rigid, moralizing, humorless man Lucas's own father was.

He'd be relieved to go to Texas. Except there was no Zoey in Texas.

For the hundredth time he thought of telling his father the

truth, explaining what had really happened two years ago when he had so thoughtlessly confessed to something he didn't do.

But his father would dismiss it as another in a long string of lies. Even his mother wouldn't believe it.

Lucas turned off the light and lay back on his bed, still in his damp clothing, and hugged the meager pillow to his chest. He stared into the darkness and saw that rectangle of light, a picture frame holding the image of Zoey, twirling across her kitchen floor and thinking of him.

Lucas

Why did I sign that confession? Do you have any idea how many times I've asked myself that question? That question has been with me ever since then, every night as I lay in my rack and listened to my cellmates snore and cry in their sleep. And worse things.

Why did I do it?

Because at the time I was in love with Claire. I would have done anything for her. I mean, my life was no Disney World attraction. My mom and dad live in a state of suspended animation, two bodies sharing the same space but nothing else. Do they hate each other? I don't know. Do they still love each other? I don't know that, either. I know I never felt like anything other than an intruder in my own home. I was this . . . this creature that stayed up too late, and ate too much, and never did anything right.

Claire was the first person who ever said she loved me. She was a beautiful, brilliant, perfect being, an angel who for some reason actually claimed to care about me. She could do no wrong. So I didn't argue as hard as I should have for her to pull over and stop the car that night. I mean, jeez, we could easily have walked home, but I didn't want to make her mad by insisting. I just made a few jokes about it, hoping she'd get the hint and pull over, but drunks aren't good at taking hints.

We hit. I climbed out through the back window and then I got Claire out of the car. Her forehead was bloody. I got Wade out, too. Funny, but at the time I thought Claire was the one who was badly hurt.

But he died very soon after. And she was in the hospital. I was terrified that she would die. Confessing was like . . . like some offering I was making to God. Please just let her live. I'll do anything, just let Claire live.

She lived. Her father came to see me and said he thought I was being a man accepting my responsibility the way I was. He had never thought I had the backbone, but now, he could see that he had misjudged me.

He said he knew my dad was having some financial troubles, and he was a banker, so maybe he could help.

You know what's funny? I didn't even understand what Claire's dad was doing till days later. Honest. I didn't understand he was telling me he'd help my dad, but only as long as I stuck to my confession.

Why did I confess? Because I loved Claire. And because even though I hate him, I love my father, too.

Neither of them ever came to visit me. Or sent letters. Or called.

I fell out of love with Claire over time. But what can you do about your dad? He's still always your dad.

TEN

AFTER SCHOOL ZOEY WENT STRAIGHT from the ferry to Lucas's house. He had skipped school that day, leaving Zoey apprehensive. As the day wore on and her imagination grew wilder and wilder, she became totally preoccupied, even fearful.

She ran straight to his house but hesitated at the front door. She hadn't run into either Mr. or Mrs. Cabral since Lucas had come back from jail. She knew that relations between Lucas and his parents were hostile, and she didn't know whether that hostility transferred to her.

She knocked and waited, trying to look pleasant. The door opened quickly. Mrs. Cabral stood there in the dark interior, wiping her hands on her long apron. She had Lucas's blond hair, made lusterless by streaks of gray. Her face was somber, her eyes expressionless.

"Hi, Mrs. Cabral," Zoey said cheerfully.

"Hello, Zoey," Mrs. Cabral said, showing neither surprise nor any great interest. "How are your parents?"

"They're fine, ma'am. They work too much, but I guess you and Mr. Cabral know about work, don't you? I mean, I know Mr. Cabral's work is really hard. And yours . . . you know, whatever it is, must be . . ." She took a deep breath. "Is Lucas home?"

"He is in his room."

Not exactly an invitation, Zoey realized. "Um, so, can I go up and see him? Or else could he come down?"

Mrs. Cabral stared thoughtfully at her for a moment. Then, with a shrug, she stood back from the door. "Upstairs."

"Thanks," Zoey said, flashing her best smile. She ran up the stairs. The door to what was clearly the parents' room was open. The other bedroom door was closed. She knocked tentatively.

"Yeah?" a muffled voice answered.

"It's me, Zoey. Let me in."

He opened the door, wearing jeans and no shirt. His face was grim. His eyes were red.

"Are you okay? Are you sick?" Zoey asked.

He closed the door behind her and turned away. "I'm not sick."

She stepped up behind him, wanting to put her arms around him, but the situation made her edgy. She was in his room, and she had never seen his bare chest before, and his mother could be right outside the door. She dropped her hand to her side. "So why weren't you in school?" she asked, feeling frustrated and nervous.

He released a deep sigh and bent over to reach into his wastebasket. He retrieved a crumpled ball of paper and handed it to her. Slowly she unwrinkled it, flattening it on the top of his desk to read the message:

YOU ARE ON THE 11:00 FLIGHT
TO HOUSTON. SATURDAY.

Zoey felt like she had been punched. Her knees gave way and she sat hard on the edge of his bed, still holding the paper. "Your father can't really mean this."

"He means it," Lucas said. He went back to his desk and opened the drawer. He held up an envelope with the logo of United Airlines at the corner. "One-way ticket, of course," he said, with a hint of his old humor. "Not even first class. You'd think when you get banished, the least you'd get is a first-class ticket out of town. I'll probably get stuck sitting between a fat guy and a lady with a screaming baby. Then again, knowing my dad, I should probably be glad it's not Greyhound."

"What can we do?" Zoey asked bleakly.

"Well, I'll tell you, Zoey, I've spent the whole night and the whole day so far asking myself that very question." He slid the ticket back in his desk and shut the drawer with finality. "And the answer is, nothing."

"The answer can't be nothing," Zoey said.

"I could try and get a job, rent an apartment, and support myself. I figured it out. If I stay in school, I could probably work about twenty-five hours a week, if anyone would hire a high school kid with a criminal record, no references, and no experience. After taxes and so on I'd probably take home as much as a hundred and seventy, hundred and eighty a week. Seven hundred fifty dollars a month if I'm lucky. With that I might be able to rent an apartment. Unfortunately, I wouldn't be able to heat it, and here in Maine it's a real good idea to have heat in the winter. Also, there wouldn't be any luxuries like clothing, food . . ."

He flopped backward onto the bed beside her. "Or I could drop out of school and get a job making burgers or working at a minimart. If I worked hard, I could still get somewhere. Make manager and so on in a few years."

"You can't drop out of school," Zoey said firmly.

"I don't want to," he said. "But I don't want to lose you, either. You are the only thing I care about."

Zoey lay against him, resting her cheek on his smooth chest. She could hear his heart beating, rising in tempo as she took his hand and squeezed it tightly.

"I love you, Lucas," she whispered.

"I love you, Zoey," he said, his voice rumbling through his chest.

She kissed the spot where his heart beat, then his collarbone, his neck, his lips as he bent to meet her. It was a kiss full of sweetness, full of her own need and desire. But she sensed a reserve in him, as if he could no longer commit himself completely.

She lay back down on his chest, listening to his heartbeat grow more regular. In his mind, she knew, he was already distancing himself from her. He was trying to save himself from the pain of leaving her by leaving her a little at a time.

Tears filled her eyes and flowed down onto his warm skin, trickling along the curve, rolling over his side to stain his sheet. And after a while she felt him sigh, a despairing sound. His arms tightened around her, drawing her up to him again.

There would be no easy way out. No leaving her a little at a time. They were in it together, to the end, whatever might happen.

Their lips met again, and this time Lucas didn't pull away.

Down on the other side of the field, cheerleaders were shouting something in unison, then throwing their right legs up, their left legs up, and falling on the ground in splits.

Claire watched with detached amusement from her perch on the bleachers. Why did girls want to do that? She certainly never had. Bouncing and shouting in front of a crowd of football fans, obsessing over whether one girl's toe was sufficiently pointed or another girl's smile was truly enthusiastic.

But then, she also didn't understand why guys liked to play football.

She turned her attention back to the line of guys bending over, resting on one knuckle dug into the grass, rear ends raised high in the air. Well, at least that part of the game was all right. Unfortunately, Jake wasn't one of the guys bent over. He was standing in back of the line, arms out from his sides.

There was a chant that amounted to a series of numbers, then everyone started running. Someone gave Jake the ball and he tucked it into his arm and ran. Another guy plowed into him, but Jake spun and ran on. Then two guys jumped him from behind, bringing him crashing down to earth.

Jake got up laughing, shaking his head ruefully. He trotted over toward Claire, pulling off his helmet as he ran, and removing a slobbery piece of plastic from his mouth.

"See that?" he yelled as he came closer.

"Yes. I hope it didn't hurt."

"Hurt?" he said as if it was a ridiculous suggestion. "I broke the first tackle and carried the second tackle with me for another five yards. I gained fifteen yards; that's a first down and then some. I'm ready for the game Friday. Big-time ready."

He ran up the bleachers and sat down beside her, sweaty but exuberant.

"So you're saying what you did was good?" Claire said.

He squinted at her doubtfully. "You're not a football fan, are you?"

"Mmmm, I guess you wouldn't say *fan*."

Jake laughed good-naturedly. "In other words, you know absolutely nothing about the game."

"I know it involves a ball. And I thought several of your teammates had nice butts."

Jake winced and shook his head. "No. No one on the team has a nice butt. The game is not about guys' butts. It's war, it's destruction, it's about power and taking the other guy's territory away from him, advancing, penetrating. Like Napoleon at Waterloo."

"Napoleon lost the battle of Waterloo," Claire pointed out.

"Yeah, well, we're playing South Portland on Friday, so it's probably a pretty good example to use," he said wryly. "They've beaten us every year since . . . actually, since Waterloo, come to think of it."

"Isn't it depressing to think you're going to lose a game?"

"Haven't you heard? It's not whether you win or lose, it's

how you play the game." Jake gave her one of his most wonderful smiles. "Sure it's depressing, but their school is twice the size of ours, so we don't feel too depressed. Besides, we might win. Their quarterback could get hit by a bus."

"I've never been to a game," Claire admitted. "I guess if I'm going to be your girlfriend, I'll have to go to all of them."

Jake looked down and kicked mud from his cleats. "Zoey only came to three or four during the year, usually," he said. "But I think I finally got her to more or less understand the game."

Claire was silent, and the silence stretched for several minutes while the rest of the team ran plays. "I guess it's way too soon for you to be over her," she said softly.

"Yes and no," Jake said. "Most of me is just so glad you and I are together that I almost don't care. But it still hurts, you know. I mean, no one likes to get dumped." His face grew dark. "Especially not when you're getting dumped for someone like Lucas."

Claire put her hand on Jake's arm. "I'm glad you've managed to stay out of fights with him. I was worried you might do something stupid."

"I would have, except I don't really need to," Jake said. "That's one of the lessons you learn in football. Don't take unnecessary hits, and don't apply unnecessary hits. When the man is down, don't pile on. If he's down, that's all that counts.

And Lucas," he said the name with a sneer, "is out of the game."

"What do you mean?" Claire asked, feeling uneasy.

"My dad talks to Mr. Cabral just about every day. Mr. Cabral fuels up at our marina. My dad says Lucas has a one-way plane ticket out of town as of Saturday. Good-bye, Lucas." Jake smiled a cold, unpleasant smile. "Zoey may have dumped me, but the guy she dumped me for has less than three more days before he's history."

A fierce current of joy and relief flooded Claire's mind, almost taking her breath away with its intensity. Lucas, gone in three days! It was like a miracle. With him gone, there would be no one around to reveal the truth. No one but Benjamin, and he had no proof, just guesses. Her secret was safe. Safe from everyone, and most of all, safe from Jake.

She leaned over and started to kiss Jake, but he pulled back.

"I'm all sweaty and dirty," he protested, "and my breath probably smells like Joe Bolt's shoe since he stuck it into my mouth on that last play."

"Joe Bolt," she said thoughtfully. "Is he the one with the nice behind?"

"Claire," Jake said reproachfully, "we are all very, very tough guys and manly men and all. No one on the team has anything nice. Except maybe me."

He kissed her, holding his body away.

"McRoyan!" the coach yelled up at him from the field. "Are you practicing or are you making out?"

"Right there, Coach!" Jake yelled back.

"Tell him you don't need practice, you're making out just fine."

He smiled, and then she noticed he was blushing and looking awkwardly down at his cleats again. "You know, Claire, I don't know if I should say this or anything, but, you know, I'm really . . . I mean, I really am starting to like you. A lot. I mean, I always liked you, just now it's more. And different. You know."

Claire felt strangely touched. There was something so sincere and utterly without deception about Jake. In a million years he would never lie to her.

Not like she was lying to him.

The thought stabbed her and made her clench her fist.

"I guess I shouldn't have said that," Jake said, looking embarrassed. "I mean, even though we've known each other forever, we've only been *together* for a little while."

"No, I'm glad you said it, Jake. Very glad."

"McRoyan, for cripes' sake, what the hell are you doing?" The coach's voice was rising in exasperation.

Jake rolled his eyes. "I have to get back to the other manly men."

"Here," Claire said, grabbing the front of his jersey and pulling him down to her. She gave him a long, deep kiss. "Give the manly men something to be jealous of."

He bounded down the bleachers, greeted by rude catcalls from his teammates. She watched him as he rejoined his team.

It would be easy to find the words to tell him the truth. *Jake, I was driving the car when Wade was killed.* But it was impossible to imagine what she would say after those ten words.

ELEVEN

"MORNING, MORNING, MORNING," NINA SAID the next morning in a low, grumpy voice. She flopped onto the bench beside Zoey, pulled a Lucky Strike from a pack in her purse, and stuck it in her mouth, drawing deeply on the unlit cigarette. She propped her Doc Martens on the back of the next seat and cast a glance around the ferry. "What's it been, two weeks? Not even, and already I can announce that I officially hate school. I mean, seriously, what are we all doing out of bed at this hour? And I was up late last night trying to figure out how it is that the Russians could be good guys in World War I, then bad guys at the beginning of World War II, changing again to good guys halfway through, then as soon as the war was over they were bad again, up until a few decades ago when they switched back to good. I think there should be a law: You pick a side, good or bad, then you have to stick with it. Hey, Eesh. You're a senior. What's the deal with the Russians? Good, bad, or just indecisive?"

Aisha stopped in front of Zoey and shook her head. "You

look bad, Zoey. What's the matter, are you sick?"

"You're sick?" Nina asked in surprise, looking at Zoey more closely. "Why didn't you say something?"

"I'm not sick," Zoey said in a low whisper.

"You look sick," Aisha said flatly. "If it's catching, stay away from me."

"If it's catching but it's not too painful, come closer. I wouldn't mind a few sick days," Nina said.

"It's not that," Zoey said. "It's Lucas."

"Don't tell me you two are fighting," Aisha said.

"His father is making him leave. He . . ." Zoey's voice broke. "Saturday. He's leaving Saturday."

"This Saturday?" Nina asked.

Zoey nodded.

"Can he do that?" Aisha asked. "I mean, Lucas is still his son."

"He's over eighteen," Zoey explained. "His dad could just kick him out the door if he wanted to. Lucas says at least his dad found him a place to stay, with his grandfather until he can finish school there."

"Texas, right?" Aisha said.

"Some crappy little town," Zoey muttered. "More than two thousand miles away. Two thousand miles."

Nina scratched her head uncomfortably and chewed the end

of her unlit cigarette. She had never seen Zoey so upset before, about anything. Zoey was always sunshine to Nina's rain. It was unnatural having her on the edge of tears, but obviously so cried out that no tears would come. She glanced over at Aisha, who just shrugged and bit her lip. *Aisha's probably dying to say I told you so*, Nina thought.

"Isn't there any way to get Mr. Cabral not to do this?" Aisha asked. "I mean, I guess Lucas has tried and all."

Zoey nodded mutely. The ferry whistle blew, and the boat began to draw away from the dock. Nina saw Jake glance in their direction, his eyes softening for Zoey, then growing hard and pitiless. Claire was close by him. She stared for a moment, too.

"I can't take it," Zoey said in her low, trembling whisper. "It's not right. No one should tear people apart who love each other."

Nina put her arm around her friend's shoulders. Aisha sat close on Zoey's other side and took Zoey's hand. Zoey found a few extra tears, which fell softly on her books, forming little dark spots on *La Langue Française*.

"What am I going to do?" Zoey wondered. "I can't go with him, can I? Where would I stay? How could I still finish school?"

Nina made eye contact with Aisha over Zoey's bowed head.

"He told me yesterday. I went up to his house because he wasn't in school. I guess he figures why bother for just two or three days. I spoke to his mother, but Lucas says she's totally under his dad's thumb. He showed me the note his father left him, not even anything on it but the time the flight leaves. His family is so cold, you wouldn't believe it."

Nina was about to break the tension with a joke about Claire, something along the lines of knowing all about cold families, but again she saw Claire across the open deck, stealing a furtive glance at Zoey. Claire's lips were pressed into a thin line, and she looked away quickly when she saw Nina watching her.

Very strange, Nina thought. *She acts like she knows why Zoey is sad.* Then again, it was a small island. Claire probably did know.

Claire glanced back again. Weird, especially given that there was an amazing pile of those really tall clouds on the horizon. Why wasn't Claire staring up at them?

"Just tonight, then tomorrow will be the last night I have with him," Zoey said, sounding hopeless. "I really love him, you guys. I really do. We kissed for hours after he told me. Hours, but it still seemed like no time at all, and I could tell he was trying to pull away from me emotionally. I can't blame him. I wish I could pull away from him, but I can't."

"This is true love," Aisha said darkly. "It's great for a while, but it always seems to lead to pain in the end." She put her hand on Zoey's. "I guess you couldn't stop yourself. Maybe there really is such a thing as fate. Maybe you were just doomed to go through this."

"It isn't doom, Eesh," Zoey said through her tears. "I mean, I'd still do it all over again, even knowing . . . knowing . . ." She succumbed to sobs.

Aisha looked troubled. She gave Zoey a disbelieving look, but Nina could see doubt there, too.

For her part, Nina felt the beginnings of tears. It had suddenly occurred to her that this could happen to any guy and girl. What if Benjamin were suddenly to disappear from her life? Not that he was exactly *in* her life. But what if she knew she might never see him again?

The first tear welled in her eye and trundled down her cheek.

"Both of you stop it, now," Aisha said, but not harshly. "How are we supposed to get through the whole day at school when we start off weeping on the ferry?"

"Sorry," Zoey murmured. She sat up straight and wiped her eyes.

Nina rubbed her friend's back slowly. "It will all work out somehow. Won't it, Aisha?"

"Sure, of course it will."

"Some dumb parent can't stop true love, can he?" Nina challenged. "Look at Romeo and Juliet. Their parents tried to stop them, didn't they?"

"They ended up dead," Aisha said.

"Oh, right. Well, I know this for a fact—Wilma's parents never did approve of Fred."

Aisha rolled her eyes to the sky. "Nina, if I ever need to be comforted, remind me not to come to you."

"Don't tell me," Benjamin said, holding up his hand. "It's . . . um, sloppy joes made with ground turkey . . . green beans . . . and, um, I want to be sure . . ." He sniffed the air carefully. "Cherry . . . no, raspberry Jell-O."

The old woman behind the lunch counter shook her head in amazement and piled Benjamin's tray high. Benjamin smiled in her general direction and pushed his tray along on the stainless steel railing.

"Okay, not to be dumb," Aisha said, just behind him in the cafeteria line, "but how do you do that? I mean, are you telling me you can *smell* raspberry Jell-O from ten feet away with the air full of sloppy joe and perfume and body odor?"

"It's easy," Benjamin said out of the side of his mouth. "They list the school lunches in the paper at the beginning of each week. Today sloppy joes, green beans, and Jell-O."

"The paper specified *raspberry* Jell-O?"

"No." Benjamin dug his lunch ticket out of his pocket and handed it to the cashier. "The guys in front of us asked what flavor it was. It's always useful to have an air of mystery about you when you're a discriminated-against minority. Don't you think?"

Aisha took his arm and led him across the crowded lunch-room to an empty table. It was one of the things Benjamin couldn't do alone, not unless he just wanted to grab the first vacant seat he stumbled into. Classrooms were different; steps could usually be counted. His English class was one step in, left seventeen steps, right nine steps, and his desk would be in the back row, halfway across the room. To get to the room itself would be sixty-three steps along the hall, up four flights of stairs, right forty-eight steps.

But in the lunchroom, tables tended to get shoved around more, chairs reassembled in different groupings each day, so whoever happened to be nearest the cashier, usually an islander but often other kids, would grab Benjamin's elbow and ask where he wanted to go or whom he wanted to sit with.

"Table's to your left," Aisha said.

He heard her sit down at the seat roughly across the table from him. He aimed his sunglasses in her direction. "Aren't you sitting with Zoey today?"

"What, you don't like my company?"

Hearing her voice again, he readjusted the aim of his shades. "I've always enjoyed your company," he said. "I was just making sure this wasn't a pity date because I don't have Claire to sit with anymore."

"You're a very prickly guy, you know that?" Aisha said.

Benjamin smiled. "I think that's why I don't have Claire to sit with anymore."

Aisha sighed. "Actually, I don't want to sit with your sister because she's just too depressing. Don't tell her I said that, but all she's done all day long is sniffle."

Benjamin frowned. "What's the matter?"

"Oh, great. You don't know? So I'm the one telling you?"

"Telling me what?"

Aisha sighed again and rearranged her silverware. "You probably *should* know," she said reluctantly. "You are Zoey's brother, and besides, I don't think she's trying to keep it a big secret or anything. I think she's just too close to having a nervous breakdown. It's Lucas."

"Oh, a romantic problem," Benjamin said. "What's up? They can't agree on whether they should get engaged?"

"Mr. Cabral is kicking Lucas out. He has to go live with his grandfather in Texas somewhere."

"What?"

"Yeah, you know. Lucas is a juvenile delinquent who has embarrassed his family or whatever. You know Mr. Cabral. He's like, uptight father squared."

Benjamin threw his fork down on his tray, making a clattering noise. He cursed under his breath, finishing with *that selfish bitch.*

"Who's a selfish bitch?" Aisha demanded. "Zoey?"

"No, no," Benjamin said quickly. "Of course not. Zoey's anything but selfish. Poor kid. Man, she got herself in the middle of it this time."

"I told her running around with Lucas Cabral would lead to trouble," Aisha said.

"Zoey's too much of a romantic to listen to sensible warnings," Benjamin said affectionately.

"Exactly. If she'd listened to reason and common sense, none of this would have happened."

Benjamin barked a short, dismissive laugh. "Aisha, if people listened to reason and common sense, we'd all still be walking around dragging our knuckles, eating bugs, and talking in grunts. We'd be baboons. Football players."

"I don't see Zoey crying and sobbing for twenty-four hours straight as part of the march of civilization," Aisha said sarcastically.

"Yeah, well, neither is sitting on the sidelines saying *I told you so.* I'm sure when the first caveman burned himself trying to start a fire with a couple of sticks, some smartass was there saying, *Hey, I told you not to play with fire.*"

He winced as Aisha slapped the table. "You know how I said you were prickly? Leave off the *l* and the *y*."

Benjamin held up his hands placatingly. "Aisha, I wasn't talking about you. We were just having a discussion."

"I know you're not talking about me," Aisha snapped. "We're talking about your sister, who is four tables away looking like someone drained all the blood out of her. Damn. Nina's giving me a come-help-me-out look. I have to go."

"Tell Zoey to be cool; Mr. Cabral will probably lighten up eventually."

He heard the scrape of Aisha's chair. "I don't know how much he's going to lighten up between now and Saturday," she said doubtfully.

"Saturday?" Benjamin said, feeling a jolt of concern. "You don't mean as in the day after tomorrow?"

"As in the morning after tomorrow," Aisha said.

BENJAMIN

Zoey is my little sister. That's just a biological fact. I was born a year and seven months before her. And all the time we were growing up, I was the traditional big brother, which, as I understood it, meant that I had two major duties: First, I was ~~rouqired~~ required by law to tease her. About her hair, her body, her ideas, her clothes, her friends, and anything else that came to mind.

The other thing a big brother did was protect. I was supposed to protect her from anyone or anything that might threaten her. That was ~~su posed~~ supposed to be a lifelong job.

My career as a big brother didn't last long, though. I was twelve when I lost my sight. I'm not supposed to say that, by the way. "Lost my sight" is negative, you see. The therapist who taught me my basic coping skills wanted me to say that I had "become differently abled." I was only twelve, but I still knew b.s. when I heard it.

Anyway. I was twelve, Zoey was ten, and all of a sudden I wasn't a "big" brother anymore. I fell behind at school till I had to race just to stay even with her. I couldn't protect anyone. Not even myself. If you've never been anyone's big brother, you don't know how pathetic it makes you feel to ~~duddenly~~ suddenly need your baby sister to lead you to the men's-room door at the mall, or find your belt because you don't remember precisely where you hung it. Or pipe up in her brave little voice and tell some punk to leave you alone, stop picking on my brother, he needs his cane.

And yet, I discovered that from time to time there were ways I could help her. I pushed myself so hard at school that soon she didn't have to pity me, or worry about how I'd feel if ~~agw~~ she was better than me at something. I drilled myself endlessly to handle getting around town and the ferry and the school, so she wouldn't have to spend her life being my guide. I worked to free her from me and, as you might expect, I freed myself at the same time.

I still can't beat guys up for her, but from time to time, in little ways, I do still get to be her big brother.

TWELVE

USUALLY NINA, AISHA, AND ZOEY met at the end of the school day to walk together down to the ferry landing. They met on the front steps of the three-story brick behemoth, and since there was always an hour to kill till the four o'clock ferry, they would wander the tiny shops of downtown Weymouth, or stop in at a hangout for ice cream.

But the usual had been suspended for now.

Nina and Aisha watched as Zoey came down the front steps, arm in arm with Lucas. *Like Siamese twins*, Nina thought. *Like they've been Superglued together.*

Not that she could blame either of them. They had tonight and tomorrow, and that was it.

"Hi, guys," Zoey said in her worn, soft voice.

"Hi, you two," Nina said.

"Are you coming?" Zoey asked.

Nina flashed a quick glance at Aisha. "No, I don't think so.

Why don't you two go on ahead, and Eesh and I will see you on the ferry."

Zoey didn't argue, just smiled a pathetically grateful smile and walked on, still hanging on to Lucas.

"You know, Aisha," Nina said, "I'm starting to think you're right. Why would anyone deliberately put themselves in a position to suffer like that?"

"Oh, so now *you* think I'm right?" Aisha said grumpily.

"I'm just saying, what's so great about falling in love if you end up like Zoey and Lucas?"

Nina hopped down off the steps and popped an unlit cigarette in her mouth. They began walking across the field, the shortcut to town. The football team was running around at one end of the field. Closer at hand, a less-organized-looking group of girls were learning how to advance soccer balls. Nina recognized Christopher, wearing shorts and a rugby shirt, teaching the finer points.

"I'm glad someone agrees with me," Aisha said. "Benjamin called me a baboon."

"A baboon? Why?"

"And on the ferry this morning did you hear Zoey? *I'd still do it all over again, even knowing boohoo*? Even now she acts like she did the right thing."

Nina took a drag on the Lucky Strike. "Love is a many-splendored thing, Eesh," she said philosophically. "Better to have loved and lost than never to have loved at all."

"Oh, shut up. I don't see you trying it."

An image of Benjamin leaning close, his lips nearly touching her ear, came to Nina's mind. It was replaced by another image, of Benjamin saying, "I never thought of you as a romantic type, Nina. Is it anyone in particular, or is that none of my business?"

"I'm like you, Eesh," Nina said wistfully. "Too big a coward to take the chance of getting dumped on."

"So now I'm a coward," Aisha said.

"Better than a baboon," Nina pointed out.

Aisha stopped and planted her hands on her hips. "Obviously everyone is just going to keep picking on me."

Nina looked at her friend in puzzlement. Suddenly Aisha was upset, and Nina had no real idea why.

"I'm not a coward," Aisha ranted. "I've gone out with lots of guys, unlike you, may I point out, Ms. Too-cool-for-everyone. I'm *not* afraid, I'm just sensible. See, I don't let other people decide what I'm going to do, or whom I'm going to go out with. That does not make me a baboon or a caveman."

"No, I—" Nina began.

"But everyone is just going to keep picking on me until I go out with him. You, Zoey, Benjamin, my mother."

"Go out with who?" Nina asked.

"Like you don't know. Don't waste your time trying child psychology on me; I'm not a child."

Or a baboon, Nina added silently.

"But just to shut everyone up, just so everyone will finally leave me alone in peace, I'll do it. All right? I'll do it."

Nina was about to ask what Aisha was going to do, but her friend spun on her heel and began marching across the field. Aisha stopped in the middle of the soccer players and planted herself in front of Christopher.

"Oh," Nina said. She flopped down on the grass, watching. Of course. Duh.

Aisha evidently asked a question, and Christopher evidently answered, because after a few seconds Aisha came marching back. Nina got up, picking bits of grass off the backs of her thighs.

"We're going out tomorrow night," Aisha said. "Are you happy now?"

"You just went right up and asked him out?" Nina said wonderingly. "Just like that?"

"Yeah," Aisha answered, trying unsuccessfully to stop a smile. "Just like that."

"And it worked, huh?" Nina asked thoughtfully.

"Of course," Aisha said. "I don't believe in all that coy girly stuff. That's why *I* won't end up like Zoey. Just because you go out with a guy, that doesn't mean anything. I just did it so you all would leave me alone. It does not mean I'm interested in him."

"Just go up and say, *do you want to go out with me*?" Nina muttered.

"Come on. I need something to wear, and the ferry's in forty-five minutes."

"It's really only been a few days," Claire said. "But I feel like . . . I feel a lot for him."

"As you pointed out, you've known Jake your whole life," Dr. Kendall said in her neutral, nonjudgmental psychiatrist's voice.

Claire shifted in her seat, making the leather creak. Dr. Kendall believed there was significance in everything, even shifting from one position to another because your left butt cheek was numb. "I know, but we were never close. Once when Zoey—that's his former girlfriend—was out of town, I kind of took a run at him. You know, a friendly kiss."

Dr. Kendall nodded.

"Maybe a *very* friendly kiss. But I was going with Benjamin, and Jake was with Zoey. But now that we've all broken up, things are different."

"Are you saying that you never really cared for Benjamin?"

Claire reflected for a moment, as memories came drifting up to her consciousness. "No, I really did care for Benjamin."

"Yet it was you who broke off the relationship with him."

Claire grinned mischievously. "Everyone needs a little variety. Benjamin was old news. Besides, he has annoying habits that get on my nerves. He is the pickiest person sometimes. Not to mention suspicious. And now with Jake I'm so much happier. I know it's sudden and all, but already I think I feel more for him than I ever did for Benjamin."

"I'm happy for you," Dr. Kendall said.

"Yeah. I'm happy, too," Claire said, feeling vaguely dissatisfied even as she said it.

"He is the brother of the boy who died in the accident, isn't he?"

"Uh-huh. Wade was Jake's brother."

Dr. Kendall fell into one of her long, dragging silences.

"I suppose you think there's something psychological going on there," Claire said mockingly.

Dr. Kendall smiled and lifted her shoulders.

"You mean like I'm going out with Jake to make up for his losing Wade? That's stretching it pretty far, isn't it?"

"That would be pretty far-fetched. Unless you had some reason to feel guilty over Wade's death."

Claire's breath caught in her throat. She forced a cough to

cover her gasp. What the hell had made Dr. Kendall say that? When she was done coughing, she apologized. "Sorry. I think I breathed in some dust."

"I'll have to ask the cleaning crew to dust more thoroughly. I was just wondering whether you felt any guilt over the death of Jake's brother. People sometimes experience guilt even over things for which they bear no responsibility," Dr. Kendall said.

"I guess that's true," Claire said. "But no, I don't feel any guilt. Except maybe, you know, feeling a little strange that I survived and someone else died."

"That's also a very common feeling."

Claire smiled broadly. "So, I'm still not crazy? Damn, and I've tried so hard."

Dr. Kendall put on the strained smile she wore whenever Claire used the word crazy. "I already gave you my opinion, Claire. You're a strikingly well-balanced person for a teenager in this day and age. You don't use drugs, you aren't promiscuous, you get along well with your father, and I believe you have adjusted well to the death of your mother. The fact that you can't remember the accident only means that you suffered a concussion that affected short-term memory."

"You probably kept me sane," Claire said insincerely.

"Our hour is nearly up. Have there been any more dreams about the accident?"

"Nope. Sorry. Although I had a dream about Sheldon, you know, the guy on *The Big Bang Theory*? That was pretty gross. I could tell you about it and throw in a few details to make it more interesting."

"Another time," Dr. Kendall said. "And no memory flashes? Nothing new on that front?"

"No. It's still as much of a blank as ever."

THIRTEEN

CLAIRE WAS NOT ON THE four-o'clock ferry, much to Benjamin's annoyance. Then he realized where she was: the psychiatrist Claire thought no one knew about. The one she'd been seeing since her mother died. Damn, he cursed himself, he should have tried to catch her there as she came out. That would have given him quite a nice little edge.

But then, he didn't know where the shrink's office was, so he would have had to be led. And then, a blind guy couldn't "accidentally" run into anyone who didn't want to be run into. He would have needed someone else along to act as his eyes, and that was unacceptable.

Instead he went to Claire and Nina's house just before seven o'clock, minutes before he knew that Claire would arrive on the later ferry. It would be tricky because he would have to avoid Nina and Mr. Geiger and somehow get to Claire alone.

He counted the steps from the corner of Center, right, with

the sound of surf to his left. He found the familiar gate and opened it.

Did Mr. Geiger know he and Claire had broken up? Probably not. But Nina certainly knew, and she was bound to think that he was there to beg Claire to come back to him.

He knocked on the front door.

"Hey, Benjamin, haven't seen you around here in some days."

Mr. Geiger. Benjamin was relieved. "Hi, Mr. Geiger. Is Claire around?"

"No, she's not home yet. But I expect she'll be up from the dock in a few minutes." He ushered Benjamin inside. The two of them had always gotten along well. "Can you stay for dinner? Love to have you."

"No, thanks, I've already eaten. You know we middle-class types eat dinner earlier than you folks with the lifestyle of the rich and famous."

Mr. Geiger let the remark go with good humor. "This rich and famous person has some work to do. Foreclosing on widows and orphans, as you always say. But Nina's upstairs. You want me to call her down?"

"No, no," Benjamin said quickly. "I'll just head on up and wait for Claire in her room, if that's all right with you."

"You know the way," Mr. Geiger said.

He did. Nineteen steps up. Turn right and follow the railing around. This was the tricky part, passing the door to Nina's room. If it was open, she'd come out and press him for some explanation. He heard music, muffled, and Nina's voice, singing along slightly off-key. Good, the door was closed. Now, fifteen more steps to Claire's room.

He found the bed and sat down, trying to look casual. A moment later he heard the front door of the house opening, closing. A pause, then a light tread climbing the steps. Good, just one person. She hadn't brought Jake home with her.

That would certainly have made things interesting.

"Benjamin. What are you doing here?"

"Hi, Claire."

"Hello, Benjamin. What are you doing here?"

Benjamin stood up and squared his shoulders. "We have to talk."

He heard Claire make a derisive noise. "I never thought you'd come begging, Benjamin. I'm with Jake now."

"That's not why I came," Benjamin said calmly, although her tone had hurt him. "Do you know that Lucas is leaving the island on Saturday?"

"I may have heard something about it," Claire said.

"You feel relieved that he's going?"

"I don't think I feel relieved, Benjamin. I'm not sorry he's going, though. No one on the island wants him around. The sooner he's gone, the sooner everything will get back to normal."

"Normal," Benjamin repeated wryly.

"Is that what you came here for? To ask me how I feel about Lucas leaving?"

Benjamin considered his answer for a moment. "In a way, yes. I was curious about how you felt, knowing that Lucas was going to suffer still more for something you did."

"That again?" Claire snapped angrily.

"That again," he answered quietly. "That again, that forever until you decide to tell the truth, Claire."

"Get out of here."

"He spent two years in reform school—well, let's call it what it was, jail. He spent two years in jail for something he didn't do. Maybe you didn't realize what was happening then. Maybe you really didn't remember back then; I'm willing to believe that. But you remember now."

"I don't remember anything, Benjamin. I know you think you're just the smartest person on the planet, but you can't read minds. You can't see inside me." She laughed cruelly. "In fact, Benjamin, you can't even look into my eyes, can you?"

Benjamin actually stepped back, stunned by her sudden fury. She had never resorted to cheap ridicule like that before. "I see enough," he said. "I know you remember."

"Why the hell do you care? Why is any of this *your* business? Why don't you deal with your own screwed-up life and stay out of mine? What's Lucas to you?"

"He's someone my sister cares about," Benjamin said.

"Oh, just get out of here."

"Lies have already cost Lucas two years of his life—"

"—I said get out!"

"And now they're going to cost him more."

"Benjamin, I swear to God I'm going to push you down the steps!"

"And they're going to cost my little sister a broken heart."

"Where are the violins? A broken heart? I can't believe I'm hearing this from your mouth, Benjamin. What do you know about anything? You wouldn't know a broken heart if you tripped over it."

A wave of sadness swept over him. She wasn't going to back down. He had failed. He felt his resolve collapsing. "I might know a broken heart," Benjamin said softly. He took a deep breath. "I'm surprised by you, Claire. I didn't think you were this far gone. I never would have believed it of you."

"Get over yourself, Benjamin."

"I could go and tell Mr. Cabral the truth," Benjamin said halfheartedly.

"And you think he'd believe you? You think he'd just accept your intuition that Lucas is innocent?" Claire laughed scornfully.

Benjamin shook his head. "No. He wouldn't believe me. He wouldn't believe Lucas, even if Lucas did try to tell him. There's only one person that anyone will believe, Claire, and that's you. You're the only one who would have nothing to gain."

"Nothing to gain," she repeated.

"Except that you would be telling the truth. This has all been about dishonesty. First Lucas lying to cover up for you, now you lying to protect yourself." He loaded his voice with weary scorn. "I never thought I would feel contempt for you, Claire."

She laughed. "You don't feel contempt for me, Benjamin."

He could feel that she was closer, feel the warmth of her body within inches of his own. Her fingers grazed his chin. He jerked his head away. But then her hand lay against his chest. He wanted to pull away, but he didn't.

She brushed his lips with her own and he moved closer, craving the contact, needing to feel her mouth on his again. But she was gone.

"See? You're not nearly as hard to figure out as you imagine, Benjamin. Now get out."

Claire listened to the sound of his slow, measured tread descending the stairs. She started to smile, but her lip was quivering. Her hands were shaking and she clasped them together to control them.

That bastard. That nosy, pushy, arrogant bastard. She *should* have pushed him down the stairs. She should have. He deserved it. Coming around here and accusing her of things. Trying to make her feel guilty.

She tore off the shirt she had worn to school and rummaged in her dresser for a sweatshirt. She realized she was throwing clothing across the room. She grabbed the next shirt that came to hand and slipped it on.

Guilt. What did she have to feel guilty about? She hadn't known. She had not remembered. It wasn't her fault that Lucas decided to be a knight on a white horse and confess. She hadn't asked him to. And if she had known the truth, she would have told everyone. She never, never would have let him go to jail for her. She wasn't that kind of person at all. That would have been cowardly, and she was no coward.

But she hadn't remembered.

Until just last week.

It was too late! It was too late to change everything. Even if she told Mr. Cabral the truth, it wasn't like he and Lucas would suddenly be best friends. Going off to Texas was probably the best thing for Lucas. He'd be better off away from the island. He would.

And as for Zoey's broken heart . . .

Well, Zoey hadn't minded breaking Jake's heart, had she? Why was this any different? In fact, if Claire were to go around blurting out the truth, that would just hurt Jake even more. And he was the main victim, not Lucas. Lucas had always been trouble. Jake was the sweetest guy on earth. He deserved to have some happiness.

Saturday morning it would be over, Claire told herself. Saturday morning it would all be over. Lucas would be gone. No one would ever ask any embarrassing questions of her father. She and Jake would still be together. Zoey would be ready to forget all about Lucas.

That would be best for everyone. History could not be rewritten.

No one would know but her and her father.

And Benjamin, who could do nothing about it.

She heard Nina's voice yelling up to her that dinner was ready.

She wasn't hungry, but it would look strange not to eat. A

quick dinner, then over to see Jake. Jake would help her to forget all about Benjamin, and Zoey crying on the ferry, and the image of Lucas climbing on a plane and disappearing, this time for good.

Jake. How good it would feel to be with him and put Benjamin out of her mind.

FOURTEEN

"I'VE NEVER SHOWN THIS TO anyone," Zoey said later that same evening, pulling a heavy bound pad from the drawer of her desk. "I've been writing in it for years."

"I didn't know you wrote," Lucas said, sitting on the edge of her bed.

"Well, I write, I just never finish anything," Zoey admitted.

"What do you write?"

Zoey made a face and smiled self-deprecatingly. "You'll just laugh."

"I promise I won't." He crossed his heart and looked solemn.

"I've written the first chapter of a romance novel about twenty-five times. Always chapter one, or else just a single scene. I have about a hundred and twenty pages altogether."

Lucas smiled. "Romance novel? You mean like those books with the covers where some half-naked guy is groping a woman whose dress is falling off?"

"Yeah, and the woman always has these big double-*D*-cup buffers squeezing out of a *B*-cup bodice. Except in mine the heroine is always normal size. Maybe even a little on the small end of the spectrum."

"And how about the hero?" Lucas asked. "Six five, big squared-off chest about a yard wide, smoldering dark eyes?"

"Lately he's been more like five ten. But he has a nice chest. And he does have smoldering dark eyes."

Lucas gave her an exaggeratedly smoldering look. "Like this?"

"Smoldering, not nearsighted," Zoey teased. Then she squealed as Lucas grabbed her and threw her back on the bed. She was still giggling and squirming when he kissed her. She closed her eyes and put her arms around his neck.

"By the way, they're not on the small end of the spectrum," Lucas said when they paused for air.

"Trust me," Zoey said. "Padding." She felt his hand move, and she caught her breath.

"Mmm, not padding," Lucas said in a husky voice.

"Lucas . . ."

"Yes?"

"That's, um . . . it's, oh . . . oh, what I mean is . . ."

"Tell me, in this romance novel you're working on, do the hero and the heroine ever make love?"

"Um, well, no. I mean, she never has."

"Never?" he asked, looking at her skeptically.

"I think I would know if the heroine had ever done it," Zoey said.

"Not even with . . . with the previous hero?" Lucas asked.

"No, not ever," Zoey said, feeling a blush rise up her neck. "She's not ready. Besides, that part always comes much later in the book after the hero and the heroine have either been married in the cathedral, or maybe been thrown into a dungeon together where they think they're going to get their heads chopped off the next day."

"Oh. Doesn't your hero *want* to, you know, make love?"

Zoey captured his hand with hers and raised it to her lips, kissing the tips of his fingers. "The hero pretty much always wants to make love. And it's not like the heroine doesn't. She has heaving-bosom syndrome, which is very common in romance novels. But being the heroine, she has to maintain a grip."

"Poor hero," Lucas said.

"Not really," Zoey said. "He just needs to learn that it's not always about having. Romance is about wanting."

Lucas made a pained face. "What if he explodes?"

"He won't," Zoey said confidently.

He kissed her deeply, a heart-stopping kiss that left them both breathless. "What if our heroine explodes?" Lucas asked in a low voice.

"Now that is . . . oh . . . a real possibility," Zoey said, closing her eyes. "But the thing to worry about is that if the hero does that again, he's going to get his hand smacked."

"Did I do it wrong?"

"No, no, you definitely did it right. Believe me. Only don't do it again." She pushed him back gently. "Maybe we should take a time-out. We have plenty of time."

Lucas's face fell, and instantly Zoey realized what she'd said was untrue. They didn't have plenty of time.

Lucas sat back and smiled at her ruefully, shaking his head. "Bad choice of words. It can happen to any writer, I guess."

"What are we going to do, Lucas?" Zoey asked, her voice betraying the desperation that came flooding over her again.

He raised his hands in a gesture of helplessness. "I don't know. I keep thinking there's something I've overlooked, some way to make it all work."

"There has to be a way," Zoey said. "It's ridiculous that some mistake you made two years ago would screw up our lives, maybe forever."

He nodded and averted his eyes.

"I'm sorry, I shouldn't have brought that up," Zoey said. "You know I think that's all ancient history. I know you're sorry for what happened, and you've already paid for it once. I just don't see why you should have to still go on paying. It's not fair."

But Lucas didn't respond. He pulled away and rested his elbows on his knees, hanging his head.

"Did I . . . did I say something wrong, Lucas?" She put her hand on his shoulder, and after a moment's hesitation he covered her hand with his.

"No. No, you didn't say anything wrong." He forced a smile and gently caressed her cheek. "Let's just not talk about it anymore. Heroes and heroines shouldn't be sad."

"Hmm," Jake muttered, thinking over Claire's question. "I guess red. It's bright, it doesn't fool around, it says, Look at me, I am definitely red. How about you?"

"Blue," Claire said without hesitation. "Blue sky, blue water."

"Can a red and a blue get along?" Jake wondered.

"Together we make purple," Claire pointed out. "Now, greens and yellows, no way. You'd get brown."

"Hmm," Jake said.

"Hmm," Claire replied.

This is good, Claire realized. *This is good, and something I could never really do with Benjamin.* She was walking along the west beach barefoot, holding hands with Jake, the two of them swinging their arms back and forth. Talking about nothing at all. Just enjoying the stars and the moon and being together.

With Benjamin she had always been so serious.

No, that wasn't really fair, but it was how she felt. And as mean as it might be to think it, it was nice to be able to share the visual universe with someone, both of you enjoying the size of the moon, or the way the lights of Weymouth sparkled on the bay.

"Between Coldplay and Maroon 5," Jake said.

"I have to go with Maroon 5."

"Coldplay," Jake said, shaking his head.

"Hmm," Claire said.

"Hmm," Jake replied.

"Okay, let's find something we agree on," Claire said. "Soft, hot, fresh-from-the-oven chocolate-chip cookies."

"I'm with you."

"Um, okay, Jimmy Fallon over Jon Stewart."

"No question," Jake agreed.

"Cats over dogs?"

"No way. Dogs."

"Well, let me try again," Claire said, biting her lip in concentration. "Pepperoni, no anchovies."

"Now you're back on track."

"Classes where the teacher lectures instead of just assigning a lot of reading."

"Definitely. Mr. Gondin instead of Ms. Boyer."

"No contest," Claire agreed. "See, we're doing pretty—*ahh*!"

"Run for your life!" Jake shouted gleefully as the surf surged suddenly, foaming over Claire's feet.

"Boy, that's cold," Claire said. "I guess the tide must be coming in. What time is it?"

"Time for you to kiss me."

"Oh, you think so?"

"You don't?" Jake asked.

"I didn't say that," Claire said. She tilted back her head and let herself melt into his arms.

"Ahhh, ah, let's move up the beach," she said, breaking away suddenly as the freezing surf rose to cover her ankles and soak the hem of her jeans. "It's coming in fast."

They climbed the slope of the beach, retreating beyond the reach of the surf, and flopped down onto the sand in a low sheltered spot between two grassy hillocks.

"I have one," Jake said. "Beaches and surf over mountains and snow."

"That's a close one for me, but I think I can go along with you," Claire said. She nestled against his chest and gazed out across the water. Weymouth was over there, not exactly a metropolis, not exactly Boston or New York, but a city just the same. Full of people who typically did not know each other, people who could come or go at random, not on whatever schedule the ferry kept. "Do you ever stop to realize how unusual it is living on this island?" Claire asked.

"Well, there are only about three hundred of us, so I guess that makes us pretty rare," Jake agreed.

"I know there are other islands—Matinicus, Monhegan, all the ones down in Casco Bay, and so on—but even if you throw in places like Nantucket and Martha's Vineyard, I'll bet there aren't as many people living on islands in this country as there are people over in Weymouth."

"The few, the proud, the islanders," Jake said ironically.

"Do you ever wonder about when we go off to college how we're going to fit into a world where you don't already know everyone?"

"I have to admit I haven't really thought about it."

"Sometimes I'm jealous of those people," Claire said wistfully. "It must be nice to be anonymous. It leaves you free to be whatever you want to be. You can reinvent yourself. If you make a mistake or do something awful, who's going to even remember? Whereas here . . . here it's just hard ever to live down your past."

Jake cuddled her up under his chin. "I don't think you have anything to live down."

"Maybe you don't know everything about me," she said in a low voice.

"I've known you all your life."

"You didn't know that blue was my favorite color," she said, trying to sound lighthearted again.

"I know what's important," Jake said confidently. "And I like it this way. See, over there in Weymouth, or I guess anywhere in the rest of the world, you can never be sure who your friends are. People can hide their true selves."

Claire waited, listening to the surf crash once, twice. "You thought you knew Zoey," she said in a near whisper.

She could feel the sudden heavy thudding of Jake's heart, the way his breathing grew shallow. "Yeah. I did, didn't I? Well, I guess that's a good point. I guess even here you can never be totally sure who you can trust."

"No, you never can be sure," Claire said.

"It's a hard lesson to learn," Jake said. "It tore me up pretty good. It still does when I think about it. Not that I'm saying I miss Zoey or anything," he added quickly.

She scooted around halfway to face him, and they kissed.

"Don't you ever do that to me, okay?" Jake said in a half-pleading, half-joking voice. "Don't suddenly turn against me. I couldn't take it twice."

Claire was on the edge of reassuring him, of saying, *Of course not, Jake, of course I'll never betray you*, but something inside her choked off the words. She was already betraying him. "Kiss me again," she said.

When he had pulled away he smiled at her, his open, honest eyes glittering in the starlight and the ocean's phosphorescence. "Just always be straight with me, Claire. That's all I'll ever ask."

The words pained her, but the darkness hid her involuntary reaction. She couldn't bring herself to answer, to add a fresh lie on top of the old lies. Instead she distracted him again. "That's *all* you'll ever ask me?" she asked archly.

"Well—" He laughed.

She kissed him again. The serious mood was dispelled. His sad, hopeful pleas had gone unanswered. It was so easy to deceive Jake. It would have been so much harder with Benjamin. Benjamin would have instantly recognized her evasiveness and been on her like a cat on a mouse.

She pushed Jake away, feeling unsettled. It was fun, trying to manipulate Benjamin. Benjamin could take care of himself. Jake could not. She could lie to Jake forever. She could manipulate Jake as much as she wanted to. She already had.

"Is something the matter?" Jake asked.

"No," she answered shortly.

"Did I do something wrong?"

She'd had two major boyfriends in her life, boyfriends that amounted to anything—Lucas and Benjamin. Neither of them easily hurt. Neither of them exactly saints. Jake was different. Jake was . . . was waiting expectantly for her to say a kind word.

"No, Jake, you didn't do anything wrong," she said, a little wearily. "I doubt you've ever done anything really wrong."

Claire

Diary:

Not much weather today, a perfectly clear night, and they say the high-pressure system may stay over the area for a week. Good weather is so boring. I need a storm.

Or maybe I'm just being cranky. I feel agitated and unhappy. I should feel great. I'm happy with Jake, really. He's such a relief after Benjamin.

Still, it's a big change. It's not just like changing clothes. I have to be different with him than I was with Benjamin. If I ever insulted Jake the way I sometimes did Benjamin, I think Jake would really be hurt. It's not that he doesn't have a sense of humor, he does. He's funny in a different way, though. Not as biting as Benjamin was. Nicer.

Nice. Decent. Sweet. Straightforward. Honest.

I like Jake a lot. I can't wait till I can be with him again. And I know he feels the same way about me. The problem is each time we're together, I feel like I'm tricking him somehow. I feel like I'm outsmarting him. And that just makes me mad, although I'm not sure if I'm mad at myself for being manipulative or at him for being so easy to manipulate.

I guess this is what it's like going out with a nice guy. No wonder Zoey finally dumped him. It's too much pressure to live up to. It's a strain being around someone who's nicer than you are.

But I can't be honest with him. I can't. He would never understand or accept the truth.

Honesty would just hurt him. So I have to go on deceiving Jake to protect him, and of course he'll go on believing me.

I could really use a storm. A major blow, lightning, thunder, driving rain. That would shake me out of this funk.

FIFTEEN

NINA THREW HER PILLOW AT the alarm clock the next morning, knocking it to the floor, where it kept right on blaring overly loud music. She climbed out of bed, reached for the clock, realized too late that her foot was caught in the sheet, and tumbled onto the floor, where she was at last able to turn off the radio. She glared up at her poster of the Black Keys.

"Is this really the way to start out a day?"

Although, it was, at least, a Friday. Even the worst Friday was better than the best Monday.

She untangled herself from the sheet, put the clock back on her nightstand, and fumbled in her bulging purse for a Lucky Strike. Only two left. She popped one in her mouth. *You'd think they'd last longer when you never actually light them*, she thought.

Friday. Cool. It was possible to survive Fridays. Fridays could be handled. There was still school, but on Friday even the teachers just wanted to end it all. Teachers tended not to do tests on Friday because they didn't want to spend their weekends grading them.

Ah yes, Friday.

She padded out into the hallway and down to the bathroom. Ha! She had beat Claire to it. Excellent. Now, to waste as much time as humanly possible and pay her sister back for yesterday morning, when Claire had left her with about seven minutes and no hot water.

How long a shower would it take to use up all the hot water?

"Let's find out," Nina said gleefully, turning on the hot-water tap in the bath as she calmly brushed her teeth over the sink.

She looked at her reflection in the mirror, which was just beginning to steam up. "This is the day," she told herself, pointing her foamy toothbrush for emphasis. The direct approach. It worked for Aisha. Why shouldn't it work for her?

"Benjamin, I would like to go out with you. Yes, on a date."

What's the worst he could say? *I love you like a sister?* Ooh, that would hurt. How about, *Nina, I just don't think of you in that way*? Not to mention, *Go away, why would I want to go out with you, you gorgon, when I can have any girl in the school, ha ha ha ha!*

She brushed some more and spit. He wasn't going to say that. She had never heard Benjamin call anyone a gorgon. Besides, how would he know if she was?

"The direct approach," she told her now-steamy reflection. "But first a long, long shower."

Aisha closed her eyes and stuck her face under the jet of hot water, rinsing away the soap, then tilted her head down to rinse away the shampoo. Conditioner?

Yes, the stuff that smelled like coconuts.

Would Christopher like that? What if he didn't like coconuts? A lot of people didn't. Maybe she should use the stuff that smelled "like spring." Everyone liked spring, though Aisha doubted anyone really knew what spring would smell like. Flowers? Rain? Birds hatching?

Who cared what Christopher liked? She wasn't going to be inviting him to smell her hair. Besides, maybe she'd use some of her mom's perfume.

Only the scent wouldn't last till the end of the day, when Christopher was going to pick her up. Which also meant that her coconut hair conditioner wouldn't smell by then, either.

Maybe she should bring some perfume with her. Some scent that would blend nicely with the cotton candy and hot dogs and pony poop at the carnival they were going to down in south Weymouth.

Or maybe she should just cancel the whole thing. It wasn't too late. Later it would be too late. Later, when they were coming back on the late ferry and he tried to get her to kiss him.

No kiss. She had decided on that. The purpose of this date was just to show that she was definitely *not* afraid to go out with him, because she, unlike Zoey, could deal with guys without losing her mind.

So no kiss.

Except maybe one small one. Just to be polite.

She twisted the faucet and slid back the glass shower door.

Claire's teeth chattered as she snatched the towel from the hook and wrapped it around herself. What did Nina do in the shower for twenty minutes? She hadn't even left any lukewarm water, let alone hot. Well, she was definitely going to straighten this out with Nina before cold weather came. She wasn't going to freeze to death every morning while Nina used up all the hot water daydreaming about new ways to annoy people.

She grabbed a second towel and wrapped it over her shoulders.

Great. Ten minutes to get ready.

Friday, she realized suddenly. It was Friday. Tomorrow was the day Lucas would be leaving.

"Stay away from Zoey today," she muttered. Zoey would be wandering around like a zombie, no doubt. Even worse than she'd been the last two days.

She pulled on her robe, sudden anger making her movements clumsy. Then she ran up the stairs to her room.

Not my fault, she told herself. It was just the way things had worked out.

She pulled off her robe, balled it up, and threw it into a corner.

I'll wear something white today, she thought, looking at the contents of her closet. *Something in a nice, innocent white.*

Zoey dressed with numb fingers, pulling up her shorts and zipping the fly, buttoning the front of her blouse. She had to look like she was going to school. And yet she wanted to look perfect for Lucas. This might be their last day together. She wanted him to have a good memory of her.

The tears started again, as they had so many times, but she wiped them away determinedly. He was not going to remember her with red, swollen eyes. She would use some Visine. Gets the red out.

Was this all right? she asked the image in her full-length mirror. She looked like she always did, like the girls in the J. Crew catalog—wholesome.

Was that what she wanted him to remember? She made an ironic face. Well, she was wholesome. It was too late for her to suddenly transform herself into Miley Cyrus or Katy Perry.

Although maybe that was what Lucas would have liked.

He wanted to make love to her. Maybe she should. Wouldn't that do more than anything else to ensure that he never forgot her? And that someday he would come back to her?

She grimaced at herself. "Yeah, he can come back to meet Lucas junior."

Although he probably had condoms.

Condoms sometimes broke.

But how could she say no when they had so little time left together? And did she really want to say no? She was getting ready to skip school for the first time in her life. Maybe it was time for another first.

She looked thoughtfully at herself and unbuttoned the top button of her blouse, showing just the edge of her white lace bra.

Then she shook her head and buttoned it again and walked from the room.

Nina desperately craved another cigarette. She knew it was insane, she knew she couldn't really be addicted because it wasn't like she even smoked the stupid things, but still, she wished she had one.

The ferry was coming into Weymouth. In two minutes it would be docking. Then she probably wouldn't have any time alone with Benjamin all day. Which would mean her next opportunity would be on the ferry coming home.

But what if someone else offered to take him to the concert? Everyone knew Benjamin liked the strangest music. Anyone might ask him out between now and the end of the day.

She bit her thumbnail, watching him from under her lowered brows as he calmly sat, reading a Braille book.

"Okay," she said, squaring her shoulders.

"Okay, *now*," she repeated.

"Really. I mean it. Now."

Suddenly she was walking, swinging her arms wide in a wild parody of nonchalance that was completely lost on Benjamin but would make her look like DORK SUPREME to everyone else on the boat.

"Hi, Benjamin," she said in some other girl's voice.

"Hey, Nina. What's up?"

"I guess Zoey skipped school to hang out with Lucas, huh?"

"Looks that way," Benjamin agreed, nodding glumly.

"Well, there's a concert, you know. Like, um, Batch."

"Batch? You mean Bach?"

"Of course that's what I mean," she giggled, blushing furiously. Was that really how you pronounced it? "Can't you tell when I'm kidding?"

"Usually," Benjamin said, looking puzzled.

Too late to stop now. "So, Bach is playing down in Portland would you like to go because I could drive my dad's car and it would be kind of fun I mean I know you like that kind of music and so do I really."

"Huh."

Nina took a breath. "Of course if you don't—"

"Are you just doing this to be nice, because I would pay for the gas and all."

Nina froze. Was that a yes? Yes, yes. It was almost certainly a yes. "It starts at eight thirty. Tomorrow. At night."

"Cool. We can catch the five ten. Grab something to eat when we get down to Portland. My treat on the food, since you're probably going to be bored all night."

"I don't think I'll be bored," Nina said, feeling almost giddy with triumph.

SIXTEEN

"SEE, THE THING YOU HAVE to do is control your fire," Christopher said, squeezing the trigger briefly and sending half a dozen very loud rounds into the target. "Most guys think because it's a machine gun they should just blast away." He squeezed off a quick burst.

"You're not hitting the little red star," Aisha pointed out, peering closely at the target.

"I'm blasting a circle *around* the star, see, then it will fall out and I'll have the fabulous blue-and-white teddy bear that I've wanted my entire life." He fired again, forming a circle halfway around the red star. "One more burst." He squeezed.

"That's it, pal," the attendant said in a bored voice.

"That's it?" Christopher demanded. "I'm out of ammo?"

"What can I say?" the attendant said with a shrug.

Christopher put the gun back in its cradle and turned to Aisha. "What can I say?" he mimicked. "No teddy bear."

"Want some cotton candy?" Aisha asked, holding out her half-eaten cone.

"No, let's go on the Ravin' Rodent," Christopher said. He pulled a bunch of tickets out of his pocket. "We've barely touched the rides."

Aisha followed him somewhat reluctantly. Thrill rides had never exactly been her thing. "Just don't blame me if I hurl pink," she said.

The line was short so late in the season, with almost all the tourists gone home. Aisha threw away the last of the cotton candy and licked her fingers clean. Then they scrunched side by side into the narrow red car. Christopher put his arm around her shoulders to make more room.

"I heard some kids were killed here when one of the cars jumped off the track, flew through the air, and crashed into the Tilt-a-Whirl," Christopher said conversationally.

"Really?"

"No. I just thought I'd make the ride more exciting for you."

"Thanks. I appreciate that."

"No problem."

Aisha tested the bar that held them down. "They do inspect these things, though. I mean, experts look at them and make sure they're all right?"

Suddenly the car jerked forward and began the slow, clanking ascent to the top. The carnival came into view around them, a sea of swirling neon surrounded by darkness. Off-key music blared from the carousel, and somewhere a persistent bell was ringing.

"I love roller coasters," Christopher said. "Especially this part. The anticipation."

"These rails look so rickety. Hey, I think there's a bolt missing. Right there." Aisha pointed at a section of track that passed beneath them. "I'm serious."

"At the top you have that pause, that first look down at the drop, and you think, Wow, what am I doing here?" Christopher offered philosophically.

"What are we—*Ahhhhhhhh!*"

"Yes!"

"Uhuhuhuhuhuh."

"Ha, look out!"

"Oh! Okay, that's enou-uhuhuhuhuh."

"Yahh yow, that was great. Here comes the loop."

"The what? Oh. Oh. *Ahhhhhh!*"

"That was excellent. I never thought such a small coaster would be that much fun. Come on, stand up."

"Is it over?"

"It's over, and they would like us to leave now," Christopher said.

Aisha opened her eyes and glared at him reproachfully. "You're a sick person, Christopher."

"I love roller coasters. If we're going to be . . . whatever . . . you're going to have to learn to like roller coasters. My great goal in life is to go to Ohio."

"Ohio," Aisha said as she walked shakily down the ramp.

"Cedar Point, the Mecca of great roller coasters. Roller-coaster heaven." He had a faraway look, his eyes shining with wistful anticipation. "Cedar Point. We could drive down next summer. Get a room at the Holiday Inn, spend all our time riding the coasters." He paused to consider. "Well, maybe not *all* our time."

"It's good to have dreams," Aisha said sardonically. "Even if there's no chance they'll ever come true."

"What, you don't think I'll ever get to Ohio?" he asked innocently.

"I don't think you'll ever get me to a Holiday Inn," Aisha said.

"Don't be so sure. You know what an overachiever I am." He laughed easily. That was one of his more attractive character traits, Aisha thought. He had a sense of humor, even about himself.

"How about a nice, slow, gentle ride?" Christopher suggested.

"Okay. Give my heart a chance to stop pounding."

"Uh-huh, right," he said noncommittally. He gave two tickets to the ticket taker and led her down the roped pathway to a row of boats.

"Does this involve plummeting down a waterfall and getting wet?" Aisha asked suspiciously.

"No waterfall," Christopher said. "See? They don't even have a safety bar, so how bad can it be?"

They climbed down into the boat together and again Christopher put his arm around her, although this time there was plenty of room. Aisha considered shrugging him off, but they'd been having a good time together and it would seem rude. Besides, he'd been perfectly well behaved so far. And it was just a little chilly in her sleeveless shirt. She had tiny goose bumps up and down her arms.

The boat meandered along an artificial stream, then slid into a dark tunnel, lit only intermittently by dim bulbs revealing dusty tableaux of plaster pirates gloating over papier-mâché gold coins.

"Sort of a low-budget Pirates of the Caribbean," Aisha remarked.

"Yeah, this ain't exactly Disney World," Christopher agreed, laughing. "But it is slow and gentle."

"I like slow and gentle," Aisha said.

She felt Christopher's arm tighten slowly around her shoulders. *That's not quite what I meant*, she thought. But instead of speaking, she just swallowed and pointed at the next tableau. "That one's really lame."

Now Christopher was sitting closer, his leg pressed against hers, his arm sliding down her back to encompass her waist. His warm breath was on her neck.

The boat slid out of the circle of light, into a still-darker part of the tunnel. There was no light. No sound but the trickle of the water and the beating of Aisha's own heart.

Now was the time to say no. Now was the time to tell him she did not want to kiss him, because she didn't really care about him one way or the other, was not attracted to him, was not interested in anything serious, was not going to fall for him just because they were both black in a nearly all-white school.

His lips were close. They brushed her cheek, searching in the dark. Then missed again, brushing her chin.

What did she have to do, draw him a road map?

She found his jaw with her fingers and guided his lips to hers.

At that precise moment, a flashbulb went off.

Aisha jumped back, startled. The boat plowed through swinging doors and emerged in the neon glow of the carnival again.

"I think that ride was a little too short," Christopher said, his voice an octave lower than usual.

She looked away, feeling confused and annoyed. And frustrated. "It ended just at the right time. I should have told you, I don't kiss on the first date."

"You don't?" Christopher said, smirking as he helped her up onto solid ground.

"That wasn't like a real kiss," Aisha said. "Besides, it was so dark I didn't even know where you were."

"Uh-huh."

"You folks care to buy the souvenir photo?" the attendant asked, holding out a Polaroid. "Two dollars."

"No," Aisha said quickly.

"Absolutely," Christopher said, pulling two dollars from his pocket. He admired the photograph critically. "Huh. You say that wasn't a real kiss?"

Aisha snatched the Polaroid from his hand and clapped a hand over her mouth. Christopher snatched the photo back.

"Why don't you just admit it, Aisha? You like me. You wanted me to kiss you, I did, and you liked that, too. Why is that so hard for you to admit?"

Aisha glared at him, then down at the photograph in his hand. Then, despite her best efforts to stop herself, she grinned sheepishly. "Okay, I didn't hate it. But I'm still not going to Ohio to ride roller coasters."

Claire pushed the last of her pecan pie halfway across the white linen tablecloth. "That is so rich," she said.

Jake looked greedily at the dessert. He had already finished his own. "You're not going to eat that?"

"You eat it," Claire invited, smiling in amazement as the last two bites disappeared almost instantly.

"I'm a growing boy," Jake mumbled apologetically.

Claire sipped her coffee. "That was a pretty good meal," she said. "Not quite as good as Passmores', maybe, but good."

Jake raised an eyebrow. "I don't know when I'm going to feel right about going into Zoey's parents' restaurant again."

"Think they'll poison you?" Claire joked.

"I don't know; it just doesn't seem quite right, you know?"

Actually, she didn't. She wasn't doing anything wrong going out with Jake instead of Benjamin Passmore. And Jake wasn't doing anything wrong by going out with her and not Zoey Passmore. Claire's inclination might have been to make that point by having dinner at Passmores'.

"I understand," she said.

"No point rubbing people's noses in things," Jake said.

This, from the guy who had punched Lucas almost the first time he saw him back from jail? But then, Claire realized wearily, that was all a part of it—it was one thing in Jake's mind to go right up and start a fistfight, because that was straight-up-the-middle. Taking Claire on a date to Passmores' would seem sneaky to him.

"You realize this is our first real date?" Claire said, breaking away from her morose thoughts.

He gave a leering wink. "Does that mean I get my first kiss all over again?"

"Anytime," she said, leaning through the candlelight to let him kiss her. It was a brief kiss, but full of tenderness. Also full of self-consciousness as Claire realized that some other patrons were watching.

"Come on, let's get out of here," Jake said, his voice low. "I already told Mrs. Savageau to put it on my dad's tab. He owes me for some work I did at the marina."

"Jake, I was going to pay half," Claire complained. "Come on, let me help out."

"No way," he said. He stood up and came around the table to pull out her chair.

Claire sighed and led the way outside, pausing only to tell Mrs. Savageau that everything was wonderful. Outside the air was cool and clear, and they strolled arm in arm along the waterfront, wandering in the general direction of Claire's home. The ferry was just coming in, rounding the breakwater, and they used the excuse to stop and make out a little, leaning against the shadowed side of a wooden souvenir shack.

"That's the ten ten," Claire commented. "I didn't realize it was so late."

"If you remember, we got a slightly late start," Jake pointed out. "Certain people weren't ready at seven sharp like certain people said they would be."

"Certain people had to make themselves look good," Claire said.

Jake stepped back and looked her up and down, then back up again. "Mmm. I take it back. Definitely worth the wait."

"Hey, look," Claire said, laughing as she pointed toward the bow of the ferry.

"Is that Aisha and Christopher?" Jake asked rhetorically. "I thought she didn't really like him."

"Has an interesting way of showing it, doesn't she?"

"It looks to me like they're getting along," Jake said dryly.

"Young love," Claire said.

"They aren't the only ones," Jake said, suddenly sounding serious. "I have totally lost it for you, Claire."

"Jake—"

"No, I mean it. I'm actually glad Zoey dumped me. I mean,

if she hadn't, you and I might never have gotten together. I've known you all my life, and yet I feel like I'd never really known you until that evening when you came to my room when I was depressed over Zoey and—" He shook his head helplessly. "It's like you rescued me."

Claire felt her hands clenching and deliberately forced herself to relax. Damn. He was going to say it, and there was no way to stop him.

"I love you, Claire." He held up his hand. "You don't have to say anything back, I know it's kind of quick and all, but I know how I feel."

"Jake, how can you know how you feel?" she asked miserably.

"Because I know you," he said.

Damn it, she raged inwardly. *Why is he doing this to me?* "You . . . look, you don't know everything about me, Jake. You really don't. I'm not exactly perfect, I'm—"

He silenced her with a kiss. "You are exactly perfect for me."

Claire returned his kiss, going through all the familiar motions. But inside she was boiling, raging. Something was gnawing at her, infuriating her and at the same time drawing a blanket of unhappiness over her mind. It was a strange, unfamiliar, unpleasant feeling.

He pulled away and whispered, "You're the best, Claire, the best."

The feeling grew, and suddenly the name for it popped into Claire's consciousness. Guilt.

Oh, Claire thought dismally as Jake held her tight to his chest, *so that's what guilt feels like.*

SEVENTEEN

ZOEY HAD SPENT THE DAY with Lucas, walking the beach, climbing the winding paths up the ridge, strolling along Pond Road. They'd covered nearly every square foot of the northern half of the island.

Lucas was saying good-bye, again, to his home.

They talked of everything under the sun, of his plans and hers, their hopes and dreams. He talked about his mother, how sorry he felt for her, a shadow in her own home. And he talked about his father, how he admired him, despite everything, for his moral code, his ability to work without complaining, even his determination.

And Zoey talked about her own family, the way she felt her parents had never really grown up, the way they both felt somehow guilty because Benjamin had lost his sight. But the more she talked, the differences became so clear. Yes, her father still had one foot in the past, still played Grateful Dead records and wore a ponytail. And yes, her mother flirted too much with the guys who came into the restaurant's bar, and was, by her own admission, not into "all that parental stuff." But what was so clear was that in her family she was loved. And despite her parents' almost daily arguments, they loved each other passionately.

She had so little to complain of, really, and Lucas had so much. Without her, Lucas was utterly alone.

They had cried, and kissed, and hugged each other till it hurt. But they had not found a way to put off the deadline that seemed now to be racing toward them at a terrible speed.

They vowed to spend every last minute they could together. They also vowed they would never give up, that they would find a way to be together.

They said good night easily at midnight, knowing that it was only a rehearsal.

Zoey went through all the motions of going to bed, lying awake in her bed until she heard her parents come home from closing the restaurant and go to sleep. At two thirty she dressed silently, stole down the stairs, and crept out the back door.

The moon was still in the sky, turning the dew that had settled in her backyard silver. She made her way up the path. She saw Lucas in his window, waiting. He held up his hand and disappeared. Seconds later the front door opened silently and she flew into his arms.

They walked at a snail's pace up the stairs and into Lucas's room.

"I knew you'd come," he whispered.

"Of course. Nothing could stop me."

They kissed passionately, hopelessly, lying on his bed, a tangled mess of arms and legs and twisted sheets.

Zoey knew he wanted to make love to her. And she didn't know how she could refuse. In five hours they would have to catch the ferry. In nine hours he would be on a plane. In less than eleven hours she would be back on the island, alone.

Alone.

He lay on his back, she lay on him, looking down at his dark face, knowing that her tears were falling to mingle with his. Sadness swept them both up, dampening the passion that had threatened to carry them away.

They lay together in each other's arms, saying nothing. After a while Zoey felt she might even be sleeping, as dream images floated through her mind. Images of them together, happy in sunshine.

She even smiled, the first time in so long, as she constructed fantasies of how they could find each other again. Then her bleary, swollen eyes focused on the blue numbers of his clock. Four o'clock. Their time together had shortened by another hour and a half.

She stirred, and her lips found his in the darkness. Her fingers unbuttoned his shirt. He seemed to have stopped breathing, and then, his fingers, nervous, fumbled at the front of her blouse.

"You don't have to do this," he whispered.

"I know," she whispered back. Was she? Was she really going to do this? Or was this just another part of her fantasy of happiness?

There was a heavy clumping on the steps and Lucas froze.

"My dad. He's going to work."

"At four in the morning?" Zoey asked.

"Lobstermen start early," Lucas said.

They heard the sound of the front door closing and footsteps crunching on the gravel driveway. He had not bothered to say good-bye to his own son, Zoey realized. And with Mr. Cabral gone, any last hope for a reprieve was gone, too.

Suddenly a voice came from the front yard. Not Mr. Cabral's deep, accented voice. They hesitated only a split second, then they raced to the dormered window, both half-dressed.

The sky was still dark and the moon had set, but the porch light showed them clearly—Mr. Cabral, standing, smoking a cigarette.

And Claire.

Zoey looked at Lucas questioningly and saw the trace of a smile on his lips.

"I'll be damned," he said softly.

They dressed quickly and went down the stairs, no longer caring what anyone thought, and emerged as Mr. Cabral was walking away.

Claire had her back to them. "Mr. Cabral," she called out. "You have to do it. You know it's the right thing."

For what seemed an eternity, Mr. Cabral stood, his cigarette burning away in his mouth, staring down toward the distant dock. At last he half turned, looking over his shoulder at his son. "Lucas," he said, giving the name an odd pronunciation. "Lucas, you better stay."

For a moment it looked as if he might have something more to add, but then, grinding the butt of his cigarette out underfoot, he set off again, rounding the corner and disappearing down Center Street.

Claire turned to face them, her mouth set in a grim line. "I suppose you're wondering what I'm doing here at four in the morning," she said, her attempt at humor falling flat.

"What *are* you doing here?" Zoey asked.

Claire ignored her, focusing on Lucas. "Look, Lucas, there's something you have to understand. I really didn't remember. After the accident I really did not remember."

Lucas nodded and remained silent.

Claire drew in a deep, shaky breath. "I just remembered a

week ago. Things just started coming together. Mostly I guess because you returned. I guess it jarred my memory. Anyway, I've known since then. I didn't speak up because of my dad . . ."

Lucas nodded again. "I understand."

"I don't," Zoey said.

Claire looked surprised. "You didn't tell her?"

Lucas made a dismissive noise. "One thing you learn right away in jail—everyone in there claims to be innocent. What was the point in one more convict running around claiming he got screwed?"

"Innocent?" Zoey said, trying to piece together some understanding.

"Lucas wasn't driving the car the night Wade McRoyan was killed," Claire said wearily. "I was."

Zoey rocked back on her heels and put a hand over her heart. "You?"

"No one knew the truth but Lucas and my father," Claire said. "Not even me. Lucas took the rap because . . . well, we were good friends."

"I loved you," Lucas said simply.

"And then my father got into the act. He helped Mr. Cabral out with a loan he needed to keep his boat. He wanted to make sure Lucas wouldn't change his mind and recant. Especially after everyone realized they were actually going to send Lucas to jail." Claire took another deep breath. "My father knows I know," she said. "I told him I'd keep it quiet. He says people might think he'd broken the law himself. The loan to your father might look like he was paying you to confess."

"I'm not going to tell anyone about that part of it," Lucas said.

Claire sagged in relief, but Zoey was outraged. "Why would you protect Claire's father?"

"I wouldn't," Lucas said. "I'd protect my dad, though. He doesn't know why Mr. Geiger arranged that loan. I know my old man's a bastard, but he would never sell me out for money, and it would tear him apart if he knew the whole truth. From here on out the story will just be that I was a dumb kid, so madly in love that I confessed to protect Claire. That's ninety percent of the truth, anyway."

Claire nodded. "That's a better percentage than we've had around here lately."

"Have you told Jake yet?" Lucas asked.

Claire hung her head and answered in a whisper. "That's next."

"Poor Jake," Lucas said sincerely.

"Yeah," Claire said. She looked at each of them, her dark-in-dark eyes almost lifeless. She tried out a smile that quivered and collapsed.

"You say you've remembered for a week, at least," Zoey said. "But you kept it a secret till now. What made you change your mind?"

This time Claire did manage a soft, sad smile. She sighed deeply. "I don't think Lucas ever had any illusions about me being perfect, back when we were together. And I know Benjamin didn't. But Jake . . . Jake thinks I'm like him. He thinks I'm sweet and honest and fundamentally decent. The more he trusted me, the worse I felt. The more he accepted my deception, the more I couldn't stand myself."

"You felt guilty," Zoey said.

"Yeah. It took me a while, but then I realized that was it." She made a sour face. "Nasty feeling. I'm going to have to learn how to get over it." She turned away and took several steps before calling over her shoulder, "You two can get back to *whatever* it was you were doing."

Lucas grinned and took Zoey in his arms. "Can we?"

Zoey gave him a quick peck on the cheek, then firmly pushed him away. "I'm very, very sleepy. I think I'll head on home."

"Will I see you tomorrow? I mean, later today?" Lucas called after her.

"Yes," Zoey said, twirling around in sheer happiness. "Actually, you will."

• • •

She tapped at the sliding glass door for a long time. The sun was just beginning to peek over the horizon, a faint glow that threw the ridge into relief, black against a pearl gray sky. Claire was exhausted. She hadn't slept at all this night.

She had tossed and turned in her bed, arguing one side and then the other. Concern for her father, fear of losing Jake, versus the sense that either way she would lose Jake. How could she ever really pretend to love someone when their entire relationship was built on deception?

And as much as she tried to dismiss it, the image of Zoey crying, having to say good-bye to Lucas, and even the image of Lucas, whom she had once loved, suffering yet again for a crime he didn't commit, kept coming back.

She tapped again at Jake's door. Sooner or later he would wake up. It wasn't even five yet, a ridiculous hour for a visit. But Claire was determined to get it all over with. She couldn't let Jake learn the truth secondhand. She had to tell him herself.

A memory popped to the surface of her mind. Benjamin, of course, just a few days earlier . . . had it really been only a few days? It seemed like forever. He'd pointed his sunglasses at her and said, "In the end, as self-serving and ruthless as you are, Claire, when the line is drawn between right and wrong, I think you'll do the right thing."

The memory brought a smile. Benjamin would feel so smug, being proved right.

The door slid open quite suddenly. Jake stood there blinking sleepily, wearing only a pair of boxer shorts. "Claire?"

"I'm afraid so," she said.

"Is something the matter?" Then his face brightened as he thought of another possibility. "Or are you just here to—"

"I have to talk to you," she said. "Can I come in?"

"Of course." He was fully awake now and obviously puzzled.

She entered the dark room. He offered to turn on the light, but she said no, the darkness was fine. They sat together on the edge of his bed.

"What's up?" he asked.

She took his hand in hers. Then she leaned over and kissed him, not a passionate kiss. Closer to a farewell.

"I don't know any easy way to say this," Claire said. "For a long time I didn't remember the details of the night Wade died."

She felt him stiffen, but she maintained her grip on his hand. "But now I do remember. We had all been drinking. Lucas and I and Wade. All of us."

"I know you were all drunk," Jake said. "But only Lucas was driving drunk."

Claire felt a tear trickle down her cheek. Damn. She didn't

want to do that, but she was just so tired. "Lucas wasn't driving," she said.

For a moment Jake froze. Then, slowly, he pulled his hand away.

"Lucas was in the backseat," Claire said. "In fact, he was saying we should pull over and walk home. But I wouldn't listen."

"You?" he whispered.

"I was the one driving the car, Jake. And the more Lucas complained, the more I would swerve around, making a big joke of it. Until that last split second when I realized we were going to hit." She took a deep, shaky breath and forged ahead. "And just so the whole truth is out, once and for all, I saw the tree, and I knew we would hit it. And at the very last second I yanked the wheel over so that it wouldn't hit my side of the car. I saved myself. And I killed Wade."

EIGHTEEN

NINA WAS UP EARLIER THAN she had ever been on a Saturday, managing to catch the usual seven-forty ferry to Weymouth. The night before, just as her father was heading to bed and was yawning and vulnerable, she had talked him out of his American Express card and half the cash he had in his wallet.

She hadn't gone on a date since . . . well, for a very long time, and she needed clothes, a purse, shoes other than boots, all the usual date stuff. Probably stockings. Lip gloss, eyeliner, breath mints.

Obviously, Benjamin wouldn't really know how she looked, but still, she didn't want to show up and have him look great and her look like crap. What if someone he knew was there and came over and said, Hi, Benjamin, how come you're going out with a girl who's dressed like a skank?

It was pretty bad if you couldn't manage to dress better than a guy who couldn't even see himself in a mirror.

Once off the ferry, she caught the bus out to the mall,

arriving just as the doors opened. Instantly she felt over-whelmed. If only she had Zoey with her. But today was the day Zoey would be saying good-bye to Lucas. Not a good day to ask her along on a shopping trip.

Naturally, she felt sorry for Zoey, but Nina's presence would not be welcome while Zoey and Lucas said their sad farewells. And as for Aisha, Nina didn't really want to try to convince Aisha to get up this early on a Saturday.

Too bad Claire wasn't the type of sister she could really share this kind of an experience with.

Plus, of course, it was Claire's former boyfriend she was going out with.

"Okay," she said, standing uncertainly at the mall's cross-roads, "all you need is one complete outfit. Sophisticated, but not like you're making a big deal out of it. Attractive but not sleazy. Conservative enough for classical music and yet with a style all your own."

She set off like an explorer through uncharted wilderness. She had shopped at the mall, of course, but usually only in certain areas. She'd never even been inside some of the shops. Possibly because she had never consciously bought anything *for* a date. Which, she supposed, did make her a little backward compared to most junior-class girls.

"Face it," she muttered, "you're a little backward compared

to most sixth-grade girls."

She didn't know why she hadn't dated very often, or why she had never dated any guy more than twice. Usually her dates amounted to meeting casually at a movie, or a quick stopoff at a burger place. She'd only ever kissed one guy and that had grossed her out.

The truth was, most guys grossed her out.

Except Benjamin. He was so different. She knew he would never be disgusting, the way guys often were. He would always treat her with respect, and that was important. Unlike when she had gone out with George O'Brien and he had kissed her and then tried to touch her breasts.

The memory made her heart race, and she realized her palms were sweaty. She had totally panicked when George had done that. So utterly uncool of her. George had gone around telling everyone she was a lesbian. Which she wasn't. In fact, she had more experience than people knew. More than Zoey and probably Aisha.

That memory made her even more uncomfortable. She beelined for a bench and sat down beside an old man. She fumbled a cigarette out of her purse and stuck it in her mouth.

"You're not going to smoke that, are you?" the old man asked.

"Actually, no," she said. She took several deep breaths and

wiped her hands on her shirt front.

Why were these things out of her past suddenly reemerging? She hadn't thought about all that in a long time. At least not outside of the dreams she sometimes still had. Was it because she was finally going out with Benjamin? Was that it?

But Benjamin wasn't George O'Brien.

And Benjamin wasn't her uncle, either.

She looked at her fingers and saw they were shaking. She sucked deeply on the unlit cigarette. *That's all in the past, Nina,* she told herself. *Years and years ago. Over and done and forgotten. Things happen, and then you go on.*

What if Benjamin tried to kiss her and the panic happened? Like it had with George? Was that why she had gagged in the movie theater when Benjamin had leaned close? Was she still capable of losing it the way she had with George?

She'd rather die than act that way with Benjamin. How would she ever be able to face him again?

But that wasn't going to happen, she reassured herself. This was Benjamin. Gentle, smart, funny Benjamin. Her friend. Her trusted friend.

And besides, he couldn't do anything she didn't want him to do. After all, he was blind, and that did give her a certain advantage she had never had back . . . back then.

"All right, shake it off, kid," she challenged herself. The

old man turned and stared. "Sorry, sir, I was just talking to the voices in my head. They want me to shoot Justin Bieber, but I'm refusing."

The old man gave her a startled stare that had the effect of instantly putting her back in a better mood.

She pulled out her father's American Express card and looked at it. "All right, let's you and me do some damage."

Nina arrived at Benjamin and Zoey's house at four forty-five, wearing a black dress, black pumps with heels that made her wobble and lurch, real stockings that itched her thighs, a silver necklace and bracelet, and enough perfume to fumigate a barn. She felt like the largest, most conspicuous dweeb on earth.

Zoey's reaction when she opened the door was not promising. "Nina? What are you . . . Nina? Is that a dress? And hose? Did someone die?"

Nina gave her a dirty look. "Didn't Benjamin tell you? We're going out to hear Bach. You know, Bach, I'm sure? Naturally I mean Johann *Sebastian* Bach, who lived from 1685 to 1750 and is considered the leading composer of the late baroque period."

Zoey stared at her. "Is this one of those cases of demonic possession? Have you been worshipping Satan again?"

Nina brushed past her into the entryway. "So tell me the

truth, is it too much? It is, isn't it?"

"That's not it, it's just that—"

"Damn," Lucas said, nodding appreciatively at her. "Little Nina is suddenly all grown up." He grabbed her around the waist and swung her in a graceful circle.

"Lucas? What are you doing here? I thought today was the day you were, you know."

"Didn't Claire tell you?" Zoey asked.

"I haven't seen Claire all day," Nina said. "I've been buying clothes and memorizing fun facts about old Johann Sebastian. Tell me what?"

Zoey exchanged a look with Lucas. "Claire should probably tell you," she said.

"I would browbeat you into telling me," Nina said, "but my thighs itch, and I'm really here to pick up Benjamin. Is he ready? We have to make the five ten, and I'm not fast in these shoes."

"I'll go get him," Zoey volunteered.

"So, what do you really think," Nina asked Lucas, holding out her arms to give him the full effect. "You're a guy and all."

"That's very observant of you, Nina," Lucas said, giving her a wink. "What do I think, as a guy? I'll tell you what I think." He grabbed her around the waist. "Quick! Before Zoey gets back! Let's do it, right here on the floor!"

Nina felt a tremor of fear before she realized that Lucas was obviously kidding. She pushed him away. "I guess that's a compliment. Kind of."

"You're a babe," Lucas said sincerely. "What are you going to do? Pick up guys down in Portland whenever Ben's out of earshot?"

"No," she said, blushing a little.

"Well, it's probably a good thing Benjamin can't see you tonight," Lucas said. "He might start thinking of you in a whole new way."

Nina rolled her eyes in exasperation. Obviously Lucas didn't get it.

Benjamin arrived with Zoey a few steps behind. He was dressed in a suit and loosely knotted tie. He took a quick turn as he came in. "Sorry to keep you waiting, but Zoey told me you were showing leg tonight. I thought I'd better go beyond my usual concert attire of jeans and a jacket and go all out and wear my dead-relative clothes. How do you like the jacket? I hear it's plaid."

Nina grinned. The suit was black, like most of what Benjamin owned, because black was an easy color to match. "I think the plaid jacket clashes just a little with the striped pants."

"How does Nina look?" Benjamin asked.

"She looks sophisticated and—"

"No, not you, Zoey," Benjamin interrupted. "What do you

know? You're a girl. Lucas?"

"She looks too good for you," Lucas said. "I give her a thumbs-up. Way up."

"You're both sexist scum," Zoey said disgustedly.

"We better get going," Benjamin said.

"Yeah," Nina agreed. "I wouldn't want to miss anything. You all know how I love baroque music."

"Oh, right," Zoey said. "You just won't shut up about baroque music."

"This is very sweet of you to give up your Saturday night for me," Benjamin said.

Nina blushed again and muttered a quick good night to Zoey and Lucas. She took Benjamin's arm, and they crossed the yard together.

"You don't have to guide me," Benjamin said. "You know I have this island down like the back of my hand."

"Oh, yeah, I did know that," Nina said awkwardly, releasing her grip. Then she saw something that made her stomach churn. "It's Claire!"

Her sister was coming up the street looking angry, or at least distracted.

Nina slapped her hands down to her side and sidled away from Benjamin. She hadn't exactly mentioned to Claire that she was going out with her recently ex-boyfriend.

Claire caught sight of them and came rushing up. "Has either of you two seen Jake at all today?"

Nina shook her head violently, still expecting Claire to lash out with some choice bit of sarcasm.

"I haven't," Benjamin said.

"Okay. Okay. Damn. Um, is Zoey in?"

"She and Lucas are both inside," Benjamin said.

"I'll go ask them," Claire said, immediately heading for the house.

"What was that all about?" Nina asked as she urged Benjamin down the road.

"I'm not sure," Benjamin said in a troubled voice.

"I can't believe she didn't give me a hard time," Nina said.

"Why would she?"

Nina shrugged. "You know. Because, you know, you were her boyfriend and all. And we're, you know . . ."

"Mmm," he said, still frowning in a preoccupied way. "It's not like she'd be jealous. I mean, it's just you and me."

Nina stopped and glared at his back as he walked on. *It's not like she'd be jealous*, she mimicked silently. *It's just you and me.* She looked down at her expensive, painstakingly chosen outfit, with her tight, uncomfortable shoes. All this, and he still didn't get it. All this effort and he still thought of her as his little buddy. Damn him to hell and back again. The insensitive toad.

"Come on, Nina," he called over his shoulder.

"I'm coming," she muttered through clenched teeth.

"Well, walk up here with me," he said crankily. "I can't talk to you when you're dragging back there. Besides, I want to make everyone who sees us jealous."

"Why would they be jealous?" she subtly mimicked his own tone.

He shrugged. "Everyone's jealous of a guy with a beautiful girl on his arm."

Nina sighed. Okay, maybe he wasn't a complete toad.

NINETEEN

CLAIRE SPILLED OUT HER FEAR to Zoey and Lucas. She had told Jake the truth early that morning. Jake had said very little, just turned his back on her, and when she had tried to put her arms around him, he had told her to leave.

Later that afternoon she had tried to call him, but there had been no answer.

She had gone over to his house. His yellow pickup was gone, and when Claire peered through the sliding glass door into his room, she had seen a pile of empty beer cans shoved half under his bed.

She had looked for him everywhere, called everywhere, but no one had seen him. She was worried. He was probably drunk, and in his truck, somewhere on the island.

"I don't know where to look that I haven't looked," she said, sitting stiffly on the chair in Zoey's room. "There's only one place . . . And I don't want to go there alone."

Lucas caught Zoey's eye. "We'll go with you," Zoey said.

The three of them piled into the Passmores' island car, a wreck even by island standards. Zoey drove along South Street to Coast Road. There was no question in anyone's mind where they should look.

At the end of Coast Road where the asphalt gave way to gravel and sand, where a huge tree still bore the scar of a deadly impact, they spotted the pickup truck parked in the ditch.

Jake was slumped over the wheel, unmoving.

Claire leapt from the car and ran, followed closely by Zoey and Lucas. She threw open the door, her heart pounding, her mind swimming in fear.

She saw Jake's breathing and, putting her hand to his cheek, felt the warmth. She nearly collapsed with relief.

"He's all right," she said. "Just passed out."

"Thank God," Zoey whispered.

Lucas gently pushed Jake back onto the seat and raised his legs into a prone position. Then, with a glance at Claire, he removed the keys from the ignition and handed them to her.

"I'll wait here with him," Claire said. "Till he wakes up."

FIND OUT WHAT HAPPENS NEXT!

ONE

THE WHISTLE SHRIEKED, OBLITERATING EVERY other sound. The ferry strained and vibrated and churned the dark water to a cheerier blue-green. It pulled back from the dock, turning clumsily away from the already failing sun, and pointed its blunt nose across the cold, oily chop toward the island.

Nina Geiger pulled the red-and-white pack of Lucky Strikes from her purse, extracted one cigarette, and popped it in the corner of her mouth. She drew deeply on it and exhaled contentedly.

The young man on the bench behind her leaned forward over her shoulder. "Do you need a light?" A yellow plastic lighter was in his hand.

"No thanks, I don't smoke," Nina said, speaking around the cigarette. She turned to Zoey Passmore, a willowy blond seated beside her. "The guy's trying to kill me," Nina said with mock outrage.

Zoey refused to look up from her book. Nina bent forward

and looked past Zoey to Aisha Gray. "What's with Zoey?"

"Studying," Aisha said with a shrug. Her eyes were closed and her head tilted back to savor the cool breeze on her face. Her mass of black curls floated and bounced like something alive.

"She doesn't need to study," Nina said to Aisha.

"Yes, *she* does," Zoey muttered.

"I'm the one who needs to study," Nina said. "Algebra. It's only the third week of school and I'm already four weeks behind."

"Who do you have for algebra?" Aisha asked, cracking open one eye.

"Ms. Lehr."

"You don't have to study for Ms. Lehr's class," Aisha said.

"Maybe *you* don't have to study for algebra, but trust me," Nina said, "I do. You can't b.s. algebra. History you can b.s. English is the ultimate b.s. subject. But not math. Math is either right or wrong."

"Aisha's right," Zoey said, still studying the book open on her lap. "I had her last year. You can't get less than a *B*-plus in Ms. Lehr's class."

"Watch me," Nina said.

Zoey looked up at last, turning amused blue eyes on her friend. "You're not listening, Nina. Ms. Lehr is all into self-esteem. Everything is self-esteem. She took some seminar or something where they taught her that students have to have self-esteem, and you can't have self-esteem when you're flunking algebra, right? So she gives everyone a good grade."

"No way."

Aisha held up her hand as if taking an oath. "True fact."

Nina laughed. "You're saying I can blow every test—"

"And you'll get a *B*-plus," Zoey said. "If you want an A-plus, you have to work a little harder."

Nina thought it over for a moment. "Wait a minute. How about if I tell Ms. Lehr that my self-esteem will be crushed unless I get an *A*?"

Zoey and Aisha exchanged a look.

"Damn," Aisha said.

"Never thought of that," Zoey admitted.

The ferry was up to top speed now, heading across the harbor with its cargo of high school students, homeward-bound shoppers loaded with bags, and early commuters hunched over folded newspapers. The trip to Chatham Island took twenty-five minutes.

Nina saw her sister, Claire, come up from the lower deck. She appeared first as a head of glossy, long black hair rising from the stairwell, then step by step revealed the body that had half the guys at Weymouth High quivering. *Okay, three quarters of the guys*, Nina corrected herself.

Claire glanced at Nina, then looked away, searching the deck uncertainly for a place to sit. Nina felt a momentary twinge of sympathy but suppressed it. Claire could take care of herself.

Jake McRoyan was leaning against the forward railing, looking thoughtful and distant, his big football player's shoulders hunched forward. Zoey's brother, Benjamin, was toward the back with his earphones on, staring sightlessly ahead through his Ray Bans and taking an occasional bite from a Snickers bar.

Poor Claire, Nina thought, without too much pity. Trying to find a safe, neutral place to sit, somewhere between her two ex-boyfriends and her sister.

Zoey nudged Nina in the side. She too had caught sight of Claire. "Come on," Zoey said. "It won't kill you to be nice to your sister."

Nina made a face. Zoey was a hopelessly nice person. But then, Zoey had spent her life growing up with kind, considerate, decent Benjamin as her only sibling, while Nina had grown up under the ruthless tyranny of Perfect Claire. Ice Princess. Holder of the Record for Early Breast Development. Claire the Zit-proof. Claire of the perfect taste in clothing who had never once worn anything to school that caused large numbers of people to wince and turn away. Claire who must have sold her soul to the devil because she certainly didn't have one that Nina had ever—

"Come on, Nina," Zoey said in a chiding voice that Nina hated.

Nina growled at Zoey. Then she called out, "Oh, Clai-aire."

Claire came over, looking reserved as always and a little skeptical. "Yes?"

"Would you like to join us?" Nina said, using her fingers to squeeze her mouth into a happy smile.

Claire rolled her eyes. "It's come to this. You're actually feeling sorry for me."

"No, we're not," Zoey said quickly.

"Yes, we are," Nina told her sister. "No one's ever seen you looking pathetic and lost and boyfriendless before."

Claire sat down beside Nina. "So, of course, you're enjoying it," she said dryly.

"No, we're not," Zoey said sincerely.

Aisha made a so-so gesture with her hand.

"You bet we're enjoying it," Nina said. "At least I was."

"How are things between you and Jake?" Zoey asked. "I mean, we haven't really talked since . . . since that night."

Claire shrugged, her eyes uncharacteristically troubled. "I told him everything. He told me to get out."

Aisha and Zoey stared at her expectantly.

"That's it," Claire said.

"You know, you're quite a storyteller," Nina said. "You really made the moment come alive."

"I went to his room. He was asleep, so I knocked louder. He eventually woke up, and I told him the truth," Claire said simply. "I said, 'Hi, Jake, you know how for the last two years you blamed Lucas for crashing the car the night your brother was killed? Well, guess what? It's all come back to me now, and it turns out *I'm* the one who was driving. I ran the car into that tree. Surprise!' " She shook her head. The lightness in her voice had turned to bitterness. "Then he told me he never wanted to speak to me again." She paused, her eyes studying her hands. "Does that make the moment come alive for you?"

Nina lowered her gaze. "Sorry."

"Yeah, so am I," Claire said sharply. "Sorry about what happened two years ago, sorry I didn't remember, sorry Lucas suffered. Where is he, by the way? I could grovel for him a little."

"He's at his parole officer's. He still has to go until you guys get all the legal stuff cleared up," Zoey said.

"Excellent," Claire said. "Another thing for me to be sorry about."

"Well," Nina said, for lack of anything better to say.

"You know, we're all still your friends," Zoey said, reaching across Nina to put her hand on Claire's arm.

"Really," Aisha joined in. "What happened two years ago

is ancient history. And just because it took you a week longer than it should have to decide to do the right thing, that's not going to turn us against you. It's not like we ever thought you were Joan of Arc."

"We know how hard it was for you," Zoey said. "And I know Lucas is cool with it."

To Nina's amazement, her sister actually looked touched. Claire nodded mutely and looked away. For a moment Nina was afraid Claire might actually cry. It was an unnerving possibility.

"So. All forgiven, all forgotten," Nina said cheerily. "I guess there's nothing left now but the big group hug."

Claire gave her sister a dubious look.

"Anyway, we're all friends, right?" Zoey asked hopefully. "I mean, you know, island solidarity and all."

"I am glad you guys don't hate me," Claire admitted.

"I never hated you," Aisha said. "By the time I found out what was going on, it was all over."

"*I* still can't stand you, Claire," Nina said helpfully.

Claire smiled her rare, wintry smile. "We're sisters, Nina. We're not supposed to get along. Although Dad will probably want us to try, for a while at least."

"What do you mean?" Nina asked. "He knows better."

"You know. While Aunt Elizabeth and Uncle Mark are here."

Nina felt her heart thud. The unlit cigarette fell from her mouth and rolled across the gray-painted steel deck, "What are you talking about?" she demanded.

"Didn't Dad tell you? They're doing the leaf-peeping thing through Vermont and New Hampshire, then they're coming to stay with us for a week. What is the matter with you, are you choking?"

Nina realized her hand was clutching at the collar of her shirt. She forced herself to release her grip. "I better pick up that cig," Nina said in a low voice. She bent over to retrieve the cigarette, but her fingers were trembling. She took a deep breath and sat back up.

"Are you okay?" Claire asked.

"Fine," Nina said with forced cheerfulness. "Fine."